THE ACCUSERS

Lindsey Davis

Century · London

Published by Century in 2003

1 3 5 7 9 10 8 6 4 2

Century
Random House UK Limited
20 Vauxhall Bridge Road, London SW1V 2SA

Random House Australia (Pty) Limited
20 Alfred Street, Milsons Point, Sydney,
New South Wales 2061, Australia

Random House New Zealand Limited
18 Poland Road, Glenfield
Auckland 10, New Zealand

Random House (Pty) Limited
Endulini, 5a Jubilee Rd, Parktown 2193, South Africa

The Random House Group Limited Reg. No. 954009

www.randomhouse.co.uk

A CIP catalogue record for this book
is available from the British Library

Papers used by Random House
are natural, recyclable products made from wood grown in
sustainable forests. The manufacturing processes conform to
the environmental regulations of the country of origin

ISBN 1-8441-3185-8

Typeset in Bembo by SX Composing DTP, Rayleigh, Essex
Printed and bound in the United Kingdom by
Clays Ltd, St Ives plc

For the Gang: Hannah, Lesley, Mary, Pamela, Pauline, Susan and Sybil
In Friendship

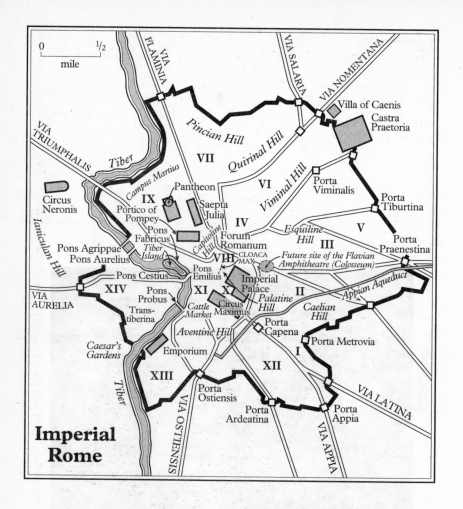

Imperial Rome

Jurisdictions of the Vigiles Cohorts in Rome:

Coh I   Regions VII & VIII (Via Lata, Forum Romanum)
Coh II   Regions III & V (Isis and Serapis, Esquiline)
Coh III Regions IV & VI (Temple of Peace, Alta Semita)
Coh IV Regions XII & XIII (Piscina Publica, Aventine)
Coh V   Regions I & II (Porta Capena, Caelimontium)
Coh VI Regions X & XI (Palatine, Circus Maximus)
Coh VII Regions IX & XIV (Circus Flaminius, Transtiberina)

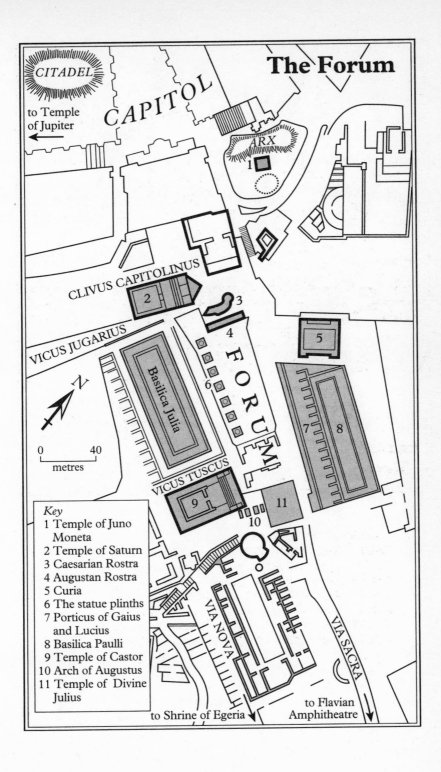

The Forum

CITADEL

CAPITOL

to Temple
of Jupiter

ARX

1

CLIVUS CAPITOLINUS

2

3

4

5

VICUS JUGARIUS

Basilica Julia

FORUM

6

7 8

N

0   40
metres

VICUS TUSCUS

9

11

10

VIA NOVA

VIA SACRA

Key
1 Temple of Juno
  Moneta
2 Temple of Saturn
3 Caesarian Rostra
4 Augustan Rostra
5 Curia
6 The statue plinths
7 Porticus of Gaius
  and Lucius
8 Basilica Paulli
9 Temple of Castor
10 Arch of Augustus
11 Temple of Divine
  Julius

to Shrine of Egeria

to Flavian
Amphitheatre

FAMILY TREE OF THE METELLI

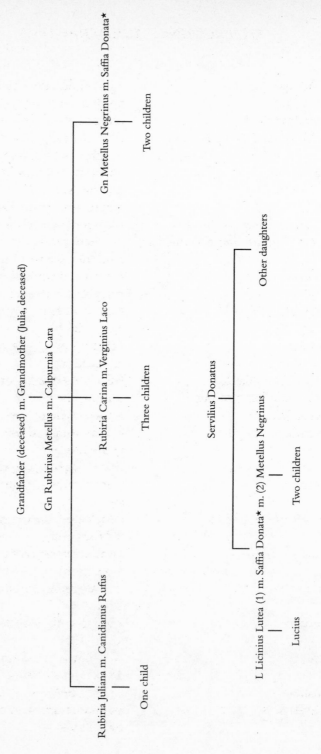

Grandfather (deceased) m. Grandmother (Julia, deceased)

Gn Rubirius Metellus m. Calpurnia Cara

Rubiria Juliana m. Canidianus Rufus

One child

Rubiria Carina m. Verginius Laco

Three children

Gn Metellus Negrinus m. Saffia Donata★

Two children

Servilius Donatus

L Licinius Lutea (1) m. Saffia Donata★ m. (2) Metellus Negrinus

Two children

Lucius

Other daughters

OTHER PRINCIPAL CHARACTERS

M. Didius Falco	a principled informer (who needs the money)
Helena Justina	the guardian of his ethics
Julia Junilla and Sosia Favonia	their children (never ill; never naughty; never loud)
Albia	a British visitor, who has seen nothing yet
Nux	a dog, who owns Falco
The Sacred Geese of Juno and The Augurs' Sacred Chickens	religious poultry's free range omelette producers
Ma	a mother shamed by impiety
Verontius	Falco's brother-in-law, as straight as a Roman road
D. Camillus Verus	Helena's father, a senator with memories
Julia Justa	her mother, a matron with connections
A. Camillus Aelianus and Q. Camillus Justinus	Falco's Associates, on a long learning curve
Ursulina Prisca	a valued client; very litigious
L. Petronius Longus	Falco's friend in the vigiles, a useful contact
Anacrites	Falco's enemy, a useless spook
Glaucus	Falco's trainer, who has seen it all
Ti Catius Silius Italicus	a high class lawyer (with a dubious past)
C. Paccius Africanus	a trusts expert (with a shady reputation)
Honorius	a legal idealist (heading for disillusion?)
Marponius	a judge with encyclopaedic knowledge
Bratta	an informer's informer
Procreus	an accuser's accuser
Euphanes	a sickly herbalist
Rhoemetalces	an apothecary who takes his own medicine

Claudius Tiasus	a funeral director with a chipped nymph
Biltis	a professional mourner, taking an interest
Spindex	a funeral clown; not laughing much
Olympia	a fortune teller; therapist to the nobility
Scorpus	aka 'Old Fungibles'; a wills expert
Scythax	the vigiles doctor, prescribing caution
Aufustius	a banker with profligate clients
Euboule	a wetnurse who fosters doubts
Zeuko	her daughter, keeping it in the family
Perseus	a door porter who knows too much
Celadus	a steward who knows what the last meal was
Julius Alexander	a loyal land agent who knows where the loot is

ROME: AUTUMN, AD 75 – SPRING, AD 76

====

I HAD BEEN an informer for over a decade when I finally learned what the job entailed.

There were no surprises. I knew how society viewed us: lowborn hangers-on, upstarts too impatient for honest careers, or corrupt nobles. The lowest grade was proudly occupied by me, Marcus Didius Falco, son of the utterly plebeian rogue Didius Favonius, heir to nothing and possessing only nobodies for ancestors. My most famous colleagues worked in the Senate and were themselves senators. In popular thought we were all parasites, bent on destroying respectable men.

I knew how it worked at street level – a hotch-potch of petty investigative jobs, all ill-paid and despised, a career that was often dangerous too. I was about to see the glorious truth of informing senatorial-style. In the late summer of the year that I returned with my family from my British trip, I worked with Paccius Africanus and Silius Italicus, two famous informers at the top of their trade; some of you may have heard of them. Legals. That is to say, these noble persons made criminal accusations, most of which were just about viable, argued without blatant lies and supported by some evidence, with a view to condemning fellow senators and then snatching huge proportions of their doomed colleagues' rich estates. The law, ever fair, makes decent compensation for selfless application to demeaning work. Justice has a price. In the informing community the price is at least twenty-five per cent; that is twenty-five per cent of all the condemned man's seaside villas, city property, farms, and other investment holdings. In abuse of office or treason cases, the Emperor may intervene; he can bestow a larger reward package, much larger sometimes. Since the minimum estate of a senator is a million sesterces – and that's poverty for the élite – this can be a nice number of town houses and olive groves.

All informers are said to be vile collaborators, currying favour, contributing to repression, profiteering, targeting victims, and working the courts for their personal advantage. Right or wrong, it was my job. It was all I knew – and I knew I was good at it. So, back in Rome, after half a year away, I had to stick a dagger down my boot and make myself available for hire.

It started simply enough. It was autumn. I was home. I had returned with my family, including my two young brothers-in-law, Camillus Aelianus and Camillus Justinus, a pair of patrician wild boys who were supposed to assist me in my work. Funds were not flush. Frontinus, the British governor, had paid us only rock bottom provincial rates for various audit and surveillance jobs, though we did secrete away a sweetener from a tribal king who liked the diplomatic way we had handled things. I was hoping for a second bonus from the Emperor but it would take a long time to filter through. And I had to keep quiet about the King's gift. Don't get me wrong. Vespasian owed me plenty. But I wanted to stay out of trouble. If the august one called my double bonus an accounting error, I would retract my invoice to him. Well, probably.

Six months was a long time to be out of the city. No clients remembered us. Our advertisements chalked on walls in the Forum had long since faded. We could expect no meaty new commissions for some time.

That was why, when I was asked to handle a minor documents job, I accepted. I don't generally act as someone else's courier, but we needed to show that Falco and Associates were active again. The prosecutor in a case in progress had an affidavit to be collected, fast, from a witness in Lanuvium. It was straightforward. The witness had to confirm that a certain loan had been repaid. I didn't even go myself. I hate Lanuvium. I sent Justinus. He obtained the signed statement without bother; since he was inexperienced in legal work, I myself took it to court.

On trial was a senator called Rubirius Metellus. The charge was abuse of office, a serious offence. The case had apparently been going on for weeks. I knew nothing about it, having been starved of Forum gossip. It was unclear what part the document we fetched had to play. I made the deposition, after which I suffered uncalled-for abuse from the filthy defence lawyer, who made out that as an informer from a plebeian district I was an unfit character witness. I bit back the retort that the Emperor had raised my status to equestrian; mentioning Vespasian seemed inappropriate and my middle-class rank would just cause more sneers. Luckily the judge was eager to adjourn for lunch;

he commented rather wearily that I was only the messenger, then he told them to get on with it.

I had no interest in the trial and I wasn't going to stick around to be called irrelevant. Once my job there was finished, I left. The prosecutor never even spoke to me. He must have done a decent job, because not long afterwards I heard that Metellus had been convicted and that a large financial judgment had been made against him. Presumably he was quite well off – well, he had been until then. We joked that Falco and Associates should have asked for a higher fee.

Two weeks later Metellus was dead. Apparently it was suicide. In this situation his heirs would escape having to pay up, which no doubt suited them. It was hard luck on the prosecutor, but that was the risk he took.

He was Silius Italicus. Yes, I mentioned him. He was extremely well known, quite powerful – and suddenly for some reason he wanted to see me.

II

I DID NOT respond well to a haughty summons from a senator. However, I was now married to a senator's daughter. Helena Justina had become adept at ignoring stares as people wondered why ever she had anything to do with me. When she was not calmly ignoring stares, she had a scowl that could fuse brass locks. Sensing that I intended to be difficult about Silius Italicus, she began to frown at me. If I had been wearing a sword-belt, the fittings would have melted to my chest.

I was in fact wearing a light tunic and old sandals. I had washed but not shaved; I could not remember whether I had combed my curls. Acting casual was instinctive. So was defying orders from Silius Italicus. Helena's expression made me squirm a bit, though not much.

We were at breakfast in our house at the foot of the Aventine. This edifice had belonged to my father and was still being renovated to our taste. It was six months since any fresco painters had bothered to show up; their pigment odours had faded and the building had reverted to nature. It had the faint musty whiff that afflicts elderly homes which have suffered flooding in the past because they were built too close to the river (the Tiber was a mere twenty feet away). The building had mostly lain empty while we were in Britain – though I could tell Pa had been camping out here as if he still owned the place. He had stuffed the ground floor with pieces of hideous furniture that he claimed were in 'temporary storage'. He knew we were back in Rome now, but was in no hurry to shift out his impedimenta. Why should he? He was an auctioneer and we had provided a free warehouse. I looked for anything worth pinching, but no reasonable customer would bid for this junk.

That didn't mean it would not be sold. Pa could convince a ninety-year-old childless miser that he needed an antique cradle with its rattle-hook missing – and that the victim could afford to have its rockers renovated by a deadbeat carpenter to whom Pa just happened to owe a favour.

'I'll throw in this fine Alexandrian rattle,' my father would say magnanimously (forgetting to do so, of course).

Since we could not climb into our dining room until my parent removed half a huge stone corn grinder, we ate upstairs in the roof garden. This was four storeys away from the kitchen, so we dined on mainly cold buffets. For breakfast, that posed no problems. Ever big-hearted, Pa had lent us a double-jointed Bithynian slave to carry up the trays. Bread rolls and honey survived, even when the sour-faced nonentity took his time. He was useless. Well, Pa would have held on to him, had he been any good.

We had family under our feet constantly. Helena and I had produced two daughters, one now two and a half and one six months. So first we had my mother weaselling in to check we had not killed her darlings while in barbarian territory, then Helena's elegant mama sailed up in her sedan chair to spoil the children too. Our mothers each expected to have all the attention, so as each arrived, the other had to be shepherded out some other way. We did this without making it obvious. If Pa walked in to mouth more excuses about the grinder, Ma would openly storm off; they had lived apart for nearly thirty years and took pride in proving it had been a wise decision. If Helena's mother were here when *her* father dropped by, he liked to play at being invisible so he had to be shunted into my study. It was tiny, so it was best if I were out at the time. Camillus Verus and Julia Justa did live together, with every sign of fond toleration, yet the senator always gave the impression he was a hunted man.

I wanted to discuss with him my summons from Italicus. Unfortunately when he called I was not at home, so he had a snooze in my one-man den, played with the children, drank us out of borage tea, and left. Instead, I was stuck with breakfast with his noble offspring. When Helena and her brothers assembled together, I began to see why their parents had allowed all three to leave their large but shabby home in the Twelfth District and share my desperate life in the much lower-class Thirteenth. The boys still lived at home, in fact, but hung around our easygoing house a lot.

Helena was twenty-eight, her brothers slightly younger. She was the partner of my life and work, that being the only way I could persuade her into my life and bed. Her brothers nowadays formed the junior sector of Falco and Associates, a little-known firm of private informers who specialised in background investigations of the family type (bridegrooms, widows and other cheating, lying, money-grubbing swine just like your own relatives). We could do art theft recovery, though that had been slack lately. We would hunt for missing persons, persuading rich teenagers to return home – sometimes even before they had been ravaged by their unsuitable lovers – or we would track down moonlit-flitters before they had unloaded their wagons at their next rental (although for reasons associated with my pauper past, we tended to be kind to debtors). We specialised in widows and their endless legacy problems, because ever since I was a light-hearted bachelor, I had done so; now I just reassured Helena they were my clients' half-mad aunts. I, the senior and more skilled partner, was also an imperial agent, a subject on which I was supposed to keep my mouth shut. So I shall do so.

Breakfast was where we all met up. In the manner of traditional Roman marriages, Helena Justina would consult me, the respected head of our household, about domestic issues. When she had finished telling me what was wrong, what part she felt I had played in causing it, and how she proposed to remedy the matter, I would gently concur with her wisdom and leave her to get on with it. Then her brothers would arrive to take orders from me on our current cases. Well, that was how I saw it.

The two Camilli, Aelianus and Justinus, had never been too friendly together. Matters had deteriorated when Justinus ran off with Aelianus' rich betrothed, thus persuading Aelianus that he wanted her after all (whereas he had been lukewarm about Claudia until he lost her) while Justinus soon saw that he had made a big mistake. However, Justinus had married the lass, for Claudia Rufina would one day possess a great deal of money and he was intelligent.

The brothers took their usual opposing attitudes to the Silius request.

'Damned chancer. Don't give him the time of day, Falco.' That was Aelianus, the elder, tolerant one.

'It's bloody interesting. You should see what the bugger wants.' Justinus, undogmatic and fair-minded, despite the bad language.

'Ignore them,' said Helena. She was older than Aelianus by one year and Justinus by two more; the big sister routine never died. 'What I want to know, Marcus, is this: just how important was the document you fetched from Lanuvium? Did it affect the outcome of the trial?'

This question did not surprise me. Women, who have no legal capacity in our system, are not supposed to take an interest in the courts but Helena refused to hear patriarchal fossils telling her what she could or could not understand. In case you are provincials from

6

maternalist societies, some sort of unfortunate Celt, for instance, let me explain. Our strict Roman forefathers, scenting trouble, had decreed that women should be innocent of politics, law and, wherever possible, money. Our foremothers had gone along with it, thus permitting the feeble sort of woman to be 'looked after' (and fleeced) while the strong sort overturned the system merrily. Guess which sort I had chosen.

'You need to know what the trial was about first,' I set about explaining.

'Rubirius Metellus was accused of trafficking in offices, Marcus.'

'Yes.' I refused to be surprised that she knew. 'While his son was the curule aedile in charge of road maintenance.' A twinkle appeared in Helena's fine brown eyes. I flashed a grin back. 'Oh, you asked your papa.'

'Yesterday.' Helena did not bother to be triumphant. Her brother Aelianus, a repressed traditionalist, tossed olives into his open mouth after a tut of disgust. He wanted a routine sister, so he could lord it over her. Justinus gave a superior smile. Helena took no notice of either, simply saying to me, 'There were a lot of charges against Metellus, though not much evidence for any of them. He had covered his tracks well. But if he was guilty of everything he was accused of, then his corruption was outrageous.'

'The court agreed with that.'

'So was your document important?' she insisted.

'No.' I glanced at Justinus, who had ridden to Lanuvium to fetch it. 'Ours was only one of a whole bunch of sworn statements that Silius Italicus produced at the trial. He was bombarding the judge and jury with examples of misconduct. He lined up every pavement-layer who had ever bought favours and had them all say their piece: *I gave the Metelli ten thousand, on the understanding it would help us win the contract for repairs to the Via Appia. I gave Rubirius Metellus five thousand to get the contract for maintaining the gullies in the Forum of Augustus. . .*'

Helena sniffed her disapproval. For a moment she leaned back with her face turned to the sun, a tall young woman in blue, quietly enjoying this fine morning on the terrace of her home. A lock of her fine dark hair fell free over one ear, its lobe bare of ear-rings this morning. The only jewellery she wore was a silver ring, my love gift from before we lived together. She looked at ease, but she was angry. 'It was the son who held the office, and who abused his influence. He was never charged, though?'

'Papa had all the money,' I pointed out. 'There was no financial mileage in accusing a legal minor who had not been emancipated from parental control. People who have no money of their own never get sued. The case still worked in court: Silius played it by painting a picture of a powerless junior, trapped under the authoritarian paternal thumb. The father was judged a worse character because he had subjected a weakling to his immoral influence at home.'

'Oh, a tragic victim of a bad father!' Helena scoffed. 'I wonder what his mother is like?'

'She was not in court. Dutiful matron who plays no part in public affairs, I expect.'

'Knows about nothing, cares about less,' Helena growled. She believed a Roman matron's role was to take strong umbrage at her husband's failings.

'The son may have a wife of his own too.'

'Some washed-out whimpering wraith,' decided my forthright girl. 'I bet she parts her hair in the middle and has a high little voice. I bet she dresses in white. I bet she faints if a slave spits . . . I hate this family.'

'They may be charming.'

'Then I apologise,' Helena said. Adding viciously, 'And I bet the young wife wears lots of dainty bangles – on both wrists!'

Her brothers had emptied all the food dishes so began to take more interest. 'When they worked the scam,' suggested Justinus, 'it probably helped that Papa received the bribes while Junior sealed the dodgy deals behind the scenes. A little separation would let them cover their tracks better.'

'Almost too well,' I told him. 'I heard Silius had a hard time winning.'

Helena nodded. 'My father said the verdict caused surprise. Everyone was sure Metellus was as guilty as Hades, but the case had dragged on too long. It was mired in bad feeling and had lost public interest. Silius Italicus was reckoned to have bungled the prosecution and Paccius Africanus, who defended Metellus, was thought to be the better advocate.'

'He's a viper.' I remembered him going for me harshly at the trial.

'Doing his job?' asked Helena mischievously. 'So why do you think Metellus was successfully convicted, Marcus?'

'He was a grubby cheat.'

'That would not have mattered.' Helena smiled drily.

'They voted against him on technicalities.'

'Such as?'

It was obvious, and quite simple: 'He thought he had the court in his pocket – he despised them and he let it show. The jury felt the same as you, love. They hated him.'

III

THE FORUM ROMANORUM. September. Not as hot as it could be in midsummer. The shade was cooler than the open sunlight, but compared with northern Europe still intensely warm. I had thought of bringing my toga, unsure of protocol, but could not face even carrying the heavy woollen folds over an arm. There was no way I would have worn the garment. Even without, patches of sweat made my tunic feel damp across my shoulders. Brilliant light pounded on the ancient cobbles of the Sacred Way, throbbed off the marble statues and cladding, heated the slow fountains and the shrinking pools in the shrines. On temples and plinths that lined the roadways, motionless pigeons lurked with their heads pulled in, trying not to faint. Old ladies, made of sterner stuff, battled across the space in front of the Rostra, cursing the trains of effete slaves, uniformed retinues of fat old men in litters who thought too much of themselves.

A mile of stately buildings lined the Forum valley. The Golden City's marble monuments towered above me. Arms folded, I took in the spectacle. I was home. Intimidation and awe are how our rulers keep us respectful. In my case the grandiose effects failed. I grinned at the glorious vista defiantly.

This was the business end of the historic area. I was standing on the steps of the Temple of Castor, with the Temple of the Divine Julius to the right – both places of nostalgia for me. To my far left, the hundred-foot-high Tabularium blocked off the foot of the Capitol. The Basilica Julia was next door, my current destination; opposite and across the worn stone piazza lay the Senate House – the Curia – and the Basilica built by Aemilius Paullus, with its grand two-storeyed galleries of shops and commercial premises. I could see the prison in a far corner; immediately below me, the office of weights and measures lurked under the podium of the Temple of Castor; near the Rostra was the building that housed the secretaries of the curule aediles, where the corrupt young Metellus had worked. The piazza was awash with priests; crammed with bankers and commodity brokers; flush with would-be pickpockets and the loitering sidekicks to whom they would swiftly pass whatever they stole. I looked in vain for the vigiles. (I was not intending to point out the pickpockets, only to demand loudly that the officers of the law should arrest the brokers for usury and the priests for telling lies. I felt satirical; setting the vigiles a task even they would shrink from would be an amusing way to rejoin public life.)

The messenger had left no directions. Silius Italicus was a grand type who expected everyone to know where he lived and what his daily habits were. He was not in court. Hardly surprising. He had had one case this year. If the convicted Metellus had paid up, Silius could have avoided work for another decade. I frustrated myself for a long time at the Basilica Julia, discovering that he was also the type whose home address was closely guarded, to stop lowly bastards from bothering the great bird in his own nest. Unlike me, he did not allow clients to call around at his apartment while he was dining with his friends, screwing his wife, or sleeping off either of those activities. Eventually I was informed that in daylight hours Silius could generally be found taking refreshments in one of the porticoes of the Basilica Paulli.

Cursing, I barged through the crowds, hopped down the steps and marched across the roasting travertine. At the twelve-sided well called the Pool of Curtius, I deliberately refrained from chucking in a copper for good luck. Amid the multicoloured marbles of the Porticus of Gaius and Lucius on the opposite basilica I expected a long search, but I soon spotted Silius, a lump who looked as if he made greedy use of the money he earned from his high-profile cases. As I approached, he was talking to another man whose identity I also knew: about the same age but neater build and more diffident in manner (I knew from recent experience how *that* was deceptive!) When they noticed me, the second man stood up from the wine-shop table. He may have been leaving anyway, though my arrival seemed to cause it. I felt they should have kept their distance, yet they had been chatting like any old friends who worked in the same district, meeting regularly for a mid-morning roll and spiced Campanian wine at this streetside eatery. The crony was Paccius Africanus, last seen as opposition counsel in the Metellus case.

Curious.

Silius Italicus made no reference to Africanus. I preferred not to show I had recognised my interrogator.

Silius himself had ignored me on the day I attended court but I had seen him at a distance, pretending he was too lofty to take notice of mere witnesses. He had a heavy build, not grossly fat but fleshy all over as a result of rich living. It had left him dangerously red in the face too. His eyes were sunk in folds of skin as if he constantly lacked sleep, though his clean-shaven chin and neck looked youthful. I put him in his forties but he had the constitution of a man a decade older. His expression was that of someone who had just dropped a massive stone plinth on his foot. As he talked to me, he looked as if it was still there, trapping him painfully.

'Didius Falco.' I kept it formal. He did not bother to return the courtesies.

'Ah yes, I sent for you.' His voice was assertive, loud and arrogant. Taken with his morose demeanour, it seemed as if he hated life, work, flavoured wine, and me.

'No one sends for me.' I was not his slave, nor did I have a commission. It was my free choice whether to accept, even if he offered one. 'You sent word that you would appreciate a discussion, and I have agreed to come. A home or office address would have helped, if I may say so. You're none too easy to find.'

He modified his confident manner. 'Still, you managed to root me out!' he replied, full of fake friendliness. Even when he was making an effort, he remained dour.

'Finding people is my job.'

'Ah yes.'

I sensed that internally he sneered at the type of trade I carried out. I didn't waste a truculent reaction on him. I wanted to get this over with. 'Down at the rough end of informing we have skills you never require at the Basilica. So,' I pressed him, 'which of my skills do you want to use?'

The big man answered, still with his offhand manner and loud voice: 'You heard what happened to Metellus?'

'He died. I heard it was suicide.'

'Did you believe it?'

'No reason to doubt,' I said – at once starting to do so. 'It makes sense as an inheritance device. He freed his heirs from the burden of the compensation he owed you.'

'Apparently! And what's your view?'

I formed one quickly: 'You want to challenge the cause of death?'

'Being paid would be more convenient than letting them off.' Silius leaned back, his hands folded. I noticed a cabochon beryllium seal ring on one hand, a cameo on a thumb, a thick gold band marked like a belt buckle on the other hand. His actual belt was four inches wide, heavy leather, wrapped around a very clean fine wool tunic in plain white with the senatorial trim. The tunic had been carefully laundered; the purple dye had not yet leached into the white. 'I won the case, so I don't personally lose –' he began.

'Except in time and expenses.' At the rough end, we were rarely paid time and expenses, and never at the glorious rates this man must command.

Silius snorted. 'Oh I can wave goodbye to the time charges. It's the million and a quarter winnings I prefer not to lose!'

A million and a quarter? I managed to keep my expression blank. 'I was unaware of the compensation limit.' He had paid us four hundred, which included a mule allowance for the ride Justinus took; we had bumped up the travel costs in accordance with the customs of our trade, but compared with his great windfall, our return wouldn't buy us a piss in a public lavatory.

'Of course I share it with my junior,' Silius grumbled.

'Quite.' I hid my bad feeling. His junior was a snivelling scrivener called Honorius. It was Honorius who had dealt with me. He looked about eighteen and gave the impression he had never seen a woman naked. How much of the million and a quarter sesterces would Honorius take home to his mother? Too much. The dozy incompetent had been convinced that our witness lived in Lavinium, not Lanuvium; he tried to avoid paying us; and when he did write out a docket for their banker, he misspelled my name three times.

The banker, by contrast, had coughed up quickly, and was polite. Bankers stay alert. He could tell that by that stage anyone else who upset me would have been sodomised with a very sharp spear.

I sensed further stress coming at me over the horizon on a fast Spanish pony.

'So why did you want to see me, Silius?'

'Obvious, surely?' It was, but I refused to help him. 'You work in this field.' He tried to make it sound like a compliment. 'You already have a connection with the case.'

My connection was remote. I should have kept it that way. Perhaps my next question was naïve. 'So what do you want me for?'

'I want you to prove that it was *not* suicide.'

'What am I going for? Accident or foul play?'

'Whatever you like,' said Silius. 'I am not fussy, Falco. Just find me suitable evidence to take the remaining Metelli to court and wring them dry.'

I had been slumped on a stool at his table. He had not offered me refreshments (no doubt sensing I would refuse them lest we be trapped in a guest/host relationship). But on arrival, I had assumed equal terms, and seated myself. Now I sat up. 'I never manufacture proofs!'

'I never asked you to.'

I stared at him.

'Rubirius Metellus did not take his own life, Falco,' Silius told me impatiently. 'He enjoyed being a bastard – he enjoyed it far too much to give it up. He had been riding high, at the top of his talent, dubious though it was. And he was a coward, anyway. Proof of something that will suit me is there to be had, and I shall pay you well to look for it.'

I stood up and gave him a nod of acknowledgement. 'This type of investigation has a special rate. I'll send along my scale of charges –'

He shrugged. He was not at all afraid of being stung. He had the confidence that only comes with the backing of huge collateral. 'We use investigators all the time. Pass your fees to Honorius.'

'Very well.' There would be an on-cost for having the awful Honorius as our liaison point. 'So let us start right here. What leads do you have? Why did you become suspicious?'

'I have a suspicious nature,' boasted Silius bluntly. He was not intending to tell me any more. 'Finding the leads is your job.'

To look professional, I asked for the Metellus address and went to get on with it.

I knew then that I was being taken for a sucker. I decided I could outwit him. I forgot all the times that manipulating swine like Silius Italicus had outplayed me on the draughtboard of connivery.

I wondered why, if he used his own tame investigators normally, he selected me for this. I knew it was not because he thought I had a friendly, honest face.

IV

RUBIRIUS METELLUS had lived in the style I expected. He owned a large home occupying its own block, on the Oppian Hill, just beyond Nero's Golden House, half a step from the Auditorium should he want to hear recitals, and an easy walk from the Forum when he conducted business. Booths for shops occupied street frontages on his home; some rich men leave them empty but Metellus preferred rents to privacy. His impressive main entrance was flanked by small obelisks of yellow Numidian marble. They looked ancient. I guessed war loot. Some military ancestor had grabbed them from a defeated people; perhaps he was in Egypt with Mark Antony or that prig Octavian. The former, most likely. Octavianus, with the nasty blood of Caesar in his veins and his eye to the main chance, would have been busy turning himself into Augustus and his personal fortune into the largest in the world. He would have tried to prevent his subordinates carrying off loot that could grace his own coffers or enhance his own prestige.

If a past Metellus had nonetheless snaffled some architectural salvage, maybe that was a clue to the whole family's attitude and skills.

I leaned on the counter of a bowl-and-beaker snackshop. I could see across the street to the Metellus spread. It had a weathered, self-confident opulence. I had intended to ask questions of the food vendor but he looked at me as if he thought he had seen me before – and remembered we had had a row about his lentil pottage. Unlikely. I have style. I wouldn't order lentils any day.

'Phew! It's taken me hours to find this street.' It was a ten-minute walk from the Sacred Way. Maybe if I looked fagged out he would pity me. Or maybe he would think I was an ignorant deadbeat, up to no good. 'Is that the Metellus house?'

The man in the apron amended his glare to suggest I was a dead bluebottle, feet-up in his precious pottage. Forced to acknowledge my question, he produced a quarter of a nod.

'At last! I have business with the people there.' I felt like a clowning slave in a dire farce. 'But I hear they had a tragedy. I don't want to upset them. Know anything about what happened?'

'No idea,' he said. Trust me to choose the outlet where Metellus deceased always bought his morning sesame cake. Loyalty makes me sick. Whatever happened to gossip?

'Well, thanks.' It was too early in the game to make myself unpleasant, so I refrained from accusing him of ruining my livelihood with his stingy responses. I might need him later.

I drained my cup, wincing at the sourness; some bitter herb had been added to much-watered-down wine. It was not a success.

The food vendor watched me all across the street. Being turned away by the door porter would be a deep humiliation, so I made sure it didn't happen. I said I was from the lawyer. The porter thought I meant *their* lawyer and I failed to put him straight. He let me in.

So far, so good. A small battered sphinx guarded the atrium pool. The wide-eyed wise one had stories to tell, but I could not dally. The décor was all polychrome floors and black frescos with gold leaf touch-ups. Perhaps an old house, revived by recent new money. Whose was that? Or was this an old grand mansion, now sinking into disarray? – I noticed an air of dusty neglect as I craned to look into the side rooms.

I did not make contact with any of the family. A steward saw me. He was an eastern-born slave or freedman, who seemed alert. Late forties, clearly with status in the household, efficient, well-spoken, probably cost a packet to purchase though that would have been some years back. I decided not to prevaricate; incurring a false-entry charge was a bad idea. 'The name's Falco. Your porter may have misunderstood. I represent Silius Italicus. I am here to check a few details about your master's sad demise so he can write off his fees. First, allow me to express our most sincere condolences.'

'Everything is in order,' said the steward, almost as if they had expected this. It was not quite the correct response to my condolences and at once I mistrusted him. I wondered if Paccius Africanus had warned them here that we would try to investigate. 'Calpurnia Cara –'

I took out a note tablet and stylus. I kept my manner quiet. 'Calpurnia Cara is?'

'My late master's wife.' He waited while I made notes. 'My mistress arranged for seven senators to view the corpse and certify the suicide.'

I held my stylus still and gazed at him over the edge of my notebook. 'That was very cool-headed.'

'She is a careful lady.'

Protecting a lot of money, I thought. Of course if it really was a suicide, the husband and wife may well have discussed what Metellus intended. Metellus may have instructed his wife to bring in the witnesses. Paccius Africanus would certainly have advised it, if he were involved. It was a chilling thought that counselling his client to die might be good legal advice.

'Do you know whether Calpurnia Cara tried to dissuade her husband from his planned course?'

'I imagine they talked about it,' the steward replied. 'I don't know what was said.'

'Was the suicide announced to the household staff beforehand?'

He looked surprised. 'No.'

'Any chance I might talk with your mistress?'

'That would not be appropriate.'

'She lives here?' He nodded. I made a small symbol on my tablet, without looking up. 'And the son?' Another nod. I ticked that off too. 'Is *he* married?'

A minute pause. 'Metellus Negrinus is divorced.' I made a longer entry.

'So.' Now I raised my eyes to the steward again. 'Calpurnia Cara ensured that her husband's death was formally witnessed by noble friends. I assume you can provide me with the seven names, incidentally.' He was already producing a tablet from a pouch. These people were expertly organised. Grief had not confused them at all. 'Was the viewing conducted before or after your master actually – ?'

'Afterwards. Straight afterwards.'

'Were the witnesses in the house while he –'

'No, they were sent for.'

'And do you mind – I am sorry if this is very painful – but how did he. . . ?'

I was expecting the classic scenario: on the battlefield a defeated general falls on his sword, usually needing help from a weeping subordinate because finding the space between two ribs and then summoning the strength to pull in a weapon upwards is damned difficult to fix for yourself. Nero cut his throat with a razor, but he was supposedly hiding in a garden trench at the time, where there may have been no elegant options; to be skewered on a dibber would have lacked the artistry he coveted. The traditional method in private life is to enter a warm bath and open your veins. This death is contained, relaxing, and reckoned to be more or less painless. (Mind you, it presupposes you live in a grand home with a

17

bath.) For a senator, such an exit from disaster is the only civilised way out.

But it had not happened here.

'My master took poison,' said the steward.

V

To INTERVIEW seven senators, I needed help. I returned home and summoned the Camilli. They had to be found first. I sent out my nephew Gaius, a lad about town recently returned from having his habits reformed in the country. It had not worked. He was still a layabout, but agreed to be my runner for his usual exorbitant sweetener. Trotting off to the senator's house to ask where the lads were supposed to be, he soon rousted out Aelianus from a bath house then rounded up Justinus, who was out shopping with his wife.

While I was waiting I did some budgeting, wrote an ode in my head, and replanted some flower tubs little Julia had 'weeded'. Helena pounced. 'I'm glad you're here. A woman called for you.'

'Oh good!' I leered.

'One of your widows.'

'Sweetheart, I promise you: I gave up widows.'

'You may do this one,' Helena assured me cruelly. 'Her name is Ursulina Prisca and she is about sixty-five.'

I knew Ursulina. She had been badgering me for a long time to take on an extremely complex wrangle involving her estranged brother's will. She was half crazy. I could have coped with that; most of my clients were. But she talked a torrent, she smelt of cats, and she drank. A friend of hers had recommended me. I had never worked out who the friend was, though I would like to have strong words with them.

'She's a menace.'

Helena grinned. 'I said you would be delighted to take on her work.'

'I am not available to the widow Ursulina! She tried to grab me by the balls once.'

'Don't make excuses.'

Luckily the lads turned up and I forgot the harassing widow.

I divided up the suicide witnesses, two to each of the lads while I took three.

'What was the point of having all these witnesses, Falco?' Aelianus asked fretfully.

'It's like getting your will ratified, if you are an important bean. Looks good. Deters questions. In theory it stops Forum gossip. In this case it also raises expectations of a good scandal.'

'Nobody will query certification by seven senators,' mocked Helena. 'As if senators would *ever* conspire to lie!'

We would be lucky if any of the seven agreed to see us. Having signed the certificate, they would hope to be left alone. Senators try to be unobtainable to the public. To be asked about their noble signatures by a pack of harrying informers would seem outrageous.

Sure enough, Aelianus failed to interview either of the men allocated to him. Justinus saw one of his.

'A strike! How come?'

'I pretended I had a good tip on a horse race.'

'Smart!' I must try that.

'I wish I hadn't bothered. He was rude, Falco.'

'You expected that, you're grown up. Tell.'

'He grudgingly said they were all called to the house by Calpurnia Cara. She announced calmly that since losing the court case, her husband had decided to seek an honourable exit from public life. She told them he had taken poison that afternoon; he wished them – as his circle of friends – to observe the scene and formally certify suicide. This, she said, would simplify matters for his family. They knew what she meant. They did not see Metellus die, but inspected the corpse. He was lying on his bed, dead. He wore a grimace, had a nasty pallor, and smelt of diarrhoea. A small sardonyx pillbox lay open on a side table. The seven men all signed the declaration, which the widow has.'

'Flaw,' I chipped in. 'Metellus did not himself tell them his intentions. Then they did not see him actually swallow any pills.'

'Quite. How can they say he did it willingly?' Justinus agreed.

'Still, well done; at least we know what song these warblers want us to listen to.'

'How did you get on, Falco?' Aelianus then asked, hoping my record with the witnesses was as bad as his. I had spoken to all three of my targets. Experience tells. Aelianus replied that it also causes pomposity.

'All my subjects told the same story,' I reported. 'One did concede it was bad form that they had not been addressed by Metellus beforehand. That's the ideal procedure in a council of friends. But they trust his wife, apparently – or they are scared of her – and I was assured that availing himself of the suicide ploy was entirely in character. Metellus hated to lose. He would enjoy thwarting his accusers.'

'He won't enjoy much from the Underworld,' Aelianus muttered.

'Right, I think we'll end up telling Silius it stinks. Before we do, we'll go one stage further.'

'You'll try to see the strangely calm widow!' Justinus thought he was ahead of me.

I grinned. 'Helena hates me seeing widows.'

'I know –' Helena herself had it right: 'He is sending me. And if I am successful in gaining entry, Falco will arrive halfway through, as if innocently collecting me to walk me home.' I had not thought of that. 'Don't do it,' she said immediately. 'Keep out of my way, Falco. Calpurnia and I may become great friends.'

'Of course. You'll go back there to swap bangles and gossip every afternoon.'

'No, darling. I just want to ask her advice on procedure, in case I ever decide things are so bad, *you* should poison yourself.'

'I'll take that as a threat! – Well if I do it, I don't want seven sleazebags invited to sit on the bed and watch.'

I waited around a corner, perching on a bollard. I might be banned from joining Helena in her visit to Calpurnia Cara, but I had brought her to the Metellus spread and I would walk her safely home. Rome is a city of dangers.

When she reappeared, looking thoughtful, I decided not to press her but to make the long hike home first. We had to traverse most of the length of the Forum, pass around the base of the Capitol and Palatine Hills, then skirt the end of the Circus Maximus. At least since moving to Pa's house, we no longer had the steep haul up the Aventine, but Helena looked tired when we finally staggered home. It was dinnertime, we had our children to attend to, and before we found a chance to talk the rest of the household was in bed. We went up to the roof terrace to watch the bright stars overhead and the dim lights down along the riverbank. A single oil lamp glimmered on a table among the trained rose trees. Insects plunged at it madly, so we sat a little apart in shadow.

'So,' I prompted. 'You were welcomed in?'

'Well, I was *allowed* in,' Helena corrected me. 'I pretended that my mother had sent commiserations. Calpurnia Cara knew she had never met me, but she may have been unsure who Mama was. In case they were old acquaintances who had talked for four hours at the last secret gathering for the Good Goddess, she felt obliged to be polite.'

I shuddered. Traditional religion has that effect. I was relieved that Helena had never expressed any interest in the notorious female goings-on in honour of the so-called Good Goddess. My own religious observance stopped short at the guano-spattered environs of the Temple of Juno, where I had duties as the Procurator of Juno's Sacred Geese – a merry jest of the Emperor's. 'So what is Calpurnia like?'

'Between fifty and sixty, as you would expect from her husband's and son's positions in the Senate. I wouldn't call her handsome, but –' Helena paused. 'She had bearing and presence.'

That sounded as if Calpurnia was a vicious old bat. Since my own life's companion certainly had presence, I was careful of my phrasing: 'She would have been no cipher in the marriage?'

'Oh no. She's a little defensive –'

'Bad tempered?'

'Let's say, very confident. Well groomed, but not wearing much jewellery. She seems cultured; there were reading-scrolls in the room. Mind you, there was a wool basket too, yet I reckon that was just for show! I can't see the lady actually spinning like a traditional good wife.'

'You suspect a slave had been sent out in a hurry to buy some wool so they could stage-manage appearances?'

'Could be. She had a mousy maid in attendance, to look modest.'

'How formal? Was she veiled?'

'Don't be silly, Marcus; she was at home. Her manner was reserved, but it should be, with nosy strangers coming to her house for days, trying to catch her out.'

'She was receiving well-wishers, though?'

'A queue of callers; I gathered I was lucky to find her alone. I felt that accepting condolences – from both genuine friends and even the wickedly curious – was an ordeal which Calpurnia Cara quite enjoys.'

'A duty?'

'A challenge.'

'She wants to test her own endurance?' I wondered.

'Oh I think she knows how capable she is,' Helena replied warmly.

The air temperature was dropping. Helena reached for her stole, which I helped to tuck around her. As usual it was a good excuse to explore her body affectionately.

'Do you want to hear this, Marcus?'

'Of course.' I was perfectly capable of groping a woman while extracting her evidence. My profession calls for a man to be physically adroit and mentally versatile, often at the same time. I could take notes while scratching my bum too.

'She told me what you already knew. Nothing added and nothing different. It seems very well rehearsed.' Despite the dusk, I knew that Helena had read my thoughts and smiled. 'That does not necessarily make it untrue.'

'Perhaps,' I agreed.

'One other thing –' There was a new note of mischief in Helena's tone. 'I didn't see the son, of course. I couldn't tell if he was in the house. They call him Birdy, by the way; I don't know why. I took the opportunity to ask one of the staff for an address for junior's divorced wife – ostensibly so I could pay condolences there too.' I said nothing. 'Unless you want to take over that visit?' she enquired, in apparent innocence.

'You know me so well.'

'I expect you will claim,' Helena scoffed, 'the divorcee may give us another side of the story. This may be a crucial breakthrough and you need to expose her directly to your experienced interrogatory skills?'

'My love, how comfortable it is to have a wife who understands my business.'

'Her name is Saffia Donata – and you need to know in advance that she is causing trouble!'

I said that sounded like exactly the kind of sweet little breakthrough I was looking for.

'She has three children and some money.' An excellent briefing. Helena Justina made a wonderful work partner – thorough, discreet, witty, and even fair to me. 'I did not ask if she is pretty.'

I said I could discover that for myself.

VI

NEXT MORNING I began to see why Silius Italicus was so secretive about where he lived: self-protection. We were still at breakfast when a message was brought up that Ursulina Prisca had arrived downstairs. I sent Justinus to get rid of her. I could be magnanimous. Let her have a few minutes of pleasure being rebuffed by a handsome, polite young fellow.

Once that role would have been mine. Now I was middle-class, middle-aged, and full of middle-rank anxieties. When you have no money there is no point worrying. Once you obtain some, all that ends.

While dear Quintus interviewed the persistent baggage, using a side room which we kept tidy for that purpose, I kissed Helena, pulled a face at the baby, tickled Julia, locked the dog in a bedroom, and slipped out of the house. (Leaving home in a hurry was much slicker when I was single.) If Ursulina decided our boy was adorable, she might dig in her talons. My youngest brother-in-law was *very* polite and hated saying no to women in distress. I knew that all women were hard as nuts, but he would easily be manoeuvred into taking the commission. Fine. He could do it. Now our team had a nagging-granny specialist.

I was off to try my skills on a much more difficult female. Forget the divorcee. My motto was hit them gently to see what happens – then hit them again, hard. I was going to revisit Calpurnia Cara.

There is a trick informers use. If you have assailed a house once in the afternoon and want another attempt, go next time in the morning. If the household is wealthy, they *may* work their porters in shifts. Mind you, many rich families work their door porters to death, thinking that the provision of a cubicle with a stool means the porter has an easy life. It's a boring career, and that can work to your advantage. On the whole though, door porters become obstructive, maybe because sitting on a stool all day cuts off the circulation painfully in their legs. It affects their brains too. They get above themselves. I hate the swine.

The Metelli, as I might by then have expected, kept their porter *in situ* all day. I observed this from the same unfriendly snackbar where I had rested my trotters on the counter yesterday. This meant I might have to wait around for hours before that other informing trick: knocking on the door at lunchtime when the porter takes his meal break. Luckily, I did not need to wait so long. While the door was open for a delivery, I heard the porter ask another slave to stand in while he went off for a pee.

Thank you, gods!

(Which reminded me again that I was Procurator of the Sacred Geese of Juno, and I ought to say hello to my fat feathered charges, now I was back in Rome.)

'Morning. My name is Didius Falco; I was here yesterday on business with your mistress. Could I possibly see her again for a few minutes, please?'

'I'm supposed to ask the steward,' the stand-in said. 'I think.' He was a kitchen worker normally; he had an apron on, stained with oil and sauce.

'That's right,' I agreed, smiling helpfully. 'The other Janus – what's his name?'

'Perseus.'

'Perseus asked the steward yesterday.'

'Oh he asked him, did he? Well, that's all right then. She's in the garden; this way, sir –'

The stand-in had left the door open. Assuming my helpful guise, I pointed out that while he escorted me to find Calpurnia Cara, wrong-doers might sneak in. That worried him. So he stayed there but gave me instructions how to cross the atrium, pass through a colonnade, and find the garden area by myself. I handed him a quarter denarius. It was the least I could do. I knew, though he apparently did not, he had just earned himself a severe beating for letting loose an informer in the house.

It was worth a quiet wander around. I like gardens. This peaceful enclosed space between wings of the silent house had a damson tree and ancient twining plants fastened up pilasters. Inside the house there was that faint impression of not having enough slaves around to keep the place smart, but the garden was well tended. Puddles and damp earth showed that plants had been watered, though whoever brought the buckets had moved on. I could see at once that Calpurnia was not there.

This was tricky. Or rather, for an informer it was excellent.

I spent a long time walking about. No town houses have enormous grounds, but I explored colonnades, peered into empty ground floor rooms, poked into stores. Though light on attendants, it seemed a well-run, organised establishment. That fitted. Corrupt nobles have to be efficient, or they get found out. True, Metellus had been exposed – but he had fallen victim to an informer, and informers notoriously target victims unfairly. Left to himself, he might have fleeced the state and its contractors for many more years and died 'with honour'.

At the back of the house soared the old Servian Walls, the ancient fortification we called the Embankment. Approaching, quite suddenly I came upon a woman alone. She was dressed in dark clothes, though I thought that reflected her glum nature rather than mourning. I had reached the farthermost part of the garden, a small patch of dry earth with vegetable trenches and a fan-trained fig tree. She was standing, apparently in a reverie, on a gravel path that was flanked by tired herbs, outside an outhouse that had been partly carved into the side of the Embankment.

'Damned wasps' nest,' she muttered, seeing me. She was pretending her eye had just been caught by something. It sounded mundane, but her face had hardened. 'What are you doing here? Who do you think you are?'

'Would you believe a wasp exterminator?'

'Stop your nonsense.'

'I apologise.' She was right about the nest. Insects were flying to and fro, entering the roughly constructed building above a corner of the doorway. 'Marcus Didius Falco –'

'Ah yes!' she jumped in, with an acid tone. 'From Silius. You sent your wife on an exploratory mission yesterday.'

She turned away from the shack, which was chained up. I noticed she was carrying a large bunch of metalwork – the traditional matron, in possession of the household keys. 'Calpurnia Cara, I take it?' I asked, a neutral response to cover up being caught out. The woman, who had a permanent expression of distaste, nodded slightly. Trying to distract her, I asked, 'What do you keep in the garden store?'

'Unwanted household goods. Your wife was unwanted too, I may say.'

It was a neat link, but I decided not to play word games: 'Helena

Justina was merely curious about the work I have taken on –'

'I am not a fool, Falco.' Calpurnia Cara was annoyed, though at the same time she somehow accepted that annoyance was bound to happen. She began to walk back to the house; meekly I went with her. She looked to be in her late fifties, a heavy woman, her step slow and a little awkward. Had she been my grandmother, I would have offered an arm, but this grand matron was far too austere. She took pleasure in telling me how she had outwitted us: 'My adviser dined here yesterday. We have to be careful; my family has attracted unpleasant notoriety. I showed him a list of visitors. Africanus spotted her.'

Paccius Africanus had taken an interest in me, then. He must already have known my connection with Helena Justina, before he saw yesterday's list. Our association was unusual, yet Helena and I were hardly well-known names in public life. So: Paccius Africanus had been digging.

'Who let you in?' Calpurnia demanded. It boded ill for my crony on the door.

'Perseus had been called away –'

'*Called away?*' I had the impression Perseus might have caused exasperation in Calpurnia before. Well, that would make him a typical door porter.

'Call of nature.' In fact I was starting to think that nothing as easy-going as nature would occur in this establishment.

'I'll see about that. . .' What did she want him to do? Pee into the atrium pool? It has been known; put-upon porters are aware that their nagging owners use the run-off from the pool as spare drinking water.

We had reached the colonnade that fronted the atrium. I was led smartly round the sphinx and the pool. I was on my way out.

'I have nothing to tell you,' Calpurnia informed me. 'So stop bothering me. I know you have been to our formal witnesses and they have affirmed all that happened.' She was keeping very well informed. The normal porter was back, looking unconcerned at his lapse, as porters tend to do. '*Perseus!* Put this man out.'

'Had your husband discussed his intentions with you?' I squeezed in.

'Metellus did nothing without my knowledge,' Calpurnia barked.

'Did that include his business life?' I enquired coolly.

She pulled back quickly. 'Oh none of that had anything to do with me!' As if a stronger denial were called for, she went on, 'Load of spiteful, invented stupidity. Viciousness. Collaborators. Silius ought to be exiled. Destroying good men –'

Goodness played no part in the business ethics of the Metelli, as I knew the facts.

I was leaving as ordered, when Calpurnia Cara called after me. 'Your wife was trying to extract the whereabouts of my ex-daughter-in-law.' I turned back. 'I am sure my staff were very helpful,' Calpurnia stated in a dry tone. 'Don't bother with Saffia Donata. She has nothing to do with any of this and she is a mischief-maker.'

'Nonetheless, I am sorry to hear of your son's so recent separation from the mother of his children.' Since the Metelli were so keen on form, or the appearance of form, the dig seemed apt.

'Child!' barked Calpurnia. 'Her other brat came from another source.' I raised an eyebrow at her wording. Had immorality occurred? 'Previous marriage,' she explained impatiently, as if I were an idiot. Clearly nothing untoward in the bedroom arena could be allowed to touch this family. 'We took her on for that reason. At least we knew she was fertile.'

'Oh quite!' Best to accept patrician motives for marriage. Choosing a bride because she is capable of having children is no more crazy than believing some girl worships you and has a sweet temper – both of which are bound to prove untrue. 'In fact, I understood that Saffia Donata has *three* children.' So Helena had said, and she would have remembered accurately.

'We shall see!' replied Calpurnia Cara harshly. 'She claims she's pregnant. It may happen. She's no loss,' opined the ex-mother-in-law, as she vanished from sight, jingling her keys.

It was nice to find relationships that so closely followed tradition. Had the harsh mother-in-law been fond of her son's wife, I would have felt disconcerted.

VII

N<small>O WAY</small> out. I needed an appointment with the fertile divorcee.

Saffia Donata lived nearby now. She had rented an apartment close to the Market of Livia, just through the Esquiline Gate. The Embankment stood between her new abode and the Metelli like a symbolic barrier. I buffed through the hawkers and puppeteers who congregate in the shadow of the ancient fortification, using an elbow where necessary. I was among a lot of smart habitation. To the east where the Metelli lived in the Fifth Region were no less than five public gardens; to the west where I was going were the elegant Third and Fourth Regions, dominated by the Gardens of Lollianus. Very nice. Not so fine, once you realise that all these glamorous green spaces have been built up with many feet of topsoil on what used to be the Esquiline Field – the graveyard of the poor. Never stop to breathe the pretty flower scents. The graves of the poor still stink.

Pregnant women do not scare me. Still, I did not roam about by myself in Saffia's new apartment. I might easily have sneaked around a bit. She was still moving in and there was chaos. When I turned up and was admitted without trouble, men were everywhere moving furniture (quality stuff; Pa would have made an offer for it). I saw a lot of treasures having their corners knocked off. Ivory items and silver-inlaid sets of delicate stuff with goats' feet were being hauled around as casually as the battered joint stools at my mother's house which people had kicked out of their way for thirty years. There were enough bronze candelabra to light an orgy. I bet some found themselves dismantled into convenient pieces and hidden in packing wraps, ready for the no-questions resale market.

Saffia was, I could report to Helena, very pretty. She was younger than I expected. Twenty-five at most. She had dark hair, tightly wound about her head. Light swathes of drapery kept her cool, but seemed almost indecently thin on her swollen torso. A maid wafted rosewater about, to little purpose. Saffia was barefoot, reclining against

29

cushions on a couch, her embroidered slippers resting on a footstool.

I could reassure my beloved that this peach was too ripe for stealing. It looked as if Saffia was carrying twins and that they were due next week. She had reached the restless stage, unable to make herself comfortable, and sick of friendly people asking how was she finding the wait?

'I am sorry to bother you —'

'Oh Juno, I don't mind,' she uttered wearily, when I introduced myself. I had said exactly what I was there for. Deluding a young, divorced woman in her home would be dangerous. 'Ask me anything!'

In view of her condition, I was surprised to be received. Something about this offhand young matron seemed common; her openness to a male stranger was out of place in the patrician world. Yet her accent was as upper-crust as Calpurnia's and her welcome soon felt acceptable. There were other attendants constantly in the room, pottering with ornaments on gilt-legged marble sidetables. She was as well chaperoned as any witness I had ever spoken to.

'I hope this is not inconvenient. I can see you are still in mid-move here — Do you mind if I ask, is your divorce a recent event?'

'Straight after the trial ended. My father was horrified by the verdict. We are a very respectable family. Papa had no idea what he was getting me into when I married Birdy. And my ex-husband was furious. He doesn't want his boy to be associated with such people.'

I ignored the self-righteous stuff and stuck to facts. 'Your first husband gave you a son, and Metellus —?'

'My daughter. She is two.'

I should have said, so is mine. But I was gruff in interrogations. To me, informers on duty are solitary grousers, not given to domestic chat. I thought it best to say, 'Would you prefer me to speak to your legal guardian, by the way?'

'That's up to you. I have one, of course.' Saffia did not seem to mind dealing with me. She did not name the guardian either. I had shown willing. The last thing I really wanted was to be fobbed off with some jumped-up freedman who had been put in charge of her contracts and accounts, just to look respectable. He was probably of low rank, and I doubted if he saw much of Saffia. This was not that frequent situation where the legal stand-in has an eye to marriage with his charge. Divorce and Saffia were no strangers. Remarriage in the highest social circumstances was what she expected, and soon. The Augustan laws would give her six months, if she wanted to avoid loss of privileges. I felt she was an expert. I could see her swapping husbands more times yet – probably raising her status every time.

'Excuse my ignorance; I don't know who your ex-husband is?' I was certainly intending to visit Negrinus; now I reckoned her first cast-off might be worth an interview too.

'Oh he's not involved at all, don't worry about him.' I guessed the first ex had begged to be kept well out of her troubles with the second; Saffia was loyal enough to comply. Interesting. Would she be so loyal to Negrinus?

'Is it rude to enquire why *that* marriage was terminated?'

'It is rude,' said Saffia. Rather rudely.

'Still, you remain on good terms?'

'We do.'

'Because of your son?'

'Because it is civilised.'

'Wonderful!' I said, as if I had fine grit between my teeth. 'And how are things between you and Birdy?'

'Unspeakable – unfortunately.' She waved a small neat hand above the unborn child. Several silver bracelets slipped on her wrist as she did so. Her draperies were held on with numerous enamel studs and pins. Even the slave mopping her brow wore a bangle.

'The mother-in-law comes into it?' I suggested with a twinkle. Saffia *was* loyal for some reason: she just pouted slightly and said nothing. Perhaps the Metelli had paid her to keep quiet. 'I met her today,' I tried one more time.

Saffia gave in. 'I expect you think them an awful family,' she told me. 'But the girls are all right.'

'What girls?' I had been caught out.

'My husband's two sisters. Juliana is sweet, though she's married to a crosspatch. The trial was a terrible shock for them both. Carina always kept her distance. She's rather strict and has a mournful air, but then I think *she* understood what was going on.'

'Carina disapproved of the corrupt practices?'

'She avoided trouble by staying away. Her husband also took a very stiff attitude.'

'Will you still see the sisters?'

Saffia shrugged and did not know. She had the knack of seeming full of disingenuous chatter but I already felt that nothing vital would be wheedled out of this witness. She gushed, but she only told me what she could afford to say. Anything she needed to keep private stayed out of bounds. Lawyers do it in court: bombard the jury with trivia while omitting anything pertinent that may harm their client.

I tried her with the main question: 'I am really looking into what happened over Metellus senior's death.'

'Oh I don't know. I wasn't there. My father fetched me, the day the trial ended.'

'You went home with your father?'

'I certainly did.' She paused. 'Papa already had a quarrel with them.'

'It happens in families,' I sympathised. 'What was at issue?'

'Oh something to do with my dowry, I know nothing of such matters . . .'

Wrong, darling. Saffia Donata knew everything about anything that concerned her. Still, women of rank like to pretend. I let it go. I can pretend too.

'So, home to Papa, at least temporarily? Of course you wanted to live in your own apartment; you are a married woman, used to your own establishment?'

Not quite. She was used to living with Calpurnia Cara, a matron who possessed – as Helena Justina had commented wryly – bearing and presence. Saffia saw that I recognised the contradiction; she made no answer.

I smiled like a conspirator. 'You have my congratulations. Living with Calpurnia must have taken stamina. I imagine she told you exactly how you should do everything –'

'*I cannot permit my son's wife to suckle!*' Saffia mimicked viciously. She was good.

'How dreadful.'

'At least this baby won't have the evil wet-nurse that my daughter was forced to endure.'

'You are glad to have escaped such tyranny.'

'If only I had.' I looked quizzical. Saffia then explained the curious procedures that are imposed on mothers-to-be who divorce from families where a large inheritance may be at stake: 'Calpurnia is insisting a reputable midwife lives with me, examines me, and monitors both the pregnancy and birth.'

'Jupiter! What's she afraid of?'

'A substituted grandchild, if my baby dies.'

I huffed. It seemed a lot of fuss. Still, Metellus Negrinus would not want to be saddled with maintaining the wrong child.

'She told me you would call.' So Saffia and the tyrant were still on speaking terms.

32

'She told *me* you are causing trouble,' I said bluntly. 'What did she mean by that?'

'I have no idea.' I could see that she did know, but she was not going to tell me.

I changed tack. 'You are very well organised. There must have been hectic activity to find you somewhere to live so fast.' Briefly, I even wondered if Calpurnia had had a hand in this.

'Oh, dear old Lutea sorted it all out for me.'

I raised an eyebrow, half amused. 'Your ex-husband?' I guessed. She blushed slightly at being outwitted. It was an unusual name. I would soon track him down. I smiled. 'Let's be frank. Do *you* believe Rubirius Metellus killed himself?'

But Saffia Donata knew nothing of those matters either. She had had enough of me. I was asked to leave.

At the door, I paused. Since I had already put away my stylus, I chewed a fingernail instead. 'Damn! I meant to ask Calpurnia something . . . I don't want to keep annoying her in her time of grief – would you happen to know, what poison was it that Metellus took?'

'Hemlock.' This was good, from a woman who had not been in the house when the poisoning occurred and who was estranged from the family.

'Hades, we're not in the wilds of Greece, and Metellus was not a philosopher. Nobody civilised takes hemlock nowadays!'

Saffia made no comment.

'Do you know where he would have acquired it?' I asked.

Saffia looked more wary. She merely shrugged.

I had now interviewed two matrons from the same family, in my opinion both deeply devious. My brain ached. I went home for lunch to my own open and uncomplicated womenfolk.

VIII

'How could you do that to me, Falco?'
Justinus was chomping his way through a bowl of chicory, olives and goat's cheese. He looked morose. I asked what I had done, knowing he referred to Ursulina Prisca. His brother, who was reading a scroll as if he despised lunch, smirked.

'Vulcan's breath,' Justinus went on. 'Your widow is so demanding. She goes nattering on about agnates –'

'Agnates?' Helena looked sceptical. 'Is that a disease or a semi-precious stone?'

'Close relatives, other than children, who are next in line to inherit.' Aelianus, for once more efficient than Justinus, must actually be learning up the finer points of inheritance law. Was that in his scroll?

'Ursulina has some claim on the estate of a brother,' I confirmed. 'Or she thinks she does.'

'Oh I'm taking her word!' Justinus marvelled. 'Ursulina Prisca has a firm grip on her rights. She knows more law than all the barristers in the Basilica.'

'Why does she need our help then?' Helena managed to put in.

'She wants us to be, as she puts it, the instruments of her legal challenge.'

'Go to court for her?'

'Go to Hades for her!' Justinus moaned, in deep gloom.

'So you accepted the client,' I surmised, laughing at him. 'You are a public-spirited soul. The gods will think well of you.'

'Even his wife doesn't think well of him,' Aelianus told me, in a curt tone. The two of them never stopped. They would be wrangling to their graves. Whoever first had the task of pouring the funeral oils over his brother's bones would be obnoxious in the fraternal elegy. 'But your litigious old widow fancies the boots off him, so he fell for it.'

I shook my head, ignored the scrapping, and gave instructions for our next move.

'Right. We have done some preliminary exploration, and identified the chief personnel. Now we have to grill the key people, and not let up. With luck we are going in before the witnesses have any more time to confer. There are two Metellus daughters and a son. We have two Camillus sons and a daughter, so I wish I could match you up neatly with opposites – but I cannot send Helena Justina to interview an aedile.'

'We have no evidence that Birdy is a womaniser,' Helena protested. 'You don't have to protect me.' Senators' daughters cannot knock on strangers' doors. Her rank barred Helena from visiting strange men.

It had not stopped her visiting *me* in my seedy informer's apartment – but I knew where that had led. 'Metellus Negrinus is a high-placed official,' I countered. 'As a responsible citizen, I am protecting him!'

'You're saving the best for yourself,' she muttered.

'Wrong. I hate corrupt state servants, especially when they hide behind feeble cries of *"I had no choice; I was unfairly influenced"*. No wonder our roads are blocked with dead mules' carcasses and the aqueducts leak. So Helena, can you try to visit Carina, the daughter who is supposed to have stayed aloof from the tricky business?'

'If I can do her sister too. I want to compare them.'

I nodded. 'All right. You take Carina and Juliana. Then Justinus, you can apply your charm to their two husbands and do a similar comparison. Their names are Canidianus Rufus and Verginius Laco. I'll take on Saffia's husband.'

'Which?' demanded Helena.

'Both.' I had no intention of letting anyone else interview Metellus Negrinus, whose role in his father's downfall had been so significant; there were curious questions hanging over 'good old Lutea' as well. His full name, I had discovered from sources at the Curia, was Lucius Licinius Lutea, and he was thought to be something of a social entrepreneur. I believed it. Not many divorced husbands would personally find a new apartment for a wife who had been married again and who was carrying the new man's child. Either the good old marital discard was risk-obsessed and looking for a scandal, or he was up to something.

'What about me?' wailed Aelianus.

'Stick with researching agnates. I have a hunch that inheritance plays some part in whatever is going on here.'

'What was in the Metellus will?'

'That's been kept rather quiet. Presumably the seven tame senators who witnessed the "suicide" had also previously witnessed the will being signed. I asked the ones I interviewed what was in it. I got nothing. Only the Vestal Virgins with whom the document was lodged during Metellus' lifetime will know details of bequests.'

'If they read it,' Helena said demurely. She pretended to be shocked that I had suggested this.

I grinned. 'Sweetheart, Vesta's holy handmaidens devour an aristocratic will within a heartbeat of accepting it for safe keeping.'

'Ooh, Marcus! You don't mean they break the seals?'

'I'll take bets on it.'

Aelianus decided to have lunch after all, like a good son of a patrician house – that is, back at home with his mother. He was learning. He had few useful contacts for our business, but Julia Justa was one he could always call on. His noble mama knew at least one senior Vestal. Julia Justa would never help me in my work, but her favourite son was different. Off he trotted to ask her.

If this failed, I knew one of the more junior Vestal Virgins myself. Constantia was a game girl. So friendly, in fact, that in the confines of my home, I preferred not to mention her.

We all worked the case for several days. At the end of that time, we knew what had happened – and what had not happened.

At least, we thought we did.

So, wanting a quick payment into our bank account, we prepared a summary and presented it to Silius Italicus as a job well done:

Evidence Reports in the Accusation against Rubirius Metellus

Interviews with formal witnesses post-death (M. Didius Falco and Q. Camillus Justinus)

Four interviews successfully conducted. Results inconclusive. Metellus was seen dead in his bed, with a pillbox on a side table. Nobody spoke with him about his intentions prior to death. All interviewees claimed suicide was in character, with intent to discommode recent prosecutors and avoid compensation fees.

All seven witnesses are senatorial, so 'above suspicion'.

Attempts to interview remaining three were abandoned; it is believed they would all tell the same story.

Interview with Calpurnia Cara (M. D. Falco)

C.C., wife to Metellus: strong-willed, hostile, resistant to questioning. Claimed to have discussed suicide with deceased; threw burden of proof on to witnesses (see above for flaws in their testimony).

Interview with Saffia Donata (M. D. Falco)

S.D., recently divorced from Metellus Negrinus, son of deceased, and pregnant by him. Not present on day of death. No direct knowledge of event, but maintained the poison used was hemlock.

[Note: Unreliable witness?]

Approach to Rubiria Carina (Helena Justina, for Falco and Associates)

Known as Carina. Younger and allegedly favourite daughter of Metellus, though believed to be distanced at time of his death. Aged thirty or under; mother of three children; holds office as priestess of Ceres in husband's family's summer residence at Laurentum; benefactress of local community at Laurentum (endowed and built a granary); was awarded statue in forum and laudatory plaque by town. These are unusual honours for a woman of her age – unless she controls great personal wealth and is thought to be of impeccable moral character.

Carina appears oddly colourless. This may be the effect of grief for a recently deceased father – or just a dull personality.

R.C. received H.J. briefly in her home, but on learning the purpose of the house call, declined to be interviewed.

Approach to Rubiria Juliana (H.J.)

Known as Juliana. Aged approximately thirty-five; mother of one infant; regular attendee at festival of the Good Goddess with her mother Calpurnia Cara; no known community good works.

Refused to receive H.J.; declined to be interviewed.

Interview with Gnaeus Metellus Negrinus, son of deceased, aka 'Birdy' (M.D.F.)

Approached at his place of work, subject agreed to be interviewed. Questioning took place at length at the aediles' secretaries' office, adjacent to the Rostra.

Negrinus aged about thirty, middle child of the deceased and Calpurnia Cara. Sandy hair, almost studious appearance. A senator since twenty-five (honourably elected 'in his year', with strong family backing to enhance his chances; came second in the field and was highly popular at home.) **[Private Note: just shows how dumb the electorate are!]** Acted as quaestor in province of Cilicia, nothing known against him. Senate career unremarkable, perhaps due to his rarely attending. With this clean record was elected a curule aedile and appointed to supervise road maintenance. Implicated in corruption trial of his father, though not himself prosecuted, hence failure to remove him from office despite charges of profiteering and contract swindles.

Against expectations, subject responded well to interview. Pleasant, affable, and helpful to our enquiry. Answered all questions put to him. (Interviewer unable to detect whether answers were honest.) Admitted father's 'rather carefree' business practices, denied own involvement in sale of contracts, claimed no knowledge of corruption. Suggested that trial charges were based on technical misunderstandings and exaggeration of minor errors; said witnesses were acting out of jealousy; declined to comment on the motives of the prosecution.

Gave statement that father's suicide was exactly that. Son was present in the bedroom shortly before death, dismissed by father. Denied that the poison used was hemlock, but believed that the cause of death was due to deliberate overdose of some medicine, obtained by father for the purpose of self-destruction (i.e. pills in sardonyx box). Thought medicine would probably have been purchased from family's herbalist, Euphanes [**see below**].

Calendar of events obtained from Negrinus runs: Rubirius Metellus senior convicted. One week later invoice for compensation arrives from prosecutor, Silius Italicus. One further week of consultation with Paccius Africanus, defence lawyer, results in negative possibilities for evading payment. Simultaneously a clemency appeal to the Emperor is turned down. Metellus determines on suicide. Informs wife and son in morning; death occurs in afternoon; formal witnessing of the body in early evening. Funeral held next day. Will formally read to close family and friends, including the original witnesses, on afternoon of funeral.

Negrinus declined to give details of will. Appeared upset when asked.

Interview with Euphanes, herbalist (M.D.F.)

Subject is a freedman of oriental origin, with usual physical traits of his profession: pallid, spotty, unhealthy looking. Sniffed throughout interview.

Euphanes regularly supplied herbs, spices and medicinal commodities to the Metellus household. Most were for the kitchen. Hemlock never supplied. Normal delivery would be alexanders, mustard seed, poppy seed, small quantities of long pepper, and Greek herbs (rosemary, thyme, cicely, catmint, wild savory). None of these is poisonous. Denied knowledge of Metellus senior's pills. Denied supplying them.

[Accountancy note: a small expense item for a gratuity arises from this interview.]

Approach to Verginius Laco, husband of Carina (Q.C. Justinus, for Falco and Associates)
Subject refused to be interviewed, citing citizen's right to privacy.

Approach to Canidianus Rufus, husband of Juliana (Q.C.J. for Falco Assoc)
Subject refused to be interviewed. Door porter commented, citing filthy temper of subject.
[Item: a quadrans to porter.]

Interview with Claudius Tiasus, undertaker, of the Fifth Region (Aulus Camillus Aelianus)
Tiasus runs a busy professional firm, operating out of a street below the Embankment. They were hired to carry the body of Rubirius Metellus to the family tomb, a mausoleum on the Via Appia, which Tiasus described as a dank old shack with a mock pyramid on the roof. There they performed the usual obsequies. They had previously acted for the family on the death of the grandfather (died of old age, about five years ago).

Metellus Negrinus presided at cremation of his father, assisted by Canidianus Rufus, a brother-in-law, together with another man, said to be a close friend of Negrinus. The body was burned, in accordance with custom, then its ashes gathered by the son and placed in an urn within the mausoleum (the urn was provided by the family, not purchased from Claudius Tiasus; it was a large green glass funerary jar, with a lid.)

They had ordered the full ceremonials: a master of ceremonies, flutes and tubas, a procession of female mourners, men carrying the masks of ancestors, and satirical clowns abusing the memory of the dead man.

Interviewer was refused access to staff or attendants from the funeral. Attempt to gain communication was viewed as bad taste and scandal-mongering; there was a loud hint that officers of the Watch would be called. Interviewer withdrew.

Interview with Biltis, a professional mourner (A.C.A.)
Biltis is a specialist funeral mourner, available for hire. A large, slovenly woman of overbearing friendliness. At a 'chance' meeting in a bar engineered by A.C.A., she responded to tactful probing with the information that the Metellus event had been 'one for your memoirs'. First, Biltis said that Tiasus hates having to take on convicts, even though committing

39

suicide had secured Metellus the right to a proper funeral. The public can be abusive in such cases, and it had been hard work persuading the family that Metellus' conviction made it a bad idea to have the bier displayed in the Forum. Then the undertakers' staff 'wet their loincloths' over the son's insistence that the script for the comedians must concentrate on personal traits of his father, while omitting all reference to the recent trial over his business practices. Although Tiasus had given the impression that this part of the funeral procession took place, Biltis said that it was omitted. This caused a huge upset with the chief mime, who lost his chance to show his mettle as a satirist – and lost his fee.

The affair was characterised by more than usual frostiness between the family mourners. At one stage, the daughter Carina had had to be restrained by her husband Laco, after loudly accusing her brother and elder sister of killing the dead man. She left early, before the ashes were collected up.

In addition, Biltis volunteered that she thought the corpse 'smelt funny'. No further details.

Biltis is a free citizen and willing to give evidence if her expenses (travel and time off work) can be refunded.

[Note: modest gratuity has already been paid.]

Interview with L. Licinius Lutea, first husband of Saffia Donata (M.D. Falco)

Subject discovered at Porticus of Gaius and Lucius, apparently after conducting business of some kind.

Marriage to Saffia occurred when she was seventeen and had lasted four years, after which divorce by mutual consent took place. There was one child, son Lucius, who lives with his mother but is seen regularly by Lutea. Lutea has not remarried. He remains on what he called spiffing good terms with Saffia; claims he helped her find a new home out of kind-heartedness plus concern for welfare of his little son. (He had a previous marriage but no other children.) Denounced bad behaviour of Metelli; cited difficulties over removal of Saffia's chattels from their home: her personal bedding (wool mattress, sheet, down pillows, embroidered coverlet) was 'lost'. Lutea reckoned this was stolen to upset Saffia.

Asked if Saffia would pursue the issue, Lutea huffed that he himself had smoothed things over, being on very good terms with Metellus Negrinus.

Asked whether this did not cause complications, Lutea snorted 'why should it?' then left the Porticus at speed, citing a business meeting with his banker elsewhere in Rome.

[Note: Information from a known source at the Porticus is that Lutea's banker

[(Aufustius, see below) works from there, and was not 'elsewhere' but present in the upper gallery.]

Interview with Aufustius, a secure money-holder and loan-provider (M.D.F.)

Aufustius has known Licinius Lutea for the past decade. Declined to comment formally, on grounds of client confidentiality.

On being bought a morning drink and a pastry, Aufustius opened up and freely mentioned that his client has been through a period of instability lasting several years. Lutea just told Aufustius that morning that he hopes to see a revival in his financial standing as a result of some unspecified turn of luck.

Asked how he thought Lutea would have been able to negotiate with landlords on behalf of Saffia, if his own credit was tight, Aufustius lost his charm and helpfulness. Accused interviewer of libel. Offered the usual threats about persons who would know where to find him on a dark night, the interviewer left.

[Expense incurred for entertainment on this interview.]

Interview with Nothokleptes, a banker known to Falco and Associates (M.D.F.)

Lutea's banker (Aufustius) is a well-known figure in the world of commerce, with a high-profile client base. Aufustius would wait patiently for a man in difficulties to recover, continuing to accept him as a customer; however, he would demand an assurance that any insolvency was temporary. This assurance would need to be detailed, eg proof of a coming inheritance.

An upsurge in his client's fortunes would be of clear advantage to Aufustius, so it is reckoned he must have good information about this if he believes Lutea's claim.

[Entertainment expense ditto.]

Interview with Servilius Donatus, father of Saffia Donata (M.D.F.)

Elderly, bald, irascible cove with large family, all daughters. Seems obsessed with manipulating their dowries; groused against obligations on a family to provide settlements in order to secure daughters' marriages, and the subsequent burdens on family estates when dowry payments fall due. Raved against Metelli for bad management of the estates which comprised the dowry of his daughter Saffia. Continually harped on losses incurred to the capital as a result of Metellus senior's mismanagement, which Donatus claims was criminal negligence; Donatus wished to sue

41

and is now considering an action against Negrinus. Special anxiety for financial losses that will affect Saffia's children by Negrinus, especially the unborn. Donatus has other grandchildren and cannot afford to take responsibility for any who are not paternally maintained.

Has no views on Metellus senior's suicide, though showed strong reaction to mention of corruption charge. Deep distaste for anyone selling contracts and offices. Old-fashioned attitude to ethics in public service. Capable of lengthy, unscripted tirade about slipping standards nowadays, with wild arm gestures and impersonation of hungry hippopotamus in full attack mode.

Blanked questions about Lutea. Treated Lutea's relationship with Saffia as past history. Went deaf when asked about Lutea's finding of lodgings and current situation between the pair. Spoke lovingly of infant grandson Lucius.

Notes on information from a female source who wishes to remain anonymous (A.C. Aelianus)

A contact with inside knowledge gave background on the Metellus family.

The parents were always pushy. The two daughters were shunted into good marriages at a very early age and have had problems resisting interference by Calpurnia Cara. Carina's husband, Laco, is thought to have put his foot down, causing strain in family relationships. Carina and Laco do not attend family gatherings such as birthdays and Saturnalia.

Elevation of Metellus Negrinus to the Senate was achieved with much manoeuvring; while not illegal, the degree of open electioneering by his father and grandfather (now dead) was felt to be unsuitable. Negrinus was only elected as aedile by the skin of his teeth; his chances of a praetorship later were thought to be low, even before the corruption case. Retaining his post as aedile after the trial may have been sanctioned because there are only a few months left in his term; it would be unfair to require another candidate to take on the office for so short a time. He may have benefited from of the Emperor's personal interest too; Vespasian may wish to minimise any failure of public confidence which might follow a formal dismissal of an office-holder.

A person in high places has revealed to our source, in absolute confidence, that the will of Rubirius Metellus contained 'unthinkable surprises'.

[Note: Falco and Associates are not free to divulge the nature or identity of this source or that of the person who advised our source on the will. However, we can assure our client that the material is impeccable.]

Interview with Rhoemetalces, an apothecary on the Via Praenestina (M.D. Falco)

Rhoemetalces, an expensive remedy-vendor of Cilician extraction, sells pills and potions from a discreet booth near the station house of the Second Cohort of Vigiles. This is within walking distance of the Metellus home. With the co-operation of the Second Cohort, Rhoemetalces was approached, in company with the vigiles officer who controls licences and secret lists in that district. After a short discussion of the terms under which he is permitted to sell goods, Rhoemetalces admitted that he had sold pills, presumably those in the sardonyx box which was subsequently seen at the bedside of Metellus senior.

The pills had been purchased, not by Metellus, his wife or his staff, but 'on behalf of her poor troubled father', by the elder daughter, Rubiria Juliana. She said her father was proposing an honourable suicide and wished for a rapid end. The apothecary claims it was against his better judgement to comply, but he felt that if he refused she would simply go to some other practitioner. He therefore assisted Juliana, in order to ensure that the deceased was not sold some slow and painful concoction by charlatans or ignorant druggists who would take advantage of the family's turmoil. He sold Juliana seeds of corn cockle, a noxious plant commonly found in wheat fields. If the small black seeds are ingested with other food, corn cockle is fatal within an hour.

Juliana then claimed she was anxious to save her father from his intended course. She wondered if there was a way he could be made to think he was killing himself, but would remain unharmed if – as she believed he would – he changed his mind. Rhoemetalces therefore persuaded her to buy (at enormous expense) pills which were contained within a coating of real gold. We are informed that this is a current fashion among wealthy invalids; the gold is said to increase the beneficial effects of the medicine. Besides, it hides any disgusting taste.

Rhoemetalces, revealing a secret of his trade, declared that he has no faith in such pills (though he sells them on request). He is convinced gold-plated pills simply pass through the patient's gut undissolved. He told Juliana the effects should be harmless, and to safeguard himself further, he offered to provide gold pills which contained only flour dust. However, Juliana said she feared that her father, a suspicious man by nature, would suspect deception and cut open a pill to check its contents. So corn cockle was included. But in the professional opinion of Rhoemetalces, the pills were safe and it is by some unique and terrible accident that Metellus was killed.

Rhoemetalces is currently in custody with the vigiles, who are explaining to him their professional view that the 'unique accident' was directly caused by Rhoemetalces supplying poisonous pills.

[Accountancy note: no gratuity necessary to the apothecary, but there will be a substantial expense item relating to a payment into the vigiles' fund for widows and orphans.]

Reappraisal of Rubiria Juliana (M. Didius Falco and Q. Camillus Justinus) Interview conducted in the presence of Canidianus Rufus

A formal application was made to Canidianus Rufus to interview his wife on a very serious matter, the nature of which was hinted. Rufus agreed, subject to his being present as her head of household, a request which was immediately granted. Rubiria Juliana was allowed two hours to compose herself, then interviewed at her home. M.D.F. directed the questioning; Q.C.J. took notes.

[Note: it is believed that the informer Paccius Africanus was present in the Rufus house during the interview, though this was not mentioned by the subjects. He was observed entering just before the interviewers, and was later seen leaving.]

Rubiria Juliana is a fine-boned, fashionable woman, pale and purse-lipped. She spoke very quietly, though without hesitation. Her husband, previously described to us as unpleasant, paced edgily about the room. He did not sit near, reassure or comfort his wife, as might have been expected. For most of the time he remained silent, allowing Juliana to speak for herself. The interviewers felt he expected her to get herself out of any trouble.

Juliana confirmed the facts as relayed by the apothecary Rhoemetalces. Her father had known that she had bought pills before, for various female ailments. He asked her to obtain a reliable poison for his intended suicide. Juliana had argued with him, and although she obeyed his request, she wanted to save him if he did change his mind. She was certain he would.

Juliana gave details of the suicide. The family had eaten a last lunch together, all except the younger daughter Carina, who had refused to attend. Metellus then retired to his bedroom. Juliana and her mother were present in the room when Metellus senior took one of the pills. He had previously talked with his son Negrinus, alone, but Negrinus had been sent outside when the women were called in. Asked why this was, Juliana said her brother was very upset by what their father wanted to do.

Metellus lay on his bed, waiting for the end. Juliana and Calpurnia Cara stayed with him for about half an hour, at which point he sat up suddenly and, as Juliana had feared, decided he did not after all want to kill himself. Calpurnia abused him for a coward, in the manner of the most stalwart matrons of old Roman history, then rushed from the room.

44

Juliana quietly told her father that the gold-plated pills should pass safely through him, and was thanked by Metellus for saving his life. Unhappily, within a very short time Metellus did collapse and die. It appeared that the apothecary is wrong; the gold does dissolve, in this instance causing the death of Metellus, even though by that time he did not wish to kill himself.

Conclusion

It is the view of Falco and Associates that the death of Rubirius Metellus should not rightly be classified as suicide. He had expressed to his wife and daughter a clear wish to remain alive.

His daughter Juliana provided him with the poisonous corn cockle pills, but this was on the basis that she believed them to be safe. Although Metellus voluntarily took one of the pills, Juliana would have come empty-handed from the apothecary, but for being told that gold-plating would render the pills harmless.

Expert opinion is needed on whether a charge can be laid against Rhoemetalces for murder, as a result of giving false professional advice.

Should such a charge fail, it is the view of Falco and Associates that Rubirius Metellus died by accident.

IX

'*P*URE GOLD *pills?*'
    Silius Italicus had received our careful report with all the thanks and all the applause we hoped for. As men about the Forum, we expected none. Just as well.

I let him rave.

'And what's this try-on, Falco? – your substantial donation to the vigiles' widows and orphans fund will obviously all be drunk by the Second Cohort at a better-than-usual Saturnalia knees-up this year!' Even for a man experienced in court rhetoric, the long, irate sentence left him winded.

If the orphans' fund was all he could find to carp about, we were well landed on the jetty. Of course the fund was a fiction, but he knew the form. The vigiles do have a fund; they look after their own – but that's the point: they keep outsiders out of it. They want the grateful widows to save their thanks for the right people – their late husbands' colleagues. Some are good-looking girls who, being paupers, have to give their thanks in kind, poor dears. Much better to keep it in the family.

Excuse me if I sound cynical. I am shocked at such goings-on, but this is what I was told by my best friend Petronius. He is a compassionate man who in his time has looked after quite a few bereaved vigiles' families. Mind you, that was before he started looking after my bereaved sister. Well, it had better be.

'I apologise for the gilded poison pastilles, Silius, but these are the facts we turned up. I put all this to you as a good-quality proof – and it's backed up by creditable witnesses. Trust me: a ludicrous story carries weight. Anything too feasible tends to be a web of lies.'

'Liars always concoct a probable story,' agreed Justinus, standing at my back.

'A mad explanation like this would be stupid – if it weren't true,' his brother added piously. As these two burbled, Silius looked even more irritated, but he soon subsided. He just wanted to be rid of us.

'I cannot take a man called *Rhoemetalces* before the praetor! I'd be laughed out of court.'

'With luck, you won't have to go to court. The praetor should be able to rule on this evidence from his warm and cosy office,' I declared. 'You know how to get justice –' I was none too sure of that. 'You should walk out with an edict in your favour the same day.'

Now Silius looked annoyed that I was teaching him legal procedure. He must think me a bumpkin, but I knew about praetors' edicts. Each year's new praetor issues a revised version of the civil code, with minor refinements where the law has not been working. When problems are brought before him during the year, he decides which 'formula' for redress from the time-honoured code will fit the problem; if necessary he issues an adjusted formula. The praetor's pronouncements are not supposed to be new law, just clarifications to meet modern times.

I did think it unlikely any wimp of a praetor nowadays would dare to make a judgment in this sticky case. It was a criminal issue, not civil, for one thing. But you have to bluff.

'Rhoemetalces,' Justinus assured Silius in his most serious and most patrician voice, 'is an old-established, very respectable Cilician name.'

He was romancing. Silius suspected it, and I was certain. I had seen the lousy pill-producer.

'Don't give me that.' Silius was no fool either. 'The apothecary will be a sinister ex-slave who probably poisoned his master in the recent past as a means of gaining his freedom – and with a forged will!' he added viciously.

'Luckily,' I teased, 'we will be producing him in a murder case, not testing him before the Board of Citizenship.'

Even Silius was beginning to be seduced by our wry sense of humour. His eyes narrowed. 'What's he like, this druggist?'

'Looks successful,' I said. 'Works out of the usual booth. Sits there with a wicker chair and a footstool, surrounded by piles of medicine blocks which he cuts up as required by customers. He seems well respected in his trade. He owns some up-to-date equipment – a pill machine, where he pushes in the paste, then it comes out extruded into strips and he slices off individual dosages –'

'Yes, yes . . .' Silius had no time for technical marvels. More importantly, he could see we would not give up. 'Oh Hades. I cannot be bothered to haggle with you rogues. The story hangs together consistently.' As soon as he said this, I could see its glaring holes. Silius seemed to have a sight problem, luckily. 'Thanks for the work. Submit your bill. We'll call it quits.'

That may have sounded as though we had seen the last of Silius and the Metelli. Somehow, I doubted it.

X

<hr>

IT WAS the off-season for law. New cases have to be brought by the last day of September which was eight weeks gone, so even if Silius decided to take up our suggestions, he was too late. Autumn passed. We sent in our bill. This time Silius proved slow in paying it. That gave me an opportunity to train the two Camilli in techniques for squeezing stubborn debtors. Since at our level of informing it was a frequent occupation, I viewed this more as work experience than the annoyance it might have been. We had the money by Saturnalia.

By then we had re-established our presence in Rome. Clients were sluggish, but we knew there would be plenty as soon as the cries of 'Io Saturnalia' died down. As always, that time of unrestricted relaxation and large family gatherings had brought out the worst in people. Marriages were breaking up on every street. As soon as Janus let in the New Year in a screaming gale, we would be offered missing persons to trace after violent fights with unknown assailants who were disguised in fancy dress (but who looked like that snotty swine from the bakery). Upset employees would hand us evidence of malpractice by employers whose Saturnalia gifts had been too miserly. Festive wax tapers had burned down homes, with the loss of crucial documents. Houses left empty had been broken into and stripped of their artworks. Could we recover the loot? The wrong people had been kissed in dark corners, only to be spied on by spouses who now wanted not only divorce, but also their rights (in the form of the family shop). Children had been abused by uncles and stepfathers during the ghost stories. Could we blackmail the bastards and stop it? Drunks had never come home. Slaves playing king-for-the-day acquired too much of a taste for role-swapping and locked crazy old masters and mistresses in cupboards while they took over the house permanently. Lonely recluses had died unnoticed, so their cadavers were now smelling out their apartments. Once long-lost offspring were found and lured back to arrange burials, a hunt would start for missing fortunes that had long ago been whisked away by swindlers, then there would be work hunting down the swindlers, then the swindlers would swear their innocence and want their names cleared – and so on.

We had plenty to do. Since dear Aulus and Quintus, my patrician assistants, thought such stuff was beneath them, I was doing it. It was beneath me, too, but I had been an informer through some desperate times and I had not learned to say no.

It had been the first Saturnalia when Julia Junilla was old enough to take an interest. Helena and I had our work cut out ensuring that she stayed awake when her grandparents came calling, or running after her when she snatched her darling little cousins' presents and insisted they were her own. Sosia Favonia, our baby, went down with some frightening sickness, which parents soon learn is inevitable at festivals; it comes to nothing as soon as you are both utterly worn out with panic, but you suffer first. Few doctors were answering their doors, even if patients were successfully rushed to them through the crowded streets. Who wants to hand their tiny baby to a medico who is falling down drunk? I tried the nearest, but when he threw up on me I just carried her home. Favonia could vomit all over my holiday tunic. She didn't need him giving her ideas.

After seven days the torture ended. Saturnalia, I mean. Favonia recovered in five.

Then Julia caught whatever Favonia had had, after which naturally Helena was stricken with it. We had a British girl living with us, who looked after the children, but she collapsed too. Albia had led a troubled life and was normally withdrawn; now she also felt terribly ill in a strange, enormous city where everyone had gone mad for a week. We were responsible for placing her in this nightmare. Helena dragged herself out of bed to comfort the poor girl, while I curled up on a couch in my office with the little ones, until I was rescued by Petronius.

My old friend Petro was escaping from the noise at the house he now shared with my sister Maia. Most of the racket was not caused by rowdy children, but by my mother and other sisters telling Maia she always made bad choices with men. The rest of the rumpus was Maia losing her temper and yelling back. Sometimes my father would be lurking on the sidelines; Maia helped with his business so he reckoned he could irritate Petro by appearing at every possible awkward moment and eavesdropping. Petronius, who until then had always thought I was hard on Pa, now understood why the sight of his grey curls and sly grin could make any sensible man climb out of a back window and leave town for three days.

He and I went to a bar. It was closed. We tried another, but it was full of the relics of riotous behaviour. I had had enough of that, looking after my sick children. The third bar was clean but still had the rioters; when they started being cheerful and friendly, we left. The only place where we could be morose was the Fourth Cohort's station house. Not for the first time, we ended up there. After seven long days and even longer nights of dousing fires caused by sheer stupidity, and then dealing with rapes, stabbings, and persons who had snapped and turned into maniacs, the vigiles were in a grim mood. That suited us fine.

'Nightmare!' Petronius uttered.

'You could have stayed single,' I reminded him. His wife, Arria Silvia, had divorced him and for a short while he had enjoyed his freedom.

'So could you!'

'Unfortunately, I loved the girl.'

It would have been good to hear Petro assure me that he loved my sister – but he was pushed to the limit and only growled angrily.

We would have been sharing a drink but we had forgotten to bring any. He leaned back against a wall, with his eyes closed. I stayed quiet. A few months beforehand, he had lost two of his daughters. Petronilla, the survivor, had been brought up to Rome to spend Saturnalia with her father. The child was taking life hard. So was her father. Enduring bereavement among the festivities had been grim; the fun and games that were always arranged by Maia's thriving brood were not the best solution for anyone. What choice was there, though? It would have been a desperate week for Petronilla alone with her mother.

'I thought I would never get through this month,' Petro admitted to me. I said nothing. He rarely broke into confidences. 'Gods, I hate festivals!'

'Has Petronilla gone back to Silvia yet?'

'Tomorrow. I'm taking her.' He paused. I knew that since he had had to admit to Arria Silvia that he was now sharing a bed with Maia, he found it easier to avoid his ex-wife. My sister had played no part in their separation, but Silvia accused Petronius of having always lusted after Maia – and he stubbornly would not deny it. 'I'd better see for myself. Can't be sure what we'll be walking into.' He paused a second time, trouble heavy in his voice. 'Silvia had a bust-up with that lousy boyfriend of hers. She was facing Saturnalia alone and not looking forward to it. She threatened –' He stopped altogether. Then he said, 'She made wild threats about killing herself.'

51

'Would she?'
'Probably not.'
We sat in silence.

It was Petronius who told me that when the courts reopened, Silius Italicus was to charge the apothecary with murdering Metellus. Petro had heard it from the Second Cohort. They were agog because not only was Rhoemetalces to be offered to the praetor as having a case to answer, but Silius was putting up Rubiria Juliana as his co-accused. Well, that mischief will have brought festival joy to yet another Roman family.

Io Saturnalia!

XI

'SILIUS IS doing this because he wants a Senate hearing,' Petro said. He was a good Roman. Legal gossip excited him. 'He's out to make his name. Parricide is a bloody good way to ensure it; the public will be avid for details. This Juliana woman is patrician, so it will go before the Curia. If the family have imperial influence it could be even better than that. To spare her the ordeal, Vespasian may himself take her case at the Palace –'

'He won't,' I disagreed. 'The old man will distance himself from this family. Ordinarily, he might have rescued them from the ordeal of a public trial, but the corruption conviction will put them on their own.'

'You mean he is an Emperor who won't fiddle things for the élite?'

'I mean, Petro, he won't want it to *look* that way.'

'Does he fiddle?' Petronius was certain that I had inside knowledge.

'Presumably. Don't they all? What's the point of ruling the world if you never fix things?'

'I thought Vespasian didn't give a toss about the upper class.'

'Maybe not. But he wants them in his debt.'

'You are a cynic,' observed Petronius.

'You get that way.'

'It's very hard for Juliana,' Helena reckoned when I went home and told her. 'To be accused of killing her papa, when she bought the pills only because he sent her.'

'Silius will argue that Juliana is lying. Why send her? Why not send out his wife or a house slave?'

'She was his daughter,' Helena said. 'She knew the apothecary. Metellus trusted her to make sure they were pills that would be quick and clean and painless.'

'Would you do it for Decimus?'

Helena looked shocked. She loved her father. 'No! But then,' she reasoned, 'Juliana tried –' Helena learned fast; she quickly swung along

53

with my caution. 'Or she *says* she tried – to thwart her father's suicide.'

'I am sure the defence will parade that claim on her behalf.'

'I'm sure the defence will bungle it!' Helena was even more cynical than me. I was not sure whether this had always been so, or whether living with me had hardened her. 'She's a woman. With scandal in the air, she will stand no chance. The prosecution will allude to the previous corruption trial whenever possible, implying by association that Juliana is corrupt too. Like father, like daughter. In fact yes, she did buy the pills – but her father had declared to all the family that he intended to commit suicide. That is a recognised device at his rank, sanctioned down the centuries. Juliana was simply his instrument.'

I sniffed. 'He changed his mind.'

'So he was a vacillating coward! But Juliana had tried to save him, so that's a double tragedy for her. And to be then accused of murdering him is vile.'

We were sitting in my office at home, me on a couch with the family dog shoving at me to make more room available, and Helena sitting on a table swinging her legs. The scrolls she had moved to clear a space for herself were squashed against a wall cupboard. From time to time she fiddled with my inkwell, while I watched, waiting for it to go over. It had a non-spill device, supposedly, which I was curious to test. 'You met the apothecary, Marcus. What did you think of him?'

I repeated what I told Silius: Rhoemetalces was a successful professional who seemed to know what he was doing. Even accused of murder, I thought he would hold up well in court. As well as he could, that is. He had sold the pills which killed a man, he could not alter that. Everything hung on the court's interpretation of Metellus senior's intentions. Suicide is not illegal, far from it. So could the apothecary be held liable for a man who changed his mind? I thought it would be unfair – but fairness and justice are two different bines on the hop.

'You met Juliana,' I reminded Helena. 'What was your opinion?'

Helena acknowledged that she had not viewed Juliana as a prospective killer. 'I wanted family background. I did not scrutinise her as a possible suspect.'

'Still, what about her behaviour struck you?'

Helena pulled back the scene from her memory. 'I saw her only briefly. She had a family resemblance to her mother Calpurnia, but younger of course, and softer. Sad and strained, but it looked well-etched, so either those were always her natural features or all this business has worn her out.'

'Happy marriage?' I asked.

'Nothing to say yes or no,' Helena shrugged. 'Juliana thought I had come to express condolences. I felt she liked that. She seemed more genuine in her feelings than her mother had been – much less conscious of how everything would look.'

'Someone had told her not to answer questions.'

'Oh yes. She was quick to bridle and she jumped up to call for more attendants, once she realised what I had really come for.'

'Was she frightened?' I wondered.

'A little. Whether scared of me and what I might ask her, or afraid of whoever had told her to be very careful, I can't say.'

'The husband?'

'Most likely. What did you think of him, Marcus?'

'Rufus? Unhelpful bastard. Not just to us – to his wife too.'

We talked about the second time Juliana was questioned, after she became a suspect, when Justinus and I had interviewed her formally, with her husband grimly sitting by. We had seen Paccius Africanus lurking at their house, so he was clearly still advising the family, including Juliana. So at what stage had it struck him that her involvement with the pill purchase might cause her problems? Presumably now he would be the defence in the new court case.

'Will you attend the trial, Marcus?'

'Love to, but it will be an impossible squeeze. If the case is heard in the Curia, only senators will be admitted inside the chamber. You know what it's like. The open doorways will be packed with nosy sightseers, most of whom won't hear a word. I can't face that.'

'You produced the initial evidence from which Silius must be working. Would he not take you, in the prosecution party?'

'He might if I had kept in with him. He has not been friendly since your brothers grabbed our fee.'

Helena looked serious. 'And how, exactly, did they achieve it?' I looked vague. She tapped a fingernail on the inkwell. 'Which of your dubious methods, Falco?'

'Oh . . . they visited the informer's underling, that useless Honorius, in his office.'

'And?'

'And persuaded him to produce a banker's order.'

'Persuaded?' asked Helena, with a glint. 'They beat Honorius up?'

'Nothing so subtle. They locked themselves in with him and stayed there until he gave in. As I heard it, Aelianus took along some reading matter and sat casually immersed in scrolls. The lads peed out of the window, but Honorius was too shy, so he was suffering. After a few hours Honorius also became very hungry; Justinus fetched out a very large lunch basket – which they proceeded to devour with relish and did not share with the scribe.'

'I suppose Honorius caved in by the time they reached the forced-meat balls?' Helena chortled.

'I think it was the giant shrimp tails that did the trick. Quintus sucks them out of their shells so very suggestively. But you get the idea.'

Helena Justina, the light of my life, gave me a look that said she was never quite sure whether to believe my rampant stories – but she rather suspected the worst of them were true. This look contained enough underlying humour to show she did not entirely disapprove. I like to think she was proud of me. After all, she was nicely brought up and would not have wished her husband to collect his debts using sordid brutality.

I had done that once. But those days were past.

We found the easiest way to take an interest in the trial was to take an interest in my noble in-laws. Helena's father, who rarely attended the Senate, was no great lover of gossip, but he was now intrigued by this case which had involved both his maverick sons and his daughter's low-class lover. Decimus trotted along every day, then most evenings either we dined with the Camilli, or we invited them to us. In this way, Julia Justa managed to see plenty of her little granddaughters, which pleased at least her.

She was about to be an even happier woman. Helena and I had popped in and out of the family home near the Capena Gate several times since we returned from Britain, but we were both preoccupied. We now realised that neither of us had set eyes on Justinus' wife, Claudia Rufina, since before we left. When she appeared at dinner, it turned out that, like Saffia Donata, Claudia was pregnant, due any day apparently.

'It's a new fashion!' I joked feebly, to disguise my shock. Fathering this baby must have been the last thing Justinus did before he left Rome with me. His languorous brown eyes, the delight of so many infatuated British bar-girls, met mine above a bread roll he was now conveniently munching. Behind it, his expression was invisible. 'You kept this quiet!' I muttered to him privately. I had been fairly sure that during our trip abroad he had decided that he would end his marriage, which had become so uncomfortable despite Claudia's financial expectations.

'I would have told you, had I known,' he answered in a quietly savage undertone. But next moment he was smiling proudly, just as a father is supposed to do when his first child is due – due while we were eating our dessert custards, judging by the size of Claudia.

She was wearing a necklace of extremely large emeralds, with the air of a girl who thinks she may as well flaunt the one aspect of her personality that her husband truly admires. If they separated now, then as soon as the baby was old enough to travel, Claudia – a bright, good-hearted young woman who understood her own mistakes all too well – would finally return to her home province of Hispania Baetica. Justinus knew the implications. He would have to repay her dowry. He would concede that so young a child should live with its mother, so he would never see the child. He would not receive a sestertius from Claudia's much-vaunted inheritance. His mother would never forgive him, his father would be quietly furious, his sister would despair and his brother would gloat.

The trapped young husband looked at me again. I kept my face neutral and congratulated Claudia.

Claudia Rufina thanked me, with the dignity we had come to expect from her. To my relief, I heard Helena asking her father about the trial.

The senator sat up on his elbow, eager to take the stage. He was a grey-haired diffident man of deep humanity. Life had made him wealthy enough to have standing, yet too poor to do much with it. Just at the moment when Vespasian – with whom he had long been on friendly terms – became Emperor, family embarrassments had held Camillus back. A relation involved himself in a stupid plot, and everyone was damned. Others in Vespasian's circle might have expected responsibility and honour at this time, but Camillus Verus knew he had lost out to Fate again.

'I'm told the preliminary approach to the magistrate was argued hard,' he said, setting the picture for us. 'The praetor tried to throw out the case, but Silius held his ground. The pre-trial hearing was then fairly mild stuff. Silius kept his denunciation short. We reckon he intends to save all his surprises for the Curia.'

'How far have they gone?' Helena demanded.

'They raced through the opening speeches –'

'Silius is prosecuting, with Paccius Africanus for the defence?' I clarified.

'Yes. They both have young fellows in support, but the big names want to speak.'

'And to take the rewards!' I commented. A prosecution can be shared among various accusers, but then any compensation after a conviction will be allocated among more than one of them too.

The senator smiled. 'There is a lot of speculation as to what will be left. If Metellus was murdered, the family have to pay the original trial bill to Silius. That's his motive for bringing the new case. But his son's father-in-law –'

'Servilius Donatus?'

'Right. He is sounding off about a prior claim for compensation for misuse of his daughter's dowry. There was land. Metellus senior had control of it – the son was not emancipated – and Metellus sold all the land.'

I whistled. 'He isn't allowed to do that. The dowry is for the benefit of the couple and their children –'

'Saffia would have had to give her approval,' Decimus confirmed. 'Her father says she never agreed. Metellus had been claiming that she did.'

'But if divorce occurs,' Claudia Rufina seemed unnervingly aware of the law, 'the dowry *has* to be paid back, so the wife can use it to remarry.'

'If she wants to,' said Justinus. He should have kept quiet.

'It's obligatory,' snapped his mother. 'The Augustan laws say she must take a new husband within six months, unless she is past child-bearing.'

'Only if she wants to be able to inherit legacies,' persisted dear Quintus. He really knew how to ensure there would be flaming rows at tomorrow's breakfast table. I had a strong feeling that divorce and its consequences must have been under recent discussion here. Helena glanced at me, with a faint look of distress. She was fond of both her brother and his wife; she hated the trouble between them.

'Well Saffia Donata wants *her* legacy,' the senator said peaceably. 'This is another peculiarity. If Metellus is deemed to have committed suicide, then his will stands – and Saffia Donata is telling people she will receive a substantial bequest.'

'But she's divorced.'

'Curious, eh?'

Now I was on full alert. 'Toppling triglyphs! Who else features in

58

this shock document? Come to that, Decimus – how do you happen to know?'

The senator winked. 'A lot of people know – though the Metelli would rather we didn't.'

'If Saffia gets a nice mention,' I begged, '*please* say – who else has been shoved aside?'

Decimus pretended he was above glorying in gossip. His wife was looking hard at a pear she was peeling: 'The son, they say.'

I was amazed. Metellus and his son had seemed so closely intertwined when they were linked in corruption. And no Roman lightly disinherits any child, let alone an only son. 'So what about the sister they are prosecuting – Juliana – do you know?'

'Well I heard,' Julia Justa wiped her fingers on a napkin, 'Rubiria Juliana will receive a bequest, but according to usual procedures it has to be set against what she has already received in her own dowry.'

'So she's had her share already. The big surprise for the court is that Juliana wasn't after money. So much for greed leading to murder.'

I was disappointed. Money is the biggest motive for killing people. If she had stood to gain a great deal – and if she had known it – then Rubiria Juliana probably did somehow fix her father's demise and we could all enjoy watching Silius denouncing her. Without that motive, Juliana was probably innocent. Which made her trial a much sadder and more sordid matter. There was no creditable reason for Silius to attack the woman.

XII

'WELL, JULIANA looked ill,' said the senator when we met next day.

'You mean, they *made* her look ill,' his wife scoffed. I had once thought that Julia Justa was a hard woman but, like her daughter Helena, she was merely impatient with hypocrisy. 'You can do so much with white lead!'

'It's a convention,' Helena complained, her feet kicking on her dining couch restlessly. She had removed her sandals or I would have been fretting about the new furnishings (we were at our house tonight, joined only by Helena's parents). 'I don't know why anybody bothers with such farcical procedures, just to attract sympathy –'

She was eager to hear the day's news. Besides, the sooner she could persuade her parents to absorb themselves in the trial details, the sooner she could stop worrying that they were glaring at Albia (whom they thought an unsuitable choice to look after our daughters) and at the meal. We had not owned a cook until recently. The one I had acquired last week from a slave dealer was resold two days after I bought him and the new one had no idea what gravy was for. Still, this was an improvement. The first one had tried to fry lettuce.

'Try these intriguing hens' eggs,' Decimus offered his wife. 'Marcus tells me they are a classic Moesian delicacy; the little black specks take days to produce.'

'What happened to that other cook you had?' my unforgiving mother-in-law demanded. After one silent glance at the hens' eggs with their curious jacket of caramelised skillet flakes, she ignored the glass comport on which they nestled.

'Resold. At a profit, I can proudly say.'

'Oh you managed to find an idiot in the buying queue?'

'I sold him to my father, actually.' I chuckled gamely. 'A double coup – except it means we cannot go and dine with him.' That was no loss, and Julia Justa knew it.

'From what I know of your father, Geminus will already have shed him – with a healthy on-cost added.' The senator had not only met Pa, he had foolishly bought things from him.

'I have this vision,' I said dreamily. 'The cook – whose name was Genius, so you know to refuse at once if you are offered him –'

'Only you could fall for that, Marcus.'

'Agreed! In my vision, Genius is now being passed around Rome, constantly gaining in value as successive owners overprice him with false stories about his dishes. Each of us needs to recoup the sales tax when we get rid of him. . . All the time he is acquiring a set of fake commendations, until he becomes a gourmet's treasure, lusted after as if he can whisk up sauces like ambrosia. . .'

'It's a new kind of investment commodity,' the senator joined in. 'Genius never needs to visit a real kitchen – which is just as well, if I may tactfully mention the after-effects of that pork marinade he made for us last week.'

'This date sauce is very good,' remarked Julia Justa very politely. She had let us know her views on Genius, but if his menu had made her ill, *she* would never go so far as to say so. 'And tonight's spiced wine excels.'

'Albia made the spiced wine,' replied Helena, not upsetting her parents by mentioning that I did the date sauce; they wanted to ignore how plebeian I was. Albia went red. We made her eat with us as one of the family when the babies were in bed; she hated it. Still, we were libertarians. Everyone was stuck with our high principles. I bought slaves who were obviously useless, because I loathed the idea of owning them and I could not bring myself to bargain as hard as you had to for anyone with real skills.

As for Albia, we had transferred her from Londinium to Rome to give her the life she had been denied by losing her family in the Boudiccan Rebellion – and she was damn well going to receive family life, even if she preferred solitude. Albia was becoming a quiet, calm, tolerant teenager. She watched the decadent world into which we had dragged her with those British blue eyes, so full of reserve; they seemed to appreciate our special Roman madness while keeping her own, much more civilised restraint. I had seen her sometimes shake her head over us, very slightly.

Still, Helena had taught her to make excellent spiced wine.

'It was Rubiria Juliana's day in court,' said the senator. I noticed Helena hitch her red dress along her shoulder where a pin was digging in. The glimpse of smooth flesh between the fastenings gave me goose pimples. Helena lay flat on her stomach – not the approved style of dining, as her mother clearly noticed; I would be given the blame for this – the low-class, bad influence husband. Helena leaned her chin on her hands, a pose unconsciously copied by Albia, though the fourteen-year-old soon stopped paying attention to what Decimus said and tucked into the food bowls again. Helena had lost interest in eating. She longed to hear her father's news.

'I assume there had been no documentary evidence, Papa?'

He shook his head. 'No. And no minor witness statements are to be brought, only what the defendants have to say for themselves. So there's Juliana, properly dressed in mourning and dishevelled – very carefully, I may say. She made us all feel as sorry for her as possible, but still looked neat enough to be respectable.'

'It is difficult for a woman,' his wife argued. 'If she were smart, you would think her a heartless piece. If she looks untidy, you still won't vote for her.'

The senator winked at me; he did it openly. 'There were pitfalls for the prosecutor too. Attack her too crudely and Silius would look tyrannical. Let her off lightly, and he might seem to be bringing the case out of personal vindictiveness.'

'Which of course you don't believe?' I queried drily.

'I think he's a bloody tricky bastard.' Such strong words were rare from Decimus. 'I remember him years ago. He was an accuser in Nero's day – that's a sordid heritage. You could see his past coming out when he was cross-examining this morning. He still has the snide political innuendo: *Were you not from such a family, you might not have known what was required* . . . As if coming from a gang of contract-traders had made the poor woman a natural dealer in death!'

'I doubt she knew anything about what went on at the aediles' office. . . . Did Silius establish any motive for Juliana to want her father dead?'

'Saving the family fortune. It would be lost if he lived and they were forced to pay their court judgment. That, of course, enabled Silius to go harping on about the corruption.'

'But what is Juliana supposed to be saving the fortune *for*? Hardly any of it would go to her, you said. She had been given her dowry, and that was her lot.'

'This is the weakness in his case.'

'How does he get over it?' demanded Helena.

'Distractions and irrelevant dirt. Those old court standbys.'

'Lots of fun to listen to!'

Her father took a marinated olive, chewed it gently, and made no comment. He had a good sense of humour, but he could be prudish about unseemly jokes. In fact, I thought Helena had spoken critically. She would listen to scandal, but she disapproved of those who peddled it simply to harm others.

'So what kind of witness did Juliana make?' I asked.

'Pretty good. She stood by her story and stood up to Silius.'

Helena asked suddenly, 'Was her sister there?'

'Yes. Didn't see her yesterday. Today, they were all present: sister, brother, mother, the two girls' husbands. Backing the accused, apparently. The defence made a decent job of things too – establishing that Juliana had always been a good daughter, was a mother, only ever had one husband – who was there in court supporting her – had not been criticised for her actions by her mother – who was ditto in court – had not quarrelled with her brother over their father's death – ditto, ditto – and she was warmly praised by her father for her love and care of him, shortly before he passed away.'

'So it was a pointless day?' Helena grumbled.

'Far from it.' Her father sat up slightly. 'There was a sensation. I would not have missed being there. After Juliana, we still had the afternoon session. They had time to start on the apothecary.'

'The man who has to take the blame!' I muttered, the cynical plebeian.

'Or worse, poor fellow,' said Decimus.

He revelled in describing what had happened when Rhoemetalces was brought into the Senate. Silius Italicus questioned him forcefully about the pills he sold to Juliana. They went over the story that I had put in my report: the pills were supposed to contain corn cockle seeds, a fast poison. Rhoemetalces said again that on its own it would kill within an hour. Again he said that he believed the layer of gold would survive digestion, leaving the person who swallowed a pill alive. 'Silius used up all the rest of his waterclock declaiming what nonsense that was.' The waterclock was used to time speeches.

'Was Silius good?' asked Helena.

'Convincing. Eventually his time ran out, so Paccius stood up. Paccius had been looking as if he had eaten something indigestible himself.'

'He's a misery. I take it he made the apothecary look small?' I still remembered how scathing Paccius had been about me at the first trial.

'He didn't bother with the expected personal attacks.' Decimus had our whole attention now. He was clearly working up a good tale.

'From the fold in his toga, Paccius produced a sardonyx box. *While you were speaking to my colleague over there, I sent someone to the Metellus house. Is this the box the pills were in?* Rhoemetalces looked startled but agreed it looked like the same one. Paccius told us it was the one found in Metellus' room when he died; Calpurnia Cara nodded. Paccius asked if Silius wanted to quibble. Silius looked black but said that if the apothecary recognised the box and none of the family objected, he would accept this. Paccius spun around to the apothecary again. *How many pills were in the box?* Six, said Rhoemetalces. *How many people would that kill?* Well, none in my opinion, Rhoemetalces insisted; the gold coating should mean the pills would pass safely through the patient. . . *There were six when you sold it and –* With a grand gesture, Paccius pulled off the lid – *there are five now!'*

The senator paused. He felt the need to ask for more wine in his goblet. We all smiled and pretended not to know he was just doing this for dramatic effect. Helena grabbed a jug, poured, added water, thrust the goblet at her father.

'It was nothing new – we all knew Metellus had taken a pill – but we were leaning forward on the edges of our benches, of course. One ancient ex-consul craned so far forward he fell off and had to be pulled to safety by his toga.' Decimus tilted the goblet to Helena in thanks, then took a sip. All senators learn basic oratory. He had mastered suspense. Mind you, this was no worse than trying to get a sensible story out of my own mischievous father, whose irritable habits were entirely self-taught. 'Everyone could tell Paccius planned some theatrical device. *These five pills are the same as the one that Metellus swallowed. And you say, the gold-coated pills are harmless?* Yes, said the apothecary. He was under pressure and probably puzzled where the questioning was leading, so he added he would stake his life on it.'

I saw Helena Justina draw a sharp breath.

Her father did not pause. *'If you are wrong, one of these pills would kill within the hour, but you are the expert and you maintain that they are quite harmless. Thank you!* exclaimed Paccius, suddenly lowering his voice. The whole court hushed. *Then take one now yourself – and show us, please!'*

XIII

'J UNO! THAT'S disgraceful – it was never allowed?' cried Helena.
     'Well, everyone was on their feet. There was uproar. It gave
Rhoemetalces a moment to think, I dare say.'

'He had no choice!' I was shocked. 'If he refused to co-operate, his
entire defence would fall –'

'Exactly! Silius jumped up and tried a few ploys – he maintained
that if the accused were to die, he would lose his rights as prosecutor.
He knew damn well that if the man took a pill and lived, we would
all go home, case ended. His protests sounded feeble. Paccius just sat
down on the bench, waiting.'

'I bet he looked smug.'

'You could choke on the condescension he exuded. But the consul
stopped the racket. He said it would be inhumane to argue over
technicalities for long. He gave the apothecary a straight choice:
would he do it, here and now, or not? Rhoemetalces asked for the
box to be brought over to him, took a pill and gulped it down straight
away.'

'I am ashamed!' wailed Helena.

'It was his decision, love –'

'No choice! He had no choice, you said so, Marcus.'

'Well, he did it.' I noticed her father was as brisk as me. We had
both wasted too many hours while woolly arguments were waffled
and decisions were avoided; this was pleasingly clear-cut. 'The consul
asked for a new waterclock to be set –'

'And you all waited? You just waited in the Curia for the next hour
to pass?' Helena was still outraged. I patted her arm, trying not to look
as if I wished I had thought of the test.

'Rhoemetalces was allowed to sit – he had been standing as he gave
evidence of course,' said her father. 'So he stayed on a bench, back
very straight, with his arms folded. Nobody dared go near him. Except
Paccius sometimes.'

'To reassure his client?' Helena scoffed. 'The client who might be dying in front of him? At his suggestion?' Decimus inclined his head, acknowledging the filthy ethics. 'This is not about the defendants at all, is it? This is purely a battle between Silius and Paccius,' Helena scoffed. 'They don't care a *quadrans* what happens to anybody else.'

The senator spoke levelly. 'They have a long-standing feud, yes. Not personal enmity, but a legal tussle for supremacy. While the man sat there, hoping, they even joked together. You could say they respect each other's professional qualities – or you could say it stinks!' He knew Helena's version. I think we all knew his. 'The rest of us milled about, people rushed to and from the Forum, the news spread, more crowds gathered outside, everyone muttered in small groups and stared over at the apothecary.'

'And what happened to him?' I was busting to know.

'Nothing happened.'

'He was right about the pills: he lived?'

'So far.'

'He may have a slow digestion,' Julia Justa commented, as if some child in her household was being watched after swallowing a denarius.

'Yes. The consul had him taken under guard to his own house, where he will stay, under surveillance, through tonight. He will be allowed neither food nor drink, lest he take an antidote. If he is alive tomorrow morning –' The senator paused. I did not begrudge him. The story was sensational.

'What do we think will happen?' I asked.

'We think – since he lasted an hour in court and still looked nervously confident – we think Rhoemetalces will survive the night.'

'That's all he needs to do.'

'It is indeed, Marcus. Then the case is over.'

That was how it turned out too. It must have been the easiest defence Paccius Africanus ever came up with. Well, easy for him. For Rhoemetalces, and even for Juliana, it would have been nerve-racking.

The defendants were freed by the consul next morning. Juliana was taken home in procession by her husband and family, amidst what many thought were unseemly signs of triumph. The apothecary, who was unmarried, returned alone to his medicine booth, where for a very short time he attracted a large queue of customers. Notoriety cast its usual sordid spells. He made a fortune that afternoon. Soon, however, people started to remember how he had owned up that he had made money from selling expensive pills which would not work.

This was no more cynical than most lying lozenge-pushers, but when he thought it mattered, Rhoemetalces had been honest. We cannot have that. Rome is a complex, sophisticated society. Truth is distrusted as much as Greek philosophy. So the customers began to stay away.

His trade diminished until Rhoemetalces could no longer earn a living. The Senate had awarded him the most meagre compensation for the court case, because of his low rank. The struggle became too hard. Eventually he took opium poppy sap and killed himself. Few people heard about it. Why should they? He was just the little man who was dragged into the troubles of the great. I seemed to be the only person who commented on the irony of his suicide.

The Metellus troubles, which were deemed so much more exciting, still continued to bubble like an unwatched pot that will thicken and splutter and slowly increase in volume until it boils over. There was bound to be more yet. The praetor had ruled that on the evidence, he could not say the death of Metellus was murder – nor could he decide that it had been an accident. Silius Italicus, an unforgiving informer, still wanted to be paid for the corruption case he won. Now he had been punched in the purse again – having to pay compensation at a senatorial level to Rubiria Juliana for the failed prosecution. Paccius Africanus would benefit from this, but even he wanted to screw yet more fame and money out of the events.

Occasionally someone would remember that if the corn cockle pills had *not* killed Metellus senior, then something else must have done.

XIV

I NEVER CARED for January and February. You might as well be in northern Europe. At least there people have fires in their huts to keep them warm and they don't even try to go out on the streets, pretending to enjoy life.

In Rome it is a period of dark festivals. Their origins are lost in history, their purpose is deeply agricultural or to do with death. I tend to dodge rituals involving seeds and I damn well hate being smeared with blood from sacrificial animals. This unhappy stuff continues until the Caristia – also hideously named the Festival of the Dear Relative. People are supposed to renew family ties and resolve quarrels. Whatever deity thought that up should be locked in a cell with a ghastly brother he hates, while close kin who have offended his most cherished beliefs and stolen his chickens gather round to smile at him lovingly until he runs screaming mad.

Fortunately my family never knows what festival is what, so we don't patch up our tiffs. Much healthier. Our grudges have the historical grandeur most families so sadly lack. Rome is a traditional city; what better way to pursue our national character than by maintaining age-old bitterness and storming out like royalty whenever too many have collected in the same room?

Amongst the offspring of the late Rubirius Metellus, there cannot have been much time for observing festivals. They were always too busy wondering who was being charged with a capital offence that week. If they visited temples, their prayers may well have been fervent, but I bet they went there heavily veiled. Even the ones who were not personally making a sacrifice that day would want to cover their faces to avoid being recognised. In particular, they needed to avoid Silius and Paccius, who must both now be owed money on a flamboyant scale.

Paccius Africanus, it was now rumoured in the Forum, had made a killing with side bets on whether Rhoemetalces would die in the Curia. Yes, gambling is illegal in Rome. There must be a special dispensation for dispensers of the law. (Think of all those gaming boards scratched openly on the steps of the Basilica Julia.) No, I don't know how Paccius got away with it. Shocking. I blame the authorities for turning a blind eye. (In fact, I blame the authorities for receiving hot tips from him.)

Cheered by his winnings, Paccius Africanus took up where Silius Italicus had left off. He charged Metellus Negrinus with bringing about his father's death.

It was not yet public knowledge. I knew. I had been favoured with an urgent request to visit Paccius to talk about the charge.

Unlike Silius, Paccius saw me at his own house. They were opposites in several ways. Silius had ordered me to see him, then did his arrogant best to be invisible. In contrast, Paccius treated me with every courtesy. He even sent a chair with liveried bearers. I was bringing the Camilli, but we decided against trying to squeeze in all three of us; they trudged behind. When we arrived, Paccius rushed out at once to greet us in the atrium. The atrium was grand. Black marble and a superb bronze nymph in the pool. He owned a smart home. Well, of course he would.

'Thank you so much for coming.' He was tidy, fastidious, looked older than his forty-odd years. His voice had a scratch in it, as if it had been overused. Close to, he had one of those lop-sided faces that look as if two heads have been glued together down the middle by an inept sculptor; even his ears were different in size. 'Ah, you have brought your assistants – I am so sorry; I failed to anticipate that. You must have walked – I would have sent directions – did you find us fairly easily? Can I offer refreshments? Do come in and make yourselves comfortable –'

This was the mean-eyed grouch who had implied I came from the gutter when he wanted to make an effect in court. I let his empty etiquette wash over me. But I noted the implication that in today's enterprise, whatever that was, we were on the same side.

I shot the lads a warning glance. Justinus assessed a tapestry as if he had seen better. Aelianus sneered directly at Paccius; truly patrician, he loved an excuse to be boorish. Both had unsmiling faces. None of us wore togas, so Paccius, who had arrived formally dressed for some reason, felt obliged swiftly to shed his. We refused food and drink, so he had to wave away a clutch of slaves with silver trays who gathered in the room he took us to.

I was still wondering about the toga. He was at home. Nobody wears a toga at home. He must have come back from some formal event. What, and who with?

'I need your help, Falco.'

I let one corner of my mouth twitch into a surly smile. 'An appeal for my skills always has charm, Paccius.'

'Shall I recite our fee scale?' Justinus pretended to joke.

'He wants us – so double the on-costs!' Aelianus croaked. We all laughed. What a merry business informing can be.

A man entered, not what I expected as a house guest. He was a stranger, but I recognised my type of operator. He wore a brown tunic, tight on the chest, no braid. A wide belt, fit for various purposes. His boots were solid, also functional. Over his arm he carried a thick dark cloak, its hood hanging down. It looked as if the fabric had been oiled, which you would do if you were constantly out in bad weather. He was ten years older than me, shorter than average, wide, muscular, huge calves. His hair was trimmed so short its colour was indeterminate. His eyes moved restlessly around the room, taking us all in.

'This is Bratta,' introduced Paccius. 'He works for me, as a runner.' Bratta was an informer, then. My type of informer. Silius used one too, he had told me. I never saw his. 'We have a problem, Falco.'

I listened. Bratta watched me listening. His expression was faintly derisive. That could just be his normal face. Mine was no better. I must be looking suspicious of Paccius. The Camilli were quiet. I could trust them nowadays. Bratta stared at them suspiciously; I hid a smile.

'Let's hear it, Paccius: what is your scenario?' If he was using Bratta, I could not see why he needed us.

'I am accusing Metellus Negrinus of killing his father. The motive is vengeance for his omission from his father's will. The method still has to be dragged out of him.' Paccius leaned back. 'You do not appear surprised?'

'Well, I thought you would have gone for the sister next – the one who keeps aloof. An easier target.' He did not respond to the snipe. 'Do you know *why* the will cuts Negrinus out?'

Paccius paused only slightly. 'No.' He was lying. I wondered why. 'My problem is this: to begin proceedings we must produce Birdy before the praetor. It is vital that he attend, to agree the facts.'

'Why is that a problem?'

'We can't find him.'

'What happens if he fails to appear?' asked Aelianus.

Paccius surveyed him indulgently. He could see I knew the reason, but he explained it patiently to my younger colleague: 'The praetor then declares him to have gone into hiding.' With these legal vultures pursuing him, hiding up seemed a reasonable course for poor Birdy. 'His estates could be sold to meet the claim, if that were appropriate. With a capital charge it does not apply.'

'A capital charge can lead to the lions. You want Birdy in the arena?' I asked.

'Don't feel sorry for him, Falco.'

'Why not? His father shamelessly used him as a medium for fixing contracts. His wife has left him when nine months pregnant. His sister was accused of killing their father – and he was cut out of the will.'

I was going to add something disparaging about his mother Calpurnia, but for all I knew, Paccius was her lover.

'So you want me to trace the man?'

Paccius nodded. 'You will be working with Bratta.' Neither Bratta nor I bothered to show how much we hated that. 'It's a real bummer, Falco. Simply getting an appointment with a praetor is a hard enough task. Negrinus has to co-operate.'

In getting himself charged? Why should he? His family had been targeted. It was a sordid game Paccius and Silius were playing; Negrinus had not agreed to join in. These vultures just marked him as their next victim.

'Tell me: why you, Paccius?'

'I beg your pardon?'

'Why you as the accuser?' I repeated patiently. 'I thought the set-up had Silius attacking the so-called killers. You were the faithful family adviser. You did it for the father, then you defended Juliana.'

'Obviously I am horrified that Rubiria Juliana was placed in difficulties due to the malfeasance of her brother!'

'Malfeasance, eh? I see.' I turned to Bratta. He was sitting quietly. Wondering what he thought of the case, I told him my opinion. 'My first moves would be: check with the mother, the sister he was close to, the other sister, the ex-wife, and the supposedly close best friend – Licinius Lutea.'

Bratta showed his teeth. They were a sorry set. Too much bad food munched at cheap food stalls while he was watching people and places. The usual. He was one of us all right. For the first time he spoke, in a voice less rough than his appearance had promised: 'Done it. None of them have seen him.'

'So they say!'

'So they say.'

I had been thinking. Now I stood up. 'Well, that's about the limit of what I can offer.'

Paccius looked surprised. 'Falco! You mean, you won't take the job?'

'No thanks.' I gestured at Bratta. 'You have a perfectly competent trace-man here, who has done the groundwork. Bratta failed to find the fugitive. There's not much left for me; I would be floundering messily. I recommend you just sit tight until Birdy reappears when he gets bored. I don't have the time or the resources to potter about.'

The Camilli were ready to leave with me. Paccius looked astonished that I had turned down the fee. I thought he was about to argue, but he then shrugged. The informer Bratta gave me a nod. I decided there was grudging respect in it. Or maybe he thought me an idiot.

I stared at Paccius. 'You want to be careful. It looks as if you and Silius Italicus have shared this out between you. He had first go, now it's your turn.'

'That would be collaborating,' Paccius murmured. 'That sort of behaviour gets our trade a bad name, Falco.'

Too right it did.

We lads of Falco and Associates stood together in the street. Use of the Paccius litter had been a one-way sweetener. We were not offered transport home.

'So that's it?' asked Aelianus. 'We are out of the case? The Metellus affair does not concern us?' He spoke warily, as if he knew there was more on my mind than I had revealed.

I gazed up at the wintry sky. A star appeared briefly through featherings of pale cloud. Then it vanished. No others replaced it and the cloud cover thickened as I looked. We would have a long, dark walk home. Still, at this time of year the street criminals liked to hibernate. Many would have stayed indoors beating up their women and children. Not that we could feel confident. Others would be on the prowl, using the darkness.

'There's no future in this case,' I said. Justinus made a small mutter of dissent. He had doubts about my motives, like his brother. I started to walk. They followed me, their steps sluggish. I heard one of them kick at a kerbstone, then yowk as he hurt his foot. They had wasted an evening. They were annoyed and dispirited.

After walking for a while, they calmed down.

'We don't have much work,' said Justinus. 'Marcus, I was sure you had decided that we would set out to find Birdy privately.'

'I thought of it.'

'But no?'

'It's winter, no money in it – and I've grown up, Quintus.'

'I was with Quintus,' his brother confessed. 'Waiting to hear you declare you would like to get to Birdy first!'

We all laughed gently.

So we marched through Rome as the winter night descended. Our steps were light and fast, keeping ahead of trouble. We stole a lantern from a portico, so wild shadows flickered around us. Ice was forming on silent fountains; there would be heavy frost by morning. At the Forum, the Camilli left me, peeling off towards the Capena Gate. I walked briskly down the Sacred Way, turned a corner after the empty Basilica, and went home to my wife.

XV

SHE WAS waiting for me. Before I put in my latch-lifter, Helena threw open the door.

She was *not* waiting for me. Ignoring me, she moved back inside and stepped to one side so somebody else had a clear space to walk out. I recognised him instantly. Albia followed; she was driving the man ahead of her. I raised my eyebrows. He had his hands up and he looked scared. I was scared too, for a moment. I saw that Albia was holding the tip of a large kitchen knife rather hard against his back.

The man stopped. Well, he had to. My own knife was out, and pressing on his chest.

'Better stand still.' I could afford to speak gently. We were eye to eye and he could see the menace in my mind. 'I don't allow the women of my household to be troubled by male visitors while I'm out.'

Albia moved back against Helena, lowering her weapon. They clutched each other, no doubt in relief. Looking over his shoulder I could see they were not too badly frightened, more pleased with themselves. I knew who the man was. He was trouble, but not in any way I couldn't handle. Helena and Albia had dealt with him successfully even without me.

I sheathed my dagger. He took heart and spoke. 'You must help me, Falco!'

I grinned at him. 'Good boy. You know the procedure. Now you'll say, *Oh Falco, I have nowhere else to turn!*'

He opened his mouth obediently – well, I already knew he was easily influenced – then he stayed silent, feeling stupid. I gripped him by the shoulders, spun him around, and marched him quickly back inside.

'Metellus Negrinus, men who have gone into hiding from a praetor's enquiry should not stand too long out in the street. We informers get paid a bounty for turning in fugitives!' ,

XVI

WE GAVE him food, watered wine, warmth, a wash in a hand basin. We promised him a bed, safety, a quiet night. First, he had to talk to us.

'Understand this,' I said tersely. Albia had brought us soup; she banged down his bowl in front of him, splashing the low table. I spooned mine up daintily. Our chattels were growing in style and quantity slowly, but we possessed rather fine bronze spoons, a gift to me from Helena years ago. I hoped Metellus would not steal any. You never know with corrupt aediles. Luckily no one had thought to let him have one of our fine-weave Spanish napkins; I had paid for them myself. 'You are charged with murder. You have refused to answer. Tomorrow your accuser will meet with the magistrate and have you formally named as a fugitive. I have enough trouble with the authorities. Once that happens, I will not harbour you in my house.'

'You should meet the praetor, face up to it,' Helena advised him.

'I can't do that.'

Our next question should have been, why not? But there was something going on here. I was prepared to probe carefully.

Helena had already told me Negrinus rushed into the house earlier that evening, demanding to see me. He was dishevelled and dirty, also greatly agitated. She had made sure Albia stayed with her. When he decided they were lying about my whereabouts, Helena became nervous and Albia, still at heart a street child, fetched the kitchen carver.

'You need a bodyguard to tangle with my ladies. You should have brought your lictors, aedile.' Since the New Year his term as aedile had ended, but I noticed he still accepted the title from me. Disgrace had not given him any sense of shame. 'It's never hopeless,' I urged. 'Your sister escaped the charges against her. The praetor may decide that a further prosecution is vindictive. He could throw out the charge against you.'

Negrinus looked up, his face aglow. 'Would he?'

Doubt descended. 'I said it was possible. Look, what has Paccius got on you?'

The sandy-haired man pushed away his bowl. He had hardly touched anything. Normally I reckoned he would be a determined eater; it had made him chubby-jowled and too round in the stomach. He did not look as if he exercised. Now he was dejected, utterly spent mentally. I could see why people shoved him around.

We were in our winter dining room. By his standards it must be plain, but we liked the dark walls with their fine tracery of golden candelabra designs, dividing formal panels. Helena gave Albia the nod that she could disappear if she wanted to; she left, after glaring at Negrinus. Never having had a home until now, she was doubly defensive of our house. I noticed she let the dog run in; Nux experimented with a sharp woof at the stranger, then lost heart and came over to lick me. Helena quietly cleared dishes aside on the low wooden serving table. I lit more oil lamps. I wanted Negrinus to know he would be here until he came clean.

'Let's go right back. Your father was convicted of evil practices involving your duties as aedile; you were implicated but not charged. Do you have any comment?'

Negrinus sighed restlessly. He must be used to this. 'No, Falco.'

'Well, it colours how you will appear. I take it you accept that? Next comes the nonsense with your sister Juliana and the apothecary; she got off, but that too paints "murder" all over your family in the eyes of a court.'

'Paccius knows that my father did not really want to commit suicide.'

'They had discussed it after he lost at the first trial?'

'Yes.'

'Paccius is likely to say so in court then,' Helena joined in. 'An accuser with personal knowledge? The court will believe anything he cares to say. Did Paccius directly advise your father to kill himself?' Her voice was low, belying what I knew to be strong feelings.

'Yes.'

'And what did you think?'

'I didn't want to lose Father. We were close. But I suppose I could see the arguments about not paying out all our money. . .' His voice faltered when he said it, however.

'If you were close, and you cared for your father – can we assume you thought he cared for you?' I asked.

'I thought so.' Negrinus spoke in the same despondent tone as when he had answered previously. 'I always thought so.'

'So why did he cut you from his will?'

A faint flush coloured the man's fine skin. Gingery types find it hard to conceal their feelings – though interpreting the signals is not always easy. 'I don't know.'

'You must have some idea.'

He shook his head.

'I realise this is upsetting – but Paccius will interrogate you when you give evidence.'

He stared at me. 'You know his intentions?'

'He tried to hire me tonight – to look for you. He told me, your distress at being omitted from the will is your murder motive. It figures. Of course you're annoyed. You are the only son. This is not just about the money, Birdy. It's your social and domestic position at stake. This is about who takes over religious responsibility in your family, who honours your ancestors, who makes offerings to the family gods. You expected to take on your father's role.'

'Ha!' For once Birdy spoke up for himself. 'I was more likely to be pleased that Papa had not handed me all his debts.'

That can be a deterrent to heirs: a bequest brings the main beneficiary full responsibility for any debts left behind. Large debts can outweigh the inheritance. In those circumstances good men sigh and accept the burden. Heirs who are light in a social conscience try to refuse their bequest. That's most heirs, naturally.

'Were there many creditors?' Helena shot in quickly.

'He owed thousands.'

'A lot of it seems to be disputed – the compensation for Silius, your ex-wife's dowry repayment . . . Still, it would mean endless trouble for any heir. So,' I wondered, 'is this will some clever legal device? Was your father strategically protecting you?'

A sly look crossed Birdy's face. 'Maybe he was!' he exclaimed, now showing excitement.

'Have you any idea,' I asked him directly, 'how Paccius thinks you killed him?'

'Hemlock, I dare say.'

I glanced at Helena. Hemlock had already been mentioned by Saffia, the pregnant ex-wife. 'That's very precise!' Helena said.

Birdy fell silent.

I leaned on my elbow, stroking Nux. She had squirmed into her favourite place, tucked against me on the couch. Her body was warm

77

under the rough curly hair and as usual she smelt doggier than I liked. I stopped. Eyes shut, the happy hound insistently nudged my hand for more attention.

'I'm still confused about the money,' Helena mused almost drowsily. 'Your father was supposed to have made a fortune from fixing contracts. How can he have had so many debts?' Birdy looked vague. It was quite possible he did not know. He had never been formally released from parental control. His father may have hogged all details of the family finances – especially if he was involved in dubious practices. 'So how did Silius Italicus discover the fraud at your office in the first place?' Helena tried next.

'He said we had an extravagant lifestyle. He kept on and on about it in court.'

'Oh that old argument!' She smiled, with apparent sympathy, then slid in briskly: 'Did you?'

'Not really.'

'What happened to the money then?'

For a moment I thought that Negrinus would admit the Metelli still had it. Then he looked at Helena and I was aware of much greater intelligence than he normally revealed. His air of innocent weakness could all be contrived. I saw a flash of stubborn will. When he then claimed he knew nothing about the proceeds of the corruption, I was not surprised and I ignored it. He knew. Most likely, his father simply ran up debts because he was a mean bastard. Cash was stashed away somewhere. But I had a feeling we might never find it.

I yawned. 'You must be tired.' I knew I was. I was sick of the Metelli too. 'This is an anxious time and you've been out on the streets. . .'

'We have a guest room where you can stay tonight.' As she began to shepherd him to his bedroom, Helena urged, 'Negrinus, you have to appear before the praetor; unless you go to ground for ever, it is unavoidable.'

I joined in. 'Paccius is going to see him tomorrow. I suggest you turn up unexpectedly and take the wind out of him. I'll come too, if you like.' Negrinus was about to interrupt. 'You need to know what he's planning. If you go before the praetor to "agree the facts", you force him to reveal his primary evidence.'

'Oh Marcus, you are wicked!' I could always trust Helena to understand what I was at. It made some parts of domestic life tricky but was useful on occasions like this. 'Paccius will hate that!'

Negrinus seemed to like the idea of offending Paccius. He agreed to my plan.

I wondered if I had the nerve to claim a fee from Paccius for finding and producing him. I thought about it for two seconds, then decided that I did.

XVII

W E STARTED badly. The praetor had already dictated a proclamation naming Metellus Negrinus as a fugitive from justice.
When I produced Negrinus it spoiled his day. His secretary had
inscribed the proclamation nicely and hated tearing up good work.

Don't ask me which praetor it was. The usual. Anyone who wants
to look up who the damned consul was four years later can work it
out. I've forgotten. All I know is he was a snide bastard, working in
an office where even the clerks looked as if we were some foul mess
brought in on the sole of a boot. They all had better things to do than
provide justice for the Metellus family.

Paccius Africanus excelled himself.

The story now was: Metellus Negrinus, first the stooge of his father,
subsequently became the weak-willed tool of his mother. After the
corruption trial, Metellus senior refused to do the decent and remove
himself from life. Calpurnia was furious. A noble Roman matron
expected her man to show self-sacrifice. To preserve the family cash
from Silius (Paccius sombrely maintained), she decided to remove
Metellus herself; this was with the aid of her son, who felt aggrieved
that he had been omitted from his father's will. Calpurnia admitted
having the idea, but Negrinus did it, with hemlock. The plan, said
Paccius, was stupidly elaborate. He rightly claimed that murders
dreamed up by amateurs often are. Calpurnia and her boy had confused the issue by telling Metellus senior he could take his daughter's
corn cockle pills in complete safety, pretend they had worked, fake his
own death, then revive and live a happy secret life. They pretended
one of their slaves would actually be killed, to provide a body they
could display and cremate. Paccius named the slave who would have
died: Perseus the door porter. The charge was that Metellus fell for the
plan, then instead, hemlock was administered to him by Negrinus at
the lunch which they later pretended was the 'suicide's' formal
gathering to say his farewells to his family.

'Are these people mad?' asked the praetor. He had listened in silence, as if preposterous ideas were constantly brought before him. No doubt he had learned that he could most easily end the torture by allowing the complainants to finish as soon as possible. In a rare flash of humour he added a heavy praetorian joke: 'No more than your family or mine, no doubt!'

His clerks sniggered. We all grinned obediently. I waited for him to dismiss the accusation.

'I take it you are writing your memoirs, dear Paccius, and need a lively chapter for the next scroll?' The man was thoroughly enjoying himself.

Paccius made a modest gesture. He managed to imply that when he did write his memoirs, the praetor would receive a free copy of that startling work. There was a strong sense that the magistrate and the informer were old colleagues. They had obviously been involved in many previous cases, and perhaps dined together privately. I distrusted them. There was nothing I could do. No point worrying that they fixed verdicts. Of course they did. It would be hard to prove – and anyone of my new rank who did expose it might as well sail into exile on the next tide.

'What do you have to say for yourself?' the praetor asked Birdy. 'Can you tell me all this is untrue?'

That was when Negrinus damned himself. 'Not all of it,' the witless flake muttered, sounding meek.

'No point denying it, is there?' exclaimed Paccius. 'You realise I have been talking to your mother!'

'Is she to be jointly charged?' the praetor interrupted.

'No, sir. Calpurnia Cara is a woman of some years, who has lost her husband recently. We believe it would be unfeeling to inflict her with a court case. In return for her complete honesty, we are waiving the right to accuse her.'

I heard myself choke with disbelief. The praetor merely shrugged, as if forgiving highborn widows who had poisoned spineless husbands was an everyday courtesy.

'Will she make a statement?'

'Yes, sir,' said Paccius. Negrinus closed his eyes in defeat. 'I shall produce her written evidence that her son administered the poison to Metellus senior.'

'Negrinus will deny it,' I said.

The praetor gave me a sharp look. 'Well, of course he will, Falco! Paccius intends to show that he is lying.' Paccius gracefully thanked the praetor for stating his case.

So if this came off and Negrinus was convicted, Silius Italicus would once again be able to grab compensation in the corruption case, because we were back with the angle that Metellus had not committed suicide. Any money that remained in possession of the Metellus family afterwards would be there to pay off Paccius, for his defence of Juliana and his attack on Negrinus – the remainder to be enjoyed by the heirs to the dead man's estate. I had no doubt now that Paccius was in league with Calpurnia in some way. Maybe her daughter or both daughters were involved too. My one-time joke that Paccius Africanus might be Calpurnia's lover now seemed less amusing. One thing was clear: Negrinus had been used, disowned – and now was to be unfeelingly dumped by his family.

The story was still fantastic. I was still waiting for the praetor to dismiss the charge.

'So you are in agreement with some of the facts,' he asked Birdy. 'Which ones?'

'We did once discuss a plan such as Paccius described.' He was out of control. He must have had an education but nobody had taught him to use logic, even when his reputation and his life were at stake. At this rate, he would truss himself up and hobble single-handed into the arena full of lions, smiling a feeble apology. 'It was just after the trial verdict. My father didn't want to die, my mother was angry, she did suggest us taking matters into our own hands. I cannot deny the conversation happened; my ex-wife was there.' So that was why Saffia Donata had mentioned hemlock. 'But of course we didn't do it,' Negrinus whined.

Too late. It had no force. He was damned.

'No choice is available to me, I fear.' The praetor maintained the pretence that he and Negrinus were civilised equals. He pretended that he hated to see a fellow-senator brought to this. 'I have heard enough evidence to allow the case against you to proceed. Parricide is a crime we Romans hate above all others. A man of noble birth has been murdered in his own house. Shocking! I am prepared to summon the Senate to judge this.' Perhaps his voice softened. Certainly he stopped enunciating edicts temporarily: 'Metellus Negrinus, get a grip! You are in serious trouble; you need the best defender you can persuade to speak for you.' Ah, what a good sport. He wanted the trial to be fun for spectators!

At the last-minute interjection, which was caused by guilt no doubt, Negrinus shuddered. His head came up and he looked the magistrate full in the face. 'What's the point, praetor? I am lost, and we all know it!' His voice became harsh. 'I stand here accused of murdering my father – and my own mother condemns me. I am an embarrassment. She just wants to get rid of me. I never had a chance,' he groaned. 'Never, never! Nobody will defend me. There will be no justice at this trial!'

I could see why he felt that way. Worse followed. I had assumed that in view of the reported feud between Paccius Africanus and Silius Italicus, Silius would act in Negrinus' defence. But then, Silius also wanted him convicted, in order that his father's alleged suicide would be disproved. So it turned out that Silius and Paccius for once had ganged up.

Even the praetor seemed slightly embarrassed as he explained the situation: 'I have another application for charges against you. Silius Italicus has petitioned too. I have decided it is not necessary for you to be present before me a second time when he states his evidence.' After this magnanimity, he turned to Paccius. 'We shall move to a pre-trial hearing in two days' time.' He looked back at Negrinus. In a routine manner, he explained: 'This will be where I decide who has the greatest claim to prosecute. I shall adjudicate on who can bring which charges, and perhaps make a pronounce-ment on how they are to divide the compensation if you are convicted.'

Paccius looked put out. 'I claim the right of first speaking at the trial!'

'Of course you do,' the praetor told him smoothly. 'And so of course does Silius!' Things were no longer going in Paccius' favour – though they were still firmly going against Birdy. He had no friends. I had come with him today, but had done so only to claim a bounty for producing him.

The hearing was over. Paccius lingered for discussions with the magistrate. I won't say they were about to share a drink and a laugh at Negrinus' expense – but a stagnant odour of connivance followed us through the spotless marble-floored corridors as I propelled the accused on our gloomy way out.

'It's not over yet, man –'

'Oh yes it is.' Bare resignation filled his voice, though he was quiet in a way he had not been last night or this morning. 'Falco, this was settled for me a long, long time ago!'

He was not going to explain, I could see.

'Look, Birdy; go home –'

I stopped. He looked at me. He let out a brief hack of bitter mirth. 'Oh no!'

I sighed. 'No.'

Home was where somebody had almost certainly murdered his father, though as we stood on the praetor's doorstep, for the first time I did feel that it might not have been this ineffectual son who committed the crime. Home was where the mother was, who had devised that crime but who intended to condemn him for it.

I had no choice now. Negrinus had lost all hope – and he had nowhere to go. I took him back again to my house. As we walked there, a heavy feeling descended that I was being sucked into a bottomless black pool in the isolated wastes of the Pontine Marshes.

Still, that must be nothing to the mood of the man beside me.

XVIII

THE CAMILLUS brothers had little expert knowledge, but they had skills to deal with Negrinus: they became lads about town together, though on my advice they did not get him altogether drunk. We wanted him capable of speech. They took him up on to my roof terrace, where the night air grew extremely cold. They began drinking slowly, chatting about nothing as if the day's business was over. Since there were two of them, it was easy to let him imbibe more than they did, while appearing to match him. While he still felt fairly sober, they decided it was chilly, so they all trooped downstairs to a salon, where smoky braziers had created a good warm fug.

Negrinus became drowsy. Justinus had actually fallen asleep when I decided to join them. We all lolled about with winecups pretty much unused on the table. I had a scroll, which I did not bother to read. Aelianus used a soft cushion in an endless pursuit of a small moth, ultimately fruitless because he could not be bothered to raise his backside far from his couch.

It was quiet enough to hear the charcoal sizzling in the braziers. Somewhere in the distance baby Favonia was wailing. I kicked Justinus awake. 'How's Claudia, Quintus?' I added for Negrinus, 'His wife is about to pod.'

'Nothing's happened,' Justinus answered primly. 'She's fed up. I'm nervous. . . Is yours born yet, Birdy?'

Negrinus shook his head. 'I suppose not. I suppose somebody would tell me.'

'Someone would call on you for maintenance!' Justinus assured him.

'Dear Quintus is not even a father yet,' his brother marvelled lazily, lunging again at his moth. 'But he has learned the rules. . . You had a stepson, didn't you, Birdy? Do you think your two will get on with him?'

'Of course they will!' Justinus interrupted, slurring his words gently. 'Their fathers are best friends, after all.'

As we had hoped, Negrinus was ready to say more than usual. He was sitting on his couch, feet stretched out, staring at his shoes and soul-searching. 'I do love my daughter; I shall love the new one. They are my children . . . None of this is their fault.'

We all murmured sympathetically.

'They are very young,' Justinus soothed him. 'They needn't know anything about it until it's all long past.' He too stared at the floor. Aelianus was hugging the cushion, keeping quite still now. Since they started to work with me, I had taught them to be synchronised at least when playing with suspects. 'It's curious, isn't it?' Justinus then mused. 'Would you ever have seen this coming? When you were a child? Were you happy?'

'Oh we were happy,' Negrinus answered miserably. 'We didn't know. I didn't know,' he repeated. We all assumed he meant the current legal matters were unforeseen. 'I want my children to be happy,' he maundered. 'Is that too much to ask?'

We gravely assured him the hope was reasonable, then Justinus went out for a pee.

Aelianus nodded after him. 'Problems with his wife. All going bad. Same as you.'

Negrinus was drinking again. Aelianus leaned forward and gave him a refill, but neither of us took up our cups. A brazier spluttered and the flame sank. I closed it down and let the room grow darker. 'Not me,' said Birdy. 'Never went bad – it was bad all along, see. I was set up. No chance. Set upon and set up . . .' He slumped even more. 'But I didn't know anything then.'

Was this the same thing he didn't know, something specific? Or was he just tipsily rambling?

Justinus returned. He must have raced to the kitchen latrine and back, desperate to make sure he missed nothing. Aelianus shot him a look, in case he had made our confider lose the thread.

'Who set you up then, Birdy?'

'Somebody!' An adolescent retort. He sounded drunk, but not for the first time I experienced a feeling that this man was armoured unexpectedly. He looked around our group with a challenge, though his attitude was amiable. 'Now listen, you naughty fellows – this is my private life!' He collapsed again. 'Private life . . . A man has to have a private life, if he is to have a public life. Have to be married. I had to get married. So I married Saffia.'

'Your best friend's wife?' I queried lightly.

'My best friend!' he exclaimed. 'My worst friend too. . .' We were losing him. Suddenly he revived again. 'Tested!' he barked. 'Knew what she was like, you see.'

'Were you happy with that?' Was Lutea, I wondered. If Lutea's marriage to Saffia had foundered for some reason, would he have wanted to see his friend pick up his departing wife? Or did Saffia actually fall for Negrinus first, so causing the Lutea marriage to fold? It seemed unlikely. Lutea would not have stayed on good terms with her.

'I was happy!' Negrinus retorted expansively. 'She was *very* happy!'

'But it's over now?' nudged Justinus gently.

Negrinus stopped. Now we really had lost him. 'Everything is over,' he explained to us in a hollow voice. 'Everything is gone for me. I have nothing, I *am* nothing –'

'Bear up! I was wondering where you can stay,' I said, sounding as helpful as possible. I had decided I could not bear him filling our house with his unhappiness and his lofty attitude. Not now I knew how much he drank. I would not be put under obligations by a weak-willed aristocrat whose name was a Forum byword. It was always possible this man made a habit of dropping hemlock into the house-holder's dinner. 'What about your pal? Wouldn't Lutea give you houseroom for a while?'

'No, I can't go there –' His tone was blank. He gave no reason; he was unaccountable to us. I resented the way we were treated like his slaves sometimes. He was in my winter salon; he was drinking my wine. He was making away with a lot of it too.

Justinus pushed him. 'But he is your best friend!'

When Birdy just shrugged, Aelianus asked rather pointedly, 'Don't you have any other friends?'

At last he responded. 'Oh, I'll find someone,' Birdy agreed off-handedly.

After a moment, Justinus came at him again, wickedly. 'Your ex-wife has a nice apartment. Lutea arranged it for her, apparently. You should see if he can find another for you!'

Negrinus gave us a swift, rather bitter smile. He dismissed the suggestion without bothering to comment.

'Have you and Lutea fallen out?' I asked him bluntly.

'Oh no. Lutea loves me!' The reply was ambiguous. It was said with some feeling, but could be either truth or a flash of rueful irony. 'Don't worry,' he assured us (trying to make me feel bad). 'I'll move on. I'll find a lodging. I won't be in your way – or anyone's . . .' His misery, or the drink, overcame him again. 'Oh gods – what am I going to do? I have nothing – I don't even know who I am any more!'

'No, no! Stop saying that,' urged Justinus, our young idealist. 'Don't give in, if you are innocent. Defend yourself!'

Negrinus looked around our group. Like a man falling off a ladder, I saw the impact coming. 'I need someone to help me. I think you people should take on my defence.'

We were all silent momentarily.

It was Aelianus who spoke first, saving the situation for us all. Having a traditionalist on the staff grated sometimes, but freeing us from nonsense because the nonsense broke rules was a useful business tool. 'It is inappropriate for us. We don't do court cases. I'm sorry. We do not have defensive expertise.'

Negrinus laughed. 'Oh I know that! But here you are, you see. I have nowhere else to turn. You have to look after me.'

He stood up. Now he was being positive again. He was thirty years old, a senator, a curule aedile. He must have been in the army. He had held other posts in government. We were mere curs in his social entourage – and he was certain that in the end we would beg for scraps.

He went off to bed. When he left us, we argued there for hours. He must have known we would. It grew too late for the Camilli to return to their father's house; they were still arguing together when they dragged themselves off to the room where Helena let them doss on guest beds if they stayed over. I had told them, there was no way we could take on pleading Birdy's defence. They had declaimed some high-flown concepts, such as Justice demanded it. I had disparaged Justice and her foolish demands. We all felt trapped. The bastard had nailed us to the wall with our own consciences.

'It's not just that he needs help.' Justinus glared at me. I understood his feelings; he had a wife and was about to be a father. He was sick of being reminded that his wife Claudia was an heiress; he wanted money of his own.

'I know. Silius and Paccius are about to make a great deal out of this. So, if Birdy asks us, why shouldn't we have a share in the proceeds?'

'I'm off to dream of cash boxes,' Aelianus muttered blatantly.

I checked the house. Doused lamps. Fastened shutters. I looked in at my children, one feverishly hot under a tangle of bedcovers, one snoring, with dribble all over her pillow. I straightened limbs and quilts. Fine. I found Helena, in our room, also sleeping, her pose strangely like that of my elder daughter, though in fairness she was not dribbling. I tucked her arm under the bedspread. Lifted up a scroll she had been annotating. . .

Fancy that. Helena Justina had been re-reading the report I produced for Silius.

Every informer needs a girl in the office who will take messages. Mine ran the accounts, kept me in order – and made commercial decisions. While we haggled, with Negrinus and among ourselves, Helena had been working over our interviews, looking for new lines to investigate. She had already decided we were working this case.

I climbed into bed, having moved an oil lamp from Helena's bedside to my own so I could just about see.

I thought about the way Negrinus had come here, first insisting that I was the only person who could or would help him, then changing his mood to moan wretchedly that his position was hopeless, yet now once again demanding that we take on the charges. If he was a victim, ruthlessly targeted by Paccius and Silius, we in turn had been targeted by him. The lads were right: there could be rich pickings here. But I wondered why I felt so sure I did not trust our beleaguered client.

I began to study Helena's marginal notes, so I would be ready with viable ideas of my own tomorrow.

The Accusation against Rubirius Metellus: Helena Justina's Notes

Interview with Negrinus
Will formally read to close family and friends, including the original witnesses. . .
- ◆ Ask the senators what it says (any ideas on Saffia?) and what happened at the reading!**
- ◆ Ask Birdy, while we've got him here.

Calendar of events. . .
- ◆ Check timings (very carefully)
- ◆◆ Date of will?

Interview with Euphanes, herbalist
Denied knowledge of Metellus senior's pills. Denied supplying them. . .
- ◆ But does he handle hemlock?
- ◆ If not, where did they get it? Who bought it? (Does Birdy know?)

Interview with Claudius Tiasus, undertaker

. . . mausoleum on the Via Appia

♦ Visit mausoleum?

Negrinus presided (at funeral), together with another man . . .

♦ Who? Lutea? (His friend, NB)

They had ordered the full ceremonials with flute players, a procession accompanied by mourners, masks of ancestors, and satirical clowns abusing the memory of the dead man. . .

♦ Find other participants, not just Biltis. Clowns?

Interview with Biltis

Overbearing friendliness. . .

♦ Did she make advances to my brother??? (Ask Aulus!) (Don't tell Mother!)

Comedians omitted

♦♦ YES! Find the chief clown – urgent! What was he going to say???

Biltis willing to give evidence if her expenses can be refunded. . .

♦ Wants the money! Unreliable.

Interview with Aufustius, money-lender

♦ Lutea and Negrinus are friends. Do they have the same banker?

♦ Re-interview Aufustius. Why was Lutea in financial difficulties? Ask about will. Is Lutea hoping to profit from Saffia's inheritance?

Interview with Servilius Donatus, father of Saffia

Donatus considering action against Negrinus re dowry

♦ The two children of Saffia/Negrinus are close together so presumably the marriage was short. Has the third instalment of the dowry been paid? If Negrinus successfully defends against compensation claim, what is the position?

♦ NB Did Metellus senior fully pay up the dowries of his own two daughters?

♦ Younger d. (Carina) has 3 children, so presumably hers was long paid. What about Juliana though? (One child. Is her marriage recent?)

Unnamed source

Will contains certain surprises

♦ WELL WHAT??? More than Saffia? Ask my mother. Ask my father – he knows something. Did he get it from my mother – or is information about this will widespread?

Interview with Rhoemetalces
Admitted he sold pills. . .
   ◆ When were these pills bought?

It was at this point that Helena must have fallen asleep.

The proposed visit to the mausoleum would be fruitless. An urnful of ashes would not tell us much; in my experience, urns were taciturn witnesses. But the rest was all wise stuff. Her rank and sex debarred Helena from walking around Rome doing my work, but she knew how investigative informing should be done. If we did take on Negrinus, we would not start with the tale he spun, but with our own evidence. I made a few extra notes, based on today's and tonight's experience. They were people to interview:

■ *Calpurnia Cara (if possible) (O silly boy, you are joking!)*
■ *Licinius Lutea (something whiffs)*
■ *Saffia (something whiffs a lot)*
■ *Perseus the nearly-dead door porter (knows he was fingered? Why was he fingered?)*
■ Rubiria Carina (doubtful: at least try her) Or husband. (Crucial: angry scene at funeral?* Why did she not attend last lunch with father?)

*in view of accusations at funeral, why was Carina not questioned at Juliana's trial? (ask Paccius) (joke!)

Then, before I blew out the lamp and lay down, I wrote in a neat box:

?? WHO WILL DEFEND BIRDY IN COURT ??

XIX

W E WERE taking the case. At breakfast, Falco and Associates all agreed: the thought of money clinched it. When Negrinus appeared, looking refreshed and more buoyant, we asked him for a deposit. To our surprise, he immediately wrote a request for a loan from Rubiria Carina, the younger of his sisters – who immediately paid it.

She and her husband then offered Negrinus a place of refuge. He seemed surprised when her messenger brought the invitation. I was just surprised we had not thought to send him there straight away.

'I heard Carina stayed aloof from your family,' I said, as I packed him off in Helena's litter. 'That's where you gain when the rest of your family dumps you, I suppose. Tell me, had they dumped Carina too?'

'There was some trouble a few years ago,' said Birdy. 'She disagreed with things. And her husband had a tussle with my father over money. . .'

Rome seemed to be stuffed with people fighting over dowries. 'Instalment of her portion not paid?' I was getting the hang of life at aedile level.

'You guessed.'

'Has it ever been handed over?'

'Yes. Verginius Laco gets his way.'

Such problems did not afflict my section of society. Helena did not bring a dowry; our children would be fed, clothed and educated out of my income and a legacy of hers. There must have been a dowry set aside for Helena once; she had been married to a senator. Given that Helena's parents were mortgaged up to their hairlines, I had done them a favour. By my forgoing a marriage ceremony, they had been able to forgo setting us up in life.

Negrinus went off to his sister's house, and I trotted into the city to research that other source of friction: the will. After they are read, wills are stored in the Atrium of Liberty. I spent a couple of hours there, growing frustrated. Eventually I was attended to by a sad-eyed public slave, some ill-nourished clerk with no hopes and no incentive. Since the Metellus will was recent, he did find it. If it had been an older deposition I would never have seen it. I had the impression I was the first member of the public who had asked for a viewing of anything.

Still, this gave me curiosity value. Finally I had access, while there was still enough light to read through the will quietly and find out its secrets. Or so I had thought.

The limp clerk laid the will on a table. It was a double-fold wooden tablet. It was tied up with legal thread – and it was sealed seven times on the thread.

'I can break these seals?'

'No, Falco!' He snatched it back and snuggled it against his tunic protectively.

I took a fierce breath. 'Oh excuse me! I thought this document had been opened and read. I came here to study its provisions.'

'Keep your temper.'

'Am I missing the point?'

The clerk still clutched it. 'This is the usual form.'

'It is the will of Rubirius Metellus?'

'Gnaeus Rubirius Metellus –' From a safe distance he showed me the label on the outside of the tablet.

'Did they not read it?'

'Yes they did.'

'So why is it still sealed?'

'*Re*sealed . . . Do you want to know the procedure?'

'Teach me!' I growled.

'Say you are holding a reading. You fetch the will from the Temple of Vesta, or wherever it was put in safe keeping. You break the seals, in the presence of all or most of the original witnesses.'

'They know what is in it?'

'Not necessarily.' The clerk paused, seeing me stare. 'The testator was not obliged to show them. Sometimes as long as they are alive they really want it a secret.'

'If the bequests are likely to cause trouble, you mean?'

'Exactly. When people first witness a will, they are merely signing to say the outside of the document has been shown to them formally as the man's testament. That,' explained the clerk carefully, 'is why they must then be present when he dies and the will is read, to see that their seals have not been tampered with. They can't vouch for the contents, you see.'

'Go on, then.'

'The will is opened and read. A copy is usually made. Then it is resealed, with thread and wax, and placed in our archive.'

'Very funny! Where's the copy?'

'With the heir, presumably.'

'And how,' I asked, 'am I supposed to know who the heir is, if you won't let me unseal the sealed original that names him?'

'Ask somebody who knows.'

'You don't have that information?'

'We only store the tablets,' he protested. 'We don't know what is written in them, it isn't our job!'

A good day. Such a typical day in an informer's life.

I went up on the Arx to clear my head. At the Temple of Juno Moneta lived the Sacred Geese who guarded the Citadel and the augurs' Sacred Chickens. I checked them out. This was my public sinecure: religious bird guardian.

'Someone was asking about you,' the custodian told me as I prodded around the chicken huts, looking for eggs. Eggs were my official perk. I could have expended time and effort pretending to investigate the feathered ones' health and happiness, but they didn't need it. I knew they were all thoroughly spoiled. Anyway, the darling geese always had a go at me. Who wants to be pecked?

'Asking for me? Who was that?'

'He didn't say.'

'So what did you say?'

'I said we hadn't seen you up here for months.'

Nobody normal who wanted me would look for me on the Arx. I had no idea what this could mean, so I did not let it trouble me.

Being in the neighbourhood, I then explored an angle I had not listed in my notes. I walked down to the Forum and gave myself another unpleasant hour of officialdom. I wanted to know more about why Metellus and his son had been exposed in the corruption case. Where better to start, than the aediles' office?

Wrong, Falco. There was a new young brat in charge of Rome's road contracts. A friendly one would have thought the sins of his predecessor were good for a gossip, but this gilt-edged dong fell back on 'issue of national security' and maintained I was not entitled to enquire into such matters. I mentioned working as an agent for Vespasian; he still blocked me. He did not know what happened under Metellus Negrinus. He could not discuss previous errors. He was far too busy with muddy streets, crooked market weights, and endless complaints about rats rioting all night by the Altar of Peace. I could go and ram myself head-first into a narrow drain.

I should have known. The corruption case had made the aediles' scams too obvious. Audits had been instituted. Procedures had been tightened. This new young fellow might have made a killing, but for the Metellus trial. How was he now to assemble enough cash to finance lavish public Games in order to obtain the votes to move up his career ladder to the next flashy post?

He clearly wished he had jurisdiction over temple maintenance, where the bribes were notorious.

Being thwarted can damage an enquiry; I get hooked on beating the system. But it makes me more determined. So never mind the fine detail of poison and timescales which I was supposed to investigate today. I decided to find Verontius. Verontius was appalling, but he would talk to me. I knew how to make sure of it.

Normally I would walk barefoot across a mile of burning bitumen before I would encounter Verontius. He was a shifty, shambling worker in the semi-public world of road contracts. He could bend figures better than a conjurer stuffing doves up his fundament. I would be lucky if I could get away from him without a burst blood vessel and having to lend him my carpentry plane (if I ever let him get his hands on it, I would never see it again). He stank of armpits and feet. He despised me. I loathed him. Except in this emergency, we would avoid each other from one Saturnalia to the next – though at Saturnalia we were always compelled to meet. Unluckily for me, he had been married to my lumpish sister Allia for the past twenty years, so we were bonded inescapably: Verontius and I were family.

Allia was out, thank the gods. A pitiful slave with scurvy let me in. I had to wade past pallid children to reach the back room where Verontius hunched like a toad down a well. He had a tablet of official-looking tables, but was doodling at speed on a separate piece of old fish wrapper. (He had a secret second job as a squid-negotiator.) He would scribble like fury, work out a long sum, then carefully insert a single figure in the tender table with a better pen and new ink. Everything about his rapid calculations suggested he was up to no good. When he was not fiddling new contract applications, Verontius worked long hours supervising the bent contracts he had already won. I won't say he and Allia lived in squalor. We all knew that they had money. It was squirrelled away somewhere. Hoarded meanly, never spent. They would both die early, worn-out victims of a hard life they need not have had.

'Marcus!' He was colourless, bald, squinty and half deaf. He always had been, even way back. Such a catch for Allia! He had long ago learned to avoid looking guilty, but I watched the doodles being smoothly shunted into a fruit bowl while the tender was speedily rolled up under his stool. Even before he knew what I had come for, Verontius was clearing a sanitised space for his nosy in-law.

Once he knew that I wanted him to finger someone else, he was happy. 'Metellus Negrinus? Lovely boy, smashing little aedile – oh we did all like him!'

'Because he was on the take? Don't go coy on me. I don't want a dangerous commitment from you – I just need to understand how it worked. You knew about the corruption, I imagine?'

Verontius winked. 'Oh no!'

'Liar.'

'I have to live, Marcus. But I'm a small player.'

'You never gave evidence at the father's trial?'

'Hardly ever encountered the father. He dealt with the mighty consortiums. For the trial, I had too little to tell about that. But I was approached!' He was proud to have been considered.

'Approached by whom?'

'One of your lot.'

'Mine?'

'An informer came scouting, just before the trial.'

'But you chose to keep quiet to protect yourself.'

'To protect a way of life, Marcus! Listen, road construction and maintenance is a specialist business. We operate in traditional ways, ways that go back centuries.'

'That old apology for cheating practices! What informer was it?'

'Don't remember.'

'Don't try too hard, you might wear out your brain –'

'Said he was called Procreus.'

'Never heard of him. What would you have told him, if he had bribed you enough?'

'Nothing.'

'Really?' I knew enough about Verontius to obtain a second version. 'Ever see that slave girl with the intriguing entablature you used to be so friendly with? What a pretty caryatid. Very architectural!'

He shuddered. She was somehow connected to his squid-peddling – that moonlight work Allia never seemed to notice, despite the smell. So my threat was about the secret money he earned, as well as his fishy playmate. Verontius still fooled around with the girl, and he knew I knew. 'O griddled goat's goolies, Marcus my son! I'm at home here –'

'So you are, Verontius old boy! Let's get the men's talk over before Allia comes back, shall we?'

It was not often I had the beautiful pleasure of extortion from a relative. Life was good for an hour. Allia came home to find Verontius a crumpled ghost of himself. By then he had confided this: the road contractors' guild always carried out background checks on new officials. Prior to his arrival in post, Negrinus had been a worry to them. He had come from his earlier position, as quaestor, with a reputation for resisting sweeteners. The road contractors were expecting this but straight away it became apparent that the father was on hand, not just open to persuasion, but insisting on it.

'Money?'

'Oh grow up, Marcus! What else? You know, there was a funny atmosphere. At first we thought,' Verontius confided, 'they had had a bust-up.'

'It looks as if the father turned against the son. Negrinus has been left out of the will –'

'Not the impression we got. They were never at odds with each other. The father gave the orders; the son followed through – but there were no fights. Something had shaken them; they were like men who had just walked away from an earthquake. The shock left them operating very much as a team, a team in frantic need of cash.'

'Failed investment? Disaster at a property? You don't know what?'

'Enquiries failed to dig it out.'

'Your guild uses the wrong people!' I grinned, but stopped it quickly. The contractors' guild members are worse than virulent headlice. I didn't want their trade. 'So Negrinus came into his aedile post at just the right moment, and they wrung it dry?'

'Correct.'

'Any idea why Silius Italicus picked on them for it?'

Verontius shrugged. 'He must have been desperate for cash too.' My brother-in-law gave me a sickly leer. 'But then he's an informer, so that figures!'

Luckily for him, that was the moment we heard my sister Allia struggling to work her latch-lifter. I let her into her house; she and I glared at one another in our customary fashion; I left.

I went back to see the archivist who had the will.

'Can I see that will you fetched out this morning again? Is there an original date on it?'

There had been a date when it was first sealed. When it was opened and resealed, that old date was efficiently blanked out.

I tore my hair.

There was more frustration awaiting me. I went to see Negrinus at his sister's house that evening. I arrived at Rubiria Carina's home in the usual state for an informer. I was tired, depressed, struggling to make any headway on the case – and ready to chuck it all in. I should have done so. Negrinus had found himself an extra defence lawyer. I could not believe it. Birdy had let himself be preyed on by the lax fathead of an assistant who had worked for Silius: Honorius.

XX

NEGRINUS WAS sitting with his sister in her elegant white saloon. The room was one of understated luxury. The furniture seemed plain, but its fittings were gilt. Gold Doric columns held lamps that burned with the finest oil. A single exquisite half-size Aphrodite adorned a hemispherical niche. The husband, Verginius Laco, must own an enviable portfolio of estates.

Carina looked very much like her sister Juliana. Birdy must take after their father; he was completely different. Unlike Negrinus with his light colouring, sharp-cut nose and diffident, almost studious face, this young woman was dark-haired, wide-cheeked and had a direct stare. Her mother's confidence glared out of her, though I could see why people called her nice to know. She was quiet in manner. Just as fashionable as Juliana, she copied the ladies of the imperial court in dress, hairstyle and jewellery. It was all more expensive than Helena would think necessary for an evening at home.

Helena had not come with me; the children were playing up. I could have used her calming influence.

'This is Honorius,' our client told me proudly. 'He wants to plead my case.'

I managed not to snort: why in the name of Olympus had Birdy taken on a spy from the viper's nest of his enemies? I caught Rubiria Carina's eye; she gave nothing away. But she was tellingly silent. An intelligent woman. Fond of Birdy, perhaps.

I sat back on the couch where I had been placed to be irritated and insulted. I let Honorius explain himself.

He still looked about eighteen, but told me he was twenty-five. Only child; father deceased; making a career for himself in law. He could use a good bout of army discipline to toughen him up – but a week of the recruits' training regime would send him weeping home to Mother. He did not mention his mother, but I could see her handiwork in his buffed shoes and beautifully braided tunic. I bet her poor old eyes were failing after stitching on those purple bands and neck-rings. I bet that signet ring had belonged to his dead father, and perhaps the old belt too. He must have come in his toga, which now lay folded over a couch back, as though the house slaves had not taken it away because they hoped to be rid of him rapidly. If he had managed to annoy them, he would annoy a court too.

'I have walked out on Silius.'

He was faintly pink. He thought he knew what I was thinking. I continued to watch him in silence, letting him worry.

In fact I was thinking that I could see why Silius Italicus had taken Honorius into partnership. He was good looking. Slightly gaunt, and the thick crinkled hair was too short, but women would go for the decent body and the eyes. He would fill out one day – but he would always be half a foot too short. I reckoned his judgment was suspect too, but most people never see past handsome bones and self-confidence. He would get by, and get by easily. Could he do the work? I withheld judgment.

The purple tunic bands confirmed he was of senatorial rank. Probably the dead father had left the family too poor to enable the son to try for the *cursus honorum*. For that he would have needed backers too. The official route of quaestor, aedile, praetor and consul might be closed to him, yet he had status and education, and an underlying sureness of purpose. Walking out on Silius must have stiffened him up. Where I had once thought him virginal, I now felt he might keep a mistress somewhere, some petulant, expensive piece whom he visited for vigorous but short-lived sex while the adoring mother believed he had gone to play handball at the gym. Then he would buy the mistress silver bracelets, and the mother flowers.

'*Why* have you left Silius?' I asked.

'We quarrelled over ethics.'

'After four years in practice with him, isn't that a bit late?'

Honorius learned fast. He copied me and held his peace.

Negrinus burst in, eager to set me straight: 'Honorius has watched Silius and Paccius combining against our family – particularly against me. He knows it is an injustice. His conscience is aroused.'

'He knows,' Rubiria Carina told me pointedly, 'that my brother will not find anyone else qualified or willing to take on his case.'

'So *you* will do it?' I smiled at Honorius. 'Highly commendable! And you should make quite a name for yourself . . .' I paused. This young man was after the money, just as we were. He must have been badly disappointed to find Falco and Associates were already handling the case. 'Sorry to be blunt, but I wonder if Silius deliberately stirred up your sense of outrage, knowing that in court you would be easy meat?'

Now Honorius went pale. If he had not thought of this himself, he managed to disguise the fact. He made out he was mature enough to know all Silius was capable of. 'I shall have to prove him wrong, Falco.'

'How?'

'Without being immodest –'

'Be truthful.'

'I am a decent advocate.' Somehow he made himself sound very modest.

'Are you? Oh face facts, man! You have attended your principal at some high-profile, highly political pleadings. You have spoken for him sometimes; I saw you in the Metellus corruption case.' Honorius had been handling minor evidence; he was competent, but the stuff was routine. 'I also know this: you are slapdash back in the office, you look to me as if you want to be a playboy, and the worst thing is – if you really came here out of idealism, that is not what we need. Your motive is naïve. You're dangerous. We don't want a luminous conscience; we need someone to kick balls!'

'Now look, Falco –'

'No. You listen. You propose taking on some wary old wolves – these are devious, manipulating chancers. You are too inexperienced and you are too straight!'

'There has to be a place for believers in justice,' Negrinus pleaded with me, as if he had overheard Aulus and Quintus last night.

'Too right! I believe in it myself. That's why, if you are innocent, I don't want to see you destroyed by an inadequate defence.'

'That's insulting,' Honorius said tightly.

'Well, you insulted me. Falco and Associates have taken on this man. We at least are an established team. You were an apprentice. You sweep in like some high-priced god, offering Negrinus redemption after no research into the evidence –'

'There is *no* evidence,' Honorius retorted, more warmly. 'That is precisely what disgusts me. I heard Silius and Paccius both admit they cannot prove that Metellus Negrinus directly took any action against his father. They say he administered hemlock, but they don't know how or when. They intend to win not with proofs but with arguments.'

I was not surprised. 'That's obvious. Blacken his character, make leering suggestions, and rely on the fact that if he *is* innocent, he won't have any idea what really happened – so he can't fight back. We can all imagine their *arguments*.' I took a big breath. 'So you defend in the case. You will have to produce better ones.'

'Not me,' said Honorius. 'Us.'

'No.'

'Yes, Falco. I need you. I need you to find out what we can produce in rebuttal. Silius has people working on it constantly. I don't have his network. I admit it frankly –'

'And how will you pay me?'

He looked shy. 'When we win.'

'*If!*' Both Honorius and Negrinus were waiting for my reaction. 'I can't answer you. I shall have to consult my associates.'

'There is no time, Falco.'

'All right.' I could take decisions. 'But we will not work for you.' Honorius ran a hand through that short hair in exasperation. I cut him off. 'Equal status. We'll work *with* you. That's the deal. No fees, but fair shares if we win.' Before he could argue I went straight into my plan. 'Tomorrow you and I will attend the pre-trial. The praetor will set the trial date, allowing time for enquiries. This is the tactic: we let the other side ask for the longest investigation delay they want. We shall not dispute it.'

Honorius leapt up. 'Falco, it's customary to –'

'To cut it short, to hamper the prosecution. Well we need investigation time ourselves. Now when they all think that's sorted, we'll throw in a surprise: we shall ask for the case to be heard not in the Senate – to which Negrinus is entitled – but in the murders court.'

Honorius was bright. I was probably right that he was useless, but he could take a point fast. 'You mean the full Senate will view me as a jumped-up boy, backed by a low-grade team, people they all despise. But in the special murders court, the judge will be keen to enjoy himself – and Silius and Paccius won't have trained him to their ways.'

I said nothing for a moment. 'Something like that.'

I watched Honorius evaluate my comments. He had stood for too long in the shadow of Silius Italicus and was fretting for more independence. He clearly enjoyed planning and making decisions. That was fine – if his decisions were the right ones. 'If Negrinus didn't kill his father, someone else did – and you intend us to discover who.' Light dawned. 'And in the delay before Birdy comes to trial – we shall go in and prosecute the real killer!'

Rubiria Carina leaned forwards attentively. 'But who is it?'

I gazed at her for a moment then stated the obvious: 'Well, your sister has been tried for it and acquitted, your brother is to be tried shortly but we say he's innocent — face it, lady: that only leaves you!'

XXI

IT WAS brutal. There was a shocked silence.

As they all began to react, I held up a hand. Looking from the brother to the sister, I addressed them quietly: 'Time to get things straight, please. If you want my team to work with you, you have to trust us and work with us. There are very big unanswered questions. Please stop dodging them. Rubiria Carina, if we were as heartless as Paccius and Silius, then you really would be the next target. You were estranged from your family, and you are known to have made loud accusations against family members at your father's funeral. Either you tell me what that was about, or I walk.'

Negrinus began to interrupt.

'The same goes for you,' I snapped. 'You make mysterious pronouncements. You clearly keep things back. Now it's time for honesty.' I half turned to Honorius. 'Don't you agree?'

Honorius agreed.

'Right.' I was terse. 'Honorius and I are going to pop out to use your domestic facilities. You two had better confer. If you decide to co-operate, I want to discuss your family background – and I want full details of your father's will.'

I jerked my head to Honorius, who meekly followed me from the room.

'Now listen, Honorius –'

'I thought we were going for a pee?'

'In a house like this it's useless for a case conference. They will have some damned one-at-a-time latrine.' I grinned. 'Anyway, your previous encounter with Falco and Associates should have taught you to keep your legs crossed.'

Remembering how the two Camilli had trapped him in his office and bullied him into paying up our fee from Silius, Honorius went red. Just thinking about it made him absolutely desperate for relief. I sat on a bench in a corridor unconcernedly, as if ready for a lengthy chat.

'I need –'

'Colleague, you need to know my thoughts. My information, gleaned today, is that Birdy and his father were on good terms – but they were cash-hungry. Why? Next, my two lads have so far failed to find out where the hemlock – if it existed – was bought. The family's usual herb supplier denies selling it –'

'That's Euphanes?'

'You have a grip on the cast list; good! So my poor juniors will have to tread the streets asking every damn purveyor of pungent greenery if they sold a bunch of hemlock way back last autumn.'

'You are not hopeful.'

'True.'

'Does it matter who bought it, Falco?'

'Very much. If we are to get Birdy off, it's no use just crying that he's a good boy and he never harmed his papa. We have to show who really did it. And this is urgent.'

Honorius was gripped by what I was saying. 'But who are we to accuse, Falco?'

'I suggest the mother.'

'Not Carina?'

'No. I was just trying to scare her. Calpurnia Cara did originally hatch the hemlock plan, if Birdy told us right. So Calpurnia is my chief suspect – with the possible connivance of Paccius.'

'*Paccius!*' Honorius looked scared. 'Paccius conspired to kill his client? You live in a harsh world, Falco.'

'Welcome to it,' I said gently.

Then, since I was getting desperate myself, I stood up and let him tag along as I searched for the household facilities.

Instead of the normal plank over a pit in an earth-floored cupboard, Carina and Laco had a well-tiled room with a stone throne; it stood over a pit, but the pit was very clean and there was a huge mound of fresh sponges beside the white marble washing bowl. I pointed this out to Honorius. 'This is why I don't suspect Carina. I don't mean because her house is unusually hygienic. I mean, the woman is damn rich.'

'She doesn't need her father's money?'

'No. Supposing there is any left . . .' Which I was starting to doubt.

When we returned, Negrinus and Carina looked subdued, but prepared to talk. I told Honorius to take Birdy off somewhere, while I flame-grilled Carina. It was the first time we had had access to her; I intended to be thorough.

'Please don't worry.' In fact she seemed unconcerned. She gazed at me with that direct, thoughtful stare. She was sitting upright, hands lying still in her lap. A maid was there to chaperon, but the elderly woman sat at a distance with her eyes cast down. 'Rubiria Carina, I am sorry we have to do this. I just want to talk to you about your family. Let's start with your childhood, if you don't mind. Were you a happy household?'

'Yes.' If she stayed so monosyllabic, this would be useless. Her husband was off out socialising somewhere; I hoped to finish before he came back to interfere.

'I imagine your mother was a little strict. What was your father like at home?'

Carina now decided to go along with it. 'He was a good father. We all liked him.'

'You and your sister were both married young. Were you both happy with your choices?'

'Yes.' Back to the stone wall. The chaperon was ignoring our discussion; I wondered if she was deaf.

'And your brother? I haven't talked to him much about this strange situation where he became the second husband of his best friend's wife.'

'It happens,' said Carina bluntly.

'I know.' I waited quietly.

'Licinius Lutea and my brother were educated together and they served in the same province for their army duty. They had been close friends all their lives. Lutea married first. They had a son. Later, he suffered financial difficulties and Saffia Donata's father insisted on a divorce.'

I raised my eyebrows. 'Hard! That's a rather old-fashioned idea, isn't it? Nowadays we tend to believe the parents should not break up happy couples.'

'I only know,' Carina said slowly, 'that Saffia did not argue with her father.'

'Any husband can go through a bad patch . . . I met Donatus. A frantic old buffer. He worries that his girls' dowries will be frittered away while in other hands.'

Carina made no comment on my hint about the old buffer's claim for negligent estate management against her own father. 'I think my brother felt sorry for his friend,' she said. 'Lutea was afraid he would lose touch with his son, who was then just a baby. My brother agreed to marry Saffia himself – he needed a wife, he was rather a shy person, and he knew Saffia. It would mean Lutea could still see little Lucius often and eventually Lucius could go and live with his father without too much disruption.'

'So Lutea would once have been a frequent visitor to your brother's home. I gather he and your brother are less close now? And Lutea still seems to be on rather close terms with Saffia?'

Carina knew what I meant. 'So he does,' she spoke drily. But she said no more.

I looked her in the eye. She was a married woman, the mother of three children. She must know the world. 'Do you think Lutea and Saffia have been playing around during your brother's marriage?'

She coloured and looked at her lap. 'I have no reason to suspect it.' She had every reason, I thought.

'Did your brother worry about them?'

'My brother is good-natured and easygoing.' If it were true that he had been cuckolded, I wondered who had fathered Saffia's as yet unborn child. Then I even wondered who had really fathered the first child in this second marriage, the two-year-old daughter.

'Some would say your brother is too easily pushed about.'

'Some would say that,' Carina agreed quietly.

'Saffia told me you were a nice woman,' I remarked. 'Would you say anything similar about her?'

'I have nothing to say about Saffia Donata,' said her ex-sister-in-law. It did not surprise me. Carina was nice. Nice – or else hiding something.

'Let's talk about your mother now. As I said before, don't be alarmed. I want to establish some background. Were your parents only ever married to each other?' A nod of the head. 'That's a rare and beautiful situation nowadays! So you children had a happy upbringing and theirs was a comfortable marriage?'

'Yes.'

'They produced three children as the law encourages –' I noticed a flicker of some emotion. Carina stilled it quickly. 'You were all born fairly close together, weren't you? Do I deduce that after your mother had her three babies, deliberate measures may have been taken –'

Abortion is illegal; contraception discouraged. Carina bristled. 'I could not possibly say anything about that, Falco!'

'I apologise. Excuse me, but your father died in "his" bedroom, I understand. Did your mother have her own room?'

'Yes,' Carina agreed, rather stiffly.

'Plenty of people do,' I assured her. 'But my wife and I find the marital bed a more companionable arrangement, I must say.' She made no comment, and I could not bring myself to ask what arrangements she and Laco preferred. 'You have a different outlook from your parents. Your mother insisted Saffia had her daughter put to a wet-nurse, I'm told. Did you farm out your own children?'

'No.' Again I saw a fleeting expression I could not place. Perhaps Carina, on the surface so composed, was uneasy about admitting she had spurned Calpurnia's strict childcare advice.

'Dare I ask, is your independent outlook why you have a reputation for being somewhat estranged from your family?'

'I am on perfectly good terms with my family,' Carina declared.

'Oh?' I toughened up. 'I heard that there had been trouble, that your husband had to put his foot down over interference – that you yourself refused to attend your father's farewell meal, and that you made an outburst at his funeral accusing your relations of killing him.'

Panic struck her. 'I don't want to talk to you any more!'

'Well are my facts right?'

'Yes. But you don't understand –'

'Tell me then.'

'There is nothing to say.'

'When your father had announced he would commit suicide, why didn't you want to see him?' She was silent. 'Do you regret that now?'

A tear did start lurking. 'It was not like that, Falco. I never refused to attend that lunch; I was not invited. I knew nothing of the discussions. Juliana had told me Papa had decided against suicide – and I even thought my brother was away.'

'So you *were* estranged?'

'No, they all thought it was easier. . .' She was trying to rationalise. She wanted to excuse them for leaving her out.

'So does this explain your accusations at the funeral? You felt you had been fed the wrong story –'

'I was upset. I made a mistake.'

'Not entirely – if it turns out that somebody did kill your father.'

'Nobody in my family.'

'You changed your mind about that?'

'I had a long talk with my brother. He explained –' She paused. 'Things I had not known before.'

'Your brother told you his story and you accepted that your father's death came from outside the family? So who did it?'

'I can't say. You must deal with it.'

'You are not helping.'

'This is a nightmare.' Rubiria Carina looked at me straight. She spoke like a woman who was being quite honest. Women who are lying always know just how to do that. 'Falco, I wish it would all go away. I want us to know serenity again. I want to hear no more of it.'

'But your brother is accused of parricide,' I reminded her. She was clearly under enormous strain and I feared she would break down.

'That is so hard,' Carina murmured bitterly. 'After all that we have suffered. After all he has to live with. It is so unfair on him.'

Her feelings were deep and explained why she had now given refuge to Negrinus at her home. Yet somehow this was not what I had expected her to say. She meant something else; I was missing it, I sensed it.

I asked Carina about her father's will. When she fell back on pretending she was only a woman and unfamiliar with family finances, I dropped the conversation, collected Honorius, and went home.

Honorius had learned little new from Birdy. Still, I expected that.

The young lawyer was not entirely useless. 'I asked who holds the copy of the will. This may, or may not, surprise you, Falco. It is with Paccius Africanus.'

I *was* surprised – but I was not going to show Honorius that.

'Don't tell me –' Informers of the Paccius and Silius type are infamous for chasing legacies. 'Paccius has had himself made the main heir!'

Unbelievably, it was true.

XXII

B IRDY'S APPOINTMENT of Honorius to work with Falco and Associates caused a storm among the associates. We made a silent, angry party when we attended the praetor's office for the pre-trial arraignment.

The situation looked black for our client. Paccius and Silius had formally joined as co-accusers. There was little to choose between the evidence each informer produced against Negrinus – as Honorius had said, there was virtually no evidence. The praetor awarded Paccius the privilege of first speaking. Paccius won this right to lead the case only because he had reached the praetor first with his original deposition.

They asked for a three-week delay for investigations. For our purposes, this was too short. Honorius asked to extend the period, but was overruled. No reason was given. He was overruled either because the praetor thought he was too junior to count, or because the praetor just hated his face. Yes, Birdy had stuck us with a liability.

Worse followed. When we requested trial in the murders court, surprisingly at first the praetor seemed to like the idea. I reckoned he was worried that a case which had already been trawled through once in the Senate might start to look like a legal mess if all the same evidence were regurgitated with a second defendant. As the arbiter of what came to trial, it might make him look indecisive. He would be even more anxious if my associates came to him in the next few weeks with yet another new accused! So far, nobody knew that part of the plan.

Caught by surprise, Paccius and Silius made no immediate objection to our request. However, they did not need to. The praetor disapproved of anything the upstart Honorius wanted. 'Metellus Negrinus is a senator, an ex-quaestor and ex-aedile. We cannot subject him to trial on a level with tavern knifings, like killers who are little better than slaves. Request refused!'

Paccius and Silius smiled at us pityingly.

I myself made a further application on Negrinus' behalf: 'Sir, the accusers' case is based on their proposition that our client was jealous and angry because he was cut out of his father's will. We appeal to have Paccius Africanus produce to us a copy of the will.'

'Paccius has it?' The praetor sat up sharply on his curule stool. Those X-shaped folding seats have no back support. A firm posture is required in the honourable magistrate who uses his symbol of authority. You see magistrates lying on massage slabs at the baths, groaning about their lumbar pain. It's a hazard of the job. In court, they tend to slump in boring moments, then jerk into a more rigid position if they are caught out by something said.

This one hated legacy-chasing. 'Paccius Africanus, can you explain this?'

Paccius rose to his feet smoothly. I gave him credit for a calm reaction. 'Sir, for legal reasons only, the deceased Rubirius Metellus assigned me his heir. I gain very little. I have to reassign everything to others. The estate is mainly governed by a *fideicommissum*.'

'Held in *trust*?' snapped the praetor. He said *trust* as if he was referring to some repulsive bodily function. 'Held in trust for who?' Long words did not trouble him, but we could tell he was startled; his grammar had slipped. When Rome's chief magistrate forgets how to operate the dative case – especially when the illustrious one is using the interrogative in its accusatory mood with a full blast of unpleasant emphasis – then it's time for the clerks from the *Daily Gazette* to take notes for the scandal page.

'Various friends and family.' Paccius eluded the question as if the outrage it suggested had never occurred to him. 'I shall send a copy immediately to Falco's home address.'

I thought the praetor shot me a look as if he longed to be asked to lunch so he could see the sensational note tablet. In view of his brusque treatment of Honorius earlier, I refused to do him favours. We then all consulted our notes, as if we were now checking for any other trivial points we could throw in to distract ourselves from serious issues. Issues like justice for the innocent.

Neither side found any, so we all went home.

To my surprise the copy arrived within a couple of hours. The will was on the inner sides of two waxed boards. That's normal. It was so short only one board was written on. Metellus senior had named Paccius Africanus his heir, thus leaving him all his debts and responsibilities, plus the religious safe keeping of the family's ancestral masks and household gods. Metellus had bequeathed small sums to each of his two daughters, after allowing for the amounts in their dowries. Both his son and his wife were specifically ruled out of inheritance, though each was given a very small lifetime maintenance allowance. I mean very, very small. I could have lived on it, but I had once been nearly starved and accustomed to cockroaches as fellow lodgers. Anyone who grew up in senatorial luxury would find the allowance tight.

Everything else went to Paccius, who was to pass on the money intact to Saffia Donata.

'This is odd.' Honorius took it upon himself to comment first. 'We need to show this to a wills expert. Silius uses one –'

'Old Fungibles is supposed to be the best,' Justinus disagreed coldly. 'We should avoid anyone who works with the opposition, Falco.'

'Old Fungibles?' I croaked.

Aelianus jumped in smartly: 'Interchangeable items; often con-sumables. . . A nickname, presumably.'

'Where did this mobile comestible come from?' I asked, still unconvinced.

'Ursulina Prisca,' Justinus grinned.

'Oho! Give me his details then,' I instructed, also grinning. We did not explain to Honorius the in-joke about our client, the litigious widow. 'I'll take along the will for advice; Aelianus can come too.' Honorius looked put out; that was tough. He was our law man, but I needed to re-establish good relationships with my own team. The Camilli cheered up, seeing Honorius snubbed. Justinus offered to hunt down more herbalists, still chasing the purchaser of the Metellus hemlock.

Justinus was now spreading out his search from the Embankment in ever-increasing circles. This tedious tramp could take him weeks. He might never track down the right seller. Even if he identified the one, he might never persuade him to give evidence in court. But for Justinus it had become a challenge.

'What can I do?' wailed Honorius plaintively.

'Read up the facts. Plan your arguments for when we go to court.'

'A defender who is familiar with the case? That will be a novelty!' Aelianus sneered.

Honorius gazed at him. 'I gather you are the cruel satirist in Falco and Associates.'

'No, that's my sister,' Aelianus returned. 'When Helena Justina assesses your professional worth, you'll come out of it like a raw grape skin after a wine-pressing.'

He made it sound as if he was looking forward to watching Honorius being pulped.

I told Honorius to make his presence felt with the Senate clerks and get Birdy a trial date.

As experts go, Old Fungibles was a babe – not the seventy-year-old I expected. More like thirty, though he looked forty. He was a grey little fellow who lived and worked in a one-room hole-in-the-wall unit, in a side road among furniture makers and metal workshops. The booth was spartan; the man seemed obsessed. He was colourless, but clearly extremely intelligent. My guess was that he had been some barrister's slave from a young age. He must have been trusted to carry out detailed work, and he had devoured information. Freed early, no doubt on the death of his master, he inherited enough legal codes to set up in his own business. Now he wrote wills and interpreted them. His real name was Scorpus. He acknowledged with good humour that we could call him Fungibles.

We all sat on stools. I wondered how the man could do brain-work here. From nearby premises clanged the ceaseless din of metal-beating. In the narrow street outside, people passed to and fro gossiping loudly. Some proprietors would have offered refreshments. Fungibles merely told us his fee (which was as basic as his living quarters, yet somehow I had faith in him), then he dived straight into our consultation.

He read the Metellus document. I outlined the family. I stuck to the facts. Aelianus described the lucrative position of Paccius. Fungibles listened. His face was expressionless. He did not take notes. When we had finished speaking, he read the will a second time. Even then, he remained calm.

'You may be aware of legal actions involving this family,' I said. 'They have featured sensationally in the *Daily Gazette*.'

He looked shy. 'I don't keep up with the Forum news. My business is domestic. If I do my job properly, people don't need any recourse to the Basilica.'

'How do you absorb new case law?' Aelianus asked. He was being himself – a lithe, athletic, rather untidy youth, who would suddenly demand answers to rather rude questions. Trust him to imply that we doubted the expert's competence.

Fungibles did not care. We had paid him, cash in advance. He would tell us what he thought; we could believe it or not. He was proud of the service he offered; he did not beg for our approval. 'A contact tips me off if something changes.'

Aelianus subsided. I nodded. Fungibles checked that the interruption was over, then he began.

'The form is correct. In Latin. Formal language. Properly names an heir first. It is, as it stands, a valid testament. There are three interesting aspects to this will. First, who it institutes as heir. Second, the bequests to the heirs of right – that's the children here, who have a claim in law. Third, the size and allocation of other gifts.'

'What about the wife?' I asked. 'Calpurnia Cara.'

'She has no claim, strictly. However, most men like to see their widows left in the style they have previously enjoyed. By custom she might expect to be provided for. I see that this lady has a maintenance allowance – though the amount is small.'

'Insultingly?'

Fungibles smiled. 'In a senatorial family, I would have thought this was – pointed!'

'Be frank.'

'Unless she holds a great deal of property in her own name, I would imagine from this will that Calpurnia Cara had violently upset her husband.'

'Fine.' Calpurnia at odds with Metellus? We only knew that *he* annoyed *her* with his reluctance to commit suicide. This was a new angle.

'First intriguing point: Paccius. Tell us about appointing him as the heir,' Aelianus demanded. He had really taken to this legal stuff – an unexpected surprise.

Fungibles was restrained. 'It is a principle which lawyers robustly uphold, that a man has the right to make his will just as he wishes.'

'He can name an outsider?'

'He can. It is frequently done. There is usually a reason – infant children can't be made the heirs, for instance. Or it can be a device when there are many debts.'

'There are debts,' I confirmed. 'According to one story. On the other hand, there may be money salted away, possibly in large quantities. We have difficulty sorting out the truth.'

'Intriguing! A problem when you name an extraneous heir, as Metellus has done, is that the nominee has the right of refusal. The heirs of right would be stuck with the duties and responsibilities – including paying off creditors – without any escape. This man Paccius could say no. Has he done so?'

'He is eager to accept.'

'Then he thinks there is money, depend on it,' said Fungibles. He pursed his lips. 'Tell me why you think he was the choice?'

'Family lawyer. He defended the deceased in a lengthy corruption case. Mind you – he lost!'

Fungibles glanced down at the will. 'Was this two years ago?'

I cocked my head. 'Last autumn. Why?'

'The will was made two years before that case occurred.'

I had not noticed that. It meant Paccius was very close to Metellus senior long before we had assumed he was taken on for the trial. And Negrinus, who was supposed to be on close terms with his father during his term as aedile, had already been disinherited when he took up office. Of course, he may not have known that. Was this what his sister Carina had meant when she complained about 'all he has to live with' and 'all we have suffered'?

'Scorpus, tell us about disinheriting sons.'

He screwed his mouth even more. 'A bad idea. I never allow my clients to do it. You said the son was not freed from parental control?'

'No. Both parents seem to have been strict, bossy types. It is why Negrinus is reckoned to have escaped corruption charges; he owned nothing. He wasn't worth pursuing.'

'And he owns nothing still,' commented Aelianus, perhaps anxiously considering his own position as a senator's son.

'But he could! He was entitled to inherit,' said Fungibles. 'He and his sisters would normally share equally. The only way to remove him was, as Metellus senior did, to disinherit him formally by name. It is sensible,' he went on slowly, 'to add a remark indicating why. I would advise it. Almost always it will be because the son lives a sordid lifestyle. Does he?'

'Birdy?' He drank thirstily at my home, but that was nothing. He was distressed that night. 'No one would call him debauched. Not in Rome. He's corrupt in business but respectable – unless he hides it well.'

'He would have to be a byword for immorality for this will to be upheld,' said Fungibles. 'Someone who pimps, or fights as a gladiator. Why is he called Birdy?'

'No idea.'

'Well, if he is an upright character, he should challenge the will.'

'So he can do that?'

Fungibles looked surprised. 'I am startled that he has not already entered his plea. It works like this,' he explained. 'The omitted heir slaps in a claim to the praetor that he is the victim of an "unduteous will". The basis is a legal device: it's saying that the testator must be deemed to have been insane to have ruled out a child so unfairly. An insane person cannot make a will. Thus – if the praetor allows the claim – and from what you tell me, this son has everything on his side – the will becomes void. Then the rules of intestacy are brought in to distribute the estate.'

'And what happens under intestacy?' Aelianus asked, taking rapid notes.

'Negrinus and his sisters would each get a third. For each woman the sum would be calculated minus her dowry. So the situation becomes very different.'

'Paccius would play no part?'

'Ruled right out. Paccius, and this female, Saffia Donata.' Fungibles looked up, almost smiling. 'So who is the woman? This lucky Saffia? A mistress of the deceased?'

'Daughter-in-law – divorced from Negrinus, however,' I stated. 'One child from the marriage, plus a heavy pregnancy. She has a child from a previous marriage, so if she carries the latest safely, she gets rights as a mother of three.'

Fungibles nodded. 'She will be hoping the baby survives. As for this curious will, her father-in-law must have taken quite a shine to her.'

'Why not make her the heir directly then?' Aelianus asked. 'Why this *fideicommissum*, dragging in Paccius?'

'That's a regular device,' exclaimed Fungibles. 'I imagine we are talking about people in the top census bracket? At that level, large bequests to a woman are illegal. It is to keep important estates in male hands – and perhaps save potentially rich heiresses from predators.' I laughed. I was glad that Helena was not present; she would have been outraged. Fungibles smiled slightly and pressed on: 'Your Metellus wished to favour Saffia Donata – for reasons we can only speculate – so he has instituted Paccius as his heir instead, to avoid the law. Paccius will have undertaken to pass on the money.'

'Instead of an illegal bequest, a perfectly legal gift?'

Fungibles was enjoying himself now. 'Intriguingly, the *fideicommissum* makes no attempt to pass on Saffia's portion to the Negrinus children after her. I find that very odd.' Fungibles clearly disapproved. 'Normally an arrangement would be made that if Saffia dies, the money then passes to her children; in fact, I would expect a deed of trust to be devised specifically with that intention. This wording here could leave the children in trouble. Saffia *may* make provision for them if she cares for them – but she may choose not to.'

'Negrinus is disinherited – so if their mother is hard-hearted, his children could be left with nothing?' Aelianus asked.

'Yes.'

'That's terrible. And it all seems dangerous. How binding is the *fideicommissum*? Will Saffia even get the money? Does Paccius have any real obligation to divert the money to her?'

'It is a promise,' said Fungibles. He was dry. 'You know what happens to promises! If Paccius has a conscience, then of course he must pass it on.'

'He's an informer! What if he has no conscience?'

'Then Saffia could sue him in the trusts court. The fact that there is a trusts court tells you it is often needed.'

'Would she win?' I threw in, still smarting from the conscience jibe.

'She might. Let's not slander Saffia Donata over her father-in-law's fancy for her – but was he closer to her than to his own children – and his grandchildren?'

'I'd say Saffia was regarded as a nuisance by the whole Metellus family,' I said. 'I'm not sure how far that goes back. She was first married to Negrinus' best friend, who is still very much on the scene.'

Fungibles looked up sharply, though he made no comment.

'What if Lutea – his name is Licinius Lutea – remarried Saffia?' I asked thoughtfully.

'He gets access to what Saffia gets –' Fungibles paused. 'If she lets him.'

'All right.' Ideas were whirling in my head. I needed to think. 'So what is your overall impression of this will, Scorpus?'

'I hate it. I would be ashamed to have helped produce it. If Metellus took legal advice, he was robbed. The formulae are all correct. But it's a weak will, immediately open to challenge by the heirs of right.'

'We could use that in Negrinus' defence,' Aelianus told me excitedly. 'It is alleged he killed his father because he was disinherited – yet he has a good claim to overturn the will, so why commit murder?'

That was true. But Fungibles wanted us to look at the document in another light. 'I cannot see what, but I would say there must be a secret. That usually explains why outsiders gain an unhealthy influence.'

His fee was tiny. But he had given good advice. Sometimes, in this disreputable world, you meet a man who disturbs the norm. Sometimes, you find somebody honest.

XXIII

AELIANUS AND I emerged from the hole-in-the-wall, heads reeling.

'That was dense – but you seem to thrive on all this legal stuff!' I commented. We started to walk. It was the kind of backstreet where you keep your hand on your purse and don't meet the eyes of passers-by. Aelianus grunted. He was always terse on anything personal. 'I like it,' I encouraged him. 'Honorius won't stick around after the case. We could use a legal specialist on our team. How about you?'

'What about Quintus?'

'What about him? His expertise is in languages.' Justinus was also much better than his brother with personality issues, though I did not say so.

'I thought he was your favourite.'

We reached the end of the street and turned a corner, into one that was if anything even dirtier and more threatening. I checked it out, looking left. Aelianus by now knew enough to do the same, looking right; I then discreetly double-checked his side. I wanted to trust my subordinates – but I wanted to stay alive. We took the direction we needed, heading back towards the Forum.

'I don't have favourites.' In fact, I had always warmed especially to Justinus, though I hoped I had not shown it. The two brothers fought continually, but I had been unaware that Aelianus harboured resentment about being shut out. 'I respect good work, Aulus.'

He said nothing.

We were walking at a leisurely pace. The day was grey and heavily overcast, with a hint of snow in the air. It was bitingly cold; I wrapped myself deep in my woollen cloak, throwing the ends over my shoulders and snuggling my reddened ears into its folds, while Aelianus fastened his garment more pedantically, pinning it dead centre with a fibula beneath his chin. The way the front edges hung, he must have a frozen gap chilling his stomach up the middle of his tunic. He made no attempt to grip the material together. He was athletic and liked to pretend he was physically hard.

We passed neglected fountains, stalls where the vegetable-sellers stamped miserably, a small temple with its doors firmly closed to prevent vagrants snuffling into the sanctum to take refuge from the weather.

When I next spoke to Aelianus, my breath formed a damp area in my cloak where it obstructed my mouth. 'Your parents would be amazed – and pleased – if you started studying.' I stretched my neck to show him a grin. 'I'd get some credit for reforming you!'

'What do you mean – reforming?'

'Oh yes, you're an upright character!' He gave me a look. 'Stories were circulating in Baetica,' I warned him. Helena and I had followed Aelianus out there after his stint working with the provincial governor. His life in Spain had been one of hunting and entertaining with the local wild young men; his dafter indiscretions seemed to include an unhealthy flirtation with the worship of Cybele. None of this had ever been mentioned at home by Aulus. He was secretive and had become quite a loner, once he was back in Rome. 'Of course I haven't gossiped, but your father is alert to your rampant past. Decimus may seem in a world of his own, but he's sharp. If he thinks that your working with me now is a cause for relief, then he was quite worried about the alternatives.'

'He still wants to see me in the Senate,' Aelianus confided.

'I know.'

'You discuss me?' He sounded annoyed.

'No. Trust me, Aulus. I won't rush to the baths and thrill your papa with some story that we've turned you into a barrister.'

He gave me one of his moody grunts. Our conversation paused as we sidestepped a man with flailing arms who was trying to detain us and sell us horoscopes; I foresaw that this was just so an accomplice could sneak out from behind a barrel of scallops and steal our belts. 'Very nice,' I said, shoving the astrologer aside bodily. Insincerity is a Roman street art. We walked on. Curses followed us. We did not react.

'Well, I find the legal details interesting,' Aelianus confessed. From him it was quite an opening up. He added, 'Helena says she's glad we're in this legal market now. She likes the fact it's all talk, so you are not involved in danger.'

'*You* have been discussing *me?*' I riposted.

Being himself again, he just grunted once more.

At the Golden Milestone we went our separate ways. I watched young Aelianus treading his firm path down the Forum away from me, a sturdy figure with solid shoulders and stout calves tramping beneath his neatly draped cloak. The intimate conversation had made me feel more than usually responsible for him. Watch it, Falco. Nannying aristocrats is a slave's task.

He could handle himself. Peddlers shrugged easily as he ignored their trays. He gave a wide berth to a dog with froth on its muzzle and stepped aside as a drunk spoiling for an argument staggered blearily into his path.

Hunched in my cloak, I bore around the shadow of the Capitol and made my way home. I was thinking about the best way forward. Our talk with Scorpus had been refreshing. Calpurnia Cara had always been on my list for investigation; his suggestion that she might have offended her husband was a good lead. It was also time we pursued the Saffia/Lutea angle, and hammered it hard. Then there was the idea that something looked amiss in the family; I trusted Fungibles on that. The peculiarities of the will must have an explanation – not that families always behave understandably. Mine were a cantankerous, deliberately stubborn lot. Maybe the Metelli were the same.

I came around a windswept corner by the cattle market, head down as I forged a path up the Marble Embankment to my house. Chilled now, I was tired and in need of sustenance. The cold was making my eyes water. As darkness began to gather, I saw the welcome sight of my own front door, flanked by two laurel bushes, with an oversized dolphin knocker that my father had installed. Cheered, I failed to notice villains suddenly homing in on me. I was at their mercy. Hands seized me from behind. Legs kicked my weary feet from under me. I was taken aback, thrown down on the road before I knew what was happening. How many there were I had no idea. I let out a disorientated cry, curled up protectively, craned around to look at them.

All I saw as I peered along the gutter was a large boot, coming straight at my right eye.

XXIV

I ROLLED. NOT far enough. Was it better to lose an eye, or to have a fractured skull? I thought I heard my neck crack as I wrenched away. The boot made contact, scraping along the upper bone of my eye socket painfully. Eyes shut against the agony, I screwed on to my back and kicked out hard, both feet together. I found someone, not with much force, but it gave me leeway to start fighting back.

No use. They dragged me over and face down again. My back was being pummelled. Thanks to my cloak, a heavy-duty item bought for long-distance travel, the effects were less than the murderous bastards intended. But I could not rise. I was stuck by the kerb, in the litter and dung. Someone stepped on my hand. Then either they were disturbed, or maybe their task was fulfilled. Now they were leaving. The parting shot came hoarsely right by my ear; the man must have bent double: 'Leave it to the big boys, Falco!'

Leave what? No need to ask.

I lay for a while where I was, thankful to be still breathing. Slowly I hauled myself across the pavement to my own threshold. Stumbling upright, I banged at the door, shaking too much to find my key. Somebody must have come to investigate. They would have looked out through the spy window, Albia most likely. The damage to my eye must have made me unrecognisable; instead of opening up, I heard the grim sounds of the bolts being shot home.

I fell down and waited to be rescued. My brain was almost empty – apart from a recurrent thought: I had recognised the boot coming at my eye.

But as usual in these situations, I had no idea where I had seen it before – or on whose foot.

Not too long afterwards, I was woken. A torch flamed, too close to my face. I was aware of a small group, with hard, professional voices.

'Shift that bloody vagrant off Falco's doorstep. . .'

'Dead?'

'Dying, I think. Give him a few kicks –' I was pulled upright, exclaiming at the pain. 'Oh dear, oh dear! Look who it is –' A voice I knew well as Fusculus, one of Petro's men in the vigiles, mocked me sadly. 'Helena Justina been knocking you about again, Falco?'

'Just a lovers' tiff. . .'

Fusculus shook his head, while banging stoutly at my door. It took some time for him to convince the occupants that it was safe to respond. 'Helena Justina, somebody does not like your husband!'

I heard Helena swiftly telling Albia to take my daughter Julia out of sight so she would not be scared. Julia was wailing anyway. 'Bring him in, will you –'

'You really must stop thumping him,' muttered Fusculus, continuing his tired joke. 'And do get him to give up the drink – This is a disgrace to a respectable neighbourhood.'

'Don't be a busybody, Fusculus.' A catch came in Helena's voice. 'Oh Juno, where did you find him?'

'Huddled on the step like a bundle of rags. It's all right – much worse than it looks –' The vigiles have a stock soothing repertoire for distressed wives. 'I've got him. Tell yourself he's just faking it, for a cheap thrill. Use your damned feet, Falco. Show me where to go, princess –'

They took me upstairs and I was dropped on my bed. I let it happen. Fusculus went off to tell Petronius, then almost at once Petro was there, with the vigiles' doctor, Scythax. They cleaned me up. As always, I refused a sleeping draught but Helena made an uncompromising nurse.

Trying to keep my fears private lest Helena worry even more, I croaked that Petro should contact the Camilli and Honorius. He had worked out that the attack was case-connected and promised safety checks.

'Warning you off, eh? This is a clear message. You could listen!'

'No chance of that,' Helena answered for me. 'He'll become more determined. You know him.'

'Yes, he's an idiot,' Petro replied frankly. 'Still, somebody thinks it matters to get rid of him. What's he doing this work for? Is there money in it?'

'It's a fight for justice, Lucius Petronius.'

'Oh I can see it's a fight,' Petro scoffed wryly. I felt his finger prod my eyebrow. 'But someone else seems to be getting the better of it, and there's no justice in that, is there?'

I buried my head under the pillow and took refuge in a drugged sleep.

Next day I woke, stiff as a post and groaning. I thought about getting up, but abandoned the plan. Helena forbade it, so I tried crawling out of bed after all. Then I dropped any idea of racing around the Circus Maximus and stayed put.

Helena brought up her wicker chair and a low footstool, to sit beside me. Now that I was being sensible, she allowed herself to straighten the coverlet then stroked my hair lovingly. 'Tell me what happened, Marcus.'

'You can see what happened.'

'Were you followed?'

'They were lying in wait.' I struggled to think straight. 'What about the others?'

'Justinus was at home – Claudia has gone into labour. I ought to go over there.'

'Your mother can look after Claudia.'

'Yes, but I need to look after Quintus. I imagine Claudia is a girl who will scream heartily. If my terrified brother skittles off to the baths to hide, she will never forgive him.'

'You can leave me.'

'I don't want to.'

I found her hand. She was close to tears. That upset me. Later, when she had calmed down over this, I would point out that plenty of householders arrived home in the evening wrecked, after being run over by badly driven carts or mugged by street thieves. 'What about Aulus?'

'At home. Honorius stayed out all night somewhere. His frail old mother had a seizure when the vigiles called, but he's turned up now. He and Aulus are downstairs in fact –'

'Let them up, then.'

'Are you fit for it?' she queried anxiously. No, I wasn't; but I made her let them up anyway.

They both shuffled in, looking nervous. I knew half my face must be a dreadful sight, but Helena had bandaged wadding on the eye, mainly to hide the mess. I was swollen and bruised, nothing worse, but the effects would be lurid for a few weeks. I would have a scar under the eyebrow when the damage healed. Scythax had sewn it neatly with fine thread. 'Look at me, the pair of you – then take your personal safety seriously from now on.'

Aelianus was the first to recover his composure. He threw himself in Helena's chair, leaving her to perch on the end of the bed. Honorius leaned against a cupboard. 'So who are we blaming?' Aelianus asked. He was too chirpy. His sister scowled at him.

'The opposition, obviously,' Honorius said. 'Presumably they used heavies, Falco?'

'I never saw much. Apart from the thug who croaked the special message, none of them spoke, either. They could have been fresh-cheeked, milk-fed shepherd boys – though I doubt it.'

Helena asked Honorius angrily, 'Are these common tactics? Did you see this bullying when you worked with Silius?'

Honorius shook his head. 'Oh no. Nothing like this was allowed!'

I sent Helena a private glance. For me, his assurance only meant that when rough stuff had been ordered – which it would have been – young Honorius had been kept in ignorance. 'Must be Paccius who arranged my treat, then!' I commented. Uneasy, Honorius fell silent.

I sipped a beaker of water. My head throbbed so it was a struggle to go on. 'Nothing changes. We still need to find out who bought the hemlock – Aulus, please.'

'The hemlock!' Aelianus was indignant at this mundane order. 'No, my brother's doing that.'

'He's off the scene,' I reminded him.

'I don't know how far he had gone –'

Helena scowled at Aelianus. 'Quintus was working in circles out from the Servian Embankment in the Fifth Region. You could start further west and work inwards, Aulus.' He began to protest. 'Don't play up,' she commanded.

'I'm no good at this. I'll feel a fool asking the question,' Aelianus whined.

'Oh Juno, don't be so feeble! Just start a conversation by saying you've been sent to find out what they recommend for dog fleas. I can tell you we rub Nux with a mixture of bitumen, olive oil and usually hellebore.' Nux, who was lying alongside me, hoping for treats, wagged her tail on hearing her name. 'Don't buy any; say you have to come home and ask me,' Helena pointed out.

'You could do this job,' her brother wheedled.

'Only if you stay in to feed the baby and nurse Marcus.'

'Don't leave me with him!' I stabbed a finger towards Honorius. '*You* can go and see Birdy. Ask whether he intends to contest his father's will.' Not receiving the response I wanted, I asked impatiently, 'Aelianus, have you told Honorius what we got from Fungibles?'

Both younger men looked vague. 'Pitiful. You haven't bothered to liaise.' Biting back my annoyance, I demanded of Honorius, 'So where were you last night, you stop-out? I gather your mother went spare when the vigiles called to warn you we were under threat.'

'I stayed with a friend.'

'Girlfriend?'

He blushed. 'My ex-wife, actually.' That was something new.

'You stayed the night with your ex?' Aelianus laughed mockingly.

'We were talking –'

'I bet you were!'

'She's intelligent. I value her thoughts. I told her I quit Silius. The conversation wandered into major issues of life and ethics, then you know how it is . . .' He tailed off, embarrassed.

'Messy. Either dump her, or get back with her properly,' I advised, not being unfriendly. He shrugged, looking vague. 'Warn Birdy too,' I said. 'Tell him he needs to live chastely to secure his rights. No late night partying.'

'Nothing,' suggested Helena, 'more sensational than an early evening song recital, organised by elderly ladies who knew his grandmother.'

'The same for you.' I winked at Honorius.

'You are joking.'

'No. You can do a lot of thinking, while listening to some bore with a harp and a fractured voice, in a venue where the wine has been watered three times to make it go further. You too, Aelianus!'

Despairing of my views on a decent social life, the two young men departed, seen off the premises by Nux.

That was fine. It left me alone with Helena, whose quietness I could tolerate even when a headache raged. We both settled peacefully, not speaking for a while.

'What are you holding back, Marcus?' When I looked at her quizzically, she gave one of her soft smiles. 'I can always tell.'

'You've never found out about my wild fling with that girl from the florist on Cumin Alley.'

'Not a problem. She'll ditch you,' Helena returned. She was game, though I thought she coloured slightly.

'Saffia,' I said, after a moment. 'She's next on my list but I don't want those two doing the interview.'

'Shall I see her?' As I hesitated, Helena laughed quietly. She rose and came to me, biffing me playfully. 'Oh, you want to do it yourself! It can wait. You'll be stronger tomorrow, I think.'

The bedroom door creaked open. Julia Junilla, our elder daughter had a new game: looking in at her wounded father, frightening herself at the grim sight, then running off, screaming. Helena went as far as the door, which she closed, latching it. All parents of small children should ensure they have a bedroom hook that only works from inside.

She came back to me, kicking off her shoes and squeezing next to me on the bed. I put an arm around her, feeling affectionate. My hand found its way up her sleeve. She was wearing a dark blue dress; she looked good in it, though she would look even better out of it. With my free hand I unhooked her gold ear-rings and tossed them gently on to the bedside table. Helena's great dark eyes appraised my intentions; she had seen me ill in bed before. I wasn't dead. I only had one wounded eye. Other parts of me still worked. In any case, some accomplishments of mine could be put into action even with my eyes closed.

XXV

SNUFFLING NOISES announced trouble. I deduced that Nux was now lying outside in the corridor, full length, with her paws against the door and her nose pressed to the gap at the bottom. I could also detect that little Julia must be prone alongside, bottom up, mimicking Nux. They could not get in. However, more competent noises told me that someone else, someone adept at domestic burglary, was working on the latch with a piece of wire expertly poked through the side crack in the door. We were about to be invaded. I had seen enough children rescued from cupboards to know who was coming to get me.

Helena was sitting in her chair, fully clad and innocent, when the door opened. Nux shot in and hurled herself on to the bed. Julia was being gripped under a firm arm.

'Hello, Ma.'

'This door sticks!' exclaimed my mother, as if she assumed I had not noticed the problem. 'What can you expect – in this house?' Her disapproving sniff referred to my father, who had owned the house previously. Then she looked me over. 'What happened to you, then?'

'I'm fine.'

'I asked what happened. Still, I see you survived.' Helena had quietly relinquished her chair, taking Julia. Julia tried the screaming-at-father trick, though in the presence of her awesome grandma she moderated the noise. My curly-haired daughter had a fine sense of who would tolerate nonsense. Ma perched in the wicker chair with a scowl like a particularly anti-social goddess of retribution.

'How are you, dear mother? How is Aristagoras?'

'Who?' asked Ma, as she always did when anyone enquired after her eighty-year-old boyfriend. I backed off. I never had the nerve to ascertain exactly what was going on. My father had asked me to find out – which was another reason not to. 'I heard there was trouble,' Ma sniffed. 'I see that's right.'

'Misunderstanding with some men who don't like my current

127

workload . . . Who told you?' I assumed it was Petronius, then I remembered that Maia and Petro were not speaking to Ma. Whereas a sane mother might be expected to feel glad that her troubled daughter had now found stability with a good-looking, salaried officer who adored her, mine kept passing remarks about Petro's estranged wife not deserving to lose him. . .

'Anacrites never forgets his poor old landlady.'

'Bull's bollocks!'

'I don't know who taught you to be so crude.' Ma sniffed, implying it was Pa.

Anacrites was the Chief Spy – a one-time follower of my sister Maia, who had turned violent when she dumped him. Even before that he was my long-term enemy – but he had been Ma's lodger and she thought him little lower than a Sun God in a twinkly diadem. I had other views about where his rays shone.

I ignored the low hint that Anacrites, who was not even family, paid more attention to my mother than I did. 'I did not want that bastard to know I was back in Rome.'

'Don't get your name everywhere in the Forum then. He says you are a byword for stupidity, because of this law work.'

'He thinks that only because I'm bringing justice to the innocent – a concept far too noble for Anacrites.'

Faced with a son who had noble motives, Ma lost interest. She lowered her voice. 'He knows Maia is back too.' She was worried, seeking reassurance. I sighed. I had none to give. If the Spy still harboured resentment, Maia was in for trouble.

Helena asked, 'Does Anacrites know about Maia and Petronius?'

'He asked me,' said Ma.

'And you told him!' I scoffed.

'He knew anyway.'

Another problem.

Helena passed Julia back to my mother. 'Junilla Tacita, if you could stay for a while and keep an eye on my brood, I should be very glad. My brother's wife is having her baby and I would appreciate a chance to go over there.'

Thrilled to be asked, Ma let a put-upon look pass over her features for a suitable moment as she pinned down Julia's plump thrashing legs. 'If they need a nurse, you have the right candidate sitting right downstairs. I was talking to her earlier – well, someone had to show some civility; poor dear, she's quite abandoned, all by herself in the hall –'

'Who, Ma?'

'Ursulina Prisca. She seems a very nice woman,' Ma told me pointedly.

'Quintus is looking after her woes.' Helena was searching for her ear-rings. My mother's keen black eyes had spotted the search and noted that the jewellery had ended up on the table. She sensed something private, though in the more interesting quest to set us straight about Ursulina, it passed without comment.

'Well, your Quintus needs to sort out that pig-farm business before the cousin ruins everything. Tell him the assessment of the walnut crop sounds *very* low to me.' Ma and Ursulina Prisca must have found each other kindred spirits. 'The valuer is a liability, and if you want my advice –' Which we didn't. 'Which of course will not be welcome as I'm just an old lady who brought up seven children single-handed, and I'm supposed to have no knowledge of the world –'

'What advice, Ma?'

'Do *not* trust the freedman with the limp!'

Helena told Mother gently that she would pass all that on to Quintus, who was very good at caring for widows.

'I wish I had someone to look after me!' snapped Ma. 'If they need a good midwife –'

'I'm sure Mother has found them one,' Helena muttered. Upon mention of Julia Justa, Ma shut her mouth like a tightly pleated furnishing feature on a smooth bolster. She had a wonderful complexion, which belied her age. It was a tribute to home-macerated face cream, brewed to a secret recipe which Ma passed off as mainly rose petals (this may have been true, but on principle my mother managed to make it sound like a bluff).

When Helena escaped to see about Claudia Rufina's progress, I claimed I was feeling poorly and needed to be left alone to sleep. After another hour of rollicking comment, my mother did leave me, removing my daughter and dog too. Exhausted, I fell into a deep slumber.

Honorius was the first of the forage party to report in.

'Negrinus refuses flatly to contest the will. No reason. I thought his sister, Carina, might argue – but she backed him up. Her husband, Laco, appeared for once – though he would not interfere.'

'So Negrinus is throwing it all away.'

Honorius sat on my bed with his arms folded. 'Negrinus is an odd body, Falco. One minute he shows all the anger you'd expect from a man in his situation. Then he suddenly implodes and seems to accept being shoved down a shit-hole by his closest relatives.'

'He is keeping something from us,' I said. 'He'll fight for himself when he's about to be charged with parricide – an offence that will get him sewn in a sack and thrown into the sea if he's found guilty. But when the penalty is less drastic, he reins back. He must have a reason to lie low.'

'So it's find the reason, then?'

'Oh yes – but you tell me where to start!'

We were both at a loss.

'I tried to see Saffia,' Honorius then told me. I refrained from throwing my water jug at his stupid head. Tantrums don't suit mature men. Anyway it was a decent jug. 'No luck. Incommunicado. Household in uproar. Males barred on the threshold. She has gone into labour, I was informed.'

'They must be putting birth-inducement powders in the aqueducts,' I growled. 'We have to see her. She seems to have gripped old Metellus by the privates – with the rest of the family all standing back helplessly to watch.'

'Well yes, but it won't look too good, Falco, if we harass Saffia for answers while she's in full birth pang!'

'You're a softie. It's just the moment.'

'That's one of your jokes,' Honorius replied stiffly.

'You're scared you'll end up snipping an umbilical cord or gathering up the afterbirth.'

The young man with the neat haircut managed not to shudder. 'Since Saffia was out, I tackled Calpurnia –' This was even worse. Honorius had no idea of following orders or working in a systematic way as part of a team. 'She was at home, I'm certain. She just refused to see me.'

With a restraint that Helena would have applauded, I begged Honorius to do nothing with our suspects and witnesses unless I asked him specifically.

'Right. So you don't want me to interview the clown, I take it?'

'What clown?' I demanded through clenched teeth.

He looked huffy. 'The one who was intended to be the satire at the Metellus funeral. I obtained his address from Biltis, that woman mourner Aelianus interviewed. Biltis,' Honorius repeated. 'Her name was in your original report to Silius. You know, before the charges we brought against Juliana . . . I'm trying to get things moving, Falco. I feel I am wasting my efforts, however.'

He finished whining, before I lost it and belted him. 'Any other suspects you've barged in on without consulting me?' I was livid. But it was good work to go back to the old report, and it was sensible to use the mourner, Biltis, to track down the clown. They were both marked up in Helena's notes as needing further enquiry. I myself had intended to look for the clown, when I got around to it.

Hurt, Honorius clammed up.

'Well, the clown was a bright idea.' Praise failed to mollify Honorius. 'Perhaps he'll know why Calpurnia upset her husband enough to be left almost nothing, and why Birdy has been written out too.'

'That's what I thought.'

I said I would go to see the clown tomorrow, but that Honorius could come with me. He quietened down.

'I wonder how funeral comedians do their research, Falco? If they just used the bland material that bereaved families supply to them, their performances would be pretty tame. At all the funerals I have attended or watched passing by, the clowns have given the dead man quite a raw deal. They can really hit on a person's weaknesses, and the crowds respond to it. Do they have methods of finding out stories the family would prefer to keep quiet?'

I smiled. 'They do. They winkle hard.' He still looked puzzled. 'They use informers, Honorius!'

Helena came home, bringing the news that Claudia Rufina had been safely delivered of a son. 'It didn't take too long and there were no panics. Claudia is sleeping; Quintus is sobbing with emotion but he'll get over it. My mother wore herself out but she's fine now – father and she are collapsed in a salon with an amphora of wine. The baby has all its limbs, and a tuft of dark hair, and seems likely to live. You're an uncle, Aulus!' Aelianus had overheard the news as he arrived. He pulled a mocking face, while presenting Nux with a large packet of skin-ailment ointment. Nux knew the scent, and hid under the bed. 'You and I have our first nephew. Be nice, and maybe they will name him after you.'

'Oh I hope not!' Helena was teasing, but her brother sounded horrified. 'I suppose now I'm expected to buy it a gold bulla to hang round its fat little neck?'

'No need, dear,' Helena told him sweetly. 'Mother has bought one to be your gift.'

Aelianus contained his grumpiness. Maybe the thought that his younger brother's bachelor spree was over had cheered him up.

As he waited for the fuss over the new baby to subside, I could see he was elated. As soon as we could politely forget about his brother, I asked what was up.

'Just as well you sent me out, not young Quintus, Falco. I started at the Forum, and was intending to work over to the eastern side, moving towards where the Metelli live. I checked all the streets at the back of the public buildings on the western side first. Around there it's bookshops and jewellers mainly, but one or two other booths can be found tucked in under the Palatine. I thought there might be incense-sellers –'

'An entirely sane presumption, given the temples.' Honorius sounded unduly straight. Aelianus shot him a surly look in case he was being sarcastic.

He let the pause linger, milking it. Then he came out with his big discovery: 'I found a man who admitted selling hemlock, last autumn.'

'Well done.' I was surprised.

'Mind you,' murmured Honorius, playing the sceptical advocate, 'was it the right hemlock?'

'It's our stuff,' smirked Aelianus. He seemed unfazed by Honorius.

'Proving this is the dose used on Metellus won't be easy after all this time –'

'This was not a simple transaction; hemlock isn't a stock item,' said Aelianus, suddenly the expert. 'You don't just turn up and pick your bunch of leaves from the bundles hanging on a stall. It was special order; the seller had to have the plant fetched from a market garden he owns out in the countryside.'

'So he had several meetings with the buyer?' I could see where Aulus was heading.

'At least two. Naturally I wanted to know more about this buyer,' Aelianus emphasised heavily to Honorius.

Honorius had an ear for a witness who was about to make a dramatic statement. 'And?'

'The seeker of endless sleep was a man in his forties. Not patrician, not a slave, probably not a freedman either. Stocky, shorn head, heavy outerwear, could be a bruiser. Familiar?' Stilled, I glanced at him. Aelianus knew I had recognised the description. Honorius nervously shook his head.

'Could almost be someone daft enough to settle up with a signature!' Aelianus grinned. 'He wanted to pay with cash, but hemlock is an unusual request and the seller was an opportunist, so the price was exorbitant. The buyer fetched out his purse, but he hadn't enough money on him. Sadly, just as he was about to write a banker's draft on his employer's account, he changed his mind.'

'Now that would have been a piece of luck for us – and absolutely daft for him!' I said. 'He never did it?'

'No. He remembered some coins that he kept in his boot. My seller joked that he could identify him by his athlete's foot.'

'Sensational in court! Enough suspense,' I chivvied. 'Who was this poison-purchaser?' I already knew, of course. So when Aelianus tried to squeeze more glory from the moment by dragging things out even longer, I myself said quietly, 'It was Bratta.'

Bratta was the informer used by Paccius Africanus. He was on my mind today. For one thing, as I lay dreaming in bed I had become sure it was Bratta's voice that had ordered me to give up this case last night. Once I had thought of him, I had no doubt it had been Bratta's boot that kicked me in the eye.

XXVI

WE TOOK stock.

'You have,' listed Helena, annoying both her brother and Honorius by the ease with which she took charge, 'an opinion that Calpurnia Cara must have offended her husband.'

'That can be built up well in court,' Honorius interposed.

'No doubt. Alternatively, Rubirius Metellus may just have been a mean old tyrant, who behaved spitefully to a wife of forty years who deserved far better!'

'But we make our point first.' Honorius smiled.

Helena shrugged. 'I see. You say, *What husband would dream of removing from his faithful wife all the comforts she has enjoyed through their long marriage – unless he believes her affection is fraudulent – maybe he even suspects she is capable of murder if he will not act as she wishes. . .*'

'Why did they not divorce?' I wondered.

'Easy,' Helena snapped. 'Metellus had written her out of his will – but Calpurnia did not know.' She gave me a long look and I made two mental notes. One, it was time I prepared a testament. Two, Helena Justina should feature in it.

'But if he hated her, why not tell her?'

'Scared, Marcus.'

'A man scared of his wife!'

'Yes, how unlikely. But we know she thought him a coward, darling . . . Then,' said Helena calmly to Honorius, 'you have a link between Paccius urging Metellus to commit suicide, Calpurnia suggesting death by hemlock, and Bratta, known to be a run-around for Paccius, buying hemlock. Yes, the defence can argue that the drug was for other purposes – but you will ask them what. There are not many uses commonly. You can dismiss any suggestion as a curious coincidence.'

'They will maintain Bratta simply bought the hemlock for use by Negrinus,' Honorius offered. 'They'll say Negrinus requested it.'

'He will deny it.'

'They will say he's a shameless liar. We can only retaliate by trying to discredit them.'

'I'll sort that,' I said. 'Your job is to imply Paccius Africanus – *now openly attacking Negrinus* – has become an evil influence in the Metellus family. Stress a dark connection between Paccius and the mother –'

'Conspiracy with Calpurnia? Unproven,' reflected Honorius, 'but any jury will assume the reasons were sexual. We don't even have to say it. They will be eager to draw the worst conclusion. Then –'

'Then Paccius had also worked on Metellus, wickedly persuading him to disinherit his son and two daughters, in favour of Saffia,' I ticked off.

'So. . . we suggest an unsuitable affinity between Metellus and his daughter-in-law, plus more immorality between *Paccius* and Saffia.' Honorius, supposedly the young idealist, came out with these shameless slurs automatically. I was impressed.

'Working with Silius has had its effect,' I commented.

'Working against Silius *and* Paccius will not be easy.'

'That's right,' I grinned. 'Be aware of the odds. Then you can't fail.'

Honorius was silent. The good-looking patrician always knew when we were mocking him, though he never knew how to respond. Taking pity, Helena asked if he would make anything of my identification of Bratta among my last night's attackers. Honorius turned to her, answering courteously, 'We do not have much else to offer the court. So yes. It always goes down well to suggest that the opposition uses thuggery.'

'Threats are viewed badly by juries – and they hate disorder in the streets,' I agreed.

Honorius had been mulling. 'I shall present Negrinus as an unworldly, innocent victim, set up by a gang of cynical bullies who habitually try to pervert justice. Keep that bandage on your eye, Falco. In fact, Helena Justina, it would help if you could pad it out to look slightly bigger. If his bruises fade, you may be able to enhance them with a little feminine eye colour –'

'Eye paint?' Helena asked frostily. I was aware that she used it on special occasions; I grinned at her.

'Yes, try orchid rouge, with smudges of blue put on afterwards.' Honorius was serious. He had done it in the past. How fortunate that this manipulator was on our side – though we had yet to see what tricks the others would play to disadvantage us.

'How will it look about Saffia getting the money?' Aelianus broke in. 'Bad, surely?'

Honorius thought. 'She will be mentioned – the accusers must go through the terms of the will in order to show how unfairly Negrinus has been treated. That's his supposed motive. Silius cannot avoid mentioning the trust set up for Saffia – I think Silius will do it, to distance Paccius. It won't serve much purpose for us to speculate on why Saffia. (Well, not unless we can find out!) But we can point up the sinister Paccius involvement. Jury members who hate informers will object to legacy-chasing.' Honorius frowned. 'That is not enough, however. Birdy simply must make a claim to overturn this will.'

'If he really won't,' said Helena, 'You can say, *however much he has lost by the unfair provisions of his father's will, he is a man of very great decency – reluctant to initiate an action while his ex-wife is in the process – the dangerous process – of giving birth to his child.*'

'Sweet,' I muttered. 'But even if he's a thoroughly thoughtful spouse and father, we have to find out why he won't start the action.'

'The two daughters have a case too,' Honorius answered. 'So they aren't helping. I asked Carina about any intentions she and Juliana have. Their story is, "We loved our father and are all determined to accept his wishes." Carina's husband, Verginius, sneerily pointed out how rich he is, and that his wife does not need the money. But Birdy does. And they may have loved their father, but Metellus has shown very publicly that he did not love *them*. You are entitled to find their declaration unbelievable.' Honorius sounded as if he were in court already.

I drew the discussion to a close abruptly. Helena and her brother hung their heads and made no comment. They both knew my major concern at present was how to stop our inexperienced, uncontrollable colleague poking into things. Honorius had to be stopped. Investigating murder is no game for amateurs.

'I'll allocate jobs to everyone tomorrow,' I said. 'Just promise me that none of you will do anything stupid.'

'Of course not,' said Honorius. 'I think I'll go and see Bratta.'

I nearly let the idiot do it. Being beaten up might make him think in future.

XXVII

'BE CAREFUL,' warned Helena as I left next day. Determined to impose my authority on my younger partners, I was heading out early. I creaked and had a blind side, but there was no choice.

'Don't worry. This business is all talk,' I replied drily, alluding to her own misplaced belief up until yesterday. A twinge caught me. 'As you see!'

I was going to talk about funerals later. It seemed the wrong moment to tell Helena that.

'Don't get into any fights, Falco.'

I winced at the pains I already felt. 'No, darling.'

First, I went to Rubiria Carina's house to re-interview her and her brother. On the subject of their father's will, I extracted no more than Honorius had done. They both meekly accepted their disinheritance and told me that so did the elder sister, Juliana.

'Birdy, Birdy, you're not helping yourself. Indignation will look much better to a court. It's more natural. We are trying to advise you; contest the will!'

'I can't,' he whimpered. As usual, he gave no reason. When I glared, he stiffened up. 'I choose not to. And I will not discuss it.' Whatever pressure he was under to make him take this attitude, it must be serious.

'If your father dumped you in favour of your wife, that might just about have been acceptable – but now Saffia has left you. Maybe your strange, devious papa might have altered his will if he had lived – but he ignored the chance. His witnesses were to be called in to swear to his suicide; he could easily have prepared an updated will and had it signed. As far as I know, he made no move to rewrite the conditions or to add a codicil. So, Negrinus, what do you have to say about this?'

'Nothing.'

'Did you know about this will?'

'Yes.'

'From the start? When it was prepared more than two years ago?'

'Yes.'

'Did you argue?'

'No. Father could do as he wished. I had no choice.'

'Did you even talk to him about his arrangements?'

A vague look came over that oddly bookish face. 'I think he meant to change the will.' Negrinus was unconvincing. We could not defend him in court with anything that sounded so insincere.

'Our father was not devious,' Carina stated frigidly. She must have been harbouring resentment over my remark.

'Your father had been proved corrupt,' I reminded her. 'Now it looks as if his personal relationships were as rocky as his business conscience.'

'Children have no options in their family heritage,' she commented. I saw Birdy heave a huge sigh to himself. His sister only assumed a look of determination.

'Why did your father favour Saffia Donata?'

'Nobody likes her,' Carina suggested. 'Papa felt sorry for her, perhaps.'

I could not bring myself to suggest to Birdy that his father had had an affair with his wife.

I did ask these legacy-spurning siblings about their parents' relationship. Why, after a marriage of forty years or more, had their father been so ungenerous to Calpurnia Cara?

'We have no idea,' Carina told me firmly. I always felt she was the tough one, but even Birdy clenched his jaw.

'Well, how do you react to this? – I believe your mother killed your father.'

'No.' They both said it. They spoke up instantly. Then, as if she could not restrain herself, Carina murmured to Birdy, leaving me out of it: 'Well, in a way she did. She made the situation unbearable, you know.'

I looked at him quizzically. He explained it as their mother trying to force the issue of their father committing suicide. I did not believe that was what Carina had meant. She clammed up, of course.

Now I did tackle Birdy on the obvious solution: 'I'm afraid your father made your wife Saffia his fancy piece – and your mother could no longer stand it.' Negrinus showed no reaction. Carina flushed, but said nothing. 'Were your parents always close to Paccius Africanus?'

'They had a business relationship with him,' Negrinus answered.

'Your mother too?'

'Why?' It came out very quickly.

'I think *her* attachment to him may have been rather too close. Still is. Perhaps that was how Calpurnia compensated for her husband's appalling behaviour with Saffia.'

'No.'

'Look, I know it's unpleasant to think about your mother fooling around with other men –' I wondered if it might be relevant that Birdy, with his thin-faced look, and Carina with her wider-cheeked features were so unlike each other.

'Our mother was always chaste, and faithful to Father,' Carina corrected me coldly.

Changing the subject, I told them about the informer Bratta buying the hemlock. 'I think he acquired it, on instructions from Paccius, for your mother to use.'

'No,' Birdy said again.

'Come on, Negrinus. You do not want to believe that your mother is a murderess, but it's her or you. See how a case can be built here. The family graft had been exposed; the family fortune was threatened. Paccius counselled your father to kill himself; your mother strongly supported it. She came up with a plan; Paccius used his man to acquire the drug. So your father took one lot of pills under pressure, changed his mind, thought he was safe – then was put down with another deadly potion like some old horse.'

'No,' said Negrinus, almost through gritted teeth. He was a man defending his mother – albeit a mother whose testimony would condemn him for parricide. 'I wish I'd never mentioned the hemlock plan, Falco. It was just a wild idea we once discussed, speculating on crazy ways to escape our financial losses. It was never serious. And never put into action.'

'Why Perseus?'

'What?'

I spelt it out patiently: 'You told me your mother wanted to kill a slave as a decoy, using his corpse so your father could go into hiding. The door porter was to be sacrificed. That's very specific: Perseus was the doomed slave. What had he done?'

'Again, that was just a suggestion . . .' Negrinus was shifty, though it could be awkwardness because he genuinely did not know.

Frustrated, I was now ready to pull out of the case. I had had plenty of clients I could not trust, but this beat all. I had never felt so much excluded, when excluding me worked utterly against the man's own interests.

'If you won't tell me the truth –'

'Everything I have told you is the truth.'

I laughed, brutally. 'But what have you *not* told me?'

I left, furious. I had not severed links. I should discuss that with my partners first. Besides, if I dropped the case, I would never learn what was going on. I had my curiosity. I wanted to know what these people were hiding.

It was mid-morning, so I paused and bought a snack at a bar just opposite. This can be a good idea, after a het-up meeting. Many a time staying on the scene had produced something helpful, once people thought I had left.

Eventually, Negrinus emerged and hopped agitatedly on the doorstep until transport was brought for him. I tailed him and was not surprised by where the smart litter headed. He went straight to his mother, like a devoted boy.

Wrong. He went to her house. But her outcast son did not want to see his cruel mama.

In the street outside the Metellus mansion with its yellow Numidian obelisks, he shed the litter and secured an observation post. He got the bar counter – which left me, when I arrived, hiding behind a stinking row of fish-pickle amphorae. He bought a beaker of hot, spiced wine; I had left my drink behind at the previous place. Typical. He was the suspicious character; I was the upright informer. The Fates would adorn him with comforts; I was stuck with a rumbling stomach and a cold arse.

What was he doing? When I realised, a sneaky fellow-feeling arose. The noble Metellus Negrinus was waiting for his mother to go out.

Calpurnia left home in *her* litter, which was a beaten-up chaise carried by two elderly bearers, one who seemed to have gout, neither in uniform. I could see she was the passenger, because the curtains were missing. A miserable female slave, shivering in a thin gown, wandered behind on foot.

She still had possession of the family home, but it looked as if Calpurnia Cara was already down on her luck. Had Paccius Africanus stepped in already and laid claim to domestic goods and slaves?

Was Paccius then absolutely sure the three children would not, or could not, contest their father's odd will?

Negrinus must have known his mama had an appointment. Once

her straggling party turned the far corner of the street, he quickly paid for his wine (was the supportive Carina giving him dole money?) then he marched straight across the street. He was using his latch-lifter when the door opened anyway. After a brief conversation, someone let him in. I allowed time for him to start whatever he was planning, then approached the fine front door myself.

I knocked nonchalantly. A slave I failed to recognise appeared after a long pause. 'About time.' I glared with my good eye.

'Wow! What happened to you?'

'I looked up and a passing eagle shat very hard in my peeper . . . So where's Perseus?'

'Having his lunch.'

'He has a nice life.'

'You bet!' It was said with feeling.

'I suppose he'll enjoy several courses and a snug flirtation with the kitchen maid, then stretch out for a relaxed siesta?'

'Don't ask me!' This lad buttoned up. He knew better than to gossip any further, but he had let me see he was unhappy. So, in Perseus we had that stock character: the uppity slave who abuses his position – and who somehow gets away with it.

I tipped the substitute. He let me in. 'He's a character!' I chortled. 'Somebody's favourite is he, your Perseus?' Not from the way I had heard Calpurnia address the lackadaisical beggar before. His neglect of his duties had made her rightly furious. But if something had gone on between Metellus senior and Saffia, and if Perseus knew about it, his arrogance would make sense.

We had a recognisable situation – though rare in a porter. More often, the uppity slave has intimate contact with the master or mistress of the house. In a boudoir maid or a correspondence clerk, abuse of status arises much more easily.

'Perseus has influence,' was all I could extract. Maybe my tip was not large enough. Or maybe the staff had learned that it was best to keep quiet.

My next contact was with the superior steward whom I had met on my first visit here. Instinct warned him of trouble and he arrived in the atrium, napkin under his chin. He glanced at my bandage but was too well trained to comment. Losing the bib suavely, plus the smear of oil on his chin from his abandoned lunch, he accompanied me on the track of Birdy. We found him in what must have been his bedroom once. He said he had come to collect clothing – fair enough, and a few desultory choices of tunics were made as he rummaged. He was looking for something else, though.

'My wife is in labour. I had a message that the baby is taking a long time. She is restless, and her women think she might be more comfortable with her own bedding . . .'

'I was told Saffia's stuff was "stolen" when she left here,' I said.

'If chattels went astray,' the steward put in indignantly, 'I knew nothing of it.'

'You should,' snapped Birdy. 'Saffia has been erupting.'

The steward believed the missing items could be found. He went off to investigate. Negrinus continued throwing his own possessions together for removal to his sister's house. Goading him, I commented, 'I was told that your communication with Saffia had broken down.'

'Ah, but now Saffia wants something!' Negrinus spoke with a new bitterness. He stood in the centre of his old bedroom. It was a finely decorated room in bluey-green, with curliculed pictures of sea monsters. His feet were planted on a well modulated geometric mosaic. All this décor went back several decades and was starting to look tired. So was Birdy. He ran his hands through his hair. He had looked neat when I first met him, but he now needed a haircut. 'Anything Saffia wants, Saffia will get!' He seemed furious, but reined it in.

'This stinks,' I said quietly. More and more I saw him as the wronged son, whose father had had an adulterous relationship with his wife. It left a very unpleasant question mark over the paternity of Saffia's unborn child.

'Oh yes! She has bled me dry. Now she is making a dramatic fuss about a few unnecessary bedclothes, although believe me, Saffia has plenty – plenty of everything nowadays.'

The bed in his own room here remained fully equipped with covers. 'Did you and Saffia share a bedroom?'

'Not during her pregnancy. She had a boudoir next door –'

I went and looked; the room was a shell. 'She's stripped out everything that would move, I see.'

'She would have us hack off the frescos,' Birdy said, 'but that would lower the value of this house when she comes to sell it!'

'You are clinging to your sense of decency.' I did not understand it though I admired his stoicism.

'She was my wife, Falco. I made a mistake there, but I live with its consequences. She is the mother of my children.' He never raised doubts over their paternity, I noticed. 'Oh, she ensured that I had children,' he exclaimed grimly. 'We are permanently tied together. And I tell myself,' he reasoned, with more feeling than I ever heard from him, 'that if I always respond courteously to each indignity this woman hurls at me, that is my one chance!'

One chance for what? More than a quiet life, by the sound of it. I dropped my voice. 'So you are a man charged with parricide – but you're hunting for pillows?'

'Pillows,' he raged. 'Bolster, under-sheet, mattress – and her damned down-padded, peacock-embroidered coverlet.'

He did not have to hunt for long. The steward returned with news of the lost items. Perseus, the door porter, had appropriated them. Metellus Negrinus let out a furious exclamation, then strode to the slaves' quarters and robustly set about retrieval.

The porter was taking his ease in his cubicle, reclining on a decent mattress which he had put on the ledge in place of a slave's thin pallet. He had surrounded himself with knick-knacks, all stolen property, I suspected. Well, Saffia Donata was to have hers returned, though I myself would not have been keen on bedding that had been used by a leering and obnoxious house slave.

Maybe she deserved that. Anyway, Negrinus threw the porter off and began to haul the mattress up through the slaves' corridor to the atrium. I brought the pillows and linen for him. The steward, waiting in the atrium, began to rebuke Perseus.

'Leave him to me!' snarled Birdy. This was a revelation. He dropped the mattress on my feet; I jumped back. Negrinus grabbed Perseus by the tunic, glancing at it briefly and swore, as if he recognised the garment as one of his own. It was closely woven green wool, with ribbed braid at the neck, an expensive item. Clearly this porter lifted anything he fancied. The steward, who mostly seemed so efficient, looked powerless in his company.

Negrinus had backed the porter up against a painted wall. 'Where's the coverlet?'

The porter feigned ignorance. Negrinus pulled him forwards then bashed his head back against the plaster. Trying to escape him, Perseus stumbled and fell to the floor. After that, the surprise hero used his feet. Negrinus was a senator. He had been in the army. When he stamped on Perseus, Perseus learned the meaning of a military training.

'I have had enough of you,' Negrinus told him. He stamped. He put his weight into it. I glanced at the steward and we both winced.

'I am sick of people hurting me, so I am going to –' *Stamp!* 'hurt –' *Stamp!* 'you!' A final stamp did the trick.

Perseus confessed that the missing bedspread might be in the garden shack. The keys were required; I had seen the place chained up. Calpurnia had said 'unwanted household goods' were stored there. Regaining his authority, the steward slid off and produced Calpurnia's bunch of domestic keys.

Still fired up, Birdy dragged the porter to his feet and strode out to the garden, pulling Perseus with him. It was a mild day, surprisingly bright for winter. By now, I had stiffened up badly from the attack on me last night, so I limped painfully at a distance as the pair approached the little hillside store. A few wasps still buzzed around the area in the late afternoon sunlight. I caught up as Birdy wrestled with the lock, while the discarded Perseus whimpered nearby beneath a fig tree. He looked ready to run off, so I stood over him. Birdy heaved open the door of the shack. He ducked inside. I heard him exclaim, so I started forwards, with a sense of dread as if I thought he had discovered a dead body.

He reappeared in the doorway, holding nothing worse than an armful of brightly coloured material. It was badly crumpled and as he was inspecting it in the light, an expression of disgust appeared on his face. He threw the coverlet down, and came towards the porter. Scared of another kicking, Perseus took the initiative and went for Birdy. They fell back into the store, fighting.

I reached the low doorway just as Birdy staggered out again. I thought he might have been wounded, though I could see no blood. He lurched past me, as the porter came towards the door. I could just make him out in near darkness; I must have been outlined against the sunlight. He started jabbing at me with a long tool, the sort used for pruning trees, with a thick curved hook. Because my back was hurting, I grabbed at the lintel to support myself. That was when I noticed that the crude roof of the hutment had a warm spot. I recognised the symptoms. After years of living in attic apartments, I knew the wasps must be right there overhead. The light was too dim to spot any ceiling stains, but above me there could be a honeycombed nest three feet across.

I dropped down, grabbed a broom and stood up sharply, holding it by the brush end. As the porter lunged at me, I rammed the stave upwards into the rough boarded roof, hard. Then I spun out of the doorway, slamming the door after me.

I heard furious wasps storm down from their shattered nest. Even at this time of year they were active. The porter started screaming. I hobbled away from the door while Birdy stared at me, white-faced.

At my feet lay the coverlet, embroidered with multicoloured threads in shimmering blues like peacock feathers. It was beautiful to view but it smelt dreadful. I could understand why it had been taken out of the house – though not why it had been hidden in the store. It reeked, and the foul odour was of rotting human excrement.

XXVIII

PEOPLE CAME from the house and dragged out the porter. He was just about alive. He was lucky. Some go into convulsions, with their mouths and throats swollen. Some die. Maybe I should have felt some remorse, but he was a blatant wrongdoer. I said I would be back to interrogate him.

Birdy seemed in shock too. I tried to talk to him, but it was useless. Thwarted, I saw our jittery client put into his litter, to be returned to his sister's house.

In an aside, I demanded of the steward what hold over the family the porter had. He just gave me a guarded look. The steward seemed bemused by the smelly coverlet, muttering obsessively that it should have been burned. Like Negrinus, he had stared at the thing in the garden, transfixed. Both of them clearly thought it had significance. I warned the steward that I would pursue enquiries into how the ruined throw came to be in that condition and why it had been locked away.

Saffia Donata's other bedding was being carried to her apartment. Leaving the hysteria at the Metellus mansion to settle down, I walked along after the slaves who manhandled the mattress and pillows through the streets; at the apartment Lutea had found for her, they gained admittance to dump their burden, but then all of us were brusquely turned away. We could hear Saffia still in the throes of labour. This woman held the key to many puzzles. There too, I took my leave but grimly promised to return.

The crazy scenes I witnessed had helped me reach a conclusion. I could not prove my newly forming theory, but the stained and stinking coverlet seemed relevant to the Metellus death. I was coming to believe that Metellus senior had not, as we had always been told, retired to his bedroom to await his end, conducting a half-hearted suicide.

I did believe he had been poisoned.

Once I suspected Metellus had not died in his own bed, my task was to find out if he had been in the bed of someone else. The coverlet pointed to Saffia – but by then she had already left the house. Besides, if guilty, why would she draw attention to herself by whining for the return of her property? So my new theory was this: Metellus senior did not die in bed at all.

And that was fun to play with. It threw up a whole bunch of exciting possibilities.

XXIX

'HEMLOCK,' I said.

The vigiles doctor, a morose blue-chinned cur called Scythax, glared at me nastily. I won't say Scythax looked unhealthy, but he was so pale and haggard that if he arrived on a cargo ship from a foreign province, port officials would quarantine him.

He was eating his lunch. It was eggs on salad leaves. He pushed his bowl away slightly.

'How's that eye, Falco?' I grimaced. He perked up. 'Hemlock, you said?'

'The philosopher's oblivion. Tell me about it, Scythax.'

'Poison parsley,' sneered Scythax. He always looked down on anything to do with apothecaries. He enjoyed manipulating splints but hated ointments. Since the vigiles acted as a fire brigade, his unwillingness to soothe burns did hamper him, but he had worked with the Fourth Cohort as long as they could remember and the vigiles dislike changed. Scythax was marvellous with broken limbs and internal crushing, but no one went to him for a headache cure. His remedy when squad members had a heavy hangover was to shower them with very cold water. They preferred to sign out sick – but that meant Petronius Longus turned up at their lodgings, cursed them for drinking, and kicked them downstairs. He could do that even with his own head splitting.

Petronius and a couple of his lads were now lounging on benches. As I quizzed Scythax, they listened in, always glad to have me in their station house bringing some new jollity from my repertoire of crazy cases.

'River-rat weed, my country relatives call it,' I told the doctor. 'I need to know, what happens to a victim, Scythax?'

'A long, slow, creeping, very permanent sleep, Falco.'

'Before the sleep, what are the symptoms?'

Scythax gave up on his food bowl. Petro and the vigiles came to attention too, mimicking their bone-setter, folding their arms with their heads cocked. 'All parts of the hemlock plant are poisonous, Falco, especially the seeds. The root is supposed to be harmless when young and fresh, but I have never tested that. The leaves –' He paused, looking at his lunch – 'have often been used to kill off the unwary when served up as a green garnish.'

I had no idea how the poison had been administered to Metellus. 'After it is ingested, how long to an effect?'

'I don't know.' It was the doctor's turn for grim humour. 'We don't get cases of poison making complaints at the visitors' desk.'

'Can you look up hemlock in a compendium? I'm consulting you about a crime, remember.'

For that I got a filthy look, but Scythax reluctantly found and pored over a scroll he kept in his infirmary cubicle. I waited. After a long interval of squinting at tiny Greek lettering in endless columns, sometimes accompanied by blotted diagrams of plants, he grunted. 'It works quickly. An initial reaction in as little as half an hour. Death then takes a few more hours. The method is paralysis. The muscles fail. The brain stays alert, but the subject slowly fades.'

'Any distressing side-effects?'

Scythax was sarcastic. 'Other than death?'

'Yes.'

'Vomiting. Evacuation of the bowels – with diarrhoea.'

I sniffed. 'They never tell you that in the lofty story of Socrates.'

'In the Greece of antiquity, the innocent were allowed their dignity.' Scythax, a man of grandiose gloom added, 'Unlike here!' He came from slave stock, and may well have had Greek origins. 'I assure you, the tragic death of Socrates will have been accompanied by gruesome effects.'

I was satisfied. 'Gruesome effects' had certainly been inflicted on Saffia Donata's embroidered coverlet. 'Would you appear as an expert witness in court for me?'

'Get lost, Falco.'

'I shall have you issued with a subpoena then.'

'You'll have to find him first,' commented Petro. 'I'm not having him hanging around the bloody Basilica; we need him here.'

'What about my case? I'm trying to nail a killer.'

'And my lads need their grazes dabbed clean.'

'Oh pardon me.' I looked down my nose at him. 'I'll have to hire some damned informer to deliver the summons, I suppose.'

They all laughed.

XXX

SOME DAYS an informer spends in endless walking. In the pursuit of comfort, I always wore hobnailed, well-worn-in boots.

My plans to pursue the issue of lethal herbage had to be put on hold; there was no time to work out how Metellus had been persuaded to imbibe or digest the hemlock, or else how it came to be administered secretly. I had promised Honorius he could come with me that afternoon to investigate the clown who had been deprived of performing at Metellus senior's funeral.

Sadly for Honorius, the logistics were against him. I was now up at the vigiles' station-house on the Aventine crest; he was right down by the river at my house. The vigiles had given me a bread roll and a drink, so I did not need to go home for lunch. Then I knew where to find Biltis; her hangout had been listed in Aelianus' original notes. The funeral firm operated in the Fifth Region, so when I left Petro's squad, it was least effort just to plod down from the Aventine at the eastern edge, skirt the Circus Maximus at its rounded end, and head off past the Capena Gate to the Fifth. Honorius would have to miss the fun.

I had already made this tiresome hike twice, going to and coming back from the Metellus house. By the time I encountered the mourner I was in a bad mood. Biltis was, as Aelianus had tersely noted, a woman who pressed too close and took too much interest in anyone who had to interview her. She was shabby and shapeless, with restless dark eyes and a mole on her chin, and was dressed in a style that proved funeral mourners are just as overpaid as you always suspect when you are arranging some loved one's last farewell. Plenty of bills that people were too distressed to query must have helped provide the glass bead edging on the woman's brightly coloured dress and the faddy fringe on her lush crimson stole.

'Of course I wear dingy tones when I'm working,' she explained, no doubt aware I was sizing up how much her zingingly gay apparel must have cost. 'All the effort goes into dishevelling the hair to tear – Some mourners use a wig, to spare their scalps, but I had some false hair fall off once. Right in the street. It doesn't impress the bereaved. Well, they are paying, aren't they? And with Tiasus they hope they are paying for quality. You have to avoid discourtesy.'

'Quite.'

'You don't have much to say for yourself, do you?'

'True.' I was listening. We had doubts about her reliability. I was trying to evaluate her from the stream of chat.

'I liked the other one.' That was a first for Aelianus. I would enjoy telling him.

'Would it be rude to ask what happened to your eye?' asked Biltis.

'Why not? Everyone else does!' I made no effort to tell the woman.

Miffed, she shut up. Now it was my turn. I ran through what she had told Aelianus about the family tensions at the Metellus funeral: strife among the relatives and Carina's outburst about her father having been murdered. Biltis confirmed the routine details too: the procession to the Via Appia and burning of the bier at the mausoleum, where Negrinus had presided with Juliana's husband and a friend who was presumably Licinius Lutea. The chief clown they had first intended to use in the procession was called Spindex. He worked for Tiasus regularly, though Biltis said it was ages since anyone had seen him.

'He went all huffy when he was dumped by the Metelli. Tiasus sent him one or two commissions afterwards but he failed to confirm or show up. He just dropped out of sight.'

'So why, exactly, was he omitted from the Metellus do?'

Exactly must have worried her. From pretending to be the expert on everything, she started to look shifty.

'Don't worry then,' I said. 'I can ask Spindex himself, if I find him. I hope he didn't go off into retirement at some homestead in a remote province.'

'Oh he has no connections,' Biltis assured me. 'He has no friends and never mentions family.'

'Probably because he spends his days being rude,' I suggested.

'And is he rude!' the woman exclaimed. 'You won't find better than Spindex for rooting out the worst in human nature. Once he gets the dirt, he does not hold back.'

'Do you know how he finds his material?'

'Digging.'

'Do it himself?'

'Half and half, I think. With a senatorial family, he would never get direct access. He has a pal with contacts, who helps him out.'

151

'I thought you said Spindex has no friends? What pal?'

'Don't know. Spindex keeps to himself.'

'And you don't know the helper's name?'

'No. I tried to find out, but Spindex got stand-offish.'

'Why did you want to find out?'

'Just nosy!' Biltis admitted with a grin.

I sympathised with the clown. People like Biltis crowd in, finding out your weaknesses along with your dearest secrets. Then they turn against you, or poison your other relationships. In the army I had met men who worked the same way.

Still, Biltis had discovered the clown's home address. She even insisted on taking me on a route march to the road where he lived and pointing out his building. We set off under grey January skies, observed by a few chilly pigeons. Spindex had a billet which turned out to be a long walk from the Fifth, all the way back to the Twelfth District. He lived opposite the Aventine, in the shadow of the Servian Walls, close to the Aqua Marcia.

'See, I had to bring you,' Biltis crowed. 'This is a terrible hole. You'd never have found your way around.'

'You're talking about my birthplace, woman.' I cursed myself for giving away something personal.

If I had not insisted she leave, Biltis would have trodden on my heels all the way up to the clown's room, where she would have sat on my knee making saucy interventions while I asked him questions. I said bluntly that I didn't need anyone to hold my note-tablet and after the obvious lewd retort from the mourner, I managed to shed her.

Alone, I approached a narrow opening that provided dark stairs upwards from the street. As she waved goodbye from outside one of the shops that flanked this entrance, Biltis called after me that Spindex was a disorderly, filthy type. 'You'll find his room, easy – just follow the smell.'

I grunted and went up the cramped stone steps. This was not a tenement approach, but a narrow insert between commercial premises. I guessed Spindex had solitary attic lodgings on the third floor, beyond the living quarters that lay above owner-occupied shops, which would be accessed from within those shops. Only Spindex and his visitors ever came up this way.

Biltis was right, perhaps more right than she knew. The reek on the staircase was strong, growing worse every day no doubt. This smell was very particular; in my line of work, it was familiar. Filled with foreboding, I tramped up and found the apartment. I was sure before I even opened the door that Spindex would be there inside. And I knew he would be dead.

XXXI

<hr>

Being a funeral clown must have all the glamour and high rewards of being an informer. There was hardly any light on the stairs. I crashed into empty wine containers on the landing. Then I entered a meagre apartment. Two dark rooms – one for being awake in misery and one for sleeping with nightmares. No cooking or washing facilities. A high-up filthy window let in a square of murky sunlight. Either the occupant had been habitually untidy, or I was looking at evidence of a struggle. It was hard to tell which. Even at my lowest ebb in my bachelor days, I had never kept my room like this. I liked to tidy up sometimes, in case a woman could be inveigled in.

This was the horrid abode of a loner; he had never visited a laundry nor bought proper meals. Nor would he have kept records of his work; I knew before I started, there would be nothing here for me. I saw not a scroll or tablet in the place; Spindex must have kept everything in his head. Easy enough. Funerals are short-term projects, of course.

I passed a table, littered with the stale relics of a drinking session. Two dirty beakers lay on their sides; one of them had rolled to the floor. There were empty flagons everywhere, plus a half-filled one with its bung abandoned in a dish of dried-up olives. Their roughly chewed stones had been spat everywhere.

The clown's body was lying on a narrow bed in the second room. From the awkward posture, I thought he might have been dragged in and dumped there after death. It looked as though he had been strangled, but it was hard to be sure. Spindex had not been seen by the Tiasus crew for months; death must have occurred way back then. I did not linger. I called in the vigiles to deal with the remains. We were just within the boundary of the Fourth Cohort, as it happened.

Petronius Longus thanked me for the task with a growl of insincerity but promised to investigate as best he could. His men, braver than I was, came out from the apartment and confirmed that a tight ligature was buried in the fleshy neck of the corpse. Tough cord:

cut and brought here for the purpose, probably. Our chances of learning who committed the crime were slim, given the time lapse.

Even while we still stood around cursing, the investigation team found out from local shopkeepers that their last awareness of the clown alive had been of him roaring back drunk from a bar, with somebody. They did not see the visitor. No one had heard the person leave.

Surprise!

The vigiles might or might not pursue this further. We had probably learned all we could hope for. The death of a low-grade entertainer, about whom nobody cares enough even to discover why he has gone missing from his work, carries little importance in Rome.

There was no point enquiring whether a funeral satirist had enemies. Petronius pointed out wryly that at least we knew most of the people Spindex brazenly mocked had predeceased him, so they were not suspects. Their relatives would be unlikely to complain, Petro believed. Everyone always knows already that the dead man was a serial seducer who lied to political colleagues, ran up hefty debts at a brothel, deliberately farted in the Basilica and was known by an obscene name behind his back. The fun is being at last free to enjoy it – with the stiffened dead lying there, unable to retaliate.

'Do you suppose, Falco, this clown was rubbed off the tablet because of something he knew?'

'Who can say? It could just have been a pointless row when he was sozzled.'

'So what do you *think* it was?'

'Oh – elimination due to something he knew.'

'Well thanks again! Do I stand any chance of learning what, or proving it?' wondered Petro.

'Do you ever, lad?'

That was too metaphysical, so we went for a drink. Long practice made this an essential part of enquiries. We asked the barkeeper if he had had Spindex among his customers. He said every barman this side of the Esquiline could boast that – until about three months ago. Could it be nearer four months? I asked, and he shrugged agreement. As I had thought, that would take us back to the time of the Metellus funeral. Of course a defence lawyer would call it mere coincidence.

Noticing the clown's absence from lolling on his bar counter, the barman had deduced that Spindex must be dead. He said it was nice to remember the old misery for a moment, and gave us a free beaker. 'I can just see him crouched here, scratching at his fleas. . .'

I tried not to feel itchy.

'Did Spindex have a regular boozing partner?' asked Petro. We had told no one yet that Spindex had been murdered.

'Not often. He sometimes had his head together with another fellow, plotting scandal they could use at funerals.'

'Would they buy wine and take it back to the clown's lodgings?'

'Oh Spindex bought a take-out flagon every night. However late he finished here, he'd get in a spare. Sometimes he emptied it before he got home, so he'd go in another bar and buy another one.'

'But did he ever go home with his friend, the plotter?'

The barman gazed at Petronius for a while. 'Was there a fight or something?'

'Do you have a reason to think that's likely?'

'I sell liquor – so I know life. So what happened to Spindex?'

'He had a fight or something,' confirmed Petronius tersely. The barman pulled a face, half surprised, half not surprised. Petro voiced the usual message: 'If you hear anything, contact me, will you? You know the main station house. I work in the Thirteenth –' The Fourth Cohort covered two regions, controlled here in the Twelfth, but Petronius based himself in the out-station. I won't say it was to avoid the tribune – but Rubella worked from the main building and Petronius loathed him. 'Any message gets passed over to me.'

I stretched, dropping coins in the gratuities bowl. 'And we would dearly like to know who his fellow-plotter was. People may gossip.'

'Or they may not!' commented the barman.

Today had now turned unpleasant. Nothing new in that. As I walked home at dusk, I wondered if high-flyers like Silius and Paccius experienced such days. I doubted it. The reek of human putrefaction or the bleakness of a lonely man's sour existence played out in filthy rooms under the shadow of the dripping aqueducts were far removed from the 'civilised' Basilica. Silius and Paccius were men who never really knew the grim side of life – or the sight of sordid death.

I went to the baths, but fragrant oil and hot water failed to expel the odours. Their foulness had ingrained itself in my clothes and skin; it remained a taste on my tongue as persistent as regurgitated acid. Only nuzzling the soft sweet neck of our baby once I was back at home gradually helped to take away the horror.

Yes, I was tough. But today I had seen too much. I spent a long time that night considering whether I wanted to be connected with this case any more. I lay awake, gripped by distaste for the whole affair. It took Helena Justina, warm, calm, perfumed with cinnamon, a girl full of honour and resolute before any injustice, to convince me I must carry on to show that our client was innocent.

I knew perfectly well that *he* would be sleeping well, comfortable and at ease.

XXXII

Rain had drizzled all night. The streets shone and would be slippery. Before I decided on my next course of action, I went up to my roof terrace. The sky was clear now. From the river came distant shouts of stevedores, with the unexplained crashes and shouts that emanate from wharves. We were out of sight of the Emporium, yet it somehow made its presence felt; I was conscious of all the commercial activity close by. Occasional mooing sounded from the other direction, the Cattle Market Forum.

It felt mild. Not warm enough to sit on the stone benches, but pleasant enough for a quick stroll among the browned roses and near-dormant shrubs. At this time of year there was little to occupy a gardening man, but I picked off a few dead twigs and left them in a small soggy pile.

Something startled me. I thought it was a large bird, diving downwards in the wide-armed fig tree Pa had planted here and half trained. But the movement that had caught my eye was a stray leaf, desiccated and loose, suddenly falling from a cleft where it had lodged among high branches. Pallid and heavy with rain water, it had sought the ground in a sudden swoop.

Most of those leaves had dropped much earlier. When the great things had first carpeted the terrace and made it treacherous underfoot, we were sweeping up heaps of them all the time. Now I had for some time been able to see the tree's skeleton. I meant to prune the taller branches. They were carrying baby fruit over the winter, but some might yet be shed. They were too high up anyway. Even if the figlets stayed on to grow and ripen next year, blackbirds would devour them the very hour they turned purple. I would never manage to harvest the fruit unless I was up a ladder every day.

The side branches needed to be cut back too. Pa had neglected it. The fig's roots had been contained in an old round-bottomed amphora but the tree was prolific. It would need a really hard prune every spring and more tidying would be advisable each year in late summer. I made a note to acquire a billhook. Like the one in the Metellus store.

That made up my mind. I was off to see Calpurnia Cara.

The first disappointment somehow failed to surprise me. Yet again the door was guarded by a substitute. When I asked after Perseus, I was told he was no longer at the house.

'What – sold? Shoved off in disgrace to the slave market?'

'No. Sent to the farm in Lanuvium.' The substitute porter flushed. 'Oops – I'm not supposed to say that!'

Why not? I knew the family had connections near the coast. Lanuvium was where Justinus went to fetch that document Silius had requested, when we were involved in the original corruption trial.

So the door porter had been carted off at short notice. Was it convalescence or a punishment for him? Had Calpurnia finally lost patience with her slave's bad behaviour? Or was it a move to thwart me?

The steward was out, or he might have denied me admittance. The substitute porter innocently told me Calpurnia had gone outside to take the morning air. He escorted me as far as the first enclosed peristyle, but then passed me into the care of a gardener.

I passed a few polite remarks about burgeoning narcissi. The gardener was slow to respond, but by the time we reached the orchard area, I was able to ask if Metellus senior had been a plantsman. No. Or handy with a pruning knife? No, again. That failed to fit a theory I was mulling, but I made one last attempt, asking who looked after the fruit trees? The gardener did. Damn.

He spotted his mistress, so he beetled off and left me to face her wrath.

Calpurnia scowled, annoyed that I had been let in. She had been standing much where I found her on my first visit, near the store and also near the fig tree. Ashes of a bonfire smoked alongside. The store had its door wide open; slaves with cloaks over their heads were pulling down the roof panels and tackling the wasps' nest. Calpurnia, veiled, was supervising in an irritated voice. If insects buzzed her, she swept them aside with her bare hand.

I walked closer to the fig. It was professionally maintained, unlike Pa's shaggy mess; I guessed here even the new fruits had been hand-thinned for over-wintering. A wall ran behind the tree. Beyond, other properties stood close. I could smell lye, the distillation used for bleaching; one of the premises must be a laundry or a dyer's. Two unseen women were having a long, loud conversation that sounded like an argument, the kind of excited declamation over nothing that echoes around stairs, porticoes and light-wells all over Rome. We were in a small sanctum of nature up against the Embankment, but the city surrounded us.

On the wall was fastened a new-looking, inscribed limestone plaque. I did not remember seeing it before, though it may have been there yesterday when I was preoccupied with Birdy and Perseus. I walked closer. It was a memorial to Rubirius Metellus – in some ways quite standard. Ostensibly in the name of a loyal freedman, praising his master in conventional terms, it ran:

> To the shades of the departed,
>
> ## Gnaeus Rubirius Metellus,
> son of Tiberius, quaestor, legate,
> holder of three priesthoods, member of the centumviral court,
> aged fifty-seven:
> Julius Alexander, freedman, land agent, set this up
> to the kindest of patrons
> And Gnaeus Metellus Negrinus, to one who was well-beloved of him.

That last line was a mystery, squeezed in using much smaller letters, where the stone-carver ran out of space. Being tagged on as an afterthought on a freedman's plaque was an odd position for the son – whose relationship and role was not even defined.

If Calpurnia Cara saw me looking, she made no mention. Nor did I. I wanted to consider this.

'I'm sorry to have missed you yesterday,' I teased.

'Oh you are full of schemes!' Calpurnia snorted. 'First you sneak in your wife, then you devise some luncheon invitation with my daughter to lure me from my house so you can creep in with Negrinus –'

'I know nothing of any lunch date; I happened to call when your son was already here –'

'Oh *he's* to blame!'

'This is his home still, surely?' I regretted that at once. The house would be assigned to Paccius Africanus as soon as the will was

160

executed; he could throw out Calpurnia today, if he wanted to. 'Why do you hate your son, Calpurnia?'

'That is stupid.'

'You have denounced him as his father's killer.'

Perhaps she looked abashed. 'Negrinus has caused too much trouble.'

'He strikes me as inoffensive – even though he apparently upset his father. Why did your husband hate you?'

'Who told you that?'

'His will says so. Why did *you* hate *him*?'

'I only hated his cowardice.'

'He was brave enough to omit you from his bequests – in a will he wrote a full two years before his so-called suicide.' She did not react. 'I gather your husband had a passion for your daughter-in-law Saffia?'

Calpurnia scoffed. 'I told you. Saffia is a troublemaker. My husband knew that better than anyone.'

'You mean he screwed her physically, then she screwed him financially?'

This time Calpurnia only stared at me. Did she simply blank it out?

'So is Paccius Africanus being generous in letting you remain here, or are you sticking tight until he evicts you?'

'He won't institute the will until the court case is over.'

That suited us; his reluctance to evict Calpurnia was one more instance we could cite to imply Paccius and she were co-conspirators.

She was growing restless. 'I do not have to talk to you, Falco.'

'But you may find it advisable. Tell me, why was Saffia's bedspread in your garden store?'

'It was too badly soiled to save. It has been burned now.'

'Disposal of evidence? How and when did it get soiled?'

'Since you ask – when my husband was dying.' That made out I was uncouth to ask such questions.

I carried on regardless. I was used to annoying the bereaved – especially when I thought they were to blame. 'Dying in his bed, according to you – so why use Saffia's quilt?'

'Because there was a filthy mess, and anything Saffia had owned was surplus to requirements.'

'Metellus had some violent gastric upset. Without insulting your cook, what was his last meal?'

'A mixed cold luncheon,' Calpurnia replied haughtily. 'And we both ate it!' That had to be a lie.

'I asked your gardener if Metellus spent much time out here. Was he given to inspecting his market garden?'

Calpurnia glanced around the patchy vegetables, before finally losing patience with me. She started walking back indoors. 'Metellus and I used to come out here,' she told me coldly, 'to be out of hearing of our household, when we were arguing.'

'And you argued a lot,' I said quietly, 'in the days before your husband died.'

'We argued a lot,' confirmed Calpurnia, as though she meant it had always happened.

'Were you arguing out in the garden when the hemlock struck your husband down?'

She stopped. She turned and stared at me. 'You have been told how my husband went to his death.'

'Lies! Metellus died out in the open.' I gestured back the way we had come. 'Wasn't he taken ill there by the fig tree? Someone ran into the house and brought Saffia's bedding to wrap him in. Then total paralysis would have taken hours.' I went up close to Calpurnia. 'I want to know what you did with him, once he was taken ill. I want to know who else knew what was happening. Did he die alone, or was he comforted – and had you locked him in that garden store? You can answer me now – or I'll see you in court.' She stared at me. 'Yes,' I said. 'I think you killed Metellus – and I intend to denounce you for it.'

'You cannot prove anything,' Calpurnia sneered.

As she stalked off, I called after her loudly: 'So what happened two years ago?'

She turned back, aglow with fury. She gave me one filthy glance without speaking, then she disappeared from view.

XXXIII

T HE STEWARD had returned and was hovering in the atrium. As he showed me out, I took a chance: 'So Perseus is parcelled off to Lanuvium?' He looked shifty, but I sensed I might squeeze him. 'Things must be getting sticky. I assume the money has run out?'

'Nothing new in this house, Falco – unfortunately!'

'I thought the Metelli had funds? Still, I assume you haven't reached the low point – when the mistress sells her jewels and seeks consolation from an astrologer?'

His voice dropped. 'Oh she did that some time ago!' It seemed unlikely – in fact, I had been joking – yet he spoke with feeling. And I had never seen Calpurnia wearing even a necklace.

I whistled gently. 'Who's her confidante?'

'Olympia.' I noted the name mentally.

'A fortune teller?'

Nodding, he glanced over his shoulder. 'Everyone's jittery. We are all waiting to hear we'll be transferred to Paccius.'

'Calpurnia says he will wait until the court case ends.'

'That doesn't help,' replied the steward.

None of the slaves had been manumitted by the Metellus will. That was mean. A quarter of the labour force, up to a hundred in number, of those over thirty years of age, could have been freed when their master died. All the Metellus slaves would have a good idea how Saffia Donata might treat them if she ever possessed them. She might take out her spiteful feelings against her husband's family on the slaves. Paccius, more likely, would be indifferent – but he would sell them.

We were on the threshold now. The slave who was acting as doorkeeper stayed back, though not far enough for me. I offered the steward, 'Look, do you get time to yourself? Can I buy you a drink?'

He knew what this was for. He smiled. 'No thanks. I'm not naïve, Falco!'

I shrugged. 'Will you clear up a domestic issue then? What was the menu for the last meal that your master had?' I thought the steward

163

blenched. He was unhappy, that was sure. 'The lunch,' I prompted. 'The last lunch with his family.'

The steward claimed he could not remember. Interesting. He was the type who would regard it as his personal daily duty to plan menus and organise the shopping; maybe he even shopped himself. The last meal eaten by a master who was subsequently poisoned should be etched into the elegant factotum's memory.

While I was in the Fifth Region I made another call, to Claudius Tiasus the funeral director. I implied I had lost a relative. Through a series of lesser players, I acted nervous; when it looked as if the sale might be lost, the great impresario came himself to clinch the deal.

He was a fat bundle with a greasy pigtail, at once subservient and sly. He had a disreputable air. His tunic was clean, and his hands were heavily be-ringed. It seemed unlikely he still carried out embalming, though when he patted my shoulder, thinking he was consoling the bereaved, I wondered where those podgy hands had been half an hour ago.

He realised I was a fraud.

'Sorry – though there is a corpse to bury, truly. Consider my visit official. The name is Falco. I am working with the vigiles on a suspicious death. It's somebody known to you.'

Tiasus had signalled to his staff to leave. We two sat in a small corridor partly in the open air, with a view over a fountain with a soppy nymph, and soft cushions on the bench. It would be suitable for discussing which scented oil had been a deceased's favourite, though it was inappropriate for being grilled by me. For one thing, I kept staring at the nymph. She appeared to have no nipples and two doves were sitting on her head, doing what doves do.

'Who is dead?' enquired Tiasus calmly. He had a light, rather high voice.

'Your clown, Spindex.'

'No!' He calmed down fast, no stranger to tragedy. 'Spindex is a freelance. I haven't seen him since, oh –'

'For about four months? Since the Metellus do? I'll be blunt: Spindex was strangled. We think he knew too much about someone. Metellus probably.'

'This is a lot to take in,' complained Tiasus. He changed position, easing his bulk on the stone seat. I could see him thinking. When Aelianus came on reconnaissance, he received the brush-off; that would not happen today.

'Sorry to rush you. Most clients must have aeons at their disposal,' I said drily.

'Not Rubirius Metellus!' Tiasus aimed it heavily.

'Explain, please?'

'He needed fast burial.' I raised an eyebrow. 'If it is all coming out, Falco –' I nodded. 'The body was . . . not fresh.'

'I know that it stank.'

'We are used to that. Even the diarrhoea . . .' He tailed off. I let him. He rallied. 'This cadaver was, in my professional opinion, over three days old by the time we were called to the house.'

'Unusual?'

'Not unheard of. But –'

'But what, Tiasus?'

'There were odd features.'

I waited again, but he had dried up. I tried encouragement: 'When you arrived to view the body, was Metellus in his bed?'

A grateful look came into the undertaker's eyes. 'So you know, then?' I pursed my lips. He took it as an answer. 'Yes, he was. But he must have recently been placed there.'

By now, this was no surprise. 'Had they put him on his back?'

'Yes. But the dark red marks – which indicate settlement of the blood in the body after death – showed me that the deceased had lain somewhere else, in a different position, for a considerable while. Nothing too odd!' Tiasus reassured me. I blinked. I had never suspected perversion. I found it disturbing that Tiasus had routinely considered it. Did he often encounter necrophilia? 'Metellus had been on his side, rather than his back, that's all. No doubt,' he suggested, with a kind of disapproval, 'the family thought he looked more peaceful face-up.'

'That's normal. But why not arrange him as soon as he died, I wonder?'

'I wondered that,' Tiasus agreed eagerly.

'Any thoughts?'

'Well . . . You know what happened at the funeral? A lot of stress – this was an overwrought family. There may well have been panic when Metellus first died. The son was away somewhere. Maybe the widow became distraught before her son came home –'

'Not *that* widow, surely?' I smiled.

'Oh you met her! Well, perhaps not.'

'The death scene will have shocked her. Metellus had taken poison, Tiasus.'

'Yes but it was suicide. They were expecting it.' Tiasus paused. 'Weren't they?'

'So I am told.'

'Have we been told the truth?' he mused portentously.

I was sure we had not.

'You really came about Spindex,' Tiasus murmured in his comforting undertaker's voice.

'Any help you can give?'

'He liked a tipple, but he was a good satirist. He went to the heart of a man's character. And he had judgement. He knew what was permissible, what was too sensitive.'

'Not in the Metellus case. The family sacked him.'

'Ah.' Tiasus took a long breath, with his mouth wide open. He had gum problems. 'Well, I don't know the story there, and that's the problem. Spindex was let go – but they never told me why.'

'Who dismissed him? Was it the son?'

'No . . .' Tiasus looked thoughtful. 'No, I think it was another man.'

'Name?'

'I never knew that.'

'Licinius Lutea? He's a friend of the son; I think he was helping Negrinus at the funeral.'

'Means nothing,' said Tiasus. 'It was a freedman who assisted. I had a few words with him in a quiet moment. Alexander, he was called.'

'Not him who paid off Spindex?'

'Er. . . No. Possibly a relative?' Tiasus quavered. This was hard work.

'A brother-in-law?' I suggested. 'Canidianus Rufus, Rubiria Juliana's husband?'

'Yes, perhaps . . .' But then Tiasus wavered yet again. 'I don't think it was Rufus. He had a right temper; I remember him! I think the second one dealt with Spindex.'

'*Second* brother-in-law? *Laco?* Verginius Laco, the husband of Carina, the woman who got upset?'

'Yes, that was him.'

Dear gods, just when you think you have scanned all the scenery, up pops some new participant.

The two doves had finished. The female preened, looking as if she wondered what the fuss had been. The male thought he might be up for another go. She shrugged off his nonsense. The deformed nymph

166

shivered mournfully. Part of her drape had been chipped off in an accident.

'Do you think Spindex discovered something about Metellus or his family, something they did not wish the world to hear?'

'Oh no doubt of it,' Tiasus exclaimed. 'It must have been a stupendous secret! Wouldn't it be wonderful, Falco, if we knew just what?'

I agreed dourly.

I went to visit Rubiria Carina's husband.

For once, he was at home and he agreed to meet me. He was more than a decade older than his wife, a thin, cultured man who implied he was being more patient than I deserved. 'You have always refused to be interviewed, citing your privacy,' I reminded him. 'Now will you answer me?'

'You can ask. I may not be free to answer.' Interesting: why?

'So what changed your mind?'

'You intend to accuse my mother-in-law of killing her spouse.'

He was a man of some refinement; I omitted the obvious son-in-law jokes. 'Do you think Calpurnia did it?'

'No,' he said.

'There is a case to answer,' I told him. 'Metellus made unhealthy provision for his daughter-in-law, and disinherited his wife. It's vicious and it's public; Calpurnia Cara must be furious. Murky circumstances cloud what happened when Metellus died.' Laco shrugged. He wanted to see what I knew. 'At first I was told that your wife refused to go to lunch that day – but she says she was not invited.'

'No.'

'Neither of you?'

'I was not close to Metellus. I would have gone if my wife did.'

I did not feel this man would lie. Yet although we had been told he and Carina stayed aloof, now I knew he had been operating on behalf of the Metellus family.

'Did you see Rubirius Metellus just before he died?'

'No.'

'Did you see Negrinus?'

'No.'

'There is a suggestion that he was away.'

'I cannot answer for his movements.'

'I'll ask him. It is important.' Laco looked surprised. 'Laco, if he was away, someone else poisoned his father and Birdy has an alibi.'

At once Laco retracted: 'He may have travelled to Lanuvium. It was around the time of the suicide.'

'It was definitely not suicide. Rubirius Metellus collapsed in his garden, not in his bed – and I know that was about three days *before* the body was paraded for the witnesses.'

Had he known this? Laco gave nothing away. He was reclining on a reading couch, where he now simply linked his hands and looked thoughtful. He had long, almost elderly fingers. With thinning hair and an old-fashioned expression he seemed too mature to be the father of three young children, though this was common enough among the senatorial class. Both he and Carina gave the impression they were content in their marriage. They were comfortable in their domesticity – and so they should be. Theirs was domesticity with battalions of slaves, and gold finials on the furniture. I had called here more than once, and not seen the same slave twice.

Nor had I heard any music, been charmed by a vase of flowers on a side table, seen a scroll lying half-read, nor caught advanced scents of dinner. This was a cold house. It had a cold, unemotional master – and yet, he allowed his wife to give sanctuary to a brother who was implicated in a corruption scandal and now charged with parricide.

'Don't ask me what really went on, because I don't know – but I will find out. I sympathise with your position.' I spoke levelly. It seemed best to show restraint. 'Your wife's family must have become an embarrassment.'

'My wife and I,' replied Laco, 'live with the troubles of her family as stoically as we can.'

'That's generous! Do you know who their banker is?'

I had abruptly changed the subject, but Laco did not seem startled. 'Aufustius.'

'Same as Licinius Lutea! What do you think of Lutea?' Laco shrugged. 'Not your type? A bit of an entrepreneur, I gather . . . Tell me,' I sprang on him, 'what happened two years ago?'

Verginius Laco made no reply.

'The Metelli were happy and prosperous,' I pointed out. 'Then they became desperate financially and something tore them apart. I think it had to do with Metellus and his partiality for Saffia Donata. Legally that was incest, of course. I can see why it is being shuffled under a mattress, so to speak . . .' Laco simply let me speculate. 'You have been helping to keep this great secret. When the clown Spindex discovered it, you undertook his dismissal.' Laco did not deny my claim. 'That was dangerous. Deprived of his fee, the clown might have sought public revenge.'

'No,' said Laco patiently. 'I paid him off, Falco.' He was not stupid. Of all the people on this case, I reckoned him the most intelligent. In his way, he was being quite open. I formed a picture of him coolly dealing with Spindex on behalf of the rest of the family – though I sensed it had needed his own money.

'You paid him well?'

He nodded, wryly. I was right about the cash.

'Spindex is dead.' I passed on the news conversationally. 'Strangled. I don't imagine you organised that, so there must be someone else with an interest in guarding the Metellus secret.'

Verginius Laco made no comment.

'Someone else knows, Laco. Spindex had a source. It may even have been his source who silenced him. I'll find the source eventually. Now it's a murder hunt, the vigiles are on it.'

Still nothing.

'I understand your position, Laco. You know the story, but you are a man of honour. You stand aside, except when you can give practical help. Maybe when you do act, it is to protect your wife. I suspect you disapprove of the way the family are handling matters. I think, if it was your choice, you would tell me the secret and have done.'

For a moment I felt Laco was about to say something.

But he did not.

XXXIV

THAT NIGHT we reviewed the case thoroughly. Time was short. We decided to opt for a trial of Calpurnia Cara now, and hope to discover more evidence as we went along. This was dangerous. I did realise that – though at the time I failed to grasp just how dangerous it would be for me personally.

'You have no direct evidence to link Calpurnia with the killing,' Helena pointed out. 'This will not be easy. She is not a woman to confess.'

'Trials are not decided by evidence, but arguments,' said Honorius, playing the expert. 'All we have to do is suggest strenuously that Calpurnia did it.'

'And I thought you were an idealist! Can this be why most people hold the law in contempt?' I asked him.

The two Camilli, who were with us for this case review, sniggered. 'We still have to persuade a jury that she did it,' said Justinus.

'Careful!' exclaimed his brother. 'Clear guilt in the accused only gets prosecutors a worse name – for indulging in the profit motive when they make charges.' Aelianus' new satirical mode was alarming.

'Well look at us!' I was angry at us myself. 'We have ganged up on this woman, we are conspiring to accuse her – and we targeted her in order to make money. If the jury decides to despise us, we may yet lose votes.'

'We are saving Metellus Negrinus,' Honorius objected.

'By making him live with the knowledge that his father slept with his wife and his mother killed his father?' Helena was unimpressed.

'What we need,' Honorius fretted, 'is not just a violent dose of poison – that usually convicts women, for some reason – but to be able to say Calpurnia used spells.'

'All she did was sell her jewellery and consult a fortune-teller,' I said. 'Plenty of women do that.'

Honorius threw back his arms above his head and let out a wild cry. '*Aah!* What fortune telling? Tell me! A bonus! *Magic practices?*

Astrologers? We've got her then! Falco, this is the most important evidence we could have.'

I recoiled from his excitement. 'Maybe she just wanted to know her own future?'

'Never mind what *she* wanted,' Honorius said, his teeth clenched. 'The court will know what to think – and it's entirely in our favour.'

I handed out queries for investigation. I would try to interrogate the banker, Aufustius. I took Justinus to help. Aelianus was to ride down the Via Appia, find the Metellus monument, and check any memorial to Metellus senior. Helena volunteered to attempt entry at Saffia Donata's apartment. Honorius would try to track down the horoscope-seller, Olympia.

First thing, however, we obtained an appointment with the praetor. Work must have been slack; he saw us within a couple of hours, the same day. We made our denunciation of Calpurnia. He was unimpressed. We mentioned the will. We alluded to Saffia and incestuous adultery. We said Calpurnia was angry. We said she used a fortune-teller. We emphasised that her husband died days before she had said he did; we claimed that she had now burned Saffia's coverlet to hide the evidence.

'It seems a hygienic precaution,' the praetor objected. He had fastened on the least important aspect, naturally.

'The precaution had been omitted for a whole three months, sir,' I pointed out. 'Calpurnia Cara only ordered the destruction of the coverlet once I had seen it.'

'Oh well. We cannot have a Roman matron, a mother of three children I notice, being a bad housewife,' grinned the praetor. This was a snob who believed a woman should work in wool and keep the home, earning that sweet lie, *'She never quarrelled'* on her epitaph; the swine probably kept three mistresses and stinted his wife on her food budget. No question, he was allowing us more leeway with a case against a woman than he would tolerate in a case against a man. He fixed a date for a pre-trial where Calpurnia could hear our evidence, and we rushed off to gather some.

Justinus and I took the banker Aufustius to lunch.

He was cautious and defensive, but then people were constantly complaining about his interest charges and pursuing him for loans. Nobody ever treated him, because his clients all thought his fees were steep enough and they did not want to look extravagant. Giving him lunch was a cheap investment. He was delighted with a plate of grilled fish and a wine chaser.

He told us the Metelli had been a well-set-up family until a few years ago; then he realised they had eaten into their reserves and were spending prolifically.

'A thought strikes me,' Justinus mused. 'After they lost the corruption trial, Silius told us his compensation as the accuser was assessed at a million and a quarter sesterces. Isn't the going rate about a quarter of the condemned man's estate?'

'It is.' Aufustius nodded. 'The figure was based on their Census return.'

'That was two years ago then.' I had been involved with the Census – a pleasant commission, and lucrative. 'Most people tried to undervalue their worth to avoid taxes. As a banker, you would know!' Aufustius sucked a fishbone and gave nothing away. 'In order to put Negrinus into the Senate the family had to have a million's worth of land – that's just to qualify. Election expenses would have been substantially more,' I pointed out. 'Nowadays these folk are at rock bottom. So where did it all go, Aufustius?'

'People do lose everything,' the banker sighed.

'True.' Justinus refilled a beaker for Aufustius. We toasted our guest, but then put down our cups. Justinus listed possible disasters: 'Volcanoes, earthquakes, ships that sink in storms, seedy confidence tricksters who run off with the deed boxes . . .'

'Their cash went down to zero,' Aufustius said. 'I assumed it was the trial.' I told him they had not paid the compensation yet. He looked puzzled.

'What about their landed estate?' Justinus asked him.

'I don't see that side. Well, except for the income. Rents and product revenues seem to have dried up. Maybe they have sold the land.'

'Who would know?'

'They had a land agent, a freedman, last I heard. What's his name . . . Julius Alexander.'

Justinus sat up slightly. 'Lives in Lanuvium?'

'Yes. That's where they came from originally.' Interesting.

Justinus looked annoyed. 'I didn't connect him directly. Why is he called Julius, not Metellus?'

'Julia was the grandmother. She must have freed him. The rest seem very fond of him.'

'Ever met him?'

'No.'

'I was impressed.' Justinus swallowed wine. 'He was organised, pleasant, good to deal with. I would think if he runs an estate, he runs it well.'

'During the son's tenure of his aedileship, did you see any of the bribes?' I asked Aufustius.

'No comment.'

'Oh go on.'

'Well, I wouldn't tell you if I had – but I never did. I was very surprised to hear about the case. I had no idea all that backhanding went on. I can't even guess where they stashed away the "gifts". It makes no sense to me. All the time, their bankboxes here were debouching coins like flood-water running off a mountainside.'

Justinus asked the waiter to refresh our bread basket. We sat in silence while he went behind the counter and returned.

With the new crunchy rolls we changed the subject. 'What's the history with Lutea?'

'This is not to be repeated, right, Falco?' Oh no. Only in court. 'I don't know what he's up to, but he thinks he's riding high. I haven't seen much coming in yet, though he keeps promising. This is a change for Lutea, understand. He knows how to bluff socially, but he was once on the verge of bankruptcy. His debts made me feel faint. I couldn't bear to tot up the damage. He and Saffia were a promiscuous couple!'

'*What?*' It was my turn to be startled, though with other people's sex lives, you should be prepared for anything. 'Lewd practices?'

'No, no. Well, not as far as I know!' Aufustius laughed coarsely. 'What they got up to in the bedroom wouldn't bother me. I meant they had no self-control –' He was enjoying himself. I looked at him sideways. 'On the bills side!'

'They spent well?'

'Oh shocking.'

'And that was why Saffia's father divorced her?' Justinus asked. 'They were in such trouble moneywise? Her papa blamed Lutea?'

'Oh she was as bad as Lutea – and Negrinus was all her idea, if you ask me. I saw the downfall happen. Her father kept her on a tight rein at home; she married young, got her hands on the dowry, then she and Lutea just ran through it.' The banker shook his head. 'Saffia always hopes for a financial miracle.'

'She seems to have found one,' I muttered. 'Her new apartment is stuffed with loot. And your client Lutea is hovering close. So now he tells you he's looking to be more solvent . . .'

'Saffia has a big legacy coming. Lutea says he intends to remarry her.' Aufustius suddenly looked troubled by his indiscretion. 'That may be confidential –'

'Or glaringly obvious! They stayed close?'

'Well, they had the boy. . . I never knew why they separated. The Metelli were very well off, but Saffia was losing all her independence with the new marriage. The wife of an unemancipated son in a household that was governed by strict and suspicious parents couldn't hope for much. Calpurnia Cara must have curbed Saffia's love of lavish shopping.'

'How about this,' I proffered. 'The Metelli lost their funds because – for some strange reason – their cash moved swiftly to the interesting Saffia?'

'But why?' asked the banker, quite baffled.

'She has some hold over them. It has to be something very big.' I was working up slowly to our solution.

'She could have known about the corruption,' Justinus offered. 'Blackmailed them over that?'

'Everyone knows about it now,' I argued. 'Yet Saffia has still got them. No, I think Saffia made herself a sweet little friend to Metellus senior.'

The banker was thrilled. 'That's rather unsavoury!'

'Especially if Lutea put her up to it.'

'A *pimp*?' Aufustius pulled a face; he almost seemed fond of Lutea as a client. 'Oh he's not that bad!'

I grinned. 'Then Saffia must have thought of it all by herself.'

'Better ask her then. But do me a favour,' pleaded Aufustius. 'Penurious clients are agony. Don't stop whatever is due to come to Licinius Lutea!'

Nothing was due to him, in my opinion. That did not mean he was not intending to take a great deal.

When we left the banker, Justinus ran a hand through his straight hair. 'We need a talk with the land agent. Someone needs to go to Lanuvium.'

'If you were not a new father, I'd be sending you.'

He volunteered anyway. He assured me that Claudia Rufina was a dear girl who would understand.

I doubted that. But Justinus was reliable and if he was daft enough to leave his wife I would let him go.

★

Helena had failed to wheedle admittance to Saffia's apartment. The baby was still not born, after an already very long labour. This did not seem the moment to walk in and ask who its father was.

'Saffia must be exhausted.' Helena's voice was subdued. She meant the struggling mother was now seriously at risk.

Honorius attended the pre-trial hearing. Not trusting him, I went along too. The praetor agreed the case must be answered. Calpurnia had appointed Paccius to defend her and be her spokesman.

'Oh by the way, praetor,' Paccius murmured, just when it seemed all over. 'The plaintiffs are alleging that Calpurnia sold her jewellery and went to an astrologer. Since magic practices are involved, may we seek trial in the murders court, please?'

The praetor glared. He was aware that he had heard this request from our side, on behalf of Negrinus, and that he had crisply denied it. This time he was not defending the right of a senator to trial by like-minded nobility. Calpurnia was merely the daughter, wife and mother of senators.

I could see why Paccius Africanus had taken up our ploy. The Senate had a long history of voting against women accused of murder by poison with mystical overtones; these sorceresses were packed straight off home to cut their wrists in a hot bath. While it was entirely in our interests that our accused should be put before the Senate, whose members would be outraged that one of their illustrious number had been slain at home by his wife, Paccius wanted to avoid it.

'Oh yes. Magic belongs in the murders court,' the praetor announced.

The chief magistrate in Rome may be a blithering incompetent, but when the magistrate makes a pronouncement, there is no appeal. We were stuck with it.

Aelianus came back cold and angry from the Via Appia. It had taken him hours to find the Metellus mausoleum in the strung-out highway necropolis. When he did identify his goal, the door was locked. Breaking into a tomb is a serious offence. By the time Aelianus, a terrible burglar, managed to effect entry, it was dusk, he was scared he had attracted notice, and he had cut his hand. Inside, he was thwarted: no proper inscription had yet been provided.

'Why, what did you see there?'

'Nothing. It was bloody dark.'

'Afraid of ghosts?'

'No, robbers. And spells. That vicinity is famous for witches and perverts. I wouldn't hang about as prey. I had a quick look. There was nothing that named Negrinus – nor his mother, come to that. I identified the glass urn that contains the ashes of Metellus senior. Over it, there was just a marble tablet erected by the two daughters. I guess the proper plaque is still lying in some mason's yard. Either poor old hopeless Birdy has forgotten to organise it, or more likely he can't pay for it and the mason refuses to hand it over.'

It fitted. We knew the impoverished son had had to beg for last-minute inclusion on a freedman's plaque. Julius Alexander, who as a land agent would be able to afford a memorial to a patron, had allowed Negrinus to be tagged on to his own inscription. It must be hard for Birdy to see an ex-slave now prospering when he was so completely luckless.

Was there something else dubious here? Julius Alexander, the mystery man in Lanuvium, could be yet another uppity one-time household staff member who was preying upon this family. I made sure that Justinus was primed to investigate when he rode off there next day.

XXXV

WE MADE one last attempt to tackle the three Metellus siblings. Helena and I went to ask the questions. We had sent a message in advance, saying we would like both sisters to be present as well as Negrinus. The women were there when we arrived, and both had their husbands for back-up. This was the first time we had seen the whole group of five assembled together. Canidianus Rufus, who had seemed eager to stay out of things when I had interviewed his wife Juliana about her role in her father's death, now appeared more at ease. The presence of Verginius Laco may have encouraged him. Helena agreed afterwards that the party all knew each other well, and they seemed fairly affectionate.

It was out of the question to demand that Saffia Donata join us, but I had said it would be helpful to invite Licinius Lutea. If asked, he did not show.

'Have you and your dear friend quarrelled?' I murmured to Negrinus.

He gave me one of his self-pitying exclamations. 'Oh no! He still speaks to me when I can be useful!'

'Does he touch you for money?' I threw at him. Unlikely, now Negrinus was disinherited.

Negrinus went very still. 'No. Lutea has never asked me for money.'

I was not yet ready to retort, *So he just uses his ex-wife, does he?* Negrinus, with a flash of his understated intelligence, looked rueful, as if he knew exactly what I thought.

At a glance from Helena I fell silent. She was to initiate the discussion, while I observed the parties.

She sat on a couch, a little way from me. Tall and graceful, she had dressed in the style of a senator's daughter, adorned with favourite semiprecious jewellery over a long-sleeved white winter gown, formally wound with a voluminous dark red stole. Holding a note-tablet, she looked like a high-class secretary – one keeping minutes for an empress who was plotting people's downfalls.

'I maintain the records of our enquiries, so my husband has asked me to begin.' She rarely called me her husband, though that was the state I had reported in my Census return. We lived together. It was accurate. But Helena knew it always gave me a shock.

She caught my eye and smiled slightly. I felt my lips twitch.

'Falco and Associates will shortly defend Metellus Negrinus. They intend to pre-empt the charge that he killed his father by showing that somebody else did so: Calpurnia Cara. This is hard for you – but I imagine it will not be a surprise.'

People began to speak, but I held up a hand and stopped them.

'At the trial we shall need to show motive and opportunity,' Helena continued. 'Metellus provided a motive by his will: his connection with Saffia. It is very unpleasant, but the issue of adultery and incest will come out in court. So what about opportunity? We no longer believe,' Helena announced in her measured tones, 'the story we have been given about when Rubirius Metellus died. All of you concurred in the fabrication – that he retired to his bed and killed himself, on the day that his body was witnessed by the seven senators. I have to be blunt. That is nonsense.'

For a quiet woman she could be acidic. When Helena spoke in that calm, unexcited way, it made the saliva dry under my tongue.

'Rubirius Metellus was presented to his seven friends, dead in his bed. But we know that the body had by then been lying somewhere else for days. So was *any* of your fable true?' She looked around the group. 'Did Metellus really have a last lunch with some of you? Did he ever discuss suicide? Were you sent from the room, Birdy because you were upset? Were you *there* – or in Lanuvium? Did Calpurnia rush off in annoyance because Metellus changed his mind? And did you, Juliana, sit quietly alongside your father while he passed away?'

Nobody answered.

'I think not!' Helena retorted scathingly.

There was complete silence.

It was my turn now.

I addressed Negrinus. 'Our case against your mother will have two bases: your father was killed with hemlock, which was Calpurnia's idea and which was bought by an agent of her legal adviser, Paccius.' That did seem to surprise them. 'Then she concealed your father's death for days – perhaps until you came home from Lanuvium – finally revealing the corpse in a staged deathbed scene. These details should condemn her and clear you. It will still leave that huge question: why ever did the rest of you, knowing about the fake deathbed, all go along with it?'

Birdy just looked depressed. It was Verginius Laco, the oldest man present, who said smoothly with authority, 'It is reprehensible – but everyone decided to say that Metellus committed suicide so they could save the family money.'

'I am sure you regret that!' I commented. 'Will you testify?'

'I have nothing to say in court, Falco.'

I had already judged Laco to be scrupulous. So was he ducking out of perjury?

Helena turned over a sheet in her note-tablet. 'I should mention that we believe there will be little money to save.' Attention returned to her again. 'Our prosecutor will emphasise how Saffia has taken possession of most of your fortune and that the rest passes to Saffia by the will. The court has to infer blackmail. We shall call her as a witness, though we cannot at present ask her how much she will admit.'

None of them spoke.

'The truth is bound to come out,' I threatened, sounding confident.

There was high tension in the room. Perhaps we might have shocked them into a revelation. But the silence was interrupted. A troubled slave entered, to say a midwife had arrived with an urgent message for Negrinus from his ex-wife. Then two women pushed in past the slave. One had a tiny, fair-haired girl clutching at her skirts, the other carried a wrapped bundle.

I stood up. That was a mistake. For, in the traditional manner of seeking paternal acknowledgement, she marched forward and laid at my feet a neatly swaddled newborn baby.

Helena Justina's fine dark eyes met mine, full of amusement at my discomfiture.

XXXVI

HELENA WAS the first to react. She laid aside her note-tablet and rose swiftly with a swish of her skirts. She came to me, stopped, and picked up the tiny bundle. I heard a feeble whimper. Handing back the child to the midwife, Helena announced crisply, 'Wrong father!'

I sat down quickly.

Helena stood beside me, one proprietorial hand on my shoulder. 'Try again,' she encouraged the woman, this time more gently. Rufus and Laco sat tight, trying not to look as though they were avoiding anybody's eye. Carina held out her arms to the small girl, who must be about two; she toddled across and climbed on her aunt's lap, clearly used to her, but then she buried her face and began to cry. Carina bent and reassured her in a low voice, one hand spread on her little head. I noticed she moved aside the hard links of her jewellery, a practised mother, ensuring the child's face was not bruised.

Metellus Negrinus had risen slowly to his feet. The woman with the baby fixed on him, hesitated, then went and placed the newborn once more on the ground between his feet. She stepped back. Negrinus did not move.

'Don't touch it!' warned Juliana, his elder sister. 'You don't know who –' She refused to finish, though we all understood her meaning.

'It is a boy,' pleaded the woman who brought it, as if she thought that might make a difference. If Birdy refused it, the child would be taken and exposed on a midden. Someone might snatch the helpless bundle, either to bring up as their own or to bring up in drudgery. Probably the baby would die. 'Saffia Donata begged us to bring the children to you,' quavered the midwife, looking around the room unsurely. 'She is fading rapidly . . .'

It was Carina who looked up from cuddling her brother's tearful daughter and ordered, 'Acknowledge your son, Gnaeus!'

Her brother took his decision as she willed him to act. With one fast movement, he bent down and scooped up the baby.

180

'It might not be yours,' wailed Juliana.

'It's mine now!' Clutching the child against his tunic, Negrinus gazed around at the rest of us, almost defiantly. 'None of my trouble is my children's fault.'

'Well done,' murmured Carina, with a catch in her voice. Her husband, the austerely decent Laco, reached out and took her hand. Even Juliana nodded resignedly, though *her* husband looked furious.

Negrinus faced the midwife. 'Is Saffia Donata dying?' His tone was harsh. 'So why have you left her?'

'Your mother appointed me; I was supposed merely to observe – Saffia had her own women to help her. It took so long . . . I am afraid she has probably gone by now.' Relief brought more colour to the midwife's cheeks. 'I am sorry to break in like this. I am sorry to bring you such news.' The woman was of obvious quality, slave-born, but probably now freed and working independently. I could see why Calpurnia Cara had chosen her to supervise the family interests. 'Saffia Donata pleaded with us to bring the children to you. She was desperately anxious about them being looked after –'

'Have no fears for them,' Negrinus broke in. He was holding the baby like a man who knew which way up they go. When it let out a complaining cry, he jogged it gently. He still looked incongruously studious, yet had the air of some historic pioneer, facing hardship stoically across the land he worked. 'So Saffia knew she was dying?' The midwife nodded. 'Did she say anything else?' This time the woman shook her head. 'A pity!' he exclaimed cryptically.

'You will need a wet-nurse for the little one; I can recommend someone clean and reliable –'

'Leave that to us,' Juliana replied, rather quickly.

'Saffia always used Euboule's daughter, I was told,' the midwife continued fussing.

'Zeuko. Oh yes, Zeuko! I don't think so.' Carina's views on Euboule's daughter Zeuko seemed uncomplimentary.

A silence fell.

'What has happened to Saffia's other son, little Lucius?' Helena asked quietly. 'He is not alone at the apartment, I hope?'

The midwife looked troubled. 'His father is there. He is with his father –' She hesitated, but left it.

A couple of household slaves peered in enquiringly and were signalled to escort the visitors away. Others came and carried off the children. We heard the baby cry as the door closed, but an elderly woman spoke to him kindly. After a moment, Carina glanced at her sister then went out herself, presumably to make arrangements.

Helena and I offered our excuses and retreated.

Birdy had slumped on a couch, his eyes glazed and his face set. Laco, the host, merely sat looking thoughtful. Neither Juliana nor her husband made any attempt to go home at that point. They were all waiting to hold intense discussions of some kind, after we were gone. It was polite to leave them to it. Besides, I wanted to rush over to Saffia's apartment to see what Lutea was doing.

'You don't need to come,' I murmured to Helena as she rescued her cloak from Carina's slaves and threw it on.

'Oh yes I do!'

I had already grabbed her hand as we hurried along. Despite the tragedy, for us this was good. This was the kind of moment we both enjoyed together – rushing through the evening streets to an unexpected rendezvous where we might witness something material.

Verginius Laco's house lay in what had been the old Subura, the area north of the Forum, once seedy but now redeveloped and upgraded since the Neronian fire. From there it took us less than half an hour to reach Saffia's apartment, across the Viminal Hill. It was now well into the evening, but her lodgings lay in near darkness. Everyone who worked here must be tired out and terrified. Not much point owning masses of brilliant bronze lampstands, if your slaves become too distraught to light the lamps. Not much point in anything, if you die in childbirth.

Saffia's body was lying unattended in a dim bedroom, waiting to be laid out. I had suspected Licinius Lutea might be found counting silverware, but I maligned him. He was sitting in an anteroom, lost in grief. He was weeping uncontrollably. I watched Helena assessing him: good-looking in a slewed way, early thirties, smart clothes, professionally manicured – apart from his shattered confidence at the moment of bereavement, he was the type she loathed. All the signs were that he had been there, lost, for hours. She left him to his self-absorption.

Helena found the little boy. Alone in his neat bedroom, silent and white-faced, he lay curled up on his bed, not even clutching a toy. After three days of hearing his mother screaming in childbirth, he must be petrified. When silence fell, his world ended. We knew he had been told his mother was dead; at four, he may not have understood. Nobody had fed him, comforted him, made any plans for him. No one had even spoken to him for a long while. He had no idea that his father was here. He let Helena pick him up, but accepted her attentions almost like a child who expected blows. Concerned, I even saw her checking him for marks. But he was sound, clean, well nurtured. He owned a shelf of clay models and when I offered him a nodding mule, he took it from me obediently.

We brought parent and child together. Lutea stopped weeping and took the boy in his arms, though Lucius went to his father with as little reaction as when Helena gathered him up. We instructed some weary slaves to look after them. It might have been the moment to catch Lutea off guard, but Helena shook her head and I bowed to her humanity.

Helena and I walked home together quietly, with our arms around each other's waists, feeling subdued. The fate of the small boy depressed us both. Little Lucius had lost more than his mother there. Saffia had done her best for the other two by sending them to Negrinus, but this boy was Lutea's property. It would never turn out well; Lucius was destined to spend his life being abandoned and forgotten. The father may have loved the mother, but neither Helena nor I now had any faith in Lutea's so-called great affection for the four-year-old. The little boy behaved as if he had very low expectations. Lutea held his supposedly adored son like a drunk with an empty amphora, staring over his head with regret in his soul, but no heart.

'At least he is weeping for Saffia.'

'No, he is weeping for the lost money.'

You may assume that sympathetic comment came from Helena and the harsh judgement from me. Wrong!

'You find me very cynical,' Helena apologised. 'I just believe that Saffia's death has robbed this man Lutea of expectations in a lengthy scheme to prey on the Metelli – and I believe he is sobbing for himself. You, Marcus Didius Falco, the great city romantic, hate to see a man bereft. You believe that Lutea was genuinely moved today by the loss of his heart's companion and lover.'

'I allow him that,' I said. 'He is distraught at losing her. But I don't disagree with you entirely, fruit. The only reason Lutea is not weeping for the money is that – in my view, and I am sure in his – he has not lost it yet.'

XXXVII

T HE FULL title of the murders court is the Tribunal for Poisoners and Assassins. Poisoning is routinely associated with spells, potions and other foul magic. Assassins may be all kinds of murderers, including armed robbers. This court thus relates to the grimiest side of human nature. I always found sessions there quite gruelling.

There is a panel of lay judges, drawn from both the upper and middle classes – a fact which irritates the senators and makes the equestrians smug. Their names are kept in a public register, the White List, which we were about to consult. A name from this album would be picked by Paccius Africanus, and if we approved, the chosen judge (with no right to refuse) would preside over our court case. The judge would not vote with the jury, though after hearing the evidence formally, if there was a guilty verdict he would pronounce punishment and fix the accusers' compensation. Seventy-five reputable citizens would act as the jury, their selection subject to challenges by both prosecution and defence. They would hear the evidence in strict silence and vote secretly; equal votes would mean acquittal.

'If there are seventy-five judges, how can there be equal votes?' I mused.

'Oh Falco!' Honorius deplored my simplicity. 'You can't expect seventy-five men to turn up without *anybody* sending a note to say he has a bad cold or must attend his great aunt's funeral.'

The judge meanwhile did not have to remain silent – and was unlikely to do so. I won't say we expected any judge to be crass, legally ignorant and biased against us – but Honorius became extremely exercised over who would be appointed.

'Paccius and Silius know the panels, and I don't. The trial could be effectively over for us, if we get the wrong man.'

'Well, do your best.' I despised them all and found it hard to care. 'All we need is someone who can stay awake. That's the purpose of choosing from the panels, I take it?'

'No, Falco. The purpose of choice is to ensure neither side has an opening to bribe the judge.'

I had not bargained on expenditure. 'Do we have to bribe him?'

'Of course not. That would be corrupt. We just need to make sure the opposition doesn't bribe him either.'

'I am glad you explained that, Honorius!' I was seeing the seedy side of law here – and the humourless side of our barrister. 'Surely all judges are appointed to panels for their fair-mindedness and independence?'

'Where have you spent your life, Falco?'

I started to take a reluctant interest. Aelianus was showing off, explaining the judges' qualifications. 'Freeborn, in good health, over twenty-five and under sixty-five, has to be a decurion or other local official, and has to have a modest property portfolio.'

I was shocked. 'Good gods, I could end up on a panel myself.'

'Feign sickness or madness, Falco.'

'Think of his tombstone,' Helena ruled. 'Aulus, I want my husband to have a whole list of dead-end, pointless positions, running off his alabaster slab.' Alabaster, eh? She seemed to have planned it already. Mention of dead-end positions reminded me to visit the Sacred Geese again. 'Marcus, be a judge but make sure every time in court, you go for acquittal. Go on the panel, but build up a reputation as a soft bastard, so you don't get picked for cases.'

'The jury decides verdicts,' I protested.

'The judge directs the course of the trial,' Honorius argued, in a hollow voice. He was definitely nervous. It might perk up his advocacy. But it made me tense.

Honorius did not like the judge Paccius first chose. There was no reason, but on principle Honorius would not take the first offer. We objected.

We made another suggestion. Paccius refused our name.

Apparently this was normal.

Then began several days of negotiating the published lists. The album of approved judges was laid out in three panels. First, two of these had to be eliminated. It was quick. Paccius rejected a panel, then we did. I could not see what grounds they had – guesswork, perhaps. I noticed that Paccius acted out a charade of deep thoughtfulness, chewing a stylus as he lengthily pondered; Honorius glanced down with an air of confidence before making a swift selection as if it hardly mattered.

That thinned the lists to a third. The remaining panel was subjected to intense scrutiny, as each side removed one name at a time alternately. We were using a panel with an uneven number of names, so we had first pick; had it been an even panel, Paccius would have started. In either case, the intention was to allow the defendant to make the final rejection. We all had to keep going until one name was left.

There was no time limit, except that if we spent too long debating we would look amateur. Hasty research was conducted. Both sides were steered by their private advisers. Paccius had a whole group of spindly specialists who looked like clerks with chest diseases. Falco and Associates were just asking my friend Petronius. He had one great advantage: he had appeared in front of most judges.

'Do you want a cretin or a meddler?'

'Which is better for us?'

'Whoever gets the larger backhander.'

'We won't pay. We are going for probity.'

'Can't afford true justice, eh?'

Nobody knew the judges in this court well. At first I thought the opposition were proceeding in some clever manner; then I spotted them off guard one day when I was half concealed behind a pillar, and I could see that where we were facetious, they were frantic. As the names were whittled down, they threw up their hands. Even with Petro's guidance, we were not removing judges on the basis of what we knew against them, but leaving them in because we had never heard of them. There was one exception. One name stayed there even though Petro and I both knew the judge. Both of us were amazed that he survived the process. We both thought it was funny; as the women who loved us sometimes remarked, Petronius and I had never grown up.

By the last three names, we had the man we knew, plus two others whom Petro said were a foul-mouthed liar and a bully (these were milder than some of his comments on others). Honorius rejected the liar. Paccius struck out the bully.

'So! Our judge is called Marponius.' Paccius turned to Honorius. 'Do you know anything of him?'

'Actually, no.'

'Me neither.'

Petronius and I hid quiet smiles.

Though on opposite sides, Paccius and Honorius had spoken as colleagues who now faced a common enemy. Their frank exchange included a trace of contempt, for these two nobles knew from a mark against his name that the judge was an equestrian.

We knew more than that. At least we knew what we were getting; that was why we had kept quiet. Petronius Longus had had many a run-in with Marponius in the murders court. Marponius and I had clashed a few times too. The man was a duff encyclopaedia tycoon, a purveyor of cheap knowledge to the rising classes, who had made money and used it to advance himself from the stews on the lower Aventine to the temple-topped crest of the hill. Being on the panel of approved judges was the height of glamour for him. He was ambitious, nasty, narrow-minded and famous for spouting bigoted drivel. He sat in his court like a warm geyser in the Phlegrian Fields, belching foul volcanic air — a risk to all the wildlife in his neighbourhood.

As he left us, Petronius said he was sure we would all find the arbiter in our coming trial to be full of talent and humanity.

'I hope not!' muttered Honorius. 'We don't want some damned interventionist.'

I told him that Marponius was famous for his innovative directions to juries. Paccius overheard me. He and Honorius glanced at each other and winced.

This was typical of Marponius. He had not even met them, yet he had upset the legal teams on both sides.

XXXVIII

MARPONIUS WAS loving it. We were informed that he was so thrilled to preside over a prestigious case (instead of bath-house stranglers and brothel batterers), he had bought himself a new toga – and forgot to request a price discount. Petronius seemed to have access to the judge's house; he knew so much about his reactions, it sounded to me as if the vigiles must be crouching under his pillow like bedbugs as the judge put himself to sleep every night with his beaker of hot camomile tea and scroll of Cicero. . .

In fact Marponius, a childless widower, lived a life of moral austerity. That was one reason Petro and his men hated him. There was nothing to work with when they wanted to influence a case in the right direction.

So keen was Marponius to feature in the *Daily Gazette*'s legal reports and to have the masses in the Forum wonder who in Hades he was, he brought Calpurnia's trial forwards and rushed through the jury selection. Marponius apparently had more influence than we supposed; he then somehow wangled himself use of the Basilica Julia. It was normally reserved for the Court of One Hundred, which dealt with inheritance. Appropriate – though Marponius probably just knew the right court official. Since the centumviral court actually had a hundred and eighty judges and occasionally sat in full session, there would be plenty of room for onlookers, though I thought Marponius was going overboard.

It was a cool day when I strolled down the Vicus Jugarius, walked under the Arch of Tiberius, and entered the historic end of the Forum near the Capitol. The Basilica stretched between the Temple of Saturn and the Temple of Castor, in a dramatic and lofty group of monuments. Overlooked by the great temples on the hill above, that part of the Sacred Way was rich in ancient sites. I came out on a corner, by the Lake of Servilius – some antique hero who once gave a horse a drink here (or maybe it was the name of the thirsty horse). Ahead were the orators' rostra adorned with prows of captured ships, the so-called Umbilicus of the City, and the mysterious Black Stone. Very historic. Somewhere for loafers to tell their friends to meet them. I found the rest of my own party gathered in the shadow of the towering statue plinths that lined the Sacred Way.

We mounted the steps in the centre. For once I noticed the elegant symmetry of the double-height rows of arches that faced us. There must be nearly twenty – I had no concentration to count them – and they are entirely constructed of expensive marble. Inside, some cutbacks occurred; there the piers are simply made of cheaper travertine with white marble veneers. The long rectangular hall, roofed in wood over a fifty-foot span, has a double row of colonnades on each long side, paved with more glittering slabs, so a ponderous chill strikes the bones in winter and an important hush lies everywhere, except when barristers are arguing among themselves in the side aisles. The colonnades have upper galleries, where people can observe proceedings, eat nuts, then throw down pistachio shells into the toga folds of the legal teams.

In our case there seemed little need for sightseers to hang over the balcony rails; a few friends and members of the public lounged on seats we had supplied, but standing room was hardly at a premium. The Basilica staff had allocated us a derisory area at one end of the huge hall. A single usher waved us in with obvious lack of interest. We greeted well-wishers hoarsely. It did not take long.

We watched Marponius strut into the Basilica Julia, followed by an official slave who carried his folding ivory stool, and a slave of his own who had brought him an unofficial red cushion to slip on to it. Marponius had a very well padded backside, which gave him a strange walk and an uneven toga hem. He had a bald crown with curly side panels, all covering what Petronius and I denounced as only half a brain. The wrong half.

He gave a cool nod to Petronius, who was backing me up on the first day in court. I received a blank stare, though that may have been because I was sporting a large assisted bruise that gave me the appearance of a mad-eyed painted statue where the artist had wanted to use up all the pigment on his palette to save cleaning it. Honorius sat between me and Aelianus; Justinus had so far failed to return from Lanuvium. Despite his previous court experience, Honorius was extremely quiet. I found it more and more worrying.

The accused entered stiffly, as if to emphasise her years. Not quite limping, but walking with some awkwardness, Calpurnia took her place between the gloomy-looking, overweight Silius and the suaver, slimmer Paccius. She had disdained to dishevel her clothing to win sympathy, though she did wear her long grey hair loose; it was caught under the matron's stole she wore tightly wrapped around her body. She had no visible jewellery, perhaps because she had sold it all. Her expression was thunderous. Her son was in court, but she never looked at him. Negrinus never looked at anyone.

Marponius took it upon himself to address the jury on their duties and the legal teams on how he wished to run his court (he phrased it another way but he meant, with both legal teams subservient to him as he rode roughshod over them). Then we began. First came the prosecution's opening speech, in which the charges would be set out. Honorius was to deliver this. As he rose, Paccius and his old senior Silius smiled tolerantly to disconcert our young man. He took it well. Adjusting his toga briefly for the best effect, and revealing little of the nerves I suspected he felt, Honorius began:

The Accusation against Calpurnia Cara: Speech for the Prosecution by Honorius

Gentlemen of the jury, this is a case in which a noble family come to ruin tragically. Founded in Lanuvium, the Metellus family has old roots and old money. They have been senators for five generations, serving Rome with honour and distinction. The present generation appeared to flourish and live happily for thirty years. The daughters married well and left home. The son married and stayed with his parents. All had children. The son was progressing through the senatorial ranks, and if not a star, he was securely fulfilling his ambitions. About two years ago, something happened.

I admit to you freely, it is not yet clear what the disaster was. Perhaps Calpurnia Cara will shed light on it. One thing is certain: this event was catastrophic. Lack of money became a problem. The father and son desperately sought to increase their funds through corruption. The father wrote a savagely unjust will. His family were then beset from all sides.

Let me list their enemies: An informer called Silius Italicus, whom you see in court today, laid formal corruption charges, in a case which he won. The son's wife, Saffia Donata, turned against her husband and, he says, stripped him of everything. Another informer who sits among us here, Paccius Africanus – with or without connivance from Silius – moved in on the family with motives that may have seemed helpful at the time but which now look only sinister. At least one of their slaves, a door porter, Perseus, seems to have discovered secrets they wanted to hide, and ran rings around them. And harboured in their midst was Calpurnia Cara, apparently a devoted wife and mother, but as we shall show you, a woman of strong passions and determined hatreds, who would not flinch from the worst possible action.

Following his condemnation in the court case, Rubirius Metellus was advised to commit suicide. This did not suit the informer who had accused him of corruption, for if the condemned man took his own life, Silius would lose his compensation. To the dismay of Silius, Metellus died. From motives we can only despise, the informer rallied; next he accused the elder daughter of poisoning her father, after Metellus had allegedly declined to take his own life. Rubiria Juliana was tried in the Senate, but was acquitted and lives blameless. Thwarted, Silius Italicus has now allied with his colleague, Paccius Africanus, to accuse the son instead, in a case which has yet to be heard. Truly, the children of the late Rubirius Metellus carry a heavy burden. It weighs worst on the son. Disinherited by his father, for reasons of which he is totally ignorant, he now learns he has a brazen and callous mother. The unnatural woman whom we have brought before you intends to give evidence that will condemn Metellus Negrinus, her only son, for his father's murder.

We, however, will be able to demonstrate that it was not the ill-fated Negrinus who killed his father – but his mother Calpurnia Cara. She may have been a blameless wife – certainly she will tell you so. You will be shocked by what drove her to the dreadful crime she committed. She had had to endure a husband who exhibited, in the most public way, a shameful partiality for his own daughter-in-law. That young woman has unfortunately died in childbed this very week and cannot be questioned. But her influence on Rubirius Metellus is demonstrated by the way he treated her financially and it is the root cause of this family's misery. The rapacious and blackmailing demands of the daughter-in-law led to an unenviable need for money, which resulted in the corruption for which Metellus was found guilty. And the unnatural favour shown to his daughter-in-law in his will led to his death at the hands of his embittered wife. You may feel sympathy for her predicament, but her unflinching dispatch of her husband and her desperate measures to conceal the crime deserve only condemnation.

Fuelled by sorrow, shame, and anger at her omission from the will of a husband of near forty years, Calpurnia Cara turned on Rubirius Metellus and removed him from the world. We shall show you that she sold her jewellery, then consulted a woman familiar with the black arts, to learn what fatal poison she should choose and how it might be administered. She arranged to obtain the noxious drug, through the medium of Paccius

Africanus – a man who must be no stranger to the disreputable side of life. They used one of his creatures, a man of such appalling habits that he has employed violence on the very streets of Rome in a foolish attempt to dissuade us from bringing this case. You can see sitting there, my colleague Didius Falco, still bearing the scars of that vicious attack.

Calpurnia arranged to have the chosen drug, insidious hemlock, secretly given to her husband in his lunchtime meal. Metellus succumbed, and far from committing suicide among his loving family as the world was informed, he may have died a lonely death. Certainly his corpse was accorded no respect. Calpurnia attempted to hide the results of her actions by concealing the body; Metellus may not even have been dead when she secreted him in a crude garden shack – but it was in that sorry place that he met his end. For three whole days the body of Rubirius Metellus lay concealed in that mean location, without the honours due to a man of his rank or the sorrowing ministrations of his children and his friends. Neither his children nor his friends were aware of what had happened.

Then the body was at last removed from its hiding place. Realising that concealment would not work, Calpurnia had invented an elaborate lie about the time and the manner of her husband's death. Under her instructions Rubirius Metellus was laid on his own bed as if he had perished there that day. A false story of his suicide was concocted. Calpurnia Cara lied to her household. She lied to her children. She lied to the seven senators who were suborned into witnessing their noble friend's supposed suicide, allegedly at his request. When we call her to give evidence, let us all be aware that this terrible woman may yet lie in court. . .'

That was a rather exciting statement. Marponius had reached the limit of his concentration. He adjourned the session.

XXXIX

THE ADJOURNMENT provided a respite and an opportunity. Honorius went off by himself, looking exhausted. Flushed with his success at tracking down the hemlock-salesman, Aelianus volunteered to seek out Olympia, supposedly consulted by Calpurnia as a fortune-teller. Honorius had previously been looking for this crone, or so he said, but with no results.

'Where will you start, Aulus?'

'I have my methods!'

I knew he had only one method, to which he stuck with a rigidity I would need to shatter. But it served here. Any highborn ladies would know how to reach this star-gazer. Once again, Aelianus was going home for lunch. There, he would ask his mother.

The principled Julia Justa would never have handed over any of her tight household budget to a fashionable seer, but she might possess acquaintances who did. I could imagine my dear mother-in-law reproving them for their daftness in her silky, sarcastic way. Even if she had been extremely rude in the past, that would not stop her now. I don't suppose her cronies would admit to being scared of the noble Julia, but she would get an address for her boy.

I was glad to have back-up from Aelianus. With Justinus away and Honorius resting (or whatever he was up to), we needed to deploy our resources well. I myself had to tackle someone else: I grabbed sustenance, then headed off to stick my mark on Licinius Lutea.

The one-time near-bankrupt lived in an apartment not far from that in which he had established Saffia. He managed to rent half a house, divided up tastefully in what had once been a rich man's mansion. Lutea had the part above the sausage shop, the least desirable to discerning tenants – though it must be handy for a divorcee who owned no slaves. I guessed he lived on hot pies from the bakery and cold pork sausage – when he was not cadging dinners from old friends who could not shake him off.

I found him in a reading room, stretched on a couch. There was not much else in the elegant space, just a couple of lamps. I call it a reading room because there was one silver scroll box; I wondered if it had been a gift from the grateful Saffia – and instinctively, I reckoned it was empty. The whole apartment was extremely bare, its décor standardised by a landlord – though one who had used expensive designers for the black and vermilion paintwork.

'Isn't this place a bit above your price?' I asked Lutea frankly. 'I heard you had no credit.'

Lutea gave me a sharp look. Rallying from his listlessness, he admitted in a louche way, 'Yes, it is. I survive, though.'

'They call you an entrepreneur. It usually means a confidence trickster, in the world I come from.'

'Then you inhabit a tragic world, Falco.'

'It's improving. How about yours?'

'One lives in hope.' He pretended to be too subdued to argue, though I wasn't fooled.

Lutea kept acting out low in spirits. Underneath, he remained the brazen, well-manicured type with a flash tunic and no conscience. I was glad I had not brought Helena. Her open disapproval would not win his confidence. I myself would feel dirty afterwards if I played the sympathetic playboy with him, but that was nothing to me. You can scrub off the taint of lousy immorality like his.

I had noticed there was no sign nor sound of a child in the house. I asked after his son.

'Lucius is being looked after. Poor little terror. It's very hard on him – well, it's hard on both of us. Oh we shall both miss darling Saffia!' That might be so, but they would miss her in different ways.

'You seemed remarkably attentive to your ex-wife. Was the split from her a subject for regret?'

'I was heartbroken. Her damned father . . .' Lutea tailed off sadly. 'I had hoped when she left old Birdy, I might bring Donatus round again. No chance of that now . . .' Every time he wafted off into misery I felt it was staged. 'Saffia and I were a wonderful team, Falco. Nobody to touch us. It can be like that, you know.'

'I know.'

He shook his finger at me. 'I see it! You have a wife and you love the girl.'

'She's very sharp,' I said quietly. That was true; Lutea was a lifelong fraud, but Helena had seen through him. Clearly he had no recollection that he had met her with me last night. He had blotted out the cold assessment with which her eyes had raked him. 'She runs the home – and she runs me.'

'Excellent!' Lutea beamed at me. 'That's how it should be. I am pleased for you.'

I was leaning on a wall, since Lutea was still lying on his couch and there were no other seats. I enjoyed myself, smiling slightly, as I thought of how Helena viewed him. Here he was, a man in his early thirties. He lived in a luxury he did not need, on promises he would never fulfil. What had he been doing before I arrived? Dreaming up schemes. Dreaming so hard that the fragile lies from which he built his life became his reality.

'Helena was anxious about your boy,' I said. 'Maybe I can see him, to reassure her?'

'No, no,' Lutea murmured. 'Lucius is not here. He went to his old nurse.'

'Someone he knows,' I said, without judgement.

'Someone familiar,' Lutea agreed, as if this excuse had just struck him.

Different men react in different ways. If my children lost their mother, I would be inconsolable. And I would never let the children from my sight.

'This is good of you,' Lutea said, fooling himself as he tried to fool others. 'Taking the trouble to bring your condolences. I appreciate that.'

I straightened up. 'I'm afraid there is more to it.'

Lutea smiled at me, allowing himself to sink into a grief-stricken half-trance. 'Nothing too terrible, I'm sure.'

'Oh no.' I walked over to him. I slung his feet off the couch and sat down with him. I shook my head like a concerned old uncle. If he stiffened up, he hid it. 'Just this. It is being said that your sweet little Saffia blackmailed the Metelli. And I think that you were in the project with her. Any comment?'

Now sitting upright, the ex-husband let a bemused expression fill his features. Maybe he had been accused of bad practice before; the display was good. 'That is a terrible thing for anyone to say about poor Saffia! Now she is dead and cannot defend herself against such accusations. I don't believe it – and I know nothing about any of it.'

'She knew their secret. Did she tell you?'

'What secret?' Lutea gasped as if the whole idea astonished him.

'Oh come on! The secret that made you two decide to move in close to them. So close, Saffia actually left you and married herself to

Birdy. Divorcing you was a sham. Poor Birdy knows it now. I wonder how long it took him to realise?'

'I have no notion what you are talking about, Falco.'

'Well that's a shame. Call yourself a friend of Birdy's? Don't you know that your very best friend is being made somebody's patball? And don't you see why the evidence is pointing straight at you?'

Lutea shook his head in wonderment. A faint whiff of fine oil came my way. As with all the best confidence tricksters, his personal grooming was immaculate. If this scam failed, he would be able to build an extensive career preying on the rich widows of exotic commodity traders. He would like that. He could plunder their attics of stored commodities, not just empty their bankboxes. The widows would get plenty out of it – while his attentions lasted. I saw them playing dice with him, their be-ringed fingers flashing in the light of many lampstands, while they congratulated themselves on their cultured catch. Better to paw a spiny sea urchin, in fact, yet there would never be unpleasantness. Lutea would leave them flat broke; even so, they would remember him with few hard feelings. He was good-looking and would play the innocent. Not wanting to believe he had deceived them, his victims would never be quite sure it really was darling Lutea who had robbed them.

I knew how it worked. I had dreamed of doing it, in the hard, lost days before I was rescued by improvements in my fate. But I recognised bad dreams for what they were. As an entrepreneur that was my tragedy. But it was my salvation as a man.

I stayed another hour. Lutea feigned shock, disgust, outrage, reproof, anger and near-hysteria. When he threatened litigation if I libelled him, I laughed at him and left.

He had confessed nothing. Still, I became certain that he and Saffia really had conspired together in a complex scheme – and one which might still be operational. Lutea denied it – but Lutea was undoubtedly lying through his teeth.

XL

H ONORIUS LOOKED more confident when he appeared in court next day. Marponius greeted him benignly. That would have scared me, but Honorius had less experience. This trusting boy would have smiled back at a Nile crocodile as it climbed out to grab him by his short legs.

He was setting out the background to Metellus' death, explaining – perhaps in too much detail – the issues behind the original corruption trial. His current argument was that Rubirius Metellus may have been a bad citizen, but he had been convicted, so the jury should dispel any feeling that in some way he deserved to die. Killing him in his home was a serious crime. Parricide – by which Honorius meant, according to Roman custom, the murder of any close relative – had been the most reviled crime since the founding of our city. It was the jury's duty to avenge the crime, lest social order disintegrate. . .

When I hear the words 'social order', I start looking around for somebody to pick a fight with.

The jury and I were thoroughly bored. I felt no conscience pangs when a message from Aelianus allowed me to make a run for it. I passed Honorius a note, did my best to make it look mysterious for the benefit of Paccius and Silius, then slid out of the Basilica like a man on the trail of hot new evidence.

The chance of that was slim. We were off to interview a fortune-teller. Presumably foresight would warn her about us before we even left the Forum.

Aelianus led me to his father's litter. He might hit the punchbag hard at the gym, but he had the natural laziness of any young man in his twenties. We crammed in and yelled at the bearers to get going as they protested at our weight. We were jogged along the Sacred Way the full length of the Forum, then waited interminably in the traffic jams around the building site for the new amphitheatre. Eventually we settled into a more regular pace along the Via Tusculanum. Olympia lived on that highway, though outside the city boundary. Cynics might think the remoteness was deliberate. For a woman who was courted by fine women who led busy lives, it seemed an awkwardly long-distance trek, though maybe the far location gave them a sense of security. A senator's wife having her stars read would have to be very discreet. If the stars under scrutiny belonged to her husband, she was breaking the law – whilst if they belonged to the Emperor, she was committing treason. To know another person's fortune smacks of wanting to control their fate for the wrong reasons.

As we jerked along, I warned my companion not to expect dead bats being thrown on to green fires. If Aelianus wanted to buy a love philtre made from the desiccated testicles of disgusting mammals, he would not find the bottles on display, well, not openly. The last fortune-teller I interviewed turned out to be a cultured piece who had three accountants and a crisp way of disposing of informers. I would not have eaten an almond cake at her house, but if she ever used witchcraft she knew how to bribe the aediles first, so they kept away. Tyche had given me a creepy feeling that if she did cast spells, they would work. *Tyche*. . . dear gods, that took me back.

Aelianus and I decided against pretending we wanted horoscopes. Olympia would know far too much about people's follies, hopes and terrors for us to fool her. Aelianus looked interested, but I warned him off.

'No seances. I promised your mother I would look after you.'

'My mother thinks you'll let her down, Falco.'

Olympia lived in a house that was primly feminine, with a manicurist in a clean little booth on the right of the front door, and a depilatory salon on the left. Rich women came out here to be pampered, to share gossip, to denigrate their husbands and deplore their in-laws, to arrange marriages for their children, and to lust after low-class lovers. The house remained very much that of Olympia herself; its rooms were completely domestic in character and she kept up a respectable front. Wooing senators' wives to visit her lair could be dangerous; she would not want to be closed down. Unsavoury couplings would occur here only rarely (though some liaisons with drivers and second-rate love-poets must have been arranged from these premises, if I was any judge).

Olympia kept us waiting, for form's sake. She had slim young girls to fetch and carry, and to lend an air of chaperoned propriety. They were too thin and too subdued to be attractive. Aelianus never glanced at them. I looked. I always do. I was checking to see if Olympia mistreated them, in case one of her woeful wenches might be met later behind the garden hedge and enticed to become a songbird for a few kind words. I was more badly bruised than they were, so I ruled that out.

When she appeared, a plump dark-skinned woman of mature age, she acted very genteel; to me she had all the appeal of mildew. Olympia had intense, pouchy eyes. She acted as if full of shrewdness, though I reckoned she was less intelligent than she supposed. Her well-spoken accent had one or two jarring vowels; she had taught herself polite Latin, but her past had followed her. She had probably worked her way into this position through several careers, careers she was keeping very quiet. Everything about her suggested a rich but sour experience of life, making her a businesswoman other women could trust. Once they did, no doubt Olympia simply preyed on them.

Aelianus smiled at the fortune-teller.

'Anything I can do for you, sweetheart?' she encouraged him, ignoring me. Suggestiveness from a woman scared him and he looked to me for help. I let him run with it.

'We have to ask about one of your clients,' he began. 'Calpurnia Cara.'

'I cannot speak about my clients.'

'There's no need to snap – she is in serious trouble –'

'Nothing will pass my lips.'

'You may be able to help her.'

'No.'

'Now less of that.' Aelianus was a bad interviewer, getting desperate. Olympia knew he was at her mercy. 'This is a legal matter. If we have to, we can subpoena you!'

I leaned forwards. Time for the man of experience to intervene. 'Aulus, don't even try that one. Olympia has to think about her *other* clients – am I right?'

She raised an eyebrow. I did not like the way she sneered.

'The ladies who patronise Olympia's establishment,' I explained to my brash colleague, 'must *never* suspect she would reveal a confidence.' I pretended to offer the fortune-teller a courteous get-out: 'Maybe we can arrange this so the ladies need never find out you helped us.'

'Yes – I won't tell you anything!' she retorted nastily.

'Alternatively,' I then said, 'all your senatorial ladies could be made to think that you *had* talked to us. . .' Sometimes subtlety is worth a try – and sometimes you should go straight to threats.

Round-eyed with mock horror, Aelianus redeemed himself: 'Oh but Falco, the customers would all run away.'

'Well, you're the bastard.' Olympia smirked at me. 'Thanks for coming clean.'

'Yes I'm the bastard,' I agreed. 'This sensitive young lad is ten years younger and he still expects good from people.'

'He'll soon turn into a bastard if he works for you.'

Aelianus had no sense of humour sometimes. He bit his lip, scowling.

We then had a more businesslike discussion – one in which I feared we were being misled.

According to this soothing soothsayer, Calpurnia Cara came to her for 'friendship'. Horoscopes were prepared from time to time, always for Calpurnia herself. The other services rendered were flattery, wise counsel, and foot massage with aromatic oils to relax the soul. (Apparently your soul is seated in your arches, so take care when buying cheap sandals.) Calpurnia, like many clients, was afflicted with bad bunions and few female friends. Well, I knew she had a limp, and was overbearing.

I told Olympia she could have made a wonderful source for informers like us. I suggested that if she helped us, we could return the favour with information on her clients. She would not co-operate. I asked if she already had a partnership with some other informer, but she denied it. I asked if she worked for the vigiles. She scoffed. I gave up on it.

'Straight questions then: Did Calpurnia ever ask you about poisonous drugs?'

'Don't expect me to comment.'

'No, of course not. I'm talking about hemlock. That was used to kill her husband, did you know?'

'I had no idea.' Olympia pursed her mouth. 'Calpurnia Cara was weighed down by troubles. She never told me what they were. My ladies have needs – illness, unhappiness, husbands, children . . . I often read Calpurnia's future, and reassured her that everything would be resolved.'

'*By her poisoning her husband?*' Aelianus snorted.

'By time and the Fates!' whipped back the seer. He had stung her into reacting, however. 'Hemlock, you say? Well once when she was very low a few years ago, she did ask me what produces a kindly death, and I told her what I had heard. As far as I knew, Calpurnia was asking for herself.'

'*Herself!*' Now I was scathing. 'That sounds like some well-thought-out excuse in the poison trade. A lawyer probably devised it. A litigation-proof contract term for the death suppliers' guild – if the woman was consulting you for solace, why should she need to do herself in?'

'Some unhappy moments cannot be smoothed away even with essential ointments,' mused Olympia.

'How did Calpurnia plan to ingest her hemlock?'

'I told her she could feed the leaves to quails, then cook the quails. That way she didn't have to think about what she was taking.'

'Or if she gave the quails to someone else, *they* didn't have to know anything!'

'You're a shocker, Falco.'

'I'm a realist.'

I then enquired whether Calpurnia sold her jewels just before her husband died, or was it about two years back? Surprised by both timescales, Olympia admitted Calpurnia had come for weekly consultations over several decades. Calpurnia had sold off her necklaces and rings many years ago – one of the 'troubles' which had required consolation. The sale was not to pay the fortune-teller's modest fees. Olympia did not know who received the money.

'Maybe she gambled,' Olympia suggested. 'Many of my ladies do. It's a bit of excitement for a lady, isn't it?' As I said to Aelianus afterwards, it would provide a lady's bit of excitement if sleeping with a boxer or with their husband's best friend in the Senate ever paled.

I could not imagine Calpurnia Cara doing any of those things. Nor could I see her ever being so depressed that she would end her own life.

'Calpurnia may have mistakes in her past,' Olympia insisted. 'It does not mean she is a murderer. Put me in court and I shall say so for her.'

I did not remind her it is a tenet of Roman law that consulting a fortune-teller damns a woman automatically. Calling Olympia as a witness would guarantee jury votes for us. But as a matter of pride, I wanted to convict the accused with proper evidence.

'You're too idealistic,' Aelianus said. This was a rare, new insult for me. 'You'll never make a lawyer, Falco.'

No; but I thought he would.

XLI

THE CAMILLUS litter had to be returned to the Capena Gate, but we had time to walk back to the Forum for the end of the afternoon court session.

As we came out into the major piazza in front of the Basilica, we were hailed from the corner of the Temple of Castor by Helena Justina. She had a lunch basket; I guessed it would be empty by now. Well, in our absence it made sense for her to eat everything, to save carrying the food home. What a scandal: a senator's daughter sitting on the Temple steps, with a large napkin spread on her lap, munching.

'You're becoming famous,' she said, after I kissed her. As I greeted her affectionately, by some sleight of hand she passed me her lunch basket. 'Even Anacrites has come to see how the case is going. We had a long chat before he went inside.'

'You hate Anacrites.'

'I won't let him see that. He would think I was afraid.'

'You should be,' Aelianus warned her.

He and I paused to sling on our togas, for once making an effort to arrange woollen pleats and to create traditional sinuses (for provincial barbarians, those are the deep folds below the left arm, where you can hide your notes or, if desperate, a dagger to stab your enemy). Helena followed us towards the Basilica.

'Dear heart,' I remonstrated fondly, 'you have already outraged ancient patricians by picnicking in the Forum Romanorum. Do not follow up your notoriety by invading the courts. Some of those traditionalists would rather see a slave rebellion than allow women in the Basilica.'

'I am a good wife to you, Marcus darling. A good wife is allowed to hear her husband make his speeches from a curtained niche.'

'You are a bad wife if you give me heart failure. Who says *I* am speaking?'

'Honorius,' smiled Helena, as she skipped away to the rear of the

Basilica, where steps led to the upper galleries. 'He wants you to do the tricky part – laying the blame on Paccius.'

I was stunned. Too late, I realised that Helena had left me to enter court carrying a large wicker hamper. This would not be viewed as a proper accessory for an orator.

I solved that. I passed it swiftly to Aelianus.

There were more spectators than previously. Too many for me.

The scene throbbed more with tedium than tension. The first person I saw was Helena's father, Camillus Verus, sharing a bench with Petronius. Petro noticed me and glared across the hall. My bugbear Anacrites was lounging on a seat, unpleasantly close to the defence party. Trust him.

Anacrites gave me what passed for a friendly wave. Most people would not have noticed his presence, but to me the Chief Spy was always a magnet; I wanted to know where he was and what he was planning in that dark mind. Habitually discreet in dress, when decked out in a formal toga he blended in even more, though his slicked-back, oiled black hair gave him away. I joined the prosecution group and pretended to give all my concentration to Honorius.

I had come at the right moment. As Aelianus and I sat down behind him, Honorius moved from his oratorical introduction into the next phase of his speech. He assumed an expression of distaste for his subject matter. Here, he would set out the events in the Metellus death, making the facts look as bad as possible for Calpurnia Cara.

Beside me, I noticed Aelianus produce a note-tablet on which he scratched regular stylus notes. A clerk was taking shorthand, but our boy wanted his own record. His system was in contrast to Honorius who, I realised, had never paid much visible attention when our investigations were discussed in his presence, yet he was now able to remember and quote many small details from interviews. Colourful facts that I had long forgotten were reappearing just when required.

Honorius knew his stuff. Once he stopped looking like a school-boy, juries would take him very seriously. If he stood on a plinth so he looked taller, it would be even better.

I slipped him a note I had prepared, covering where we found Olympia, Calpurnia's long association with her, the excuses for consultation, and the jewellery issue. He read it while he was speaking.

I settled down to enjoy the scene. Honorius was now blackening the character of our accused and her associates. For a young man of apparent refinement, he was laying it on thick:

The Accusation against Calpurnia Cara: Honorius on the Accused

I shall not, in default of evidence, try to woo your votes by denouncing the accused with endless stories of an unsavoury life –

The court revived. We all recognised the signal. His denial promised sensationally grubby details. That's the joy of rhetoric: Honorius had reached the juicy bits.

Marponius leaned forward. He sounded kindly, but Honorius was a target. 'Young man, if you are intending to regale us with scandals, may I suggest you keep it short? Some of us are elderly and our bladders cannot take too much excitement.' The old-timers in the jury ranks fluttered nervously. The rest laughed as if Marponius was a great wit.

Honorius stumbled, though he should not have been surprised. Things had gone our way for far too long. The judge was ready to cause trouble.

Gentlemen, the accused lived her married life in apparent propriety –

'Elucidate, please!' Marponius must be in a tetchy mood. This unnecessary interruption was to make Honorius look amateur. It also made Marponius look foolish, but juries are used to that from judges.

We might expect a matron of Calpurnia's status to affiliate herself with temples. Honouring the gods would be a duty. If she had money she might even endow altars or sanctuaries. One of her own daughters is just such a benefactor to the gods and the community in Laurentum; she is so admired that a statue in her honour has been erected there by the townspeople.

'Is the daughter on trial here?'

'No, your honour.'

'Respectable woman, wife of a senator – what are you doing dragging her into this? Strike out the daughter!'

I guessed Marponius had eaten his lunch too fast. Now the glutton had indigestion. He had probably been to Xero's pie shop, his special haunt when he wanted to look like a man of the people (and to overhear, incognito, the public's views on how he ran his case). Petronius had long threatened to put something in Xero's rabbit pie and eliminate Marponius. He reckoned Xero would like the publicity.

Calpurnia Cara's spiritual expression took a different course. For decades she consulted a notorious practitioner of magic, one Olympia. This sorceress lives outside the city boundary, where she is able to run an unlicensed establishment and escape the notice of the vigiles. According to her, our supposedly happy matron has been troubled in her soul for many years. She has looked to magic for solace, as women in torment sometimes do, and yet – either because she felt constrained by her position or because her difficulties were simply too terrible to share – she has never revealed what troubled her. With no mother or mother-in-law, no sisters or close friends to advise her better, she has struggled to find a confidante, clearly unable to share her thoughts with the man who had married her and unable to bear the lone burden. By the time she had daughters who could have consoled her, the pattern was set. Her jewellery had long been sold – we are informed that it was *not* to pay the sorceress, but how can we believe that?

'Are you calling the sorceress?' Marponius had aroused himself from a doze.

'I shall do so, sir.'

'That's the end of the accused then!' The judge subsided.

Paccius, smooth as ever, shook his head at this anticipation. Silius pursed his lips. Honorius contented himself with a polite smile.

I mimed at Petronius my opinion that Marponius had finished off the rabbit pie with a large jug of Falernian. Petro mimed back that it was a jug and a half.

Is it hard to imagine that a woman of this type – the respected wife of a senator, a mother of three children, seemingly a matron all Rome should admire, and yet internally racked by unhappiness – might one day resort to extreme measures?

Calpurnia herself tells us she and her husband regularly quarrelled – quarrelled so badly they would resort to a grove at the furthermost end of their garden, lest household members overhear their furious arguments. When we consider the events that clouded the end of their marriage, it is all too easy to imagine how Calpurnia's life was blighted throughout the whole course of her ill-fated union. We are not here to try her husband, Rubirius Metellus; I remind you that that has been done in the Senate. The verdict was harsh. It truly reflected the man. Everyone says that Metellus had an unforgiving character. He took delight in the discomfiture of others. That he was morally corrupt is established beyond doubt: he sold contracts and accepted favours, using his son's high position. He corrupted contractors; he abused everybody's trust; he relegated his own son to the role of a cheating cipher; it is estimated he made thousands of sesterces – none of which has ever been recovered for the Senate and People of Rome.

You may enquire, is it any wonder that with a wife who was discontented and who regularly quarrelled with him, Rubirius Metellus found it hard to resist a sweeter presence, in his cheerful and good-natured young daughter-in-law? I shall answer with another question: is it any wonder that Calpurnia herself could never bear to speak to anyone of her husband's predilection – and still denies it? Is it any wonder if, with her spirit twisting and turning with rage against him, Calpurnia Cara felt this grim adultery was the final indignity?

Let me now tell you about Saffia Donata. She was young, pretty, full of life and smitten with a love for good things. She had once been married to the best friend of Calpurnia's son; she had a child by her first husband. When that marriage ended, somebody suggested that she be joined to Metellus Negrinus. Negrinus was a young man of promise, embarking on the cursus honorum; he was soon to become an aedile. Well, that shows the kind of man he was, because he won the votes of the Senate then to award him that position of honour. It means that now as an ex-aedile he should be qualified to serve in this very court, on a jury with you. But that will never happen. His reputation has been destroyed by the actions of his father. However, at that time, he was blameless. He is by nature a quiet man, almost diffident, a man who may not have seemed very interesting to an experienced, worldly wife. He married Saffia simply because he knew her and was not shy of her. His mother approved because Saffia had shown herself to be fertile. His father's views are not known to us, but we may raise our eyebrows over the welcome he offered.

So let us think now of what must have happened in that household, as Metellus senior fretted against his own unhappy wife and Metellus junior, who became a father himself, worked long hours in the service of the state. Saffia Donata was her father-in-law's pet. So dearly did he regard her, that he made a will which disinherited his wife and son by name, leaving them the most meagre acknowledgements. He could not legally bequeath his estate directly to Saffia, but he made an arrangement to do it through somebody else – an arrangement which you may find significant. More of that in a moment.

Saffia and Metellus clearly had an unhealthily close relationship. If evidence is needed, we may look to his will. No father openly makes the distinction Metellus has done unless he has completely abandoned his sense of propriety. He does not care if the shocked world sees his shameless feelings for the woman whom he makes the recipient of his generosity. He does not care how much he hurts members of his legitimate family. Whatever went on with Saffia before he died, it is certain that both Calpurnia and her son were aware of it. What monumental verbal storms must have taken place at the end of the garden then! Imagine the accusations that flew. In whose bed did the incestuous assignations take place? Were they confined to secret occasions when the wronged wife and son were away from the house? Was the disgusting betrayal more daring than that? Did Metellus actually court discovery by his wife and son? Did he flaunt his behaviour viciously and salaciously in front of their household slaves?

Negrinus ignored it all, for the sake of his children. He still remains silent. He will not protest. His dignity is astonishing. His mother's reaction was all too different. Calpurnia took her own action.

Her torment is easy to understand. She had lost everything. Her household was once so wealthy that informers did not scruple to cite her family as having an 'extravagant lifestyle' – though her son says nothing so reprehensible and un-Roman really happened. But it is certain they had a good life, such as those who serve the state expect. They kept a handsome, noble home, to which guests and clients could be invited, a home which reflected the status of Rubirius Metellus and his son. Today, Calpurnia sees herself stripped of every natural convenience; rooms in her house are already standing empty while her possessions and slaves are due to be handed over to a fortune-hunter. Over the years, everything she came to expect from life as a woman in a family of distinction was slowly taken from her – the worst blow being that her only son was tainted with corruption, his promising career halted for ever when his father was accused and convicted. If it is a mother's duty to bring up her children well, if we praise those noble women who do so with intelligence, wisdom and the best moral example, then the disgrace inflicted on young Metellus Negrinus must also blacken the name of his mother. So one more horror fell upon her. One last hope of a good reputation had been inexorably withdrawn. She tried desperately to convince her husband to commit judicial suicide and save the dregs of the family honour; he refused her.

That is the kind of man Metellus was. I am sorry to say it. But we have to understand. That was the man who had destroyed this woman's serenity and happiness for over thirty years.

At such a moment, to whom should she turn for guidance? My colleague Didius Falco will be the next speaker. He will explain how Calpurnia Cara allied herself in her trouble to the worst possible adviser.

Marponius shot me a filthy look. He had remembered we had a history.

'We are enjoying this too much, Falco! Better take a break and calm down.'

Our case had reached a climax. There was a buzz in court. Sightseers had crowded in to watch; even the lags who played draughts all day outside on the Basilica steps had abandoned their games.

Someone else was looking good and getting the attention in his court. So naturally Marponius stopped proceedings and adjourned overnight.

XLII

MARPONIUS MAY have broken the mood but the disruption had advantages. This way, I could at least write my speech in advance. I would not bring a written version to court – that would be seen as an insult by the judge and jury – but I had acquired preparation time.

Anacrites strolled up. 'Tomorrow should be lively. You're risking it, Falco!'

'Come and watch.' I forced a grin. 'You might learn something.' My eyes must have narrowed. 'So – what's *your* interest?'

Anacrites glanced over his shoulder. He adopted a genial manner and lowered his voice. 'Watching brief on the corruption file.'

'That's a wrap-up. The perpetrator's dead, for one thing.'

Honorius was pretending to roll scrolls neatly, but I could see him listening. Aelianus sat quiet, openly observing us.

Anacrites continued to pretend he and I were old Palace colleagues sharing confidential back-corridor news. 'The file may be in the dead stacks – but it stays sensitive. The old man has a reputation for placing rapacious officials in key positions, so they can squeeze the job for all it's worth.'

I knew that. 'Vespasian and his famous fiscal sponges! Soaking up loot for the Treasury. How is this relevant to my case?'

Anacrites shrugged. 'There are rumours – quite unfounded, says the Palace – that if an official then gets tried for extortion, Vespasian is even happier. If the official is found guilty, the state wins a large slice of the compensation.'

I sucked my teeth, as if shocked. 'Dreadful! But come off it; you're forcing the issue. Rubirius Metellus was not the official. Negrinus was never charged so he can't be called an imperial "sponge". Silius Italicus would like you to think him public-spirited in charging the father, but he acted out of self-interest. If the Treasury obtained any benefit, it was an unsought bonus for them. I'd say the Emperor is about the only party who can be absolved from having a prejudicial interest.'

'Just seeing which way the wind blows,' murmured Anacrites.

'Was it your idea?'

'Your friend Titus Caesar.'

Titus Caesar was no friend of mine, but Anacrites never ceased to be jealous that I might possess some influence he himself lacked.

We were interrupted by Paccius Africanus. 'I look forward to my grilling,' smiled my prospective victim, but there was threat in his tone. I was meant to be unnerved.

As Paccius left, Anacrites made sure he shook his head ominously. Even Aelianus, standing silent beside me, gripped his fists in annoyance. Honorius, who had dumped this situation on me without warning, pretended not to notice any of it.

I had been a prosecutor on other occasions; the process held no fears. What I had never done was to attack a man of such high rank as Paccius Africanus. If I accused him of conspiracy with Calpurnia, it would blacken his reputation – and he was far too powerful to accept that. Everyone in court today – including both Paccius and Silius – knew tomorrow would bring trouble to somebody. Most thought Paccius would try something devious. So whatever happened could only harm me.

By the time we had gathered our documents and made our way outside, Helena was waiting for me at the top of the steps. She was talking to her father. He was still togate, though endearingly rumpled; his sprouting hair stood even more on end than usual, as if he had been running his hands through it obsessively. Both of them had heard my coming speech announced; both looked apprehensive as I left the Basilica.

I wanted to go straight home to prepare. Instead, Camillus Verus gathered me up. 'I'm taking this fellow to the gym,' he said nonchalantly to Helena.

'Oh, Father. Not "going to the gym"? That's what Marcus says when he's off womanising and gambling.' Helena looked surprised by her father. So was I.

He winked at her, playfully. 'Drinking bout. Don't tell your mother.'

'Hmm. A hangover won't help when he's in court tomorrow.'

'It's a ploy,' breezed Decimus. 'It tells the opposition you are so confident you can go out to a party when you ought to be at home studying your notes.'

'I never heard that Demosthenes went on the wine when he had a big speech coming up . . .' Helena capitulated. 'Look after him.'

'Of course. But Marcus may be late home.'

Now *I* was worried.

Helena Justina raised her eyebrows even higher. They were heavy, like her father's. 'I'll tell myself he is safely talking to you.'

'I shall be talking,' her father declared. 'Marcus will be taking notes.'

His tone had changed. I had seen him serious before, though never quite so straight-faced. In fact I could not remember us ever going to the gym like this together; normally we met by chance. We saw each other in domestic contexts, but otherwise were not socially close. He was a senator and I was an informer. Nothing ever changed that.

We had not far to go. We both frequented premises at the back of the Temple of Castor. I had introduced him, for not even a senator could gain membership of this gymnasium without a recommendation. It was run by my trainer, Glaucus, on the lines of a club. Clubs were illegal, lest persons of inflammatory politics congregate in them to plot against the government. I like to avoid that sort of trouble. But a private gym such as Glaucus set up was seen as acceptably sociable. Exercise is healthy. Dumbbell clowns who can't even spell 'republic' swing their arms about and heave heavy weights on to their mighty, hairy chests – don't they?

Glaucus admitted a certain quiet class. Some, like me, had professional reasons for wanting to train. Others just preferred the refinement of a place where rowdy or crass social monsters were barred. There were no loud voices, no roistering inebriates – and no oily bastards looking out for pretty boys either. There was little room for spear-throwing, but wrestling and swordplay were available. For a steep fee, Glaucus would give you a lesson that was almost as uncomfortable as being ridden down by murderous tribesmen galloping on wild horses – or you could relax in a small courtyard and read poetry. There was even a library, though nobody much used it. You could find a delightful young lady to trim your fingernails, or buy an excellent pastry adorned with toasted pistachio nuts. Perhaps the manicurist offered extra services, but if so, she didn't push it; I always settled for a nutty slice instead, believe me. I doubt if the senator even had that; his wife was making him watch his weight.

We bathed. Decimus usually had a slave to scrape him down, and today so did I. I stood lost in thought, while the boy expertly plied the strigil. Afterwards, Decimus swam in the tiny pool. I never did, though I carried out a few exercises, continuing after my companion hauled himself from the freezing water and huddled in a robe while he chatted to Glaucus.

'Your name is on a lot of lips,' said Glaucus, when I joined them. He disapproved. So did I. Fame may be attractive to many, but in my trade it is an encumbrance. Informers should keep anonymous.

'People will soon forget.'

'Depends what kind of fool you make of yourself, Falco.' My trainer never reckoned to keep his clients with flattery.

'Oh I'll be the usual fool,' I admitted.

He laughed harshly. 'That's all right then!'

The senator had finished drying off and pulling on tunics. At sixty plus, he kept himself well layered up in winter. He hauled me to the library; now I knew what it was there for: plotting. Glaucus had arranged to have a brazier sent in. Snacks and wine followed.

'Should I fetch my note-tablet?' I wondered.

'Better not.' The mood was now distinctly sombre. It had nothing to do with winter's early darkness closing in. 'Marcus, you'll prefer not to write down what I tell you.'

I settled on a reading couch. 'And what,' I asked, still slightly askance, 'will that be, Decimus?'

'All I know,' replied Helena's father quietly, 'about the past careers of Silius Italicus and Paccius Africanus.'

My jaw dropped. 'You can give me some dirt?'

'Remind you, maybe. It came up in the Senate.'

'I confess I don't recall either of them featuring.'

'Well, I was there. So that helped it stick. It was in the early sessions, when Vespasian first became Emperor.' Decimus paused slightly. 'Had things worked out differently, I might have hoped to benefit from the accession. So I was a regular in the Curia – and it was riveting.' We both looked pensive. Camillus Verus had been destroyed politically, around that time, through the actions of a relative. He lost out on what could have become a big career; five years later, the taint still badly damaged him and his sons.

He rallied and continued: 'Young Domitian was still presiding in his father's name; this was before he went too far and had his wings clipped.' Vespasian and his elder son Titus preferred not to dwell on the early career of Domitian. In fairness, the Emperor's younger son was only twenty at the time, representing his father five years before he would normally have been an acceptable face in the Senate. 'This is dangerous material. I cannot advise you how to handle it, but Marcus, I'll do my best to give you all the history.'

I was impressed by the fact that Camillus had brought me here, rather than contaminate either of our homes with what he had to say. He was a man of curious refinement.

As I said, the library was rarely used. Tonight I thought that was just as well. It would not do for others to know we had held this conversation.

We spoke for a long time, until I was well rehearsed.

Afterwards, I returned home silently, my head thronging with ideas. Helena accepted my stillness. Maybe her father had hinted at how he intended to brief me.

None of what he told me was a secret. Six years ago I had despised the Senate and jeered at its day-to-day proceedings. Maybe I read about the relevant debates in the *Daily Gazette* columns, but it had little impact at the time. We were awash with news then. Vespasian's accession had come at the end of a long period of lurid events. Evaluating every one was impossible. Our main concern had been that the civil wars and city famine should end, along with street fighting, fires, destruction and uncertainty.

That night, I could not decide what to do. I was nervous about using this hot material in open court. I talked to Helena; she encouraged me to be bold. Some members of our jury would have been present when the debates happened, after all. Dragging up old sensitivities was dangerous, however. I would be reviving a political scandal, which in a highly political city is always sinister.

I slept all night. Long training helped. I was still undecided when I left home with Helena next morning. But as soon as I walked into the Basilica, saw the long rows of the jury and felt the hall humming, I knew: this was risky – but too good to ignore.

I glanced up at the upper gallery. Peeking around the corner of a curtain, Helena Justina read my thoughts and smiled at me.

The Accusation against Calpurnia Cara: M. Didius Falco on C. Paccius Africanus

My young colleague Honorius spoke to you yesterday with great eloquence. I have been impressed by his setting-out of the issues. I congratulate him on the way he has addressed difficult material. In describing Calpurnia Cara's predicament, he has been most even-handed, while never forgetting the demands of justice for a terrible crime.

Since he has done such an excellent job so far, you may be wondering why we have decided that I should address you on the next subject. Honorius is of senatorial rank, a promising advocate, who will without question make a fine career in both the special courts and the Senate itself. Gentlemen, having made such a start, he is eager to conclude the business before you; it is indeed hard for him now to hand over to me. He has stepped back because I have particular insight into a certain type of person who may have influenced the accused.

My name is Marcus Didius Falco. I am of equestrian rank, a position for which I have to thank the personal interest of the Emperor. Some of you – and our most excellent judge, Marponius, who knows me well – will be aware that this is by no means the first time I have appeared before the murders court. I have made it a habit to identify killers and bring them to trial. I have had some success. If I were to explain myself for the benefit of those who do not know me, I would say I make it a speciality to investigate wrongs which are not suitable for the vigiles or for which the hard-pressed vigiles lack immediate resources. Sometimes I have been commissioned officially for enquiries in the community, and I may say to you that on occasions, my commissions came from the highest level. By its nature, I may not discuss that work. I mention it only so you may appreciate that people of shrewd judgement in powerful positions, the Emperor's closest advisers in fact, hold my services in some regard.

Why am I talking so much about myself? Because of this: my profession, if I may boldly call it that, is that of the informer. I hardly know how I can have named it – for informing is so often a term of abuse. If we were to go out into the Forum Romanorum now this minute, and ask passers-by to define informers, I believe their answers would include: immoral patricians, men who are intent on rising rapidly despite lack of personal talent, men without principle, and lowborn toadies hanging around the skirts of power. They might describe vicious ambition and pitiless manoeuvring. They might suggest that informers target victims for their own benefit, under cover of serving society by cleaning it up. They would undoubtedly complain about men who leap from extreme poverty into questionable wealth, men of insignificance who acquire inexplicable prestige. They would say that informers ruthlessly attack their victims, using means that are often of doubtful legitimacy. Worst of all, remembering the excesses and abuses under emperors like Nero, a creature now 'damned to the memory' for his appalling crimes, people would fear that the role of informers may be still that of secret, subversive informants, whispering poison in the ear of the Emperor.

In making these statements about my own profession, I am speaking to my disadvantage, but I want to show you how fair I am. I know that these are the opinions of many, but I hope to suggest that there is another view. I put to you that ethical informers do exist. They do valuable work, their ambition is commendable, and their motives have morality and integrity. I myself have taken up causes where I knew there would be no financial reward, merely because I believed in the principles involved. Of course you are laughing –

They certainly were. Mind you, they were all listening.

Well, that shows you what an open and honest man I am!

More laughter. With my thumbs tucked into my belt under my toga, I was grinning myself.

Thinking about it, I removed the thumbs.

Perhaps the worst prejudice against informers is that they have, in the past, involved themselves in manipulating government. Fortunately, it is well known that our new Emperor, Flavius Vespasianus, abhors such behaviour. He is famous for opposing secrecy in political circles. One of the first acts of his administration – before Vespasian himself even returned to Rome from Judaea as Emperor – was to require all senators who had acted as informers under Nero to swear a solemn oath about their past actions. Without swearing the oath, such people would no longer be acceptable in public life. Honourable men would in this way exonerate themselves from the taints of the past. But any who perjured themselves would be prosecuted – as some were. . .

'Objection!' Paccius was on his feet. 'None of this has relevance.'

Marponius was eager to do me down – but he wanted to know what was coming. 'Falco?'

'Your honour, I shall show that the accused and her family have associations with informers of the type I am now discussing. Their connection directly affects what happened to Rubirius Metellus.'

'Objection denied!'

Paccius, accustomed to unfair rulings from judges, was already resuming his seat. Was I wrong, or did he glance sideways at Silius? Certainly Silius leaned forwards as if he had a monumental stomach ache in that overfed gut.

Marponius, who normally hunched slackly, had sat bolt upright on his judicial stool. Nobody had warned him that this seemingly domestic killing might have a political dimension. Luckily, he was too dim to be frightened, though even he realised that my naming Vespasian meant the Palace would inevitably focus on his court. Paccius and Silius were now staring at Marponius as if they expected him to warn me to exercise caution.

A better judge would have stopped me.

Gentlemen of the jury, I want to take you back – briefly, let me reassure you – to those heady days immediately after Vespasian accepted imperial power. You will clearly remember the turmoil of those times. Nero's reign had disintegrated into madness and chaos. The Empire was in uproar, the city lay in ruins, people everywhere were battered and grief-stricken. Armies had trampled through the length and breadth of the provinces, some were in open rebellion. We lived through what is now called the Year of the Four Emperors – Nero, Galba, Otto, Vitellius. Then we welcomed the fatherly figure who brought us rescue from that terror –

I was concentrating on Marponius and the jury. For some reason I noticed Anacrites. He was watching with no expression. But I knew him. I was discussing the imperial family. The Chief Spy was intently noting all I said. When he reported back – as he would report, because that was his job – he would twist it to reflect badly on me.

I was a fool to do this.

You will recall that after he departed from Judaea, leaving Titus Caesar to complete the work of crushing the local rebellion, Vespasian travelled first to Egypt. In his absence, Rome was guided on his behalf by the capable duo of young Domitian Caesar and the Emperor's colleague and minister, Mucianus. It was they who assisted the Senate to address the urgent task of rebuilding a peaceful society. It had to be shown that the abuses under Nero would be fiercely nipped out. There was resentment against all those who had destroyed innocent people by making cruel accusations, especially where it had been done from motives of profit. Some wanted recriminations and punishment. The new regime rightly sought peace and conciliation, but it was necessary to show that the evil practices of the past would be ended.

In this situation, at one of the earliest sessions of the Senate a request was made for permission to examine imperial records from the time of Nero, to see which Senate members had acted as informers. This was an investigation which nobody could undertake lightly. The whole Senate had been forced to collaborate with evil prosecutions and to condemn to death those who were convicted; important men, potential holders of the highest office, would come under scrutiny for having been Nero's prosecutors – a role which, it could be argued, they had been powerless to refuse. Men of undeniable talent might be lost to the new administration if they were disgraced. The Senate might now be torn apart by revelations.

In his father's absence, Domitian Caesar wisely ruled that the requested inspection of the archives would require the Emperor's personal permission. Instead, senior members of the Senate devised an alternative. Every senator swore an oath – a serious ordeal in itself. Each swore by the gods that he had imperilled no man's safety under Nero and had received no reward or office at the expense of another's misfortune. To decline the oath was a confession of guilt. Known accusers who did take the oath were convicted of perjury.

'Objection!'

'Paccius Africanus, I have already considered this. Objection denied.'

Three prominent informers vanished from our sight for ever: Cestius Severus, Sariolenus Voccula and Nonius Attianus no longer disfigure our courts. Others could not be so certainly identified: consider Tiberius Catius Silius Italicus –

'Oh objection!'

'Silius Italicus, you are not taking part in this case. You are not entitled to speak. Objection overruled!'

As Silius grumpily slumped back in his seat, I saw Paccius lean sideways and mouth something to him. Silius then spoke in an undertone over his shoulder to a junior, the replacement for Honorius, who accompanied him to the daily court sessions. The junior rose and quietly left the hall. Anacrites watched this with great interest. I should have done.

Silius Italicus is the man who just rose and addressed the judge. Consul two years before Nero went to his death, he was thought to have prosecuted several of Nero's enemies, and to have done so *voluntarily*. For this he incurred general loathing. Yet later, his decency was not in question – I imagine he will make no objection to the judge when I raise this point – later he negotiated between Vitellius and Vespasian in the cause of peace. Perhaps for that reason, he was never prosecuted for perjury, so you may wonder why I have mentioned him in this section of my speech. My purpose is not to give you a history of an unpleasant aspect of the past, but to show how it affects the accused. Silius Italicus now likes to imply he has given up accusing – yet he it was who laid corruption charges against Rubirius Metellus, and in order to recoup his compensation award, he is soon to accuse Metellus Negrinus of killing his father. I was criticised for beginning this discussion of informers, but now, gentlemen, you can see why it is entirely relevant. And there is more.

Next I shall come to a person whose influence on the Metelli is even more baleful. I have named three famous informers who were tried for perjury. Now let me name another one.

'Objection!'
'Sit, Paccius.' Marponius did not even look up from his notes.

Caius Paccius Africanus – I hardly need to point out that you know him, for he has been so constantly on his feet today that his boot-mender must be expecting plenty of work –

'Objection!' intervened Marponius wittily. 'The private expectations of the defender's boot-mender have no obvious connection with the case. Unless you are proposing to call the cobbler as a witness –'
'I withdraw the comment, your honour.'
'Well, no need to go that far, Falco.' I could see my friend Petronius chortling as Marponius indulged himself. 'We like a good joke in the murders court – though I have heard you do better.'
'Thank you, your honour. I shall try to improve the quality of my humour.'
'I am obliged to you. Continue!'

Let me sketch something of this man, Paccius Africanus. He too is of very great eminence. He has served the state through all the ranks of the *cursus honorum* and I note, with some amusement, that when he was a quaestor he presented games dedicated to Honour and Virtue! Perhaps Honour and Virtue have been better served.

He too had been a consul, the year after Silius Italicus. Now when the senators all swore their oaths, Paccius was accused of perjury. Everyone knew he had brought about the deaths of the Scribonius brothers. Paccius had pointed them out to Nero as famous for their wealth and therefore ripe for destruction; at the behest of Nero's obnoxious freedman Helius, the brothers were tried and condemned for conspiracy. Perhaps there really had been a conspiracy. If so, which of us today would think that a conspiracy against the infamous Nero was wrong? Paccius and his colleagues would incur our hatred just as much for revealing it, if the plot were genuine. What is certain is that the Scribonii died. Nero grabbed their wealth. Paccius Africanus presumably received his own reward.

When he was called to account in the Senate, Paccius could only fall silent, cowed, daring neither to confess nor to admit his actions. It is a measure of the times that one of his most persistent and damaging hecklers in the Senate that day was also an informer, Vibius Crispus – on whom Paccius then roundly turned, pointing out that Vibius had been an accomplice in the very same case, prosecuting the man who was supposed to have hired out his house for the purposes of the alleged conspiracy. Those who had made a living from targeting victims were now targeting each other. What a terrible picture it makes.

In the event, Paccius Africanus was convicted of perjury. He was then forcibly ejected from the Curia. Yet he has never been stripped of his senatorial rank. Now he endeavours to rehabilitate himself by quiet work in a special court. Perhaps you have noticed how at home he seems to be here in the Basilica Julia; that is because it is his frequent workplace. Paccius is an expert in cases which involve inheritance trusts. He operates in the trusts court which normally meets in this very hall, the court relating to fideicommissum. And that, we shall see, is not just relevant but peculiarly significant.

Paccius was on his feet again. He had learned: 'Your honour, we are hearing a lengthy speech of great importance. Clearly it will continue for some time yet. May I request a short adjournment?'

Big mistake. Marponius remembered that his rabbit pie yesterday had caused a pain in his gut. Today, he was giving Xero's pie shop a miss.

'I am perfectly comfortable. It seems a shame to interrupt such an interesting oration. I would hate to disturb the flow. How about you, Falco?'

'If your honour allows me to continue, I shall be content to do so.'

Gentlemen, I am about to address why the connection with Paccius Africanus affects the accused. I shall speak for no more than half an hour.

When Silius Italicus charged Rubirius Metellus with corruption, Paccius Africanus stepped in to defend Metellus. You may perhaps suppose that it was the first time Paccius had any influence on the family. Not so. Rubirius Metellus had already made his will. He had written and deposited it two years before the corruption charges. Paccius Africanus was the expert who drafted it. That was the famous, very brutal testament in which Metellus disinherited his only son and his wife, leaving them no more than tiny allowances. The bulk of his estate was left, through that type of trust which we call a *fideicommissum*, to his daughter-in-law, Saffia Donata, of whom my colleague spoke to you previously. Not being allowed to inherit, she was to receive her fortune as a gift from the appointed heir. Now listen to this, please: the appointed heir was Paccius Africanus.

At this point the jury could no longer contain themselves: a gasp ran around the Basilica.

I am not an expert in such matters, so I can only speculate on the reasons for this arrangement. You, like me, may very well think it significant that someone who was a trusts expert, who worked in the trusts court on a daily basis, should advise Metellus to use this device – and to nominate himself as its instrument. When I first saw the provision, I can tell you my thought was that informers have a bad reputation for chasing legacies and that this was an example. I believed Paccius Africanus must have set this up so he would in some way obtain all the money himself. Of course I was wrong about that. The holder of a legacy which is governed by a trust will have promised to pass over the money to the intended recipient – and a person of honour will always do so. Once Metellus died, Paccius would obtain the Metellus wealth, but give it to Saffia Donata. Paccius, as the famous saying goes, is an honourable man. I believe it, gentlemen, despite what I have told you about his stricken silence when asked to swear the oath denying harm to others.

I can see two curiosities, as I will call them, arising from the very particular conditions in our case. I apologise to Paccius for mentioning them; no doubt when he comes to make his speech for the defence he will explain. He is an expert in this field and will understand everything.

To me, however, it looks rather odd that two years after he advised Metellus on this will – with its strange provisions – it was Paccius Africanus who, in the aftermath of the corruption case, told Metellus that he should commit suicide. Suicide had the specific aim of safeguarding the family wealth – wealth which in form at least had been bequeathed to Paccius. This result was no doubt a sad quirk of Fate, one which cannot possibly have been what Paccius originally intended; he was an ex-consul and pillar of Roman life (even though, as I have told you, he had once been forcibly removed from the Senate for perjury). To have planned something devious regarding the will, he would have had to know, at the time it was written, that corruption charges were to be laid by his colleague Silius Italicus in two years' time. It was surely impossible for him to have known that. For one thing, everybody reckons that Paccius and Silius have a feud.

I must say if this is right, in my experience it is a rather civilised feud. I have seen them in the Porticus of Gaius and Lucius taking morning refreshments at a pavement bar like long-term friends and colleagues. I suspect they dine together formally, which you would expect in two men of distinction, fellow ex-consuls from adjacent years, who have so many elements in common from their past. After the informing oath, they have both been accepted back as members of the Senate – even the evicted Paccius is now restored as a member – and both must be waiting impatiently to see what further honours will be bestowed upon them. They have too much in common to ignore each other. You, gentlemen, have seen them sitting close together in this court, even though Silius plays no part in our trial. You have seen them talking together during adjournments and even exchanging notes during the speeches. We can all say, these men are close. But that does not entitle us to believe they were part of some carefully planned, drawn-out conspiracy to plunder the Metelli, its plot put together at wine bars in a porticus over several years.

Let me abandon that byway. I apologise for ever beginning it. Paccius had the unpleasant duty – which is how I am sure he must have seen it – of advising his convicted client that the only honourable course was suicide. Paccius was in a very difficult position, one with which we should sympathise. He was about to benefit greatly from the will – even if it was intended that his benefit should be brief. To bring about the premature death of Metellus could look rather bad. I must confess I am a coward. If I had been in his position, I would have been afraid that advising suicide might look so biased it would damage me. I congratulate Paccius on having the bravery to do it.

There is another interesting point on which I hope Paccius will soon give us clarification: what happens now? He is a trusts expert, so he is bound to know. The problem is this: Saffia Donata has died. She died in childbirth, which for a young married woman is always a tragic possibility. A fate, you may think, that could have been foreseen as possible when Paccius wrote the will. You may indeed feel that a good trusts adviser would have mentioned it to Metellus and asked him to write in alternative provisions; however, that was not done. So now, the will of Metellus has yet to be executed. Saffia can no longer receive her money. Paccius Africanus is the appointed heir. Paccius will have the bequest, with nobody to pass it on to. This was clearly not the intention of Rubirius Metellus when he wrote that will – under the guidance of Paccius, an inheritance expert. It seems to me, Paccius can now keep everything. I hope you will eventually explain to us, Paccius, whether I am right or wrong?

Gentlemen of the jury, I am sure you will be seeing plenty of this man, when he is given the floor to defend the accused. He was close to her husband, and he has remained indispensable to members of the family. When Rubiria Juliana, the elder daughter, was accused by Silius Italicus of killing her father, it was Paccius who defended – which I must say, he did with extraordinary skill. You may have heard that he actually persuaded the apothecary who was supposed to have supplied the poison to take one of his own pills in open court, in order to demonstrate his claim that they were harmless. I shall not be asking anyone to swallow the hemlock which we believe did finally kill Metellus. It was bought by a man called Bratta; he is an intermediary who works with Paccius. At least, that Bratta bought the poison is what I believe, on the evidence of a reliable witness who sold him the hemlock, though Bratta has suddenly disappeared from Rome, so we cannot ask him.

Let me sum up: Tomorrow my colleague Honorius will return to the details of the killing. He will talk about the poison and its terrible effects; he will discuss who suggested it to Calpurnia, and who then bought it for her to use. Poisoning her husband was her idea, she administered the fatal dose, and she covered up the murder. But we know she had consulted the family adviser, Paccius Africanus, about whether her husband ought to live or to die. Awkwardly, she was asking him, the appointed heir, to advise on whether the time had come for him to enjoy his bequest. He told her that Rubirius Metellus should die. He then supplied the man who bought the poison that she used.

When Paccius Africanus begins to defend Calpurnia Cara – which undoubtedly he will do with great skill – I hope that what I have said today will stay in your memory and help you, gentlemen, to view his fine words in their proper context.

XLIII

I WAS FEELING good. I should have known better.

There was a noisy breaking up of the court, with much chatter among the jury members. This was better than we could ever have hoped. They were not only taking an interest, they were enjoying themselves. Marponius, backside prominent, strutted off in procession; he afforded me a gracious head gesture. If I had impressed him, we were home. Forget any belief in the impartiality of juries. No judge allows wishy-washy freethinking in his court. He makes sure the benchers know exactly how to vote. What would be the point of a presiding judge, if he just read out the verdict when the voting urns were emptied and the count taken?

Marponius might be a jumped-up new man scrabbling shamelessly for recognition, but from where I stood he had one advantage. He and I were both Aventine boys. He had made his way with the encyclopaedia cribs, where mine was through a different route – but we both grew up in the shadow of the Temple of Ceres, we both played in the gutters under the Aqua Marcia, we had the same mud on our boots and we recognised one another for lowborn tykes with equal disadvantages and the same points to prove. If the senatorials tried to be too clever, Marponius would side with me. If the fancy troupe got up my nose, I might even start flattering Marponius. I was despised as a low-grade informer, but he too was despised – as a self-made interloper.

I had gone into this with huge anxiety. Now I cheered up. By the end of that day we had made serious progress. Paccius and his client hurried off, a little too fast to impress anyone. Calpurnia looked grim. She must think her choice of defender had damned her. Silius was still standing about, but after my insinuations of collaboration, he had to distance himself from Paccius.

I joined Honorius and Aelianus. Holding our elation in check in public, we gathered up our scrolls and styluses.

An usher approached me. 'Didius Falco? There is a man waiting to speak to you, outside the court.' I decided to take no notice. I was exhausted. But anyone who wanted me would soon see me emerge from the Basilica. For all the observers, it was important that Honorius, Aelianus and I stuck in a tight group, smiling together and looking confident. Keeping up an air of suave good cheer, we all walked briskly through the colonnades to the exterior.

The Basilica Julia has several steps leading down from it, steeper at one end, then petering away to cater for a rise in the Forum level nearer to the Capitol. Most of the jury members were still milling about on the long steps, where as if by chance they formed an inquisitive audience. I noticed Silius Italicus very near, looking watchful. Not far away lurked Anacrites. I could even see Helena Justina, standing down at street level; she waved to me, then I saw her falter. Her father was not there; we had agreed he would sit in the upper gallery while I spoke, then he and I would not be seen together.

By magic, as I appeared through the colonnade, everyone parted. A man I had never seen before had planted himself a few levels below, waiting for me. We had the whole Forum stretched out around us. Behind me Honorius muttered abruptly, *'Shit, Falco!'* He stopped himself. Aelianus breathed in sharply. Like me, he cannot have known what was happening, but we all sensed trouble.

I stepped down once, on my own.

The man who stood in my way was a stranger. Thin, tall, long-faced, drably clad, neutral in expression, he looked insignificant, yet everything about him implied that his business with me was dramatic. He had official sanction. He was sure of himself. If he had pulled a knife and run at me, I would not have been surprised. But his intention was more formal. He was a messenger, and for me the message was deadly.

'Didius Falco!' Some helpful swine had told him which sweaty toga was me. 'I summon you to appear before the praetor to answer serious charges of abuse of office!'

Well that was fine. I did not hold any offices.

Yes, I did.

'What charges, you upstart?'

'Impiety.'

Well, that was a word. The sightseers gasped.

'Accused by whom – of what impiety?'

'Accused by me – of neglecting your duties as Procurator of Juno's Sacred Geese.'

O Juno!

O Jupiter and Minerva too, frankly. I would need the complete Olympian triad to get me out of this.

Honorius stepped to my left side, playing the ventriloquist: 'That's Procreus. He is Silius' regular informer. We had to expect something.' It was the low, admiring murmur of a man who had worked with Silius and seen what he could do. *'The bastards!'* he whispered. 'I never thought of this . . .'

Aelianus rather unexpectedly was on my right, gripping my elbow supportively. His solid response was a new treat.

We walked down the steps, smiling.

'I am at the praetor's disposal,' I told Procreus pleasantly. I refrained from punching his crossed front teeth through the back of his thin neck. My companions were grasping my arms too hard for me to take a swing at him.

We did not stop. Honorius and Aelianus walked me to my house, propping me up like a pair of bossy caryatids. It felt as if everyone in the street stared at us. Helena Justina followed us, silent and anxious. Only when I was safely indoors did I drop the fixed smile and start swearing.

Helena was white. 'Given that you have just had a charge of impiety slapped on you, Marcus, bad language is not a smart reaction.'

'Start thinking!' Aelianus instructed me. He was flushed with excitement, trying not to get hysterical. He had been an army tribune. They had taught him logical responses to setbacks. If regrouping in a square and doubling our guard would have helped, Aulus would have organised it. He assessed my situation perfectly: 'When exactly was the last time you straightened any feathers on those bloody geese? And, Marcus, it had better be recent – or you are finished!'

XLIV

MPIETY? I was innocent. My views on the gods might not be flattering, but I kept those views to myself.

My post as Procurator was ludicrous, but I carried out my duties at the temple, more or less. The job showed the world that the Emperor had recognised me. And besides, it carried a salary.

No one could spot any fiddles. I was a market gardener's grandson. Country matters were in my blood. The Sacred Geese and the Augurs' Sacred Chickens were safe in my hands. If, after tending them, I carried home stolen eggs, I knew how to stuff them in my tunic invisibly.

But there was a problem. Last year, I could not deny it, there had been a long period – over six months – when I did not oversee the geese at all. I was in Britain. I was working for the Emperor. I had a genuine excuse – but one I could not use in open court. The whole point of the tasks I had carried out in Britain was that Vespasian wanted them kept secret.

I could hardly summon the Emperor to vouch for me. One alternative existed: Anacrites. If he swore I was away on imperial business, nobody would need to know why. Even the praetor would shrink from querying the Chief Spy. But if Anacrites was my only solution, I would rather be condemned.

Helena tried to calm me down. 'Procreus, and his manipulator Silius, know perfectly well you are innocent. Making the charge is a ploy. You dare not ignore an accusation of impiety, let alone in a position that was your personal gift from the Emperor.'

'Too right. Tomorrow I shall be pacing the corridors, waiting for an appointment with the praetor. Something tells me he will be in no hurry to oblige me. I know just how they will fix it. Procreus won't show; without him to state his evidence, I'll be stuck in limbo.'

'Well, Marcus, if he really never shows, there is no charge . . . You must convince the praetor there is no case to answer – and demand a retraction.'

'I won't get that! But you understand, my darling. I have to put this right before I can show my face in court again. We cannot have Paccius Africanus helpfully pointing out to the jury that one of Calpurnia's accusers has been denounced for offending the gods.'

Today was wasted. I had just made the best speech of my life – and instantly the professionals had wiped me off the board.

'It was a good speech,' agreed Helena approvingly. 'I was proud of you, Marcus.'

She gave me a moment to bask in her sweet praise. She held me and kissed me. I knew what she was doing, but I melted.

Then, having soothed me, Helena whipped out a calendar and a clean note tablet, so she could work out my past visits to the Temple of Juno in order to rebut Procreus' charge.

XLV

'YOU MAY not want to hear this, Falco.'

'I'm low, lad. You can't make it worse.'

Petronius Longus was one of a long stream of visitors. Most were excited relatives, thrilled that I was in real trouble, trouble their neighbours had heard about. They had been barred by Helena. Petro was allowed in, though only because he said he had something to tell me about the Metellus case. He at least was not thrilled. He thought I was an idiot. Tangling with ex-consuls headed his list of untouchable social stupidities.

'Paccius was bound to turn on you.'

'Actually, my accuser works with Silius.'

'– who works with Paccius! By the way, Falco, do you know you have people watching this place?'

He was right. I took a squint through a crack in the shutters. A couple of shady characters in bum-starver cloaks and woollen caps were lurking on the Embankment outside. It was too cold for them to be fishing in the Tiber. Incompetent burglars who were casing a house too openly? Clerks who wrote the *Daily Gazette* scandal page? Sidekicks of Silius, hoping to witness me march up to the Capitol and threaten the man who herded the geese? No chance. Earlier, I did consider telling the gabby gooseboy just how he had landed me in it – but I had been dissuaded by my level-headed wife.

'They are pretty obvious.'

'Want me to move them on?'

'No. Their masters will just send others.' Petronius did not ask me, what masters.

Helena came in to join us. I glanced at Petro, and we moved away from the window. Helena glanced at us suspiciously.

'Did you hear Marcus make his speech?'

Petronius sprawled on a couch, stretching his long limbs. Helena and he looked at one another, then at me, then they both beamed. 'You and your mouth!' he commented, perhaps fondly.

Helena's smile faded slightly. 'It all needed to be said, Lucius.'

'Well,' said Petro, drawling quietly, 'our boy made a big impression.'

I joined him on the couch. 'You feel I should not have done it?'

My best friend gazed at me. 'You broke some rules today. I worry for you.' That was unlike him.

'If he wants to move among the big bad bastards,' Helena murmured, 'I would rather see him break their rules and offend them, than become what they are.'

'Agreed. Nothing he said was safe – but nothing he said was wrong either.'

For some time then we all sat musing.

'So,' Helena asked Petro eventually, 'Lucius, what is your news that affects the court case?' As if by chance, she went and straightened a window shutter, quickly glancing out to see what we had been looking at earlier.

Petronius massaged his scalp with both hands, then squeezed his fingers along his neck wearily. He watched Helena checking up on us. She spotted the observers. She shot me a glance of annoyance, but then came back and sat with us.

'Falco, I don't know if this is good or bad, but you need to know about it.'

I nudged him. 'Cough up.'

'The lads in the Second Cohort have been following the news. It finally struck them that Metellus senior died in his house and the death may be unnatural. So somebody ought to have tortured the slaves.'

He was right: I did not know whether I was happy or not.

Whenever a free citizen – well, one of a rank the authorities admire – is murdered at home, the legal assumption is that his slaves may have done it. They are all automatically tortured, to find out. This is good in one way, because their evidence is then acceptable in court; slaves can only be court witnesses if they are speaking under torture. On the other hand, evidence extracted under torture has a large flaw: it is quite unreliable. 'So nobody thought of it originally, because Calpurnia said the death was suicide and everyone believed her?'

'Nobody ever called the vigiles in. I can get you a sight of the report,' Petro offered. Then he pulled a prim face. 'Of course, the Second are under their own pressure. I can't promise to show it to you before it reaches that bastard Paccius.'

'Well, thanks for trying.'

'What are friends for?'

I could hear small thundering feet. One of my children was heading my way. Nux was barking. Any moment now, the great orator full of lofty thoughts would have to crawl around the floor making a mess of the rag rugs.

'Have the Second actually started?' I enquired quickly.

Petro winced, as Julia burst in on us and flew at me. 'Believe so.'

'Anything come out of it?' I coughed, from a prone position at floor level, with my daughter bouncing on my chest. I was thinking of putting her forward to the army as a new type of artillery. The dog was trying to kill my boot, even though I was wearing it. Helena pretended to think I liked it, and let them both carry on with their attack.

'The usual.' This would be confidential, but Petro trusted me. 'Most swear they knew nothing about anything. One croaked that we should "Ask Perseus".'

'Door porter. I already know he's no good.'

'Missing. The Second are hunting him. No luck so far.'

'He's a sassy wretch – and leaning on the family –' It sounded as though the Second Cohort were working along lines I liked. Besides, my old friend was keeping an eye on them. 'They could try for him in Lanuvium.'

'Yes, they've gone there looking.' *Io!* Things were moving fast. Suddenly it seemed too fast.

I grabbed Julia, holding her off me while she squealed and thrashed in ecstasy. I kicked feebly, failing to shake off Nux from my leg. 'Who was the slave who pointed at Perseus?'

'Some kitchen greaseball.'

'Probably the doodle who gets to stand in when Perseus fancies a rest . . . I assume they are pressing him for more?'

'We know our job!' Petro grinned. His face grew more serious. 'Well, the Second seem to enjoy it too much. I'm sure they were careful – but the slave who talked is currently out of it.'

'Crazed?'

'Raving.'

'Oh really, Petronius!' Helena hated rough stuff. 'Marcus knows about Perseus – there was no need to damage some innocent!'

I held Julia still, and hauled myself upright. 'Can you ask them to be gentler if they ever tackle Perseus?'

Petro nodded, wordlessly.

'Try the steward,' I suggested, after a moment's thought. 'I reckon he's ripe – and he would have ordered lunch that day.'

I liked the steward, but he had had his chance. He could have talked to me. Now he would have to take his chance with the heavy-handed Second Cohort.

XLVI

NEXT DAY, I was still preparing for my ordeal with the praetor when Honorius turned up. He had done some smart work with Marponius, persuading him to call a full adjournment for today.

So Marponius was on our side. All the more reason to press on, and not to be held up by distractions like imagined impiety. Marponius might be with us now – but if we left him stewing too long, somebody would get to him. I had always distrusted Paccius and Silius, but now I had seen just how they worked. Marponius thought himself incorruptible. He wouldn't last five minutes.

Honorius loved my news about the Second examining slaves.

'This is excellent, Falco. Juries love a case where the slaves have been tortured. Some prosecutors deliberately try to drag in a treason charge so they can do it.' He looked thoughtful. 'Actually, treason is an aspect we could introduce. Am I right that after the original corruption case, the Metelli made a clemency appeal to the Emperor?'

I nodded. 'Where's the treason in that?'

'Vespasian refused them?'

'Yes.'

'And so they were angry . . . any chance you can find me a letter they wrote afterwards.'

'What letter?' Nobody had mentioned letters.

'Any letter. It needs suspicious marks alongside the Emperor's name. Well, no. It needs to be in a suspect's own hand, that's all. We can blur in some suspicious marks ourselves; I have a friend who can match ink –'

I laughed. 'That's fraud, you idiot!'

'Evidence of suspicious conversations would be even better.'

'Honorius, compose yourself please. We are not that desperate.'

'Well how about a suspicious trip somewhere . . . ?' He tailed off. Cheery thoughts frolicked behind those handsome eyes. 'Did we ever find out why Birdy went off to Lanuvium?'

'Seeing the land agent, we think. Justinus is supposed to bring back details.' That reminded me: where was Camillus Justinus? His absence was becoming suspicious too. I hoped he had not run into some voluptuous Lanuvium barmaid.

'Well anyway,' Honorius stopped speculating so wildly. 'Interrogating the slaves is good. Even if they never say anything.'

Helena was watching me, so I tackled Honorius: 'Isn't that a waste of effort – not to mention cruelty?'

Honorius patted my arm. He had a very cold hand. 'Falco, the point is to have it *known* that they were tortured.'

'So we need not really cause them pain?'

Honorius had sensed our antagonism. He replied rather carefully: 'A few screams never come amiss. Rumours of the screaming soon reach the jury.'

All this time, Helena had been listening with a set expression. She was patiently holding my toga across her outstretched arms, ready to deposit the garment around me. The glint in her expression needed no interpretation. Her look was so hostile that a bronze lamp (a winged bootee, a tasteless Saturnalia gift I had not yet dumped) was shivering against its stand. Finally my tight-lipped female dresser had to speak: 'Honorius, would it not be better to stop relying on supposition and cheap legal tricks – and gather a solid trail of evidence?'

Honorius looked startled. Helena glared at him. He decided he had things to do elsewhere.

'Oh by the way, Falco – this will tickle you. My old senior seems impressed by us . . . Silius came to see me last night.' He blushed, already regretting this confession. 'I can't imagine how he found me; I was at my ex-wife's house –'

'What,' I demanded curtly of the reminiscing lover, 'did Silius want?'

'Oh. . . He tried to buy me off, that's all.'

I kept my temper. 'What did he offer?'

'My old position back.'

'You walked out, remember.'

'And a large cash welcome. . . Don't worry,' Honorius assured me quietly. He met my eye, looking confident. 'It didn't work.'

I let him go.

Growling to herself, Helena draped me in my toga for the praetor. With care, she positioned the first end on my left shoulder, brought the bulk around me from behind, tucked in the front, placed the free end back over my shoulder, tidied the pleats neatly and checked that my hem lengths were not ludicrous. She kissed me, very gently. Only then did she comment.

'Next time, Silius will offer him more.'

Worse was awaiting me downstairs in my reception hall. The one person who would unfairly believe Procreus' impiety charge accosted me: 'Well, you look awkward! Is that your brother's toga? He knew how to wear it.' If Paccius and Silius were trying to demoralise me, they were amateurs.

'Hello, Mother.'

'Will my troubles never end? – Oh, the shame of it. Now I hear that somehow I produced a blasphemer!'

'Ma, just tell your nosy friends: I have been incorrectly called a slacker by troublemaking slanderers.' I waved the tablet with the carefully concocted record of my movements. 'Your boy is innocent.'

'We'll see!'

Once again I kept my temper valiantly. 'Yes, we shall.'

I could not attend on the praetor while wound up with irritation. Besides, when I opened the door, I found rainstorms sweeping down the street. Helena made me wait while her litter was fetched to keep my precious toga dry. I stood on the step, feeling bitter, lashed by the weather anyway. Nux came and joined me, barking at the wind. 'Stupid dog!' I picked her up to carry her in. Wet dog hairs adhered to my formal attire in unattractive clumps.

Helena tried to distract Ma. She was grieving that my father would love this disaster. She pretended he would say it was her fault. Helena suggested that they should blame Pa. That thought improved my mother's mood.

Meanwhile we had another visitor: Ursulina Prisca had come again to haunt us, hoping to bother Justinus. In his absence, her feelers had twitched out that Honorius was legal and she had detained him with the long story of her disputed inheritance. The short man's handsome face creased with apprehension as he tried to fend her off. Helena moved in smoothly. She retrieved the desperate Honorius, hooking a capable hand under his elbow and drawing him to safety.

'Honorius, Silius will not give up. He will increase his offer – and next time I dare say you will take it.'

'I told you –'

'I know.' Helena's smile was silken. 'But you are a young idealist. You want to do good work, prosecuting bad people. The old fox will persuade you that work of such a high standard can only be found

234

with him. Just remember what he really does – and why he is asking you.'

Honorius may have hoped to hitch a lift with me, but Helena steered him straight outside and pushed him off into the storm by himself.

Now she turned her attention to Ursulina Prisca. 'I am so glad to see you. I wanted to ask something. You were a midwife, weren't you?'

'Yes, she was!' cried Ma.

'I am trying to find a wet-nurse –'

'Not for our little Sosia!' Ma protested loudly. Even Ursulina sucked in breath. She must know we had a baby. She had been here enough times; she must have heard Sosia Favonia yelling.

'No, no; I'm still nursing her myself. I wouldn't dream –' Helena realised that it sounded as if she wanted to abandon breast-feeding. (I knew she did, which added to her guilt.) The disapproval of two witchy crones fastened on her. To mention baby teeth and weaning on to porridge would just sound like special pleading. Helena battled on: 'Marcus needs to interview a wet-nurse in connection with our case –' It was news to me, but I never argued with her hunches. 'If I go, she may speak more freely . . .'

The concept of fooling some other woman pleased both Ma and our litigious client, Ursulina. Sisterhood was not their style. They were eager to help.

'Do you know Euboule's daughter?' Helena asked as they perked up. 'I believe her name is Zeuko.'

Ursulina reeled back. She acted out horror like a creaking tragedian at the least popular day of some tired and dusty festival. 'Far be it from me to insult people –'

'Oh go on!' urged my mother, wickedly.

'These are bad women.'

'What's wrong with Zeuko?' frowned Helena. 'Is she dirty? Lazy? Does she drink?'

'Oh she's competent, some would say.'

'She has had high-ranking customers.'

'They are fools. Her mother's a legend and I wouldn't let Zeuko foster a dead rat.' Ursulina Prisca shuddered dramatically. 'I can find her. But don't take your own along – you might never get the little darling back.'

Helena asked Ma to look after the baby and Julia – but Ma, playing against type, quickly claimed Albia could do that. 'If you're going to see the wet-nurse, I'll come too.'

No wonder I was an informer. Nosiness was in my blood.

The litter was brought. I was borne away on my hopeless errand. By now, the praetor would have a long queue of supplicants. And there were still dog hairs on my toga.

XLVII

Time: afternoon.
Place: patrol house, Aventine.
Subject: conversation between L. Petronius Longus, Fourth Cohort of
    Vigiles, and M. Didius Falco, informer.
Mood: depressed.

'How was your morning?'
    'Dire.'
    'Procreus turn up?'
    'No.'
    'Praetor see you?'
    'No.'
    'Charges dropped?'
    'No.'
    'Back again tomorrow?'
    'Damn well have to. Any good news for me?'
    'Sorry; no.'
    'The Second made any progress?'
    'No. Perseus is not found yet, and your steward's a no-go. He's a
freedman. They can't touch him. They threatened him – but then he
threatened them with appeal to the Emperor.'
    'He could talk voluntarily.'
    'He says no: he's too loyal.'
    'Who's he loyal to?'
    'He's too loyal to say.'
    'Stuff him then. Stuff everything.'
    'That's right. Take the tolerant view!'
    'I'm off home.'
    'Best thing, lad.'
    'Thanks anyway.'
    'That's all right. What are friends for?'

XLVIII

Time: evening.

Place: a town house full of wet cloaks, sodden shoes drying on the stairs, below the Aventine.

Subject: conversation between M. Didius Falco, informer, and Helena Justina, confidante.

Mood: stubborn.

'Where are you?'

  'Here.'

  'Where's here?'

  'In this room.'

  'Which room? I'm not a fortune-teller. Oh there you are.'

  'Yes I told you I'm here. Hello, Marcus.'

  'Hello, awkward. Ask about my day.'

  'Looking at you, I'd rather not.'

  'Right. How was yours?'

  'Curious.'

  'Any use?'

  'Possibly.'

  'Help me out; I'm tired.'

  'Sit, and I'll pull your boots off. . . Well, I saw Euboule – a fright, eyes sliding off in all directions guiltily. I couldn't see why Ursulina hates them so much, but your mother thought the whole set-up was sinister. They live well. There's a crèche of several infants. They've been doing the job for years. Euboule was a wet-nurse for Calpurnia, her daughter for Saffia. Trusted retainers, it seems.'

  'That so? Do they have the Negrinus new baby?'

  'No. Juliana and Carina did seem set against them – that's why I was curious. But, Marcus: I did see one child I recognised. He was very quiet, but playing happily. He seemed quite at home. Little Lucius.'

  'Lutea told me Lucius had gone to his "foster mother" . . . So she's the wet-nurse? That's odd.'

'Why, Marcus?'

'Saffia made out Calpurnia Cara insisted she use a nurse to feed the Negrinus daughter. Saffia pretended to hate it. Yet she had previously farmed out Lucius voluntarily to Zeuko? Why would Saffia lie?'

'Marcus, maybe you'll want your boots back on, if I tell you about Zeuko —'

'Zeuko wasn't there today?'

'No. She had rushed off in hysterics because of her lover.'

'Zeuko's having a fling?'

'I'd guess, one of several. But this one matters — to us, that is. Somebody saw this man being dragged into the local vigiles' patrol house this morning.'

'I think I've guessed.'

'I'm sure you have, Marcus. Euboule and her daughter live in the Fifth Region. The local vigiles are the Second Cohort. And Zeuko's lover is called Perseus.'

XLIX

Time: evening.
Place: patrol house, Second Cohort of Vigiles, Fifth Region.
Subject: conversation between an unknown squad member and M.
   Didius Falco, informer. In the presence of Q. Camillus Justinus,
   informer's associate.
Mood: angry.

'Be reasonable. We need to know what the door porter says.'
   'He's unavailable.'
   'Is he still getting the treatment?'
   'I can't comment.'
   'Can I speak to your persuasion officer?'
   'He's busy.'
   'Still in session?'
   'We never reveal that.'
   'You just invented that edict! Don't you think you owe us co-
operation? I've heard all about how you got hold of this slave. If it
wasn't for Justinus bringing him back to Rome, you'd have had to flog
all the way to Lanuvium. We've saved you a long trip and a longer
runaround – it took Justinus a three-day effort to root out the porter
from where he was hiding up.'
   'Get lost, Falco.'
   'Listen –'
   'No, you listen. Either leave this station-house right now – or you'll
be flung into a cell.'

L

Time: evening.
Place: patrol house, Fourth Cohort of Vigiles, Aventine.
Subject: conversation between L. Petronius Longus and M. Didius
    Falco, in the presence of Q. Camillus Justinus.
Mood: tense.

'I've got the story for you.'

'Something happened. That's obvious.'

'Look, Falco –'

'You're sounding defensive.'

'I'm damn well not.'

'Well, damn well get on with it.'

'Perseus refused to tell them anything. And he's no longer available.'

'Translate that, Petro. What pretty vigiles excuse is "no longer available"?'

'He's dead.'

'They *killed* him?'

'It's not their fault.'

'Oh please!'

'The courts expect a high standard of battery, if it's to count as torture legally.'

'Oh I'd really call this a "high standard"!'

'They are not all as skilled as Sergius –'

'Oh Quintus, don't you like the comparison? Sergius is the penalty man in this cohort. Here, torture is no more dangerous than a sheep-shearing picnic in the Apennines. Here they can squeeze your goolies off so delicately you stay alive and keep on making helpful statements for absolutely *weeks*.'

'Spare me your sarcasm. The Second slipped up, Falco. Sometimes it's a risk.'

'Some risk. These incompetents have removed the one witness who might have told us the truth.'

LI

I WAS BITTERLY angry. But in fact there were still other possible witnesses.

I badly wanted to sort this. The one thing that had always bothered me about accusing Calpurnia was that her family had a secret, one I still did not know. I was working blind. And that meant I could be caught out by some angle I had failed to anticipate. I was right to be wary: by the end of that evening I would know it too.

I was keen to pressurise Zeuko. Anything Perseus had known was likely to have been passed on by him to her – unless he had learned it from Zeuko in the first place. Unfortunately, since the wet-nurse had stupidly run to the Second's patrol house when she heard Perseus was in custody, the Second were now holding Zeuko herself as a suspected accomplice of the dead slave. (They had had no charge against Perseus – except that he had let himself be killed under torture, clearly a suspicious act.) To mollify me, Petro volunteered to try to inveigle himself in to examine Zeuko, but he warned me the Second were jumpy.

'I'm doing you a big favour, Falco –'

'Ah well,' I sneered, throwing his own words back to him. *'What are friends for?'*

That left the Metellus steward. As the Second could not touch him because he was a free man, they had released him and he had gone home. Although it was late, I returned to the Fifth Region to attempt an interview. I went alone. Justinus had pressing reasons to unload his travel packs at the senator's house; he needed to make his peace with his wife over absconding to Lanuvium. He was upset about losing Perseus too. He would tell me the full story of his journey tomorrow.

I found the Metellus spread in darkness, apparently deserted. Maybe Calpurnia had gone into retreat. Perhaps one of her daughters had offered her hospitality. The trial was bound to be distressing her. And she had no slaves, because they were all being processed by the vigiles.

Even the steward had failed to gain entry to the house. He possessed no latch-lifter or key; well, there had always been a porter to let people in. I found him drinking himself senseless at the nasty bar opposite. I told him about Perseus, hoping shock would make him open up. No use. He was still singing the old song: he knew that a secret shadowed the Metellus family, but had no idea what. Perseus had discovered it, but never revealed his blackmail material. Perseus had boasted that the family were at his mercy – and he intended to keep it that way.

The door porter had not been entirely immune, however. He was a slave still. His age was under thirty, so in law he could not be manumitted. And because he was a slave, when he finally went too far, Calpurnia had lost her temper and dispatched him to Lanuvium to be kept under control by the trusted freedman, Julius Alexander.

'So Alexander knows the secret?'

'He must do, but he's one of the family. He won't tell. Anyway,' maundered the steward. 'Alexander is in Lanuvium.'

No he was not. Justinus had persuaded him to come to Rome. I kept that to myself.

I offered to help the steward break in to the house, but he was content to stay in a room above the bar that night. I had the impression he would probably not bother to crawl up the stairs to a sleeping-pallet, but would remain propped up against the counter, pouring in drink like a man who had just discovered wine. He had lost all his elegance. He was as dishevelled and inarticulate as any street dosser who was down on his luck. It looked as if this steward was heading for a grim future.

Once more I encouraged him to go home. Drunkenly refusing to budge, he repaid me for my thoughtfulness by dropping me right in it.

'You asked me once, Falco – what was the last meal my master ate. I do remember –' He had never forgotten. 'It was cold meats and salad. What we always had. But my master had been sent a present, she said it was to seek his forgiveness . . . Lying little cow.'

Something cold tickled my upper spine. 'What present?'

'Two nice quails in a silver dish. We never had quails. Calpurnia finds little birds creepy. I never buy larks or fig-peckers. . . But my master liked them. He laughed and told me he would never forgive the woman, but he was very fond of game so he told me not to mention the present – then he ate the quails.'

You can feed hemlock to quails, and then eat the quails . . . 'Have you told anyone else about this?'

'Nobody asked me.'

That old nonsense! This steward was either too scared – or he had hoped for some gain for himself.

'So who sent the present? Who are we talking about?'

'Who do you think? Saffia.'

I warned the steward to take life easy, then I left him and went home. I walked slowly. I took the longest route I could think of. I had a lot to think about.

There was no doubt from the way the trial had been going – and the other side's desperate reactions – that we were winning. We could convict Calpurnia Cara successfully. But somebody else had killed Metellus.

For my partners and me, this was disastrous. No way out: we had to look into it. If the steward's claim was substantiated, our charge was untenable. Everything had been for nothing. And before I even dared to break the news to the others, I knew we could not sustain the damage. We had wrongly accused a woman of senatorial rank. She had a top defender on her side. The charge was a dreadful slur on the innocent; the case had been a terrible ordeal for her. Paccius Africanus, whom I had so fiercely humiliated two days ago, would demand compensation – on a grand scale.

Marponius would lose his chance of glory with the case, so he would hate us. Why blame him? We had made the accusation and if we withdrew, we were liable. Damaging a person of status with a fraudulent petition had always been slammed with heavy penalties. Marponius would award our victim whatever Paccius asked.

I dared not even think how high the price would be.

I knew the result, though. Falco and Associates were finished. The two young Camillus boys and Honorius would be named jointly in the penalty award. I could not shield them, even if I wanted to. I had some savings, but no financial capacity to cover their commitment. Nor could we recoup our loss through a petition for murder against Saffia Donata; Saffia was dead. My resources would go nowhere. My future, and the future of my family, had just been wiped out. We were all ruined.

LII

I HAD PLANNED to keep it to myself. Helena winkled it out of me. She seemed less troubled than I was, but then she had never lived too long in abject poverty. Our days in my old apartment up in Fountain Court had passed like an adventure for her. The cramped conditions, leaky roof and unpleasant, violent neighbours had been soon superseded by a larger, quieter set of rooms. Though not much better than our first dreadful nest, for Helena even they had now faded to a memory.

It all came back to me readily. The bugs. The creaking joists, threatening to cave in at any heavy footfall. The dirt. The noise. The theft and battery; the disease and debt. The threats from fellow-lodgers, the smoke from wonky cooking benches, the screaming children. The smell of urine on the stairs – not all of it coming from the vats in Lenia's laundry. Lenia bawling drunkenly. The filthy, filthy-hearted landlord . . .

'If you were just to withdraw, honestly telling Marponius that you made a mistake, Marcus –'

'No. It's no let-out.'

'So you began the case – and you have to finish or become liable?'

'We could keep quiet, of course. Convict Calpurnia, and send her to her death. . . My conscience won't cope with that.'

'Anyway,' murmured my sensible girl, 'somebody else might come forward with evidence. Keeping quiet would be too dangerous.'

I fell asleep shortly afterwards. I was holding Helena, smiling against her hair – smiling at the ridiculous thought that this model of rectitude might have let us cover up the truth if she thought we could get away with it. She had lived with me too long. She was becoming a pragmatist.

Helena herself must have lain awake for much longer. She knew how to keep still, shielding her busy thoughts from me. For her, if we could not hold back the new evidence, then we would damn well fight to minimise the damage. She was planning how. Her first move was to ensure that the steward's tale was true.

By the time I was up, she had started. While it was still dark, she summoned the others, explained the situation, ordered them not to panic, then addressed avenues to be explored. Honorius was due in court again today. He was to warn Marponius that we had a new witness whose testimony we thought it fair to investigate; he would request a short adjournment. We might be allowed a day; longer was unlikely. Meanwhile, Justinus was to take a full, formal statement from the steward. Aelianus was to revisit the funeral director, Tiasus; Helena had looked through the old case-notes and had spotted that originally we were told the Metellus funeral was to have had 'clowns', plural. She told Aelianus to find out who the others were, and ask them for anything they knew about the background enquiries carried out by the murdered Spindex before he was paid off by Verginius Laco.

'Especially, ask who Spindex used as his informer,' she was instructing Aelianus as I came to the breakfast table. Going vague on her, he was assessing me. I had the slow walk of a man facing disaster. Helena kept talking, as she set fresh bread in front of me. 'The vigiles haven't discovered who killed Spindex, or I presume Petronius would have told us, but you can check at the station-house, Aulus, if you have time.'

'Don't tell Petro we've been idiots,' I said.

All three young men stared at me. They were in shock too.

'Petro's not stupid,' said Aelianus bleakly. 'He'll work it out.'

'Just don't think about the penalty,' Helena advised everyone quietly. 'We have to carry on, being scrupulous about double-checking. Just because we say we have a new witness, Paccius won't immediately know we are at his mercy.'

'He will demand to know who the witness is,' Honorius said gloomily.

'Say the query arose out of the vigiles torturing the slaves,' Aelianus suggested – another of the Camillus family who was willing to bend the truth. 'Paccius will waste time following up with the Second Cohort.'

'No, Paccius will scent victory,' Honorius disagreed. I had always suspected lack of funds was a big problem for him; he seemed utterly deflated by our dire situation. He would need watching.

'Forget Paccius!' Helena retaliated crisply. Her eye landed on her younger brother. 'Quintus, you're quiet. I suppose you thought you would be the centre of attention today, with your news from Lanuvium?'

246

He shrugged. When I saw him last night he had been weary, stressed by his encounter with the vigiles and livid that they had killed Perseus. Now he was down, but seemed glad to be here with us. His wife must have greeted him with a lively scene. 'I'll tell you very quickly. I had a hard time getting anything out of the freedman to start with; he sees it as his role to act as guardian over the Metellus family troubles. He refused to admit that Perseus was there, then he did everything he could to prevent me finding the porter. Still, I tracked him down on the sly, roped him up and was bringing him back a prisoner.'

'Didn't Alexander spot you leaving his property?' I asked.

'No, Perseus was on a different farm. Alexander runs a big outfit in his own right – but I found another place locally in which he has a disguised interest. Marcus, I reckon this is where the money from the corruption was salted away.'

'So Julius Alexander may have bought property at Lanuvium anonymously?'

'He did indeed, although he denies it. Perseus told me.'

'But did Perseus confess what the real secret is?'

'No. He only started gossiping about the property to stop me asking other questions – and we were almost back in Rome by then.'

'Just at that point, you ran into the vigiles?'

'Yes. If I had known,' Justinus growled, 'I would have thrown Perseus in a ditch and hidden him. In fact, I might as well have killed the cocky bastard myself and at least enjoyed it. When the Second pulled us over and asked who we were, Perseus piped up and admitted his identity. The vigiles snatched him off me, and tore back to their station-house with me panting after them, unable to get word to you.'

'It's not your fault.'

'We could not have held on to him.' Honorius sounded pompous. 'Stealing a slave is bad enough if you deprive his master of possession – depriving the vigiles would be madness.'

Annoyed at his pedantry, Helena briskly stirred her hot drink. 'Don't forget: we think that Saffia poisoned Metellus. We think we know how she did it too – but we still have no idea why.'

'Impatient to get at her legacy,' Aelianus replied.

'If they were lovers, it could be a love quarrel.' His brother, so used to wrangling with his wife, gloomily put up a counter-suggestion.

'I don't believe they were ever lovers.' Helena looked as if she had a theory. 'I suspect Saffia Donata was just a very efficient blackmailer.' She would not tell us more. She said she did not have time to look into it today; she was going to see her father, to warn him we were all bankrupt. Meanwhile, she had one last instruction, this time for me. I had to visit the midwife Euboule, and her daughter Zeuko too, if the vigiles had released her.

That was a waste of time. Zeuko was still in custody, but if she was as hard-bitten as her mother, I would have obtained little from her.

Once I made my inspection of their house, I agreed with Helena that the children seemed well cared for and treated with kindness; there was no apparent reason why Ursulina Prisca had heaped disparagement on the two women. The house itself was well furnished and warm. A couple of young slave girls were playing with the children, who had a large toy collection. Walls and floors were covered in a collection of Eastern carpets, a highly unexpected luxury. Helena and I had no walls tapestried with Eastern carpets, even though they were attractive, useful as an investment, and difficult for casual thieves to whip away. My father had a few. But carpets were for auctioneers and kings; they were well out of our reach.

Euboule was a boot-faced, belligerent old bag of bones in layers of green and blue, with a heavy antique necklace that looked like real gold. I wondered how she had acquired it. The granulated links lay on a skinny chest. There was so little meat on her it seemed unlikely she had ever been full of milk for other women's babies, but no doubt her daughter was fully endowed now.

She stood up to my questioning like a hardened criminal. If I had not known she was a nurse and foster-mother, I would have thought she kept a chop-house with an upstairs brothel, or one of those back alley bath houses that are famous for perverted masseurs. She seemed ready for me; expecting to be tackled; determined not to give.

Taken with the expensive carpets, I knew what it meant: Euboule and Zeuko were being paid for their silence. Whether the income was current or only in the past, I could not tell. But at some point in their history this pair had been paid a great deal.

My sense of foreboding deepened. I went to my banker for a run-down of my own assets; I was unimpressed. At least when I warned him I was done for, Nothokleptes scarcely blinked; he had heard this so often in my bachelor days. He would learn how serious it was now. A new villa at Neapolis was out, that was for sure.

It was another dreadful day, with thunder in the storms. Lightning flashed around the Forum as I made my way to the Basilica. Honorius must have persuaded Marponius to hold up the trial. Nothing was going on. Tomorrow we would have to come clean, though. I nearly decided to ask for a meeting with Paccius, but held off and went home to find out what the lads had turned up for us.

The Camillus brothers joined us that evening. Honorius was supposed to come too, though he never appeared.

Justinus had done a thorough job with the steward. He had learned that his name was Celadus. Now we had a written transcript of the story about Saffia's quails, plus further details about how Rubirius Metellus had begun feeling ill shortly after he ate them. Celadus had seen Metellus go out into the garden, gasping that he needed air. The steward then confirmed the sequence I had previously worked out: Calpurnia found her husband helpless and dying; she herself fetched a quilt for him; then when he passed away she hid the body. Negrinus was away in Lanuvium. Celadus thought he had gone to explain to Julius Alexander that Metellus had decided not to kill himself. When Negrinus returned to Rome, Calpurnia brought the body into the house and faked the scene of suicide.

'After Calpurnia was accused of the crime – come to that, when her daughter was accused first – why didn't the steward declare what he knew about the quails?'

Justinus pulled a face. 'Greed, Marcus.'

'Greed?'

'He was planning to blackmail Saffia.'

'Dear gods, everyone was at it! That explains why the family never produced this as a rebuttal. They guessed hemlock was to blame – but they had no idea where it came from.'

'If Celadus hadn't started drinking yesterday, he might never have coughed.' Justinus sympathised with the man in some ways. 'He's a freedman, from a family who have lost all their money. He has no expectations, unless he creates them for himself. But Saffia's dead. And then he heard that you had done a stonking job in court, Marcus.'

I laughed bitterly. 'So Celadus thinks his mistress is for the lions – and since silence no longer holds a profit for him, he finds he's loyal enough to save her!'

Still, it was only one man's word. We could behave like true informers: since it spoiled our case, we could hide this. The silver dish on which the quails arrived would have been long ago washed up. Nobody else knew it ever arrived from Saffia. If we chose to press on with the Calpurnia case then discrediting a freedman who had kept quiet for so long would be easy; we could discount Celadus and his evidence. But in this miserable week, I guessed that now we were looking for it, corroboration would be found. The steward's evidence would stand. Anyway, we all had consciences.

Aelianus, meanwhile, had contacted some other funeral comedians who were subcontracted to Tiasus. They could not say what the secretive Spindex had discovered about the Metelli, but they did know the name of the informer – and drinking partner – with whom Spindex had often worked. His source when he needed dirt on senators was called Bratta.

Well, that fitted. That was neat as a nut. At once I sent word to Petronius that Bratta was implicated in the Spindex killing; Petro issued my description and an arrest warrant. Not that I expected a result. The vigiles are ex-slaves, most of whom cannot read. The description would be recited to them, if we were lucky. They would nod wisely. Perhaps some would remember. Generally they have too much to do bashing in the heads of villains they met last night to worry about somebody who might have killed somebody else on a different night six months ago.

To gear them up, we had to prove a link. But Bratta was a professional. He had left no clues. Mind you, even if he had left evidence all over the clown's apartment, and if a witness on the spot had seen him strangling Spindex, Paccius Africanus would get him off.

'Anything else?' I asked Helena. She was our duty officer. I was too depressed to think.

'Only that my father wants to help with your impiety charge. After I talked to him, he went to see someone.'

'He's a gem – but I can't deal with that at present.'

'You can't dodge out of it, Marcus. Just as well Papa is trying to look after you!'

We were due in court on the Calpurnia case next morning. It was unavoidable. I had wanted to debate tactics with Honorius, but he had never showed up. I was about to find out why. Before the morning session started, I made an attempt to nudge things our way. It was doomed, but I had nothing to lose. I took myself for an early stroll at the Basilica Paulli, looking for Paccius and Silius. Ever optimistic, I was hoping to fix up some plea bargaining.

LIII

I FOUND THE two elder statesmen sharing their usual friendly cake and tisane. Honorius was with them. Maybe he too wanted to sort out something helpful for Falco and Associates. Who was I fooling? Our colleague was here to protect his own interests.

Nobody seemed surprised to see me. Silius, that manoeuvring overfed blob, used his foot to hook over a seat from another table. Although not part of our case, he stayed on, looking a misery as usual. I seated myself. Paccius, ever restrained in society, moved their plate of almond fancies slightly; I declined. All their togas were piled in a heap together on another bench. I kept mine folded on my knees. I needed the warmth. It was a cold day and I was in company that chilled me.

Here we sat, among the fine Doric columns of black and red marble in the Porticus of Gaius and Lucius, named for the grandsons of Augustus, lost golden boys whose early deaths symbolised dashed hopes. We occupied a peaceful corner outside the shops, close to one of the staircases that took people up from this gracious porch-like frontage to the richly ornate upper gallery of the Basilica Paulli. This was sophisticated living. Or it should have been. But I was doing business with men who lacked all honour, faith and decency.

I gazed at Honorius. Never had his well-shaved handsome young visage seemed so objectionable. 'I take it we have lost your fine presence from our team, Honorius?'

He knew I meant he had stuffed us.

'I am sorry, Falco.' If he was abashed, his regret was cursory. 'It seems best to go back to Silius.'

The idealist had turned realist and I told him not to apologise. It was Metellus Negrinus who took Honorius on. I had known what he was from the start. Privately, my concern now was what he had told his two manipulating masters. He was bound to have told them *something*; it would be the price of their welcome home to the wanderer.

I turned to Paccius. 'You will have gathered from our approach to the judge yesterday that we have had to reconsider the evidence.'

'You accept that Calpurnia Cara is innocent?'

'No, I think she has a lot to answer for. But we shall withdraw our murder charge.'

'My client will be delighted,' Paccius said mildly. He had no need to gloat and he was too subtle to mention huge damages. His calm air of self-assurance made the prospect all the more frightening.

I pressed on with trying to negotiate. 'Silius, our new evidence means your petition against Negrinus will not hold up. He did not kill his father. If you go for it, we can wipe you out. Be grateful: we are preventing you from embarking on a fruitless case.' Silius laughed. Paccius pretended to be politely absorbed in something else, while Honorius looked embarrassed. 'But you still need to prove formally that Rubirius Metellus did not commit suicide, so you can claim your compensation. We know what happened. I can offer you a bargain –'

'I'm not buying,' said Silius, enjoying himself. 'I know that Metellus was murdered by Saffia.'

Honorius was staring at the ground. Since I arrived, an almond cake crimped with one forlorn bite had lain untouched in front of him. I was right: Silius had bought him. Now I knew how. Paccius, in league with Silius despite their alleged feud, had promised Honorius he would waive any Calpurnia compensation which Marponius awarded against him. So Honorius had given this pair my saleable information.

I kept my thoughts to myself. Expressionless, I stood up and said I would see them in court.

Maybe Honorius had a conscience – though if so, it would not last among those liver-pecking eagles. As I went back across the Forum to the Basilica, he did rush after me. He was agitated.

'Falco! Just let me say this: my leaving is not as bad as you think.'

'Oh no?' At the base of a statue plinth I rounded on him. 'You mean, you have *not* dumped us because we're in trouble – and you did *not* tell those bastards we identified Saffia as the killer?'

'I've left you,' he conceded. 'And the timing stinks. But they already knew about Saffia.'

I paused. 'They knew?'

'Paccius knew Bratta bought the hemlock for her. And she told Bratta she wanted it for her father-in-law.'

'Well, that was correct!' I stopped. '*How* did Paccius know?'

'When Saffia left Negrinus, Paccius advised on their divorce. He sent Bratta to help with her removals. She knew what kind of work

Bratta did. When she asked about buying poison, Bratta reported straight back to Paccius.'

'So did Paccius encourage – or better still, order – Bratta to help acquire the hemlock . . . ?' Honorius and I knew we would find no answer to that red hot question.

Paccius Africanus was tangled up in this business to a degree that I would call unethical – had ethics had any place in his world. If he was party to Bratta's purchase, we could charge him with incitement, or with being an accessory to murder. But I would never prove it.

I was wondering whether Paccius realised Bratta might have killed Spindex. I doubted if Honorius knew. Even Paccius might be in the dark: Bratta may have acted on his own initiative. None of them knew yet that Bratta was wanted by the vigiles. Perhaps a sordid backstreet killing which Paccius had never authorised might yet be used to topple the informers' elaborate schemes. 'Bratta has disappeared, Honorius. Do they know where he is?'

'Bratta? Paccius has the rogue as a house guest at his own mansion.'
Hmm. I wondered if we could lift Bratta. Not that Petronius Longus, whose remit was the Aventine, would agree to go north of the Forum. He wouldn't want to raid an ex-consul's grand abode either. I would have to extract Bratta myself.

'One last thing – Did they *both* know about Saffia? Paccius and Silius?' Ashamed of his new compatriots, Honorius nodded. 'And did they know from the start?'

'I suppose they may have done.'

At long last I saw it all. If the two informers knew all along who killed Metellus, everything since had been a set-up. They had deliberately failed to prosecute Saffia herself. They had toyed with Rubiria Juliana, then worked around to Metellus Negrinus. They manipulated me, hoping I would make a counter-charge – one they always knew could not hold up. They could have stopped the Calpurnia prosecution at any time. They had Bratta as a star witness. With his tale of buying the poison for Saffia, they were all set to run up their compensation claim against Falco and Associates.

As it turned out, being ethical idiots, Falco and Associates had saved them the bother.

I wondered if Paccius and Silius had deliberately planted Honorius amongst us as a spy. For a moment I even wondered if they had primed the steward to spout his story about Saffia's quails now, at a time that suited them. However, I guessed their information all came from Bratta.

Something else struck me. Maybe the two informers' crafty tricks went back much further than I had realised. If they knew about Saffia and the quails, maybe they knew whatever secret Saffia had used to blackmail the Metelli.

Finally, I began to grasp the scale – and the long timescale – of their devious plans. They had lined up the Metelli as victims years ago.

I, too, could take advantage of my opponents' weaknesses. When pushed, I abandoned all scruples. At the Basilica Julia, I left a message for Petronius. I dared not say much; any court official might be in Paccius' pay. But I asked Petro to wait for me outside. That sounded innocuous. Then I set off alone.

At the elegant home of Paccius Africanus, I gave a false name. The suave slaves were not competent enough to remember me. They accepted my fake byline, though they then denied that Bratta was indoors. I sent in word for him anyway. I said Paccius had run into setbacks and wanted Bratta urgently at the court.

Bratta came out eventually. Emerging from a doorway, I followed him. He walked with an informer's gait, confident but unobtrusive. He was checking for observers, but he never spotted me. I grew so jumpy I found myself glancing behind me in case Bratta had brought a shadow, who might now be tailing *me* . . . Apparently not. He just walked on, sometimes swapping the side of the street, but not bothering to use double-backs. He was methodical, but must have felt secure.

When he reached the Forum, he seemed to grow more wary. He crossed the historic piazza by way of the narrow, little-used path between the Regia and the back end of the Temple of Divine Julius. From the shadow of the Arch of Augustus, he checked for trouble, hoping he would see it first. He failed to spot a tall, quiet man in brown standing immediately above him on the steps of the Temple of Castor: Petronius Longus. Petro had seen Bratta lurking by the Arch, and he had seen me.

Bratta stepped out on to the Sacred Way. Lifting him would be easy. What would be hard was lifting him without the public noticing.

I moved closer. Petronius remained still. All around us were people at their normal tasks, weaving to and fro across the Forum in intricate patterns. Bratta was too hesitant; a garland-seller bumped into him. He had lost his rhythm; he was knocking against people. He had sensed his mistake. He was nervous. This was too public, and he was starting to doubt that my message had been genuine. But he still had not seen us. I signalled to Petro and we both moved in.

We reached him together. We had surprised him, but he was extremely strong. We took him, after a struggle. He was almost at the Basilica steps by then. He had kicked me in the guts, and he had bitten Petro. There was blood streaming down his tunic, where he had ignored my threatening knife. Petronius had finally subdued him, using vigiles aggression.

Bratta had never called for help. A loner by trade, he may not even have thought of it. As we hustled him away down a sidestreet, nobody saw us go.

'Thanks, Petro. This is Bratta – to be dumped in a very secure cell. Don't bother to tell anyone you have him. Don't tell them, even if they come asking.'

Some of Petro's men appeared. They surrounded our prisoner. Out of sight of passers-by, he must have received some nasty punishment. I heard him grunt. Petronius winced. Then he slapped my shoulder. 'I knew it must be something good, if you were not bothering to go to court. Best trot in there now, though.'

'I'll just instruct you first –'

'Don't bother: I'll persuade the brute to admit he strangled Spindex.'

'Easy on the persuasion.'

'Unlike the Second, we keep them breathing; Sergius is a cat with a mouse. He enjoys watching little creatures trying to survive – he can stay playful for a very long time.'

Petro had aimed his remarks at Bratta, but I lowered my voice. 'Well, don't just get him on the killing – make him confess who ordered it. If it was Paccius or Silius, tell me before you tell the Urban Praetor.'

Petronius nodded understandingly. Linking the two élite informers to a sleazy murder seemed my only hope of escaping from the mess I was in. 'Falco, get into court. You want to be present when the bastards shaft you.'

He was right. I retrieved my toga, which I had earlier left with an usher, and slid into the Basilica just as Paccius was having fun tearing my reputation to pieces. Luckily I never had much.

Apart from Petronius, everyone I knew seemed to be there listening. Well, they would be. People love to see their friends brought down, don't they?

The Accusation against Calpurnia Cara: C. Paccius Africanus on M. Didius Falco

. . . Consider what type of man he is. What is known of his history? He was in the army. As a young recruit he was sent to the province of Britain. It was the time of the Boudican Rebellion, that savage event in which so many Roman lives were lost. Of the four legions then in Britain, some were subsequently honoured for their bravery and the glory of their victory over the rebels. Was Falco among their number? No. The men in his legion disgraced themselves by not responding to the call from their colleagues for help. They stayed in camp. They did not fight. Others were left to achieve honour, while the Second Augusta, including Didius Falco, abandoned them, earning only disgrace. It is true that Falco was obeying orders; others were culpable – but remember, as a servant of the Senate and People that was his heritage.

He claims he was then a scout. I can find no record of this. He left the army. Had he served his time? Was he wounded out? Was he sent home with an honourable diploma? No. He wheedled himself an exit, under terms that are shrouded in secrecy.

We next hear of this man, operating as the lowest type of informer from a dingy base on the Aventine. He spied on bridegrooms, destroying their hopes of marriage with slanders –

'Objection!'

'Overruled, Falco. I've seen you do it.'

'Only to naughty fortune-hunters, Marponius –'

'And what does that make you?'

'Objection sustained, your honour.'

He preyed on widows in their time of bereavement –

'Oh objection, please!'

'Sustained. Strike out the widows. Even Falco has a conscience.'

Let's not quibble, gentlemen: Didius Falco did seedy work, often for unpleasant people. Some time around then, he had a stroke of enormous luck for a man of his class. The daughter of a senator fell in love with him. It was a tragedy for her family, but for Falco it proved a passport to respectability. Ignoring the pleas of her parents, the headstrong young woman ran off with her hero. Her noble father's fortunes declined sharply from that moment. Her brothers were soon to be inveigled into Falco's web – you have seen the young men in this court, subject to his incorrigible influence. Now, instead of the promising careers that once lay ahead, they are facing ruin with him.

And what is his occupation now? Accusing a respectable matron of murder. The most hateful crime – in which even Falco now admits he 'was mistaken'. There was 'other evidence', which proves that 'somebody else did it'.

I shall pass over the slurs and scandalous barbs he has aimed at me personally. I can withstand his attacks. Those who know me will not be influenced by them. Any hurt I have felt personally as I listened to his insulting tirade will pass.

Your honour, it is for you that I feel most angry. He has used your court as a platform for an ill-considered charge, backed by no evidence and fronted only by his bravado. As you can see, my client, Calpurnia Cara, is simply too distressed to attend the court today. Battered and assaulted from all sides, she is reduced to a wraith. I know she sends her apologies and pleads to be excused. This noble woman has withstood enough. I ask you, I beg you, to acknowledge her wounded feelings with exemplary damages. May I suggest that what Calpurnia Cara has suffered requires nothing short of a million sesterces to remove the harm done?

Dear gods. I must have an ear affliction. He cannot have said that. *A million?*

Well, he made a mistake, then. The great Paccius had overplayed it. Marponius was an equestrian. When the financial entry for the judge's own social rank is only four hundred thousand, to ask the price of qualification to the Senate, on behalf of a woman, was crazy. Marponius blinked. Then he belched nervously – and when he gave the award he reduced the figure asked to half.

Half a million sesterces. It was a hard struggle to stay calm.

The Camilli might bring in something, but I expected little from them. In our partnership, insofar as we had ever discussed money, I was using the brothers as unpaid apprentices. This was down to me. I was stuck with a personal debt I could in no way afford. My banker had told me bluntly: I could not raise half a million even if I sold everything I owned.

I closed my eyes and somehow managed not to scream or weep.

That was just as well. Looking fraught would have been bad at my next appointment. While the court was still closing, I received a message that the praetor wanted to see me right now about my impiety case. There was no escape. He had sent one of his official

257

bodyguards to enforce my attendance. So, escorted by a lictor complete with his bundle of rods (and feeling as if I was about to receive a public beating), I was marched off. At least it got me out of the Basilica, before anyone could voice their insincere regrets over my downfall. I was now poorer than the average slave. At least a slave is allowed to salt away some pocket money. I would need every copper to pay Paccius and Calpurnia.

The lictor was a brute but he refrained from using the rods on me. He could see I was a broken man. There would have been no fun in it.

LIV

JUST BECAUSE he had sent for me did not mean the praetor was ready to receive me. He liked to toy with his victims. The lictor dumped me in a long corridor, where benches stood all along the walls for those the great man was keeping waiting. Bored and unhappy petitioners were already lined up, looking as if they had been there all day.

I joined them. The bench was hard, backless and a foot too low.

Almost immediately Helena Justina arrived and found me; she squashed in alongside. She must have spotted me being marched off so she had scurried after us. She took my hand, winding her fingers tightly among mine. Even at that low ebb, I looked sideways and gave her a half-smile. Helena leaned her head on my shoulder, eyes closed. I moved a gold ear-ring; the granulated crescent was pressing into her cheek. Then I slumped against her, also resting.

Whatever our fate, we would have each other.

We would have two infants and various hangers-on as well – no chance of returning to a two-room doss in a tenement. We both knew that. Neither of us bothered to say it.

Eventually a clerk with a buttoned-up mouth and a disapproving squint called us into an anteroom. He got my name wrong, on purpose probably. The praetor had recoiled from an interview with me. His clerk was to do the dirty work. The bureau beetle buried his nose in a scroll, lest he inadvertently made human contact. Somebody had told him that just looking at an informer can give you impetigo and a year's bad luck.

'You are Marcus Didius Falco? The Procurator of the Sacred Geese?' He could hardly believe it; somebody in the secretariats must have nodded off. At least the judgmental swine could understand why my appointment had gone wrong. 'The magistrate is greatly perturbed by this accusation of impiety. Irreverence to the gods and dereliction of temple duties are shocking misdemeanours. The magistrate regards them as abhorrent and would impose the highest penalty if such charges were ever proven –'

'The charges are trumped up and slanderous,' I commented. My tone was benign but Helena kicked me. I elbowed her back; she was just as likely as me to interrupt this parakeet.

Repartee was not in his script so the clerk continued for some time, rehearsing the magistrate's pompous views. They had been helpfully recorded on the scroll – ensuring that somebody's back was well covered. Wondering exactly who needed to clear themselves for posterity, I let the insults roll. Eventually the stylus-pusher remembered that he had a lunchtime meeting with his betting syndicate. He shut up. I asked what was to happen. He forced himself to give me the news. The mighty magistrate's opinion was: charges dismissed; no case to answer.

I managed to hold out until we reached the street outside. I grasped Helena by the shoulders and pulled her around until she faced me.

'Oh Marcus, you are furious!'

'Yes!' I was relieved – but I hated having things manipulated for me. 'Who fixed it, fruit?'

A glimmer of mischief smouldered in those huge brown eyes. 'I have no idea.'

'Who did your father trot off to see last night?'

'Well, he went to see the Emperor –' I began to speak. 'But Vespasian was busy –' I fell silent again. 'So I believe father saw Titus Caesar.'

'And what did bloody Titus have to say?'

'Marcus darling, I expect he just listened. Papa was quite angry that you had been left to your fate. My *father* said, he could not stand by while his two darling little granddaughters were damned – incorrectly – with a charge of having an impious father, so although you felt obliged to stay silent about your recent imperial missions, Papa himself would go to court and give evidence on your behalf.'

'So Titus –'

'Titus likes to do a good deed every day.'

'Titus is an idiot. You know I hate all patronage. I never asked to be rescued. I don't want to sweeten the conscience of an imperial playboy.'

'You'll live with it,' Helena responded cruelly. 'I understand Titus Caesar suggested that the praetor – with one eye on his future consulship – could probably be brought to see (with his other eye presumably; how lucky he has never had a spear-throwing accident . . .) that Procreus has no evidence.'

'I'm stuck then.' I gazed at her. Ridiculous humour sparkled back at me. 'I don't care a duck's fart if my daughters are labelled with impiety – but to provide for them, I have an urgent need to be respectable.'

'You make a perfect head of household,' Helena told me lovingly. She could smarm like a minor goddess on the loose from Olympus for the night. Any shepherds out roaming the Seven Hills had better jump in a ditch to hide.

'I give in. Helena Justina, the law is wonderful.'

'Yes, Marcus. I never cease to be glad that we live in a society with a fine judicial system.'

I was about to say, as she expected from me, 'and systematically corrupt'. I never did. We stopped joking, because while we stood there bantering, her brother Justinus came running to find us. As he bent double, catching his breath, I could tell from his expression he had brought upsetting news.

'You had better come, Marcus. Calpurnia Cara's house.'

LV

As we walked, Quintus explained hastily. He had gone back to pressurise the steward, Celadus. Celadus was still snoozing at the bar this morning, though he had had to sober up because the bar-keeper had complained that his drunkenness was bad for trade. While Quintus talked to him again, they saw a messenger from Paccius, sent to find out why Calpurnia had not appeared in court today. As usual, nobody at the house answered the door.

If even her lawyer did not know where she was, that was worrying. Justinus and Celadus broke into the house. They found Calpurnia dead.

By the time we returned there, a small crowd had gathered. However, nobody was trying to go in. Sightseers had gathered in the street by the two empty shops and remained there. We walked down the passage to the yellow Egyptian obelisks.

The front door stood ajar. Inside, Celadus was sitting on the back of the sphinx in the atrium, his head in his hands. He was cursing himself for loitering at the bar when he could have prevented what happened. Still loyal to his patrons, he was mightily upset. Justinus stayed in the atrium with him. Helena and I walked swiftly to the bedroom. The house was cold and echoed emptily. Nobody had been here for several days.

We found Calpurnia Cara lying on her bed. She was fully clothed and positioned on top of the bedcovers. Her dress was formal, her grey hair neatly pinned – though her manner of dying had caused convulsions that disturbed her careful layout. Only her shoes had been removed before she took up her place; they stood together on a floor rug. She wore a single gold necklace, which we now knew was probably the only piece of jewellery she still owned.

It was perfectly clear that what had occurred here was suicide. On a table beside her lay an open sardonyx box, mocking the scene she had staged previously for her dead husband. It looked to be the same box purchased all that time ago from Rhoemetalces for Metellus. Flimsy fragments of gold leaf were scattered beside the box, which was empty. There would have been four corn cockle pills left, after the apothecary swallowed one in court. Calpurnia must have broken open all four remaining pills and removed the outer shell of gold. Then she swallowed the corn cockle seeds, which she washed down with water from a glass that had afterwards fallen beside her hand on the coverlet.

A sealed letter addressed to her children was on the side table. I took it, then we left hastily. The side-effects of the poison were unpleasant and the corpse had deteriorated since she died.

Calpurnia must have killed herself the day she was last seen in court. That was when the charge against her had seemed likely to hold up, before we knew she was innocent. She never knew we had withdrawn the charge.

It would have been easy to blame myself. And believe me, I did.

We took the steward with us, making the house secure again behind us. To be certain all was in order, I asked Justinus to wait outside until the family sent someone. Helena went home, knowing I would join her shortly.

With Celadus silent beside me, I walked to the younger daughter's home. That was closest, and I knew Carina better than Juliana. I would have to speak to the husband first; I preferred to broach Verginius Laco rather than the ill-tempered Canidianus Rufus, who always seemed so irritated by his in-laws' misfortunes. I found Laco in. I told him the news, offered our sympathies, passed him the letter from Calpurnia (which I noticed was addressed only to her two daughters, not to Negrinus). I mentioned to Verginius Laco that I hoped this would mean the family secret could now be revealed.

Since Laco had always seemed a decent sort, and since within limits I trusted him, I brought him up to date on the murder of Metellus senior by Saffia. Licinius Lutea had been Saffia's associate in the blackmail and could have known about the poisoning, though he would deny all of it. Whatever Lutea knew about the Metellus family could still trouble them. The secret might come out anyway. I told Laco I thought both Silius Italicus and Paccius Africanus had known all along that Metellus had been murdered, and who really did it. Bratta was in custody over a related issue and might be persuaded to confess all sorts of things to the vigiles; Petronius would let Bratta think he would receive favourable treatment in the Spindex killing if he offered other information.

These points were important to Negrinus. The murder charge against him was still down to be heard in the Senate. As far as I knew, the two informers had made no move to withdraw their petition. So what would they do now? Silius still, after all this time, needed to show that Rubirius Metellus had not committed suicide. Would they now demonstrate that it was Saffia who killed him? 'Laco, I have come to view these men as shameless in their self-interest. I had supposed Paccius was keeping Bratta at his house to stop me finding the man. But perhaps it was for more despicable reasons. Paccius may have been making sure he could turn Bratta in, if he needed to support a scheme to denounce Saffia.'

Laco pursed his lips, looking thoughtful. 'The vigiles are holding this man. But will he clear Negrinus?'

'I have brought you Celadus, who can do that. Corroboration from Bratta would be useful, but it's probably not essential.'

Verginius Laco, as was his wont, heard me out in silence, thanked me politely, and gave away nothing.

Even so, I was not too surprised when, three days, later, Helena and I, and her two brothers, were invited to visit the Metelli that evening. Clearly it was not a social invitation, or we would have been offered dinner first. Hoping that somebody wanted to open up, we dressed carefully – Helena in a matching dress and stole in tawny shades, with a full set of silver jewellery; me in a clean tunic, one with itchy rope-patterned braid cluttering up the edges. At Helena's pointed suggestion, I had had myself shaved. While I was submitting myself to the cut-throat blade, she read through all our case-notes.

We travelled in her litter, snuggling up under a rug, which helped the time pass as the bearers trudged slowly through the winter night. For reasons of her own, Helena had made them take a long detour, going up and over the Aventine above our house. It was a steep climb, apparently just so Helena could pop in with a bunch of winter celery for my mother.

Ma cannot have been expecting this treat, for she was entertaining Aristagoras. He was her eighty-year-old man-friend, a source of much curiosity and highly strung gossip in the family. When we arrived, the amiable fellow grinned a lot then tottered off like an arthritic grasshopper; Ma claimed that he had just called to bring her some cockles.

While I looked around for a new shellfish jar and failed to find it, Helena got down to her real business: 'Junilla Tacita, we are on our way to see some people and I don't have time to track down Ursulina Prisca. I wondered if by any chance you could help me clarify something. . .'

'I know nothing about anything,' Mother moaned, in a pathetic mood. Evenings tired her. She was ready to nod off in her armchair, and probably glad we had driven out her admirer.

'Oh, you know everything! I was so glad you came with me to see that wet-nurse –'

'Euboule? Don't trust her!'

'No, I didn't care for her at all,' Helena agreed. 'But one thing puzzles me. I have remembered that Ursulina told me not to take baby Favonia there because, she said, "you might never get the little darling back" –'

'Have you done anything for that poor woman, son?' Swiftly distracted, Ma rounded on me.

'Ursulina? Our next job, Ma,' I lied.

'Oh you take your time, my boy! She's only desperate.'

'No, she's not. She's stirring up trouble in her family – something I would never do in mine, of course.'

'The woman needs help.'

Ursulina needed another interest in life. I just said mildly, 'We will help her, but she may have to wait. I'm desperate myself. I have to find half a million sesterces for a vicious compensation claim –'

'So you let someone down?' sneered Ma, so unimpressed by my plight she had failed to take in the large figure.

'He was tricked by wicked men,' Helena defended me. She managed to get back to her original query: 'It may help Marcus if he knows what Euboule and Zeuko have been up to. He needs to know tonight.'

Ma stared at her. Luckily she was weary, wanting to be left alone. Her normal readiness to spar was weakened. 'Oh you know what those wet-nurses are like . . .' Helena waited. 'Rich women dump their babies there, and half the time – so Ursulina says – they forget what the children even look like. They have no idea if what they get back after a year or two is even theirs.'

'I would recognise Sosia Favonia!'

'Of course you would. Then again –' Ma, who disapproved of wet-nursing, went off into a rant. 'Of course some of those women do it on purpose. They don't want another pregnancy so if they've got a sickly little thing they take it along and make sure the wet-nurse replaces it if misfortune strikes –'

'That's horrible.'

'Not if it suits everyone. I could have exchanged a few of mine quite happily!' Ma cackled, and made sure she glared at me.

Helena Justina rocked back on her seat and stared at the ceiling, her mouth pursed.

'Still,' said Ma crisply. 'We know exactly what happened in this case of yours.'

'We do?' I asked.

Ma sounded complaisant. 'Oh, Ursulina and I worked it all out for you.' I breathed slowly, keeping my expectation in check. 'We could have solved it for you days ago.'

'Well pardon me, why didn't you say something? So, Mother darling, what's the dirty secret?'

'Son, it's obvious. Someone creeping up the stairs by moonlight.'

'What?'

'Euboule and her daughter probably know. That woman, Calpurnia must have put one over on her husband. Good for her!' chortled my mother. 'She must have had a boyfriend. Don't ask me who – it's your job to spot the culprit. Friend of her husband's, or a pretty slave. So this young man the fuss is all about –'

'Her son, Negrinus?'

'You ask them, Marcus. I bet he was not her husband's child.'

'You could well be right,' Helena said. 'The wife upset her husband, which could mean that he found out one day; the son was disinherited; people blackmailed the family. They call the son Birdy –'

'He's a cuckoo,' snorted Ma. 'A rich little cuckoo in the fancy nest.'

Helena fetched Ma her house slippers. I made her a warm drink. Then we continued on our way to visit the Metelli. Perhaps we were about to learn their family secret. Perhaps we already knew it.

On the other hand, nothing was simple in connection with this family. Helena agreed that it was quite likely the children of Calpurnia Cara still harboured some surprises.

LVI

We were escorted into the white salon. Fine oils burned in the gilded lamps, gleaming on the nifty bronze Aphrodite in her matt plastered niche. The two sisters, Rubiria Juliana and Rubiria Carina, were displaying handsome jewellery as they sat in genteel postures on the best-positioned ornate couch. Their husbands spread themselves on other plush upholstery, one on each side of the women. Negrinus sat gloomily one along from Verginius Laco, feet planted in front of him and elbows on his knees; beyond Negrinus was a tanned, thickset man we had never seen before. Helena and I took places near the scowling Canidianus Rufus, forming a half-circle. We ended up opposite the stranger. He stared at us curiously, and we returned the compliment.

The Camillus brothers arrived last, though fortunately not too late. They redeemed themselves by their smartness. Each wore well-buffed leather boots, tight belts, and identical white tunics; I detected their mother's hand in their overall neat turnout. Neither had his usual hair parting and I reckoned the noble Julia Justa had tackled them both with her fine bone comb before letting them loose.

Justinus immediately nodded a greeting to the thickset man. That confirmed he was Julius Alexander, the freedman and land agent from Lanuvium. Despite their tussle over Perseus, when the lads stationed themselves on the remaining seat Justinus sat adjacent to the freedman. Both then leaned over the curled arms of their couches and muttered in an undertone about the vigiles' fatal handling of the door porter.

Silent slaves handed trays of savoury fancies, which we mostly left untouched in case they crumbled disastrously in our fingers; others brought delicate silver thimbles of rather sweet white wine. Not a lot was said. Everyone was waiting for the attendants to withdraw. Carina gave the signal early, and they vanished. People tried surreptitiously to find somewhere to discard their little wine tots. I bent forward and placed Helena's and mine on the floor beneath our couch, giving myself heartburn. Out of sight behind my back, Helena massaged my ribs. She always knew when I was in danger of emitting an unseemly belch.

Since nobody else seemed keen to break the silence, I began. 'This meeting follows the death of your mother, presumably? Has that freed you to be more open?'

Verginius Laco, thin, austere and understated, now seemed to be the family leader. 'There has been a long disagreement about making public a certain situation.'

'Calpurnia wanted to keep the secret?' I smiled politely. 'If it helps, Falco and Associates already assume that all your problems centre on the parentage of Birdy.'

Carina jumped. 'Please don't call him that!' I had tried it out deliberately. None of my party was surprised when his sister said unhappily, 'That was his wife's name for him. None of us ever use it.'

'We understand.' Helena was sympathetic. She dropped in the answer almost as if it hardly counted: 'Saffia employed an unkind nickname to remind everyone of what she knew: that Negrinus was not really his father's son.'

'Took you long enough to guess!' Canidianus Rufus seemed to be here on sufferance. Always edgy, his unhappiness was worse tonight. Whatever was about to be exposed, he hated it. His wife, Juliana, stared down at her lap.

'Once you know,' I agreed, 'it explains a great deal.' Rufus humphed.

More relaxed than his brother-in-law, Laco leaned sideways on a couch arm, hands linked, surveying me. He had made a habit of holding back, waiting for me to reveal what I knew before he spoke up. Expecting candour, I suddenly had a feeling that he was still testing me, still ready to disguise the facts. I became more careful.

'So, Falco –' He was pretending to be friendly. 'You understand us now?'

I paused, then went with the theory that Negrinus was illegitimate. 'Around two years ago, Rubirius Metellus – who thought himself the father of a happy family, with a son moving up through the Senate – was shocked to discover that that son was not his own. I suppose this information had long been known to the wet-nurse who cared for Negrinus as a baby – Euboule. She somehow discovered his parentage from Calpurnia Cara. Over the years, she heavily blackmailed Calpurnia with the threat of telling her husband, causing Calpurnia enormous grief – not to mention the sale of her jewellery.'

As I unravelled the story, Laco and the others listened quietly. Negrinus had his chin up slightly, but he was taking it well – so far.

At my side, Helena moved slightly. 'In time,' she began conversationally, as if talking this through quietly at home with me, 'Euboule was not alone in blackmailing the family. It is obvious that she told her daughter Zeuko, who told the porter, Perseus. His demands must have seemed the final indignity. But long before then, enormous damage had been done by someone else – Saffia Donata.'

This time at the mention of her name, everyone tensed. I carried on the story. 'Rubirius Metellus was given the bad news when Saffia Donata began to squeeze. Saffia had found out during her first marriage to Licinius Lutea. She had placed their son Lucius for nursing with Zeuko. For Saffia, picking up an indiscreet remark from a wet-nurse must have been a godsend. She and Lutea had money troubles. The Metelli were very wealthy. Saffia formed an audacious plan to divorce and remarry herself to Negrinus. Getting right in among the family must have helped her apply pressure – and it will have disguised from other people what she was up to.'

'It is shocking,' said Helena. 'We have rarely heard of such determined abuse. But once she had produced a child to tie her to the Metelli, Saffia began a vicious programme of extortion. Not just occasional payments; she wanted everything.'

Carina broke in: 'I want to make it plain, there was *never* any sordid relationship between my father and Saffia.'

'No,' Helena agreed gently.

Carina, once said to have been estranged from her family, seemed most keen to defend Metellus. 'My father was a man who stood up for himself. Some people found him aggressive – but he was just as strong in his loyalty to Negrinus. When he found out the truth, Father refused to reject him, you know.'

'We can see that,' I reassured her. 'And Saffia relied on it. Without your father's feeling for Negrinus, Saffia's plan would have collapsed. She needed the family desperate to cover up the secret. So Negrinus and his father were in shock together. Money flowed out of the coffers until Saffia's demands drove them to corruption.'

'We *were* desperate!' Negrinus himself spoke up. This was the first time we had heard him acknowledge what happened during his term of public office. 'Saffia had drained our coffers. As an aedile, you have to keep up your style in society –'

'You don't have to plunder the state!' I commented.

'There was nothing else we could do. Saffia was insatiable. Father

269

even sold the land that had formed her dowry – he said it served her right.'

'Why on earth did you stay married to her?' I scoffed.

'One of her conditions for keeping quiet. Part of her cunning. She was always with us, making sure she kept up the pressure.'

'Besides, she pretended she was fond of you?'

Negrinus flushed and fell silent. I had only met her once, but she was memorably pretty. That explained the second child he and Saffia produced together. Whether it was his son or not, he must have reason to suppose it might be. At least the newborn stood more chance with him than with Lutea.

'And the will?' I asked. 'Furious and heartbroken when the truth came out, Metellus changed his will, disinheriting both you and your mother who had betrayed him?'

'Saffia made him do that,' Negrinus insisted, writhing with unhappiness.

'And that was when your father called in Paccius Africanus to advise on how she could receive a huge legacy? A big mistake, I fear.' I leaned forward. 'Paccius had to be told the reason for the gift to Saffia? So two years ago, when you were first running for aedile, Paccius Africanus learned that you were illegitimate?'

Negrinus nodded and said weakly, 'Paccius has always been professional.'

'Oh I am sure he kept it confidential!' I mocked.

Verginius Laco also sat forward. 'I am with you, Falco. In retrospect, I believe Paccius told Silius Italicus – who then lay in wait until he could institute corruption charges. It was calculated.'

'And callous.' I asked Negrinus slowly, 'Did Paccius actually suggest to your father that he use your post as aedile to make money?'

Negrinus was surprisingly astute about that: 'You mean, can we mount corruption charges against Paccius? No. Father never said where the idea came from.'

'Nor, for that matter,' Laco added, 'can we *prove* that Paccius informed Silius of the situation.'

'You lose all round,' I told the victim.

'I do.'

Aelianus, frowning, wanted to go back a step. 'I don't understand,' he asked, '*why* Paccius had to be told the reason for giving money to Saffia?'

His sister shook her head at him. 'Think about it, Aulus. Experts say the will is open to contest. Paccius had to know why the Metellus children would not make a claim against it. He had to be told that the daughters would hold off to protect Negrinus – while Negrinus himself had no real claim in any case.'

'Your illegitimacy –' Aelianus never knew how to be sympathetic to a loser – 'bars your inheritance?'

'What inheritance? There is nothing left,' Juliana's husband snorted. Then Rufus leapt up and stomped out. His wife briefly covered her mouth in distress.

People had called him bad-tempered; I could see why he might be. His respectable marriage to a daughter of a wealthy family had turned very sour. He had probably even lost financially. He had tolerated the scandal until now. But he had had enough. I caught sight of Juliana's face. She knew she was heading for divorce.

I breathed slowly. 'So will you now admit the truth about Negrinus?'

'This was my father's wish,' replied Carina. 'After the corruption charges, Father decided to take a stand.'

'It made my mother very angry,' said Juliana, 'but my father really did refuse to commit suicide. He said he would pay the compensation to Silius Italicus, and he would publicly declare the truth.'

'Your mother must have hated that. It was her deceit. When your father died anyway –'

'Mother was a very determined character. She said we had to rally round and back her up,' Juliana said. I was starting to think it was not so much Negrinus who was pushed around in this family, but her. She had carried the main burden of the 'suicide', with her elaborate fake story of sitting with Metellus on the day he died.

Helena clasped her hands, absorbed by the revelations. 'Your father's decision to reveal the true story caused Saffia to leave. She then had no reason to stay. And she knew she would lose her source of plunder?'

'She left at last. But then she decided she would murder my father,' said Carina bitterly.

'She had had so much –' Juliana agreed bitterly. 'She wanted her bequest, and she refused to wait. She wanted everything.'

'And she got it!' Negrinus growled.

There was a pause, as we all considered this.

It was Camillus Justinus who tackled the next aspect. 'You had defensive measures in place, however? Money that went missing has been quietly put into land – in Lanuvium, and perhaps other places?'

I turned to the freedman, Alexander. 'We had wondered whether

271

you were among the blackmailers —' Julius Alexander heard this dispassionately. He was one of those solid ex-slaves who are held in great regard, close to the family who freed him, and in command of himself.

'But no,' Justinus corrected me, with a smile. 'I think Alexander remained loyal to a remarkable extent – and if I am right, he has positioned an estate where Negrinus can restart his life.' It made sense. The Metelli had come from Lanuvium, only a few generations ago; Negrinus would go back there, then retrace the procedure that had brought them wealth and status. He had probably gone to Lanuvium to make final arrangements, when Metellus senior died. 'Is that so?' Justinus insisted.

The freedman deliberately folded his arms. Calmly he refused to speak. All the others were silent too. Well, most of them were used to keeping secrets. What was one more? Justinus was wasting his time; nobody here would own up.

If Rubirius Metellus had been the defiant character they said, I could believe that he had surreptitiously removed money from Saffia's grasp and invested it where the son he had loved could benefit. It would be untraceable, no question. If it was the proceeds of the corruption, he would have had to make sure even the Treasury could not unravel his dealings and reclaim the cash. It would have been cash, of course. Backhanders are.

Aelianus now joined in with his brother, addressing the freedman in a haughty tone: 'People will think that you are Negrinus' father. Are you?' he badgered, always blunt.

'No.' Julius Alexander had long mastered self-control. It was the first time he had spoken. He might as well not have bothered.

'You should be prepared for people to believe it!'

'If it helps,' Alexander smiled.

'But why must you leave?' Justinus rounded angrily on Negrinus. 'Why not admit there is a question mark over your origins, and just brazen things out? Rome is stuffed with men who have suspect paternity. Some great names, starting with Augustus, have been subject to rumours.'

Helena touched my arm. 'Leave it alone,' I ordered her brother.

She stood up and went over to him. 'Quintus, imagine it. For thirty years Metellus Negrinus had thought he belonged to a family –'

Justinus was beyond stopping. 'Yes – and if his parents and his sisters had all turned their backs when they found out, Negrinus would have lost everything, including his identity. But he has their support. He's

272

lucky. It's clear his father – even though he was *not* his father – loved him.'

Rubiria Carina now went to Negrinus. She put her arm around him. 'We all love him. He grew up with us. He is part of us. Nothing will ever change that.'

'You were the angriest,' Justinus reminded her. 'You even caused a scene at the funeral.'

'That was before I knew the truth,' Carina retorted. Though she was a charitable woman, as she remembered being left out of the secret, her face darkened. 'All I saw for several years was bad feeling and inexplicable financial mismanagement.'

Helena continued with Justinus. 'Allow him a new beginning, Quintus. He will take his young children and make what he can of the world. I believe he will do it stalwartly.'

Justinus capitulated. He had always been a decent sort. We could trust him not to inflict unnecessary pain on people.

Verginius Laco made the formal speech to finish – or so he intended.

'We are most grateful for your discretion. We all feel you have acted in a most supportive manner to Negrinus. He will be leaving Rome shortly with Julius Alexander, and in due course as you surmise, he will begin a new life under a new name, we hope in far happier circumstances.'

He had not reckoned with my two young associates. They were still boiling over. 'But Negrinus cannot leave Rome. What about the court case?' demanded Justinus, finding a new reason to argue.

Laco quietly had the answer: 'It was announced today that there will be no court case.'

'Silius and Paccius have withdrawn?' Aelianus exclaimed eagerly.

'Reason prevails!' Laco remarked drily, before adding, 'The Senate will not allow the charge to proceed. The grounds cited in the *Daily Gazette* will be that the Senate will not permit the pursuit of public wrongs for the purposes of private vengeance.'

'This makes no mention of Saffia killing Metellus? So it appears,' I said, 'as if everything relates to the original corruption case? Paccius and Silius are being reprimanded for hounding the Metelli –'

'As they have done,' said Laco, rather curtly. 'Everyone can see that.' I began to suspect his influence in this Senate vote. In fact, he looked tired. I wondered if he had been spending hard effort on lobbying colleagues. He admitted frankly, 'It is of no interest to us to have it made known what Saffia did.'

Of course not. Never mind that she was a murderess. If they damned her in public, her blackmail had to be explained; the secret she knew would become public knowledge.

'She is dead. We cannot punish her. And we have to protect her children. Her father,' said Laco, 'has stepped in with remedies. Donatus, a decent type, is to adopt Saffia's young son Lucius – Lutea has agreed to it – and Donatus is pleased to do so, having no sons of his own. Then, to protect Lucius and the other children from being sullied by their mother's past actions, Donatus will make certain payments from the money and goods Saffia had carried off. He will take responsibility for the payment Silius Italicus won in the corruption case. And I believe he will also cover certain "expenses" for Paccius Africanus.'

'The compensation was a million and a quarter,' Helena reminded him coolly.

Verginius Laco smiled. 'I understand Silius will accept a lesser sum, as a compromise.'

'Why?' Like her brothers, Helena did not shy from the awkward question, though her tone was less abrasive.

'Why?' Laco seemed surprised to be challenged.

'Why is Silius Italicus prepared to compromise?'

Without her insistence, Verginius Laco would not have paid the compliment: 'The ethical queries raised by Didius Falco against both Silius and Paccius may be a factor. They were embarrassed by the speech he made. It could interfere with their present and future standing.'

Helena Justina gave him a gracious smile. 'Then we are glad Falco made the speech! And what about the loss of Rubirius Metellus?'

Laco was terse. 'Donatus will make reparation.'

His children had accepted a payoff. Perhaps that was justice. Certainly the law would say so.

'So the family is content. But are you sure,' I asked him, 'neither Silius nor Paccius will want a formal verdict on the murder? Are their payments from Donatus enough to make them forget such a terrible crime was committed?'

'They are informers,' said Laco. Perhaps he forgot I was one. 'Pursuing money appeals to them more than pursuing wrongs.'

We had one last awkward question. Just when everything seemed over, Aelianus doggedly came out with it: 'There is just one thing nobody has explained yet. All the fuss has been because Negrinus is an interloper. So – who was his real father?'

Helena was too far away to cuff him round the ears. Rubiria Carina spoke up at once: 'That we do not know. And since my mother is now dead,' she continued wanly, 'I am afraid we will *never* know.'

Aelianus suspected she was lying. A raised finger from his own sister made him hold his peace.

I myself thought that Carina was telling the truth. Though, like the rest of them throughout this sad story, she was not telling all of it.

LVII

I T WAS made apparent subtly that we were to take our leave. Falco and Associates withdrew from the white and gold salon, leaving the family of Rubirius Metellus to reflect on the end to their difficulties.

The Camillus brothers stood with Helena and me as we waited for our bearers. Canidianus Rufus, who had stormed out earlier, was already prowling the atrium; his wife's litter stood ready and he was hanging around for Juliana.

After a glance at the others, I walked across to him. 'All very enlightening!'

He grunted. As a mode of expression it was minimal, but suited his personality. Even amongst a family he approved of, this man would have been restless and abrasive. Today he was ready to boil over. He glared at me through eyes like slits.

'Of course they have not admitted the whole story.' I implied that I knew anyway. 'I don't care for letting a murderess get away with it – and they haven't thought about Lutea. He intends trouble, depend on it. He needs money far too much to stop.'

Canidianus Rufus was hopping from foot to foot, praying for his wife to arrive and free him. But they had brainwashed him into keeping their secrets and he managed to remain silent.

I pretended not to notice his discomfiture. 'I do applaud Laco for sewing it all up with Donatus – Laco must have been working his arse off over all this . . . Curious family,' I commented. 'Though strangely loyal. And now they will get away with it –'

'It stinks!' Rufus could no longer hold back.

I shrugged. Thinking of how old Donatus was now taking on little Lucius, I suggested, 'So much could have been avoided by a quiet adoption process, surely?'

Helena had crossed the atrium to join us. She slipped her hand through my arm. 'Oh no, Marcus. Adoption is for families of good birth only. The Metelli never had that option.'

'Because his father was unknown?' I pulled a face. Canidianus

Rufus stood silent, either unaware how we were playing him, or helpless to escape. 'Negrinus would take his mother's rank, Helena – what's the problem? Adultery is the fashion; there is no stigma nowadays.'

'Keep your voice down!' Helena hushed me, drawing Rufus into our gossip. 'Marcus is so innocent. Not knowing a father is awkward, love, but common enough. But their situation is just unworkable. They have only admitted half of it. Rubirius Metellus was not his son's father – but nor was Calpurnia Cara his mother! Am I right, Rufus?'

Canidianus Rufus was desperate to share his anger: 'Oh you're horribly right, young lady!'

'Did Calpurnia bear three children?' hissed Helena. 'Two girls and a boy?'

'Yes,' said Rufus.

'And the boy died?'

'Yes.'

'So Calpurnia obtained a substitute from Euboule?'

'Yes!'

'But that's appalling.' I joined in as if the thought had only just struck me. 'Such a child was a disaster. Negrinus could be anyone!'

Canidianus Rufus could no longer contain his true feelings. 'It's disgusting!' he roared, not caring who heard him. The Camillus brothers looked startled and came over towards us. 'She should have been divorced, the minute Metellus found out. Passing off a child on him? He should have charged the bloody woman with deception. As for the so-called son –' He was livid. 'Don't ask me to use his name again – he has no right to it. That sham! It's a bloody disgrace that decent people are expected to go on dealing with him. He should never have been allowed in the Senate. Never put up for aedile. Never kept in the family. I simply can't believe it! They should all stop cosying up to him – and kick him back where he belongs!'

Overcome with revulsion, Rufus stomped off. We four stood there stunned – not only by the revelation. The outburst from Rufus showed the full force of senatorial snobbery. And his self-righteous prejudice showed exactly why the Metellus family had been trapped.

After a moment Aelianus whistled quietly through his front teeth. 'Well?' he asked Helena.

She took a deep breath. 'I just guessed. Calpurnia Cara's own son must have died whilst being nursed by Euboule. Because fear or distaste made her not want to have another baby, Calpurnia chose not to tell her husband, but she let Euboule substitute another child. It worked. It worked for thirty years. But Calpurnia had to pay Euboule extortionately to keep the secret – and in the end Euboule or her daughter began to tell others.'

'It was always bound to happen,' Justinus observed.

'Calpurnia Cara made a terrible mistake,' Helena agreed. 'When Saffia told Metellus, there was no way out. Calpurnia wanted to keep the secret for her own sake, and Metellus knew he could not allow anyone in good society to know. Metellus may have stood by Negrinus – who was the innocent victim – but he raged at Calpurnia. I can even see why she lost any feeling for Negrinus. Well, she always knew he was not her child. She let him be falsely accused of killing Metellus. She came to hate him for the trouble he had caused, and must have wanted him out of the way. It's only astonishing that neither his father nor his sisters would abandon him.'

'That's the one good part of this.' I took up the story quietly. 'Metellus senior had brought up Negrinus as his own and could not reject him. Yet he had to keep the secret. No alternative. It's more than merely scandalous. This supposititious child could have any parentage. To blackmail Calpurnia, you can bet Euboule suggested the very worst.'

'What's that?' asked Aelianus.

'Well, Negrinus could be Euboule's own child, in itself no recommendation. There are terrible alternatives, as the poor man must know. To be slave-born will make him a slave too; in theory, an owner could still claim him.'

Appreciating the problem now, Aelianus chimed in: 'Either of his parents could be infamous. If he is the child of an actor, a pimp or a gladiator, he's a legal outcast. Rufus was right – he is completely disqualified from the Senate.'

'That's nothing. He has even lost his citizenship,' I added. 'He has no birth certificate, we can be sure. His marriage was illegal. His children are now nobodies as well.'

'However much his sisters want to help,' Helena groaned, 'they cannot give him any status. The worst of all is – he doesn't even know who he is. I bet Euboule won't tell him.'

'Whatever she does say, he won't feel able to believe her,' Justinus groaned.

What Verginius Laco had hygienically called the 'situation' was dire. There was no chance of passing off Negrinus as of senatorial rank now. He and his children were lost souls. He could only leave Rome and begin afresh. Many have done it. In the Empire, a man of character could achieve much. But it would be hard for anyone who had been brought up, as he was, with such vastly different expectations.

We had our own problems. This case had left us with serious troubles. But when our transport came and we said farewell to her brothers, Helena and I went home that night in a subdued mood, not thinking of ourselves. 'Gnaeus Metellus Negrinus' had been a diffident, well-meaning young man, a good father with strength of character. Now he could no longer even use his name. To be born with nothing was grim. But to be born with everything, then to lose it, was far more cruel.

LVIII

I WAS RECONCILED to never knowing what happened to our client. Since we never defended him, because his trial was aborted, we could not even send a bill. I know, I know. Only a hard-hearted bastard – or an informer – would have thought of it. Still, I too had informers waiting for a payment. Unfortunately, my debt was a large one.

Spring was beginning to waft advance notice of its presence. Light breezes rustled the desiccated leaves that collected in the corners and crannies of fine buildings in the Forum of the Romans. Occasional shafts of sunlight reminded even hard-baked cynics that ours was a city of light, warmth and colour, any of which could reappear slyly any day now to disconcert us. The inconveniences of spring floods and flower festivals were waiting to make the streets impassable. The swollen Tiber oozed with murky silt. Birds were getting excited. Even I was, sometimes. And one fine, rather bright morning, when I thought the keen edge of their enmity might have mellowed, I took myself to the Porticus of Gaius and Lucius, to share a cup of cinnamon wine and a honey cake with two acquaintances.

Silius Italicus had lost a few pounds; Paccius Africanus looked a little greyer. I myself felt lean and sour, but that was old news. I was tough; we all acknowledged, they were tougher. Sitting at ease with morning refreshments on a napkin-laid tray and with their togas bunched over their shoulders ready for that day in court, they just hid their ruthlessness better than I did.

We exchanged courtesies. I asked after Honorius; he was at his exwife's wedding. He had expected she would return to him, but she dumped him and chose someone else. They said he had grown bitter. I said, I was glad he was learning. If the remark carried an undertone we all pretended otherwise.

I told them about Bratta. I had heard he was to be sent to the arena, for murdering Spindex. They were surprised, since they were unaware there had been a trial. I was able to tell them that sometimes the vigiles were so efficient with hardened criminals that killers were processed and condemned in the murders court before anybody noticed; the discretion was to prevent the populace becoming fearful that society was dangerous. Paccius asked why Bratta had not gone to the lions yet, and I explained that the vigiles were confident they could screw more confessions out of him. He had been told that if he coughed up enough information, he would be spared the wild beasts. Of course that was untrue. Murder is always punished, I said.

Which reminded me: I wondered whether Silius and Paccius had any plans to set their sights on Licinius Lutea? Silius told a funny story about Lutea recently buying (on credit) a highly expensive gourmet cook called Genius, whom those with inside knowledge believed to be a complete fraud. They cautiously admitted Lutea was a long-term prospect for them. His first wife had told them he was a real chancer; they were waiting to see what he chanced next. One way or another, he remained in their pending scroll box.

I told them that I did admire how they set up cases in advance, even if they had to wait years for a resolution. The informers smiled, hiding any indication that they knew what I was hinting.

'Do you ever see anything of Procreus?' I asked Silius.

Silius looked vague for a moment, then he pretended to remember who Procreus was and said, no; he had not had occasion to use him for a long time.

'That's sensible,' I murmured. 'There was a very disappointing outcome when he aimed that impiety charge for you, wasn't there?'

Paccius drank from his wine beaker, dainty as a bird. Silius flicked a cake crumb off his tunic.

I smiled gently. 'I had a narrow escape. I am grateful it was recognised that it was a fabricated charge. Of course damage has been done to me. Rumour ran rife. People were shocked . . .'

'What do you want, Falco?' asked Paccius wearily.

It was my turn to take my cup and enjoy a moment savouring the warm brew. 'My reputation suffered. Others, innocents all, have been stigmatised. My wife, who is a senator's daughter. My associates, her brothers, who hold the same noble rank. My little daughters, taunted as the children of an impious man. The slur does not die easily. My wife wants me to make an issue – sue for slander.'

'How much?' enquired Silius. He was blunt, though not unpleasant about it. I was dealing with decent businessmen. Paccius, pretending to be bored, knew it was Silius' sidekick who laid the charge, which he may have thought absolved him.

'Well, listen: I suggest we keep it neat. Save us troubling our bankers and paying their damn charges. How about the figure you were awarded in the Calpurnia Cara case? You pay me the same and it all negates nicely.'

'This is for you, dear colleague,' Silius observed, turning to Paccius. Neither of them quibbled about me assuming they had always worked in tandem, I noticed.

'Half a million? Falco, you're not worth the same as a senator's wife.' Paccius was calm, despite the amount involved.

'But you two are,' I answered. I was calm too. I had nothing to lose except my temper, and there was no point in that.

'Have I missed something?' asked Silius, paying more attention. My demand was outrageous, so why was I making it?

'I was fortunate in that impiety issue,' I explained frankly. 'I had imperial support; I don't know if you realised. Titus got involved. That was why the praetor barred the case.' I saw the two men glance at each other. 'My honour at the Temple of Juno was an imperial gift; casting doubt on my suitability was a thrust at Vespasian, you know. . . I thought it best to warn you,' I said, in a genial tone.

I sat back and sipped my spiced wine, allowing them time to adjust their thoughts.

'If I insist on a public hearing to clear my name,' I pointed out, 'with Titus Caesar backing me, your reputations will be shredded. You may be hoping for further advancement in the *cursus honorum* – surely two ex-consuls must be hoping for governorships? I know you won't want Titus screwing up your postings with a veto . . . Half a million is a small sacrifice to secure your next honours, don't you think?'

After a long silence, the sacrifice was made.

I ate my cake, then walked away from them across the Forum. I hid a smile. I knew that Titus Caesar had told the senator he would intervene with the praetor only on condition that the charge died, with no repercussions. Titus would never have backed me publicly. Still, Silius and Paccius must both be aware that sometimes in legal bargaining it is necessary to bluff.

My post as Procurator of the Sacred Geese was abolished shortly after all this, in a round of Treasury cutbacks. I was disappointed. The salary had been useful; losing it curtailed Helena's plans to build an outdoor dining room with a shell-lined nymphaeum and miniature canals.

Besides, the Sacred Geese of Juno and the Augurs' Chickens were good layers. When I was looking after them, I used to enjoy my omelettes.

I had begun this enterprise disenchanted – and had all my prejudice confirmed. I would wait in vain to see the grizzled old legals come good despite their cynicism. It was equally futile to hope that their idealistic apprentice, Honorius, would stay clean. I had escaped harm, more or less. Perhaps in some circles I had even increased my reputation.

Nobody was ever convicted of the murder of Rubirius Metellus, but nobody was wrongly condemned either. Saffia was dead, so she was beyond the courts. If Licinius Lutea escaped temporarily, he had become a target for the most patient of predators. So perhaps despite the efforts and machinations of my prosecuting colleagues, justice would one day be done.

The state had its own perspective. The following year, Ti Catius Silius Italicus was awarded a powerful post as proconsul of the province of Asia, while C. Paccius Africanus became proconsul of Africa. These were the Empire's chief prizes – honourable governorships where unscrupulous men could, by applying the right kind of diligence, acquire enormous wealth.

But that would be only greedy and corrupt proconsuls, of course.